The Eye
of Zeitoon

Books by Talbot Mundy

Avenging Liafail
Black Light
Caves of Terror
Full Moon
Hira Singh: When India Came to Fight in Flanders
I Say Sunrise
Jimgrim
King – of the Khyber Rifles
Lud of Lunden
Om, the Secret of Ahbor Valley
Queen Cleopatra
Rung Ho!
The Eye of Zeitoon
The Gray Mahatma
The Ivory Trail
The Mystery of Khufu's Tomb
The Nine Unknown
The Purple Pirate
The Winds of the World
Told in the East
Tros of Samothrace

The Eye of Zeitoon

TALBOT MUNDY

30 Oct 2016

Սիրելի Գոյգոշ,

to my new compatriot
with all best
wishes for a great
discovery.

x Nanbian

WILDSIDE PRESS

Doylestown, Pennsylvania

The Eye of Zeitoon
A publication of
WILDSIDE PRESS
P.O. Box 301
Holicong, PA 18928-0301
www.wildsidepress.com

Chapter One

Parthians, Medes and Elamites

SALVETE!

Oh ye, who tread the trodden path
And keep the narrow law
In famished faith that Judgment Day
Shall blast your sluggard mists away
And show what Moses saw!
Oh thralls of subdivided time,
Hours Measureless I sing
That own swift ways to wider scenes,
New-plucked from heights where Vision preens
A white, unwearied wing!
No creed I preach to bend dull thought
To see what I shall show,
Nor can ye buy with treasured gold
The key to these Hours that unfold
New tales no teachers know.
Ye'll need no leave o' the laws o' man,
For Vision's wings are free;
The swift Unmeasured Hours are kind
And ye shall leave all cares behind
If ye will come with me!
In vain shall lumps of fashioned stuff
Imprison you about;
In vain let pundits preach the flesh
And feebling limits that enmesh
Your goings in and out,
I know the way the zephyrs took
Who brought the breath of spring,
I guide to shores of regions blest
Where white, uncaught Ideas nest
And Thought is strong o' wing!
Within the Hours that I unlock

All customed fetters fall;
The chains of drudgery release;
Set limits fade; horizons cease
For you who hear the call
No trumpet note — no roll of drums,
But quiet, sure and sweet —
The self-same voice that summoned Drake,
The whisper for whose siren sake
They manned the Devon fleet,
More lawless than the gray gull's wait,
More boundless than the sea,
More subtle than the softest wind!

                                        *

Oh, ye shall burst the ties that bind
If ye will come with me!

*I*t is written with authority of Tarsus that once it was no mean city, but that is a tale of nineteen centuries ago. The Turko-Italian War had not been fought when Fred Oakes took the fever of the place, although the stage was pretty nearly set for it and most of the leading actors were waiting for their cue. No more history was needed than to grind away forgotten loveliness.

Fred's is the least sweet temper in the universe when the ague grips and shakes him, and he knows history as some men know the Bible — by fathoms; he cursed the place conqueror by conqueror, maligning them for their city's sake, and if Sennacherib, who built the first foundations, and if Anthony and Cleopatra, Philip of Macedon, Timour-i-lang, Mahmoud, Ibrahim and all the rest of them could have come and listened by his bedside they would have heard more personal scandal of themselves than ever their contemporary chroniclers dared reveal.

All this because he insisted on ignoring the history he knew so well, and could not be held from bathing in the River Cydnus. Whatever their indifference to custom, Anthony and Cleopatra knew better than do that. Alexander the Great, on the other hand, flouted tradition and set Fred the example, very nearly dying of the ague for his pains, for those are treacherous, chill waters.

Fred, being a sober man and unlike Alexander of Macedon

in several other ways, throws off fever marvelously, but takes it as some persons do religion, very severely for a little while. So we carried him and laid him on a nice white cot in a nice clean room with two beds in it in the American mission, where they dispense more than royal hospitality to utter strangers. Will Yerkes had friends there but that made no difference; Fred was quinined, low-dieted, bathed, comforted and reproved for swearing by a college-educated nurse, who liked his principles and disapproved of his professions just as frankly as if he came from her hometown. (Her name was Van-something-or-other, and you could lean against the Boston accent — just a little lonely-sounding, but a very rock of gentle independence, all that long way from home!)

Meanwhile, we rested. That is to say that, after accepting as much mission hospitality as was decent, considering that every member of the staff worked fourteen hours a day and had to make up for attention shown to us by long hours bitten out of night, we loafed about the city. And Satan still finds mischief.

We called on Fred in the beginning twice a day, morning and evening, but cut the visits short for the same reason that Monty did not go at all: when the fever is on him Fred's feelings toward his own sex are simply blunt bellicose. When they put another patient in the spare bed in his room we copied Monty, arguing that one male at a time for him to quarrel with was plenty.

Monty, being Earl of Montdidier and Kirkudbrightshire, and a privy councilor, was welcome at the consulate at Mersina, twenty miles away. The consul, like Monty, was an army officer, who played good chess, so that that was no place, either, for Will Yerkes and me. Will prefers dime novels, if he must sit still, and there was none. And besides, he was never what you could call really sedative.

He and I took up quarters at the European hotel — no sweet abiding-place. There were beetles in the Denmark butter that they pushed on to the filthy tablecloth in its original one-pound tin; and there was a Turkish officer in riding pants and red morocco slippers, back from the Yemen with two or three incurable complaints. He talked out-of-date Turkish politics in bad French and eked out his ignorance of table manners with instinctive racial habit.

To avoid him between meals Will and I set out to look at the historic sights, and exhausted them all, real and alleged, in less than half a day (for in addition to a lust for ready-cut building stone the Turks have never cherished monuments that might accentuate their own decadence). After that we fossicked in the manner of prospectors that we are by preference, if not always by trade, eschewing polite society and hunting in the impolite, amusing places where most of the facts have teeth, sharp and ready to snap, but visible.

We found a khan at last on the outskirts of the city, almost in sight of the railway line, that well agreed with our frame of mind. It was none of the newfangled, underdone affairs that ape hotels, with Greek managers and as many different prices for one service as there are grades of credulity, but a genuine two-hundred-year-old Turkish place, run by a Turk, and named Yeni Khan (which means the new rest house) in proof that once the world was younger. The man who directed us to the place called it a kahveh; but that means a place for donkeys and foot-passengers, and when we spoke of it as kahveh to the obadashi — the elderly youth who corresponds to porter, bellboy, and chambermaid in one — he was visibly annoyed.

Truly the place was a khan — a great bleak building of four high outer walls, surrounding a courtyard that was a yard deep with the dung of countless camels, horses, bullocks, asses; crowded with arabas, the four-wheeled vehicles of all the Near East, and smelly with centuries of human journeys' ends.

Khans provide nothing except room, heat, and water (and the heat costs extra); there is no sanitation for any one at any price; every guest dumps all his discarded rubbish over the balcony rail into the courtyard, to be trodden and wheeled under foot and help build the aroma. But the guests provide a picture without price that with the very first glimpse drives discomfort out of mind.

In that place there were Parthians, Medes and Elamites, and all the rest of the list. There was even a Chinaman. Two Hindus were unpacking bundles out of a creaking araba, watched scornfully by an unmistakable Pathan. A fat swarthy-faced Greek in black frock coat and trousers, fez, and slippered feet gesticulated with his right arm like a pump-handle while he sat on the balcony-rail and bellowed orders to a crowd mixed of Armenians, Italians, Maltese, Syrians and a Turk or two, who labored with his bales of cotton goods below. (The Italians eyed everybody sidewise, for there were rumors in those days of impending trouble, and when the Turk begins hostilities he likes his first opponents easy and ready to hand.)

There were Kurds, long-nosed, lean-lipped, and suspicious, who said very little, but hugged long knives as they passed back and forth among the swarming strangers. They said nothing at all, those Kurds, but listened a very great deal.

Tall, mustached Circassians, with eighteen-inch Erzerum daggers at their waists, swaggered about as if they, and only they, were history's heirs. It was expedient to get out of their path alertly, but they cringed into second place before the Turks, who, without any swagger at all, lorded it over every one. For the Turk is a conqueror, whatever else he ought to be. The poorest Turkish servant is race-conscious, and unshakably convinced of his own superiority to the princes of the conquered. One has to bear that fact in mind when dealing with the Turk; it colors all his views of life, and accounts for some of his famous unexpectedness.

Will and I fell in love with the crowd, and engaged a room over the great arched entrance. We were aware from the first of the dull red marks on the walls of the room, where bed bugs had been slain with slipper heels by angry owners of the blood; but we were not in search of luxury, and we had our belongings and a can of insect-bane brought down from the hotel at once. The fact that stallions squealed and fought in the stalls across the courtyard scarcely promised us uninterrupted sleep; but sleep is not to be weighed in the balance against the news of eastern nights.

We went down to the common room close beside the main entrance, and pushed the door open a little way; the men who sat within with their backs against it would only yield enough to pass one person in gingerly at a time. We saw a sea of heads and hats and faces. It looked impossible to squeeze another human being in among those already seated on the floor, nor to make another voice heard amid all that Babel.

But the Babel ceased, and they did make room for us — places of honor against the far wall, because of our clean clothes and nationality. We sat wedged between a Georgian in smelly, greasy woolen jacket, and a man who looked Persian but talked for the most part French. There were other Persians beyond him, for I caught the word poul — money, the perennial song and shibboleth of that folk.

The day was fine enough, but consensus of opinion had it that snow was likely falling in the Taurus Mountains, and rain would fall the next day between the mountains and the sea, making roads and fords impassable and the mountain passes risky. So men from the ends of earth sat still contentedly, to pass earth's gossip to and fro — an astonishing lot of it. There was none of it quite true, and some of it not nearly true, but all of it was based on fact of some sort.

Men who know the khans well are agreed that with experience one learns to guess the truth from listening to the ever-changing lies. We could not hope to pick out truth, but sat as if in the pit of an old-time theater, watching a foreign-language play and understanding some, but missing most of it.

There was a man who drew my attention at once, who looked and was dressed rather like a Russian — a man with a high-bridged, prominent, lean nose — not nearly so bulky as his sheepskin coat suggested, but active and strong, with a fiery restless eye. He talked Russian at intervals with the men who sat near him at the end of the room on our right, but used at least six other languages with any one who cared to agree or disagree with him. His rather agreeable voice had the trick of carrying words distinctly across the din of countless others.

"What do you suppose is that man's nationality?" I asked Will, shouting to him because of the roar, although he sat next me.

"Ermenie!" said a Turk next but one beyond Will, and spat venomously, as if the very name Armenian befouled his mouth.

But I was not convinced that the man with the aquiline nose was Armenian. He looked guilty of altogether too much zest for life, and laughed too boldly in Turkish presence. In those days most Armenians thereabouts were sad. I called Will's attention to him again.

"What do you make of him?"

"He belongs to that quieter party in the opposite corner." (Will puts two and two together all the time, because the heroes of dime novels act that way.)

"They're gypsies, yet I'd say he's not —"

"He and the others are jingaan," said a voice beside me in English, and I looked into the Persian's gentle brown eyes. "The jingaan are street robbers pure and simple," be added by way of explanation.

"But what nationality?"

"Jingaan might be anything. They in particular would call themselves Romany. We call them Zingarri. Not a dependable people — unless —"

I waited in vain for the qualification. He shrugged his shoulders, as if there was no sense in praising evil qualities.

But I was not satisfied yet. They were swarthier and stockier than the man who had interested me, and had indefinite, soft eyes. The man I watched had brown eyes, but they were hard. And, unlike them, he had long lean fingers and his gestures were all extravagant. He was not a Jew, I was sure of that, nor a Syrian, nor yet a Kurd.

"Ermenie — Ermenie!" said the Turk, watching me curiously, and spitting again. "That one is Ermenie. Those others are just dogs!"

The crowd began to thin after a while, as men filed out to feed cattle and to cook their own evening meal. Then the perplexing person got up and came over toward me, showing no fear of the Turk at all. He was tall and lean when he stood upright, but enormously strong if one could guess correctly through the bulky-looking outer garment.

He stood in front of Will and me, his strong yellow teeth gleaming between a black beard and mustache. The Turk got up clumsily, and went out, muttering to himself. I glanced toward the corner where the self-evident gypsies sat, and observed that with perfect unanimity they were all feigning sleep.

"Eenglis sportmen!" said the man in front of us, raising

both hands, palms outward, in appraisal of our clothes and general appearance.

It was not surprising that he should talk English, for what the British themselves have not accomplished in that land of a hundred tongues has been done by American missionaries, teaching in the course of a generation thousands on thousands. (There is none like the American missionary for attaining ends at wholesale.)

"What countryman are you?" I asked him.

"Zeitoonli," he answered, as if the word were honor itself and explanation bound in one. Yet he looked hardly like an honorable man. "The chilabi are staying here?" he asked. Chilabi means gentleman.

"We wait on the weather," said I, not caring to have him turn the tables on me and become interrogator.

He laughed with a sort of hard good humor.

"Since when have Eenglis sportmen waited on the weather? Ah, but you are right, effendi, none should tell the truth in this place, unless in hope of being disbelieved!" He laid a finger on his right eye, as I have seen Arabs do when they mean to ascribe to themselves unfathomable cunning. "Since you entered this common room you have not ceased to observe me closely. The other sportman has watched those Zingarri. What have you learned?"

He stood with lean hands crossed now in front of him, looking at us down his nose, not ceasing to smile, but a hint less at his ease, a shade less genial.

"I have heard you — and them — described as jingaan," I answered, and he stiffened instantly.

Whether or not they took that for a signal — or perhaps he made another that we did not see — the six undoubted gypsies got up and left the room, shambling out in single file with the awkward gait they share in common with red Indians.

"Jingaan," he said, "are people who lurk in shadows of the streets to rob belated travelers. That is not my business." He looked very hard indeed at the Persian, who decided that it might as well be suppertime and rose stiffly to his feet. The Persians rob and murder, and even retreat, gracefully. He bade us a stately and benignant good evening, with a poetic Persian blessing at the end of it. He bowed, too, to the Zeitoonli, who bared his teeth and bent his head forward something less than an inch.

"They call me the Eye of Zeitoon!" he announced with a sort of savage pride, as soon as the Persian was out of earshot.

Will pricked his ears — schoolboy looking ears that stand out from his head.

"I've heard of Zeitoon. It's a village on a mountain, where a man steps out of his front door on to a neighbor's roof, and the women wear no veils, and —"

The man showed his teeth in another yellow smile.

"The effendi is blessed with intelligence! Few know of Zeitoon."

Will and I exchanged glances.

"Ours," said Will, "is the best room in the khan, over the entrance gate."

"Two such chilabi should surely live like princes," he answered without a smile. If he had dared say that and smile we would have struck him, and Monty might have been alive today. But he seemed to know his place, although he looked at us down his nose again in shrewd appraisal.

Will took out tobacco and rolled what in the innocence of his Yankee heart he believed was a cigarette. I produced and lit what he contemptuously called a "boughten cigaroot" — Turkish Regie, with the scent of aboriginal ambrosia. The Zeitoonli took the hint.

"Yarim sa' at," he said. "Korkakma!"

"Meanin'?" demanded Will.

"In half an hour. Do not be afraid!" said he.

"Before I grow afraid of you," Will retorted, "you'll need your friends along, and they'll need knives!"

The Zeitoonli bowed, laid a finger on his eye again, smiled, and backed away. But he did not leave the room. He went back to the end-wall against which he had sat before, and although he did not stare at us the intention not to let us out of sight seemed pretty obvious.

"That half-hour stuff smacked rather of a threat," said Will. "Suppose we call the bluff, and keep him waiting. What do you say if we go and dine at the hotel?"

But in the raw enthusiasm of entering new quarters we had

made up our minds that afternoon to try out our new camp
kitchen — a contraption of wood and iron we had built with
the aid of the mission carpenter. And the walk to the hotel
would have been a long one, through Tarsus mud in the dark,
with prowling dogs to take account of.

"I'm not afraid of ten of him!" said I. "I know how to cook
curried eggs; come on!"

"Who said who was afraid?"

So we went out into darkness already jeweled by a hundred
lanterns, dodged under the necks of three hungry Bactrian
camels (they are irritable when they want their meal), were
narrowly missed by a mule's heels because of the deceptive
shadows that confused his aim, tripped over a donkey's
heel-rope, and found our stairway — thoroughly well cursed
in seven languages, and only just missed by a Georgian
gentleman on the balcony, who chose the moment of our
passing underneath to empty out hissing liquid from his
cooking pot.

Once in our four-square room, with the rags on the floor
in our especial honor, and our beds set up, and the folding
chairs in place, contentment took hold of us; and as we
lighted the primus burner in the cooking box, we pitied from
the bottom of compassionate young hearts all unfortunates
in stiff white shirts, whose dinners were served that night on
silver and laundered linen.

Through the partly open door we could smell everything
that ever happened since the beginning of the world, and hear
most of the elemental music — made, for instance, of the
squeal of fighting stallions, and the bray of an amorous he-ass
— the bubbling complaint of fed camels that want to go to
sleep, but are afraid of dreaming — the hum of human voices
— the clash of cooking pots — the voice of a man on the roof
singing falsetto to the stars (that was surely the Pathan!) —
the tinkling of a three-stringed instrument — and all of that
punctuated by the tapping of a saz, the little tight-skinned
Turkish drum.

It is no use for folk whose fingernails were never dirty, and
who never scratched themselves while they cooked a meal
over the primus burner on the floor, to say that all that
medley of sounds and smells is not good. It is very good

indeed, only he who is privileged must understand, or else the spell is mere confusion.

The cooking box was hardly a success, because bright eyes watching through the open door made us nervously amateurish. The Zeitoonli arrived true to his threat on the stroke of the half-hour, and we could not shut the door in his face because of the fumes of food and kerosene. (Two of the eggs, like us, were travelers and had been in more than one bazaar.)

But we did not invite him inside until our meal was finished, and then we graciously permitted him to go for water wherewith to wash up. He strode back and forth on the balcony, treading ruthlessly on prayer-mats (for the Moslem prays in public like the Pharisees of old).

"Myself I am Christian," he said, spitting over the rail, and sitting down again to watch us. We accepted the remark with reservations.

When we asked him in at last, and we had driven out the flies with flapping towels, be closed the door and squatted down with his back to it, we two facing him in our canvas-backed easy chairs. He refused the "genuine Turkish" coffee that Will stewed over the primus. Will drank the beastly stuff, of course, to keep himself in countenance, and I did not care to go back on a friend before a foreigner, but I envied the man from Zeitoon his liberty of choice.

"Why do they call you the Eye of Zeitoon?" I asked, when time enough had elapsed to preclude his imagining that we regarded him seriously. One has to be careful about beginnings in the Near East, even as elsewhere.

"I keep watch!" he answered proudly, but also with a deeply grounded consciousness of cunning. There were moments when I felt such strong repugnance for the man that I itched to open the door and thrust him through — other moments when compassion for him urged me to offer money — food — influence — anything. The second emotion fought all the while against the first, and I found out afterward it had been the same with Will.

"Why should Zeitoon need such special watching?" I demanded. "How do you watch? Against whom? Why?"

He laughed with a pair of lawless eyes, and showed his yellow teeth.

"Ha! Shall I speak of Zeitoon? This, then: the Turks never conquered it! They came once and built a fort on the opposite mountainside, with guns to overawe us all. We took their fort by storm! We threw their cannon down a thousand feet into the bed of the torrent, and there they lie today! We took prisoner as many of their Arab zaptiehs as still were living — aye, they even brought Arabs against us — poor fools who had not yet heard of Zeitoon's defenders! Then we came down to the plains for a little vengeance, leaving the Arabs for our wives to guard. They are women of spirit, the Zeitoonli wives!

"Word reached Zeitoon presently that we were being hard pressed on the plains. It was told to the Zeitoonli wives that they might arrange to have pursuit called off from us by surrendering those Arab prisoners. They answered that Zeitoon-fashion. How? I will tell. There is a bridge of wood, flung over across the mountain torrent, five hundred feet above the water, spanning from crag to crag. Those Zeitoonli wives of ours bound the Arab prisoners hand and foot. They brought them out along the bridge. They threw them over one at a time, each man looking on until his turn came. That was the answer of the brave Zeitoonli wives!"

"And you on the plains?"

"Ah! It takes better than Osmanli to conquer the men of Zeitoon!" he gave the Turks their own names for themselves with the air of a brave fighting man conceding his opponent points. "We heard what our wives had done. We were encouraged. We prevailed! We fell back toward our mountain and prevailed! There in Zeitoon we have weapons — numbers — advantage of position, for no roads come near Zeitoon that an araba, or a gun, or anything on wheels can use. The only thing we fear is treachery, leading to surprise in overwhelming force. And against these I keep watch!"

"Why should you tell us all this?" demanded Will.

"How do you know we are not agents of the Turkish government?"

He laughed outright, throwing out both hands toward us. "Eenglis sportmen!" he said simply.

"What's that got to do with it?" Will retorted. He has the unaccountable American dislike of being mistaken for an Englishman, but long ago gave up arguing the point, since foreigners refuse, as a rule, to see the sacred difference.

"I am, too, sportman. At Zeitoon there is very good sport. Bear. Antelope. Wild boar. One sportman to another — do you understand?"

We did, and did not believe.

"How far to Zeitoon?" I demanded.

"I go in five days when I hurry. You — not hurrying — by horse — seven — eight — nine days, depending on the roads."

"Are they all Armenians in Zeitoon?"

"Most. Not all. There are Arabs — Syrians — Persians — a few Circassians — even Kurds and a Turk or two. Our numbers have been reinforced continually by deserters from the Turkish Army. Ninety-five per cent., however, are Armenians," he added with half-closed eyes, suddenly suggesting that masked meekness that disguises most outrageous racial pride.

"It is common report," I said, "that the Turks settled all Armenian problems long ago by process of massacre until you have no spirit for revolt left."

"The report lies, that is all!" he answered. Then suddenly he beat on his chest with clenched fist. "There is spirit here! There is spirit in Zeitoon! No Osmanli dare molest my people! Come to Zeitoon to shoot bear, boar, antelope! I will show you! I will prove my words!"

"Were those six jingaan in the common room your men?" I asked him, and he laughed as suddenly as he had stormed, like a teacher at a child's mistake.

"Jingaan is a bad word," he said. "I might kill a man who named me that — depending on the man. My brother I would kill for it — a stranger perhaps not. Those men are Zingarri, who detest to sleep between brick walls. They have a tent pitched in the yard."

"Are they your men?"

"Zingarri are no man's men."

The denial carried no conviction.

"Is there nothing but hunting at Zeitoon?" Will demanded.

"Is that not much? In addition the place itself is wonderful — a mountain in a mist, with houses clinging to the flanks of it, and scenery to burst the heart!"

"What else?" I asked. "No ancient buildings?"

He changed his tactics instantly.

"Effendi," he said, leaning forward and pointing a forefinger at me by way of emphasis, "there are castles on the mountains near Zeitoon that have never been explored since the Turks — may God destroy them! — overran the land! Castles hidden among trees where only bears dwell! Castles built by the Seljuks — Armenians — Romans — Saracens — Crusaders! I know the way to every one of them!"

"What else?" demanded Will, purposely incredulous.

"Beyond Zeitoon to north and west are cave-dwellers. Mountains so hollowed out that only a shell remains, a sponge — a honeycomb! No man knows how far those tunnels run! The Turks have attempted now and then to smoke out the inhabitants. They were laughed at! One mountain is connected with another, and the tunnels run for miles and miles!"

"I've seen cave-dwellings in the States," Will answered, unimpressed. "But just where do you come in?"

"I do not understand."

"What do you propose to get out of it?"

"Nothing! I am proud of my country. I am sportman. I am pleased to show."

We both jeered at him, for that explanation was too outrageously ridiculous. Armenians love money, whatever else they do or leave undone, and can wring a handsome profit out of business whose very existence the easier-going Turk would not suspect.

"See if I can't read your mind," said Will. "You'll guide us for some distance out of town, at a place you know, and your jingaan-gypsy brethren will hold us up at some point and rob us to a fare-you-well. Is that the pretty scheme?"

Some men would have flown into a fury. Some would have laughed the matter off. Any and every crook would have been at pains to hide his real feelings. Yet this strange individual was at a loss how to answer, and not averse to our knowing that.

For a moment a sort of low cunning seemed to creep over his mind, but he dismissed it. Three times be raised his hands, palms upward, and checked himself in the middle of a word.

"You could pay me for my services," he said at last, not as if that were the real reason, nor as if he hoped to convince us that it was, but as if he were offering an excuse that we might care to accept for the sake of making peace with our own compunctions.

"There are four in our party," said Will, apropos apparently of nothing. The effect was unexpected.

"Four?" His eyes opened wide, and be made the knuckle-bones of both hands crack like caps going off. "Four Eenglis sportman?"

"I said four. If you're willing to tell the naked truth about what's back of your offer, I'll undertake to talk it over with my other friends. Then, either we'll all four agree to take you up, or we'll give you a flat refusal within a day or two. Now — suit yourself."

"I have told the truth — Zeitoon — caves — boar — antelope — wild boar. I am a very good guide. You shall pay me handsomely."

"Sure, we'll ante up like foreigners. But why do you make the proposal? What's behind it?"

"I never saw you until this afternoon. You are Eenglis sportmen. I can show good sport. You shall pay me. Could it be simpler?"

It seemed to me we had been within an ace of discovery, but the man's mind had closed again against us in obedience to some racial or religious instinct outside our comprehension. He had been on the verge of taking us into confidence.

"Let the sportmen think it over," he said, getting up. "Jannam! (My soul!) Effendi, when I was a younger man none could have made me half such a sportmanlike proposal without an answer on the instant! A man fit to strike the highway with his foot should be a judge of men! I have judged you fit to be invited! Now you judge me — the Eye of Zeitoon!"

"What is your real name?"

"I have none — or many, which is the same thing! I did not ask your names; they are your own affair!"

He stood with his hand on the door, not irresolute, but taking one last look at us and our belongings.

"I wish you comfortable sleep, and long lives, effendim!" he said then, and swung himself out, closing the door behind him with an air of having honored us, not we him particularly. And after he had gone we were not at all sure that summary of the situation was not right.

We lay awake on our cots until long after midnight, hazarding guesses about him. Whatever else he had done he had thoroughly aroused our curiosity.

"If you want my opinion that's all he was after anyway!" said Will, dropping his last cigarette-end on the floor and flattening it with his slipper.

"Cut the cackle, and let's sleep!"

We fell asleep at last amid the noise of wild carousing; for the proprietor of the Yeni Khan, although a Turk, and therefore himself presumably abstemious, was not above dispensing at a price mastika that the Greeks get drunk on, and the viler raki, with which Georgians, Circassians, Albanians, and even the less religious Turks woo imagination or forgetfulness.

There was knife fighting as well as carousal before dawn, to judge by the cat-and-dog-fight swearing in and out among the camel pickets and the wheels of arabas. But that was the business of the men who fought, and no one interfered.

Chapter Two

"How did sunshine get into the garden? By whose leave came the wind?"

A TIME AND TIMES AND HALF A TIME

When Cydnus bore the Taurus snows
To sweeten Cleopatra's keels,
And rippled in the breeze that sings
From Kara Dagh, where leafy wings
Of flowers fall and gloaming steals
The colors of the blowing rose,
Old were the wharves and woods and ways —
Older the tale of steel and fire,
Involved intrigue, envenomed plan,
Man marketing his brother man
By dread duress to glut desire.
No peace was in those olden days.RHope like the gorgeous rose sun-warmed
Blossomed and blew away and died,
Till gentleness had ceased to be
And Tarsus knew no chivalry
Could live an hour by Cydnus' side
Where all the heirs of evil swarmed.
And yet — with every swelling spring
Each pollen-scented zephyr's breath
Repeats the patient news to ears
Made dull by dreams of loveless years,
"It is of life, and not of death
That ye shall hear the Cydnus sing!"

We awoke amid sounds unexplainable. Most of the Mos-

lems had finished their noisy ritual ablutions, and at dawn
we had been dimly conscious of the strings of camels, mules
and donkeys jingling out under the arch beneath us. Yet there
was a great din from the courtyard of wild hoofs thumping
on the dung, and of scurrying feet as if a mile-long caravan
were practicing formations.

So we went out to yawn, and remained, oblivious of everything but the cause of all the noise, we leaning with elbows
on the wooden rail, and she laughing up at us at intervals.

The six Zingarri, or gypsies, had pitched their tent in the
very middle of the yard, ambitious above all other considera-
tions to keep away from walls. It was a big, low, black affair
supported on short poles, and subdivided by them into
several compartments. One could see unshapely bulges where
women did the housekeeping within.

But the woman who held us spellbound cared nothing for
Turkish custom — a girl not more than seventeen years old
at the boldest guess. She was breaking a gray stallion in the
yard, sitting the frenzied beast without a saddle and doing
whatever she liked with him, except that his heels made free
of the air, and he went from point to point whichever end
up best pleased his fancy.

Travelers make an early start in Asia Minor, but the yard
was by no means empty yet; some folk were still waiting on
the doubtful weather. Her own people kept to the tent.
Whoever else had business in the yard made common cause
and cursed the girl for making the disturbance, frightening
camels, horses, asses and themselves. And she ignored them
all, unless it was on purpose that she brought her stallion's
heels too close for safety to the most abusive.

It was only for us two that she had any kind of friendly
interest; she kept looking up at us and laughing as she caught
our eyes, bringing her mount uprearing just beneath us
several times. She was pretty as the peep o' morning, with
long, black wavy hair all loose about her shoulders, and as
light on the horse as the foam he tossed about, although
master of him without a second's doubt of it.

When she had had enough of riding — long before we were
tired of the spectacle — she shouted with a voice like a mellow
bell. One of the gypsies ran out and led away the sweating

stallion, and she disappeared into the tent throwing us a laugh over her shoulder.

"D'you suppose those gypsies are really of that Armenian's party?" Will wondered aloud. "Now, if she were going to Zeitoon — !"

Feeling as he did, I mocked at him to hide my feelings, and we hung about for another hour in hope of seeing her again, but she kept close. I don't doubt she watched us through a hole in the tent. We would have sat there alert in our chairs until evening only Fred sent a note down to say he was well enough to leave the hospital.

We found him with his beard trimmed neatly and his fevered eyes all bright again, sitting talking to the nurse on the veranda about a niece of hers — Gloria Vanderman.

"Chicken in this desert!" Will wondered irreverently, and Fred, who likes his English to have dictionary meanings, rose from his chair in wrath. The nurse made that the cue for getting rid of us.

"Take Mr. Oakes away!" she urged, laughing. "He threatened to kill a man this morning. There's too much murder in Tarsus now. If he should add to it —"

"You know it wasn't on my account," Fred objected. "It was what he wrote — and said of you. Why, he has had you prayed for publicly by name, and you washing the brute's feet! Let me back in there for just five minutes, and I'll show what a hospital case should really look like!"

"Take him away!" she laughed. "Isn't it bad enough to be prayed for? Must I get into the papers, too, as heroine of a scandal?"

The head missionary was not there to say good-bye to, life in his case being too serious an affair to waste minutes of a precious morning on farewells, so we packed Fred into the waiting carriage and drove all the way to Mersina, where we interrupted Monty's mid-afternoon game of chess.

Fred Oakes and Monty were the closest friends I ever met — one problem for an enemy — one stout, two-headed, most dependable ally for the lucky man or woman they called friend.

"Oh, hullo!" said Monty over his shoulder, as our names were called out by the stately consular kavass.

"Hullo!" said Fred, and shook hands with the consul.

"Thought you were due to be sick for another week?" said Monty, closing up the board.

"I was. I would have been. Bed would have done me good, and the nurse is a darling, old enough to be Will's mother. But they put a biped by the name of Peter Measel in the bed next mine. He's a missionary on his own account, and keeps a diary. Seems he contributes to the funds of a Welsh mission in France, and they do what he says. He has all the people he disapproves of prayed for publicly by name in the mission hall in Marseilles, with extracts out of his diary by way of explanation, so that the people who pray may know what they've got on their hands. The special information I gave him about you, Monty, will make Marseilles burn! He's got you down as a drunken pirate, my boy, with no less than eleven wives. But he asked me one night whether I thought what he'd written about the nurse was strong enough, and he read it aloud to me. You'd never believe what the reptile had dared suggest in his devil's logbook! I'm expelled for threatening to kill him!"

"The nurse was right," said the consul gloomily. "There'll be murder enough hereabouts — and soon!"

He was a fairly young man yet in spite of the nearly white hair over the temples. He measured his words in the manner of a man whose speech is taken at face value.

"The missionaries know. The governments won't listen. I've been appealed to. So has the United States consul, and neither of us is going to be able to do much. Remember, I represent a government at peace with Turkey, and so does he. The Turk has a side to his character that governments ignore. Have you watched them at prayer?"

We told him how close we had been on the previous night, and he laughed.

"Did you suppose I couldn't smell camel and khan the moment you came in?"

"That was why Sister Vanderman hurried you off so promptly!" Fred announced with an air of outraged truthfulness. "Faugh! Slangy talk and stink of stables!"

"I was talking of Turks," said the consul. "When they pray, you may have noticed that they glance to right and left. When they think there is nobody looking they do more, they stare deliberately to the right and left. That is the act of recognition of the angel and the devil who are supposed to attend every Moslem, the angel to record his good deeds and the devil his bad ones. To my mind there lies the secret of the Turk's character. Most of the time he's a man of his word — honest — courteous — considerate — good-humored — even chivalrous — living up to the angel. But once in so often he remembers the other shoulder, and then there isn't any limit to the deviltry he'll do. Absolutely not a limit!"

"I suppose we or the Americans could land marines at a pinch, and protect whoever asked for protection?" suggested Monty.

"No," said the consul deliberately. "Germany would object. Germany is the only power that would. Germany would accuse us of scheming to destroy the value of their blessed Baghdad railway."

A privy councilor of England, which Monty was, is not necessarily in touch with politics of any sort. Neither were we; but it happened that more than once in our wanderings about the world things had been forced on our attention.

"They would rather see Europe burn from end to end!" Monty agreed.

"And I think there's more than that in it," said the consul. "Armenians are not their favorites. The Germans want the trade of the Levant. The Armenians are businessmen. They're shrewder than Jews and more dependable than Greeks. It would suit Germany very nicely, I imagine, to have no Armenians to compete with."

"But if Germany once got control of the Near East," I objected, "she could impose her own restrictions."

The consul frowned. "Armenians who thrive in spite of Turks —"

"Would skin a German for hide and tallow," nodded Will.

"Exactly. Germany would object vigorously if we or the States should land marines to prevent the Turks from applying the favorite remedy, vukuart — that means events, you know — their euphemism for massacre at rather frequent intervals. Germany would rather see the Turks finish the dirty work thoroughly than have it to do herself later on."

"You mean," said I, "that the German government is inciting to massacre?"

"Hardly. There are German missionaries in the country, doing good work in a funny, fussy, rigorous fashion of their own. They'd raise a dickens of a hocus-pocus back in Germany if they once suspected their government of playing that game. No. But Germany intends to stand off the other powers, while Turks tackle the Armenians; and the Turks know that."

"But what's the immediate excuse for massacre?" demanded Fred.

The consul laughed.

"All that's needed is a spark. The Armenians haven't been tactful. They don't hesitate to irritate the Turks — not that you can blame them, but it isn't wise. Most of the money-lenders are Armenians; Turks won't engage in that business themselves on religious grounds, but they're ready borrowers, and the Armenian money-lenders, who are in a very small minority, of course, are grasping and give a bad name to the whole nation. Then, Armenians have been boasting openly that one of these days the old Armenian kingdom will be reestablished. The Turks are conquerors, you know, and don't like that kind of talk. If the Armenians could only keep from quarreling among themselves they could win their independence in half a jiffy, but the Turks are deadly wise at the old trick of divide et impera; they keep the Armenians quarreling, and nobody dares stand in with them because sooner — or later — sooner, probably — they'll split among themselves, and leave their friends high and dry. You can't blame 'em. The Turks know enough to play on their religious prejudices and set one sect against another. When the massacres begin scarcely an Armenian will know who is friend and who enemy."

"D'you mean to say," demanded Fred, "that they're going to be shot like bottles off a wall without rhyme or reason?"

"That's how it was before," said the consul. "There's nothing to stop it. The world is mistaken about Armenians. They're a hot-blooded lot on the whole, with a deep sense of national pride, and a hatred of Turkish oppression that rankles. One of these mornings a Turk will choose his Armenian and carefully insult the man's wife or daughter. Perhaps he will crown it by throwing dirt in the fellow's face. The Armenian will kill him or try to, and there you are. Moslem blood shed by a dog of a giaour — the old excuse!"

"Don't the Armenians know what's in store for them?" I asked.

"Some of them know. Some guess. Some are like the villagers on Mount Vesuvius — much as we English were in '57 in India, I imagine — asleep — playing games — getting rich on top of a volcano. The difference is that the Armenians will have no chance."

"Did you ever hear tell of the Eye of Zeitoon?" asked Will, apropos apparently of nothing.

"No," said the consul, staring at him.

Will told him of the individual we had talked with in the khan the night before, describing him rather carefully, not forgetting the gypsies in the black tent, and particularly not the daughter of the dawn who schooled a gray stallion in the courtyard.

The consul shook his head.

"Never saw or heard of any of them."

We were sitting in full view of the roadstead where Anthony and Cleopatra's ships had moored a hundred times. The consul's garden sloped in front of us, and most of the flowers that Europe reckons rare were getting ready to bloom.

"Would you know the man if you saw him again, Will?" I asked.

"Sure I would!"

"Then look!"

I pointed, and seeing himself observed a man stepped out of the shadow of some oleanders. There was something suggestive in his choice of lurking place, for every part of the oleander plant is dangerously poisonous; it was as if he had hidden himself among the hairs of death.

"Him, sure enough!" said Will.

The man came forward uninvited.

"How did you get into the grounds?" the consul demanded, and the man laughed, laying an unafraid hand on the veranda rail.

"My teskere is a better than the Turks give!" he answered

in English. (A teskere is the official permit to travel into the interior.)

"What do you mean?"

"How did sunshine come into the garden? By whose leave came the wind?"

He stood on no formality. Before one of us could interfere (for he might have been plying the assassin's trade) he had vaulted the veranda rail and stood in front of us. As he jumped I heard the rattle of loose cartridges, and the thump of a hidden pistol against the woodwork. I could see the hilt of a dagger, too, just emerging from concealment through the opening in his smock. But he stood in front of us almost meekly, waiting to be spoken to.

"You are without shame!" said the consul.

"Truly! Of what should I be ashamed!"

"What brought you here?"

"Two feet and a great good will! You know me."

The consul shook his head.

"Who sold the horse to the German from Bitlis?"

"Are you that man?"

"Who clipped the wings of a kite, and sold it for ten pounds to a fool for an eagle from Ararat?"

The consul laughed.

"Are you the rascal who did that?"

"Who threw Olim Pasha into the river, and pushed him in and in again for more than an hour with a fishing pole — and then threw in the gendarmes who ran to arrest him — and only ran when the Eenglis consul came?"

"I remember," said the consul.

"Yet you don't look quite like that man."

"I told you you knew me."

"Neither does today's wind blow like yesterday's!"

"What is your name?"

"Then it was Ali."

"What is it now?"

"The name God gave me?"

"Yes."

"God knows!"

"What do you want here?"

He spread out his arms toward us four, and grinned.

"Look — see! Four Eenglis sportman! Could a man want more?"

"Your face is hauntingly familiar," said the consul, searching old memories.

"No doubt. Who carried your honor's letter to Adrianople in time of war, and received a bullet, but brought the answer back?"

"What — are you that man — Kagig?"

Instead of replying the man opened his smock, and pulled aside an undershirt until his hairy left breast lay bare down to where the nipple should have been. Why a bullet that drilled that nipple so neatly had not pierced the heart was simply mystery.

"Kagig, by jove! Kagig with a beard! Nobody would know you but for that scar."

"But now you know me surely? Tell these Eenglis sportman, then, that I am good man — good guide! Tell them they come with me to Zeitoon!"

The consul's face darkened swiftly, clouded by some notion that he seemed to try to dismiss, but that refused to leave him.

"How much would you ask for your services?" he demanded.

"Whatever the effendim please."

"Have you a horse?"

He nodded.

"You and your horse, then, two piasters a day, and you feed yourself and the beast."

The man agreed, very bright-eyed. Often it takes a day or two to come to terms with natives of that country, yet the terms the consul offered him were those for a man of very ordinary attainments.

"Come back in an hour," said the consul.

Without a word of answer Kagig vaulted back across the rail and disappeared around the corner of the house, walking without hurry but not looking back.

"Kagig, by jove! It would take too long now to tell that story of the letter to Adrianople. I've no proof, but a private notion that Kagig is descended from the old Armenian kings. In a certain sort of tight place there's not a better man in

Asia. Now, Lord Montdidier, if you're in earnest about searching for that castle of your Crusader ancestors, you're in luck!"

"You know it's what I came here for," said Monty. "These friends of mine are curious, and I'm determined. Now that Fred's well —"

"I'm puzzled," said the consul, leaning back and looking at us all with half-closed eyes. "Why should Kagig choose just this time to guide a hunting party? If any man knows trouble's brewing, I suspect be surely does. Anything can happen in the interior. I recall, for instance, a couple of Danes, who went with a guide not long ago, and simply disappeared. There are outlaws everywhere, and it's more than a theory that the public officials are in league with them."

"What a joke if we find the old family castle is a nest of robbers," smiled Monty.

"Still!" corrected Fred.

I was watching the consul's eyes. He was troubled, but the prospect of massacre did not account for all of his expression. There was debate, inspiration against conviction, being fought out under cover of forced calm. Inspiration won the day.

"I was wondering," he said, and lit a fresh cigar while we waited for him to go on.

"I vouch for my friends," said Monty.

"It wasn't that. I've no right to make the proposal — no official right whatever — I'm speaking strictly unofficially — in fact, it's not a proposal at all — merely a notion."

He paused to give himself a last chance, but indiscretion was too strong.

"I was wondering how far you four men would go to save twenty or thirty thousand lives."

"You've no call to wonder about that," said Will.

"Suppose you tell us what you've got in mind," suggested Monty, putting his long legs on a chair and producing a cigarette.

The consul knocked out his pipe and sat forward, beginning to talk a little faster, as a man who throws discretion to the winds.

"I've no legal right to interfere. None at all. In case of a massacre of Armenians — men, women, little children — I could do nothing. Make a fuss, of course. Throw open the consulate to refugees. Threaten a lot of things that I know perfectly well my government won't do. The Turks will be polite to my face and laugh behind my back, knowing I'm helpless. But if you four men —"

"Yes — go on — what?"

"Spill it!" urged Will.

"— should be up-country, and I knew it for a fact, but did not know your precise whereabouts, I'd have a grown excuse for raising most particular old Harry! You get my meaning?"

"Sure!" said Will. "Monty's an earl. Fred's related to half the peerages in Burke. Me and him" — I was balancing my chair on one leg and he pushed me over backward by way of identification — "just pose as distinguished members of society for the occasion. I get you."

"It might even be possible, Mr. Yerkes, to get the United States Congress to take action on your account."

"Don't you believe it!" laughed Will. "The members for the Parish Pump, and the senators from Ireland would howl about the Monroe Doctrine and Washington's advice at the merest hint of a Yankee in trouble in foreign parts."

"What about the United States papers?"

"They'd think it was an English scheme to entangle the United States, and they'd be afraid to support action for fear of the Irish. No, England's your only chance!"

"Well," said the consul, "I've told you the whole idea. If I should happen to know of four important individuals somewhere up-country, and massacres should break out after you had started, I could supply our ambassador with something good to work on. The Turkish government might have to stop the massacre in the district in which you should happen to be. That would save lives."

"But could they stop it, once started?" I asked.

"They could try. That 'ud be more than they ever did yet."

"You mean," said Monty, "that you'd like us to engage Kagig and make the trip, and to remain out in case of — ah — vukuart until we're rescued?"

"Can't say I like it, but that's what I mean. And as for rescue, the longer the process takes the better, I imagine!"

"Hide, and have them hunt for us, eh?"

"Would it help," I suggested, "if we were to be taken prisoner by outlaws and held for ransom?"

"It might," said the consul darkly. "I'd take to the hills myself and send back a wail for help, only my plain duty is here at the mission. What I have suggested to you is mad quixotism at the best, and at the worst — well, do you recall what happened to poor Vyner, who was held for ransom by Greek brigands? They sent a rescue party instead of money, and —"

"Charles Vyner was a friend of mine," said Monty quietly.

Fred began to look extremely cheerful and Will nudged me and nodded.

"Remember," said the consul, "in the present state of European politics there's no knowing what can or can't be done, but if you four men are absent in the hills I believe I can give the Turkish government so much to think about that there'll be no massacres in that one district."

"Whistle up Kagig!" Monty answered, and that was the end of the argument as far as yea or nay had anything to do with it. Prospect of danger was the last thing likely to divide the party.

"How about permits to travel?" asked Will. "The United States consul told me none is to be had at present."

The consul rubbed his thumb and forefinger together.

"It may cost a little more, that's all," he said. "You might go without, but you'd better submit to extortion."

He called the kavass, the uniformed consular attendant, and sent him in search of Kagig. Within two minutes the Eye of Zeitoon was grinning at us through a small square window in the wall at one end of the veranda. Then he came round and once more vaulted the veranda rail, for he seemed to hold ordinary means of entry in contempt. His eye looked very possessive for that of one seeking employment as a guide, but he stood at respectful attention until spoken to.

"These gentlemen have decided to employ you," the consul announced.

"Mashallah!" (God be praised!) For a Christian he used unusual expletives.

"They want to find a castle in the mountains, to hunt bear and boar, and to see Zeitoon."

"I shall lead them to ten castles never seen before by Eenglismen! They shall kill all the bears and pigs! Never was such sport as they shall see!"

He exploded the word pigs as if he had the Osmanli prejudice against that animal. Yet he wore a pigskin cartridge belt about his middle.

"They will need enormous lots of ammunition!" he announced.

"What else would the roadside robbers like them to bring?"

"No Turkish servants! They throw Turks over a bridge-side in Zeitoon! I myself will provide servants, who shall bring them back safely!"

It seemed to me that he breathed inward as he said that. A Turk would have added "Inshallah!" — if God wills!

"Make ready for a journey of two months," he said.

"When and where shall the start be?"

It would obviously be unwise to start from the consulate.

"From the Yeni Khan in Tarsus," said Will.

"That is very good — that is excellent! I will send Zeitoonli servants to the Yeni Khan at once. Pay them the right price. Have you horses? Camels are of no use, nor yet are wheels — you shall know why later! Mules are best."

"I know where you can hire mules," said the consul, "with a Turkish muleteer to each pair."

"Oh, well!" laughed Kagig, leaning back against the rail and moving his hands palms upward as if he weighed one thought against another. "What is the difference? If a few Turks move or less come to an end over Zeitoon bridge —"

It was only for moments at a time that he seemed able to force himself to speak as our inferior. A Turk of the guide class would likely have knelt and placed a foot of each of us on his neck in turn as soon as he knew we had engaged him. This Armenian seemed made of other stuff.

"Then be on hand tomorrow morning," ordered Monty.

But the Eye of Zeitoon had another surprise for us.

"I shall meet you on the road," he announced with an air of a social equal. "Servants shall attend you at the Yeni Khan. They will say nothing at all, and work splendidly! Start when you like; you will find me waiting for you at a good place on the road. Bring not plenty, but too much ammunition! Good day, then, gentlemen!"

He nodded to us — bowed to the consul — vaulted the rail. A second later he grinned at us again through the tiny window. "I am the Eye of Zeitoon!" he boasted, and was gone. A servant whom the consul sent to follow him came back after ten or fifteen minutes saying he had lost him in a maze of narrow streets.

His latter, offhanded manner scarcely auguring well, we debated whether or not to search for some one more likely amenable to discipline to take his place. But the consul spent an hour telling us about the letter that went to Adrianople, and the bringing back of the answer that hastened peace.

"He was shot badly. He nearly died on the way back. I've no idea how he recovered. He wouldn't accept a piaster more than the price agreed on."

"Let's take a chance!" said Will, and we were all agreed before he urged it.

"There's one other thing," said the consul. "I've been told a Miss Gloria Vanderman is on her way to the mission at Marash —"

"Gee whiz!" said Will.

The consul nodded. "She's pretty, if that's what you mean. It was very unwise to let her go, escorted only by Armenians. Of course, she may get through without as much as suspecting trouble's brewing, but — well — I wish you'd look out for her."

"Chicken, eh?"

Will stuck both hands deep in his trousers pockets and tilted his chair backward to the point of perfect poise.

"Cuckoo, you ass!" laughed Fred, kicking the chair over backward, and then piling all the veranda furniture on top, to the scandalized amazement of the stately kavass, who came at that moment shepherding a small boy with a large tray and perfectly enormous drinks.

Chapter Three

"Sahib, there is always — work for real soldiers!"

WHERE TWO OR THREE

Oh, all the world is sick with hate,
And who shall heal it, friend o' mine?
And who is friend? And who shall stand
Since hireling tongue and alien hand
Kill nobleness in all this land?
Judas and Pharisee combine
To plunder and proclaim it Fate.

Days when the upright dared be few
Are they departed, friend o' mine?
Are bribery and rich largesse
Fair props for fat forgetfulness,
Or anodynous of distress?
Oh, would the world were drunk with wine
And not this last besotting brew!

Oh, for the wonderful again —
The greatly daring, friend o' mine!
The simply gallant blade unbought,
The soul compassionate, unsought,
With no price but the priceless thought
Nor purpose than the brave design
Of giving that the world may gain!

So we took two rooms at the Yeni Khan instead of one, not
being minded to sleep as closely as the gentry of Asia Minor

like to. Will hurried us down there for a look at the gypsy girl. But the tent was gone and the gypsies with it, and when we asked questions about them people spat.

Your good Moslem — and a Moslem is good in those parts who makes a mountain of observances, regarding mole-hills of mere morals not at all — affects to despise all giaours; but a giaour, like a gypsy, who has no obvious religion of any kind, he ranks below the pig in order of reverence. It did not redound to our credit that we showed interest in the movements of such people.

Monty brought an enormous can of bug-powder with him, and restored our popularity by lending generously after he had treated our quarters sufficiently for three days' stay. Fred did nothing to our quarters — stirred no finger, claiming convalescence with his tongue in his cheek, and strolling about until he fell utterly in love with the khan and its crowd, and the khan with him. That very first night he brought out his concertina on the balcony, and yowled songs to its clamor; and whether or not the various crowd agreed on naming the noise music, all were delighted with the friendliness.

Fred talks more languages fluently than he can count on the fingers of both hands. He began to tell tales in a singsong eastern snarl — a tale in Persian, then in Turkish, and the night grew breathless, full of listening, until pent-up interest at intervals burst bonds and there were "Ahs" and "Ohs" all amid the dark, like little breaths of night wind among trees.

He found small time for sleep, and when dawn came, and four Zeitoonli servants according to Kagig's promise, they still swarmed around him begging for more. He went off to eat breakfast with a khan from Bukhara, sitting on a bale of nearly priceless carpets to drink overland tea made in a thing like a samovar.

All the rest of that day, and the next, sleeping only at intervals, while Monty and Will and I helped the Zeitoonli servants get our loads in shape, Fred sharpened his wonder-gift of tongues on the fascinated men of many nations, giving them London ditties and tales from the Thousand Nights and a Night in exchange for their news of caravan routes. He left them well pleased with their bargain.

Monty went off alone the second day to see about mules.

The Turk with a trade to make believes that of several partners one is always "easier" than the rest; consequently, one man can bring him to see swifter reason than a number can. He came back that evening with twelve good mules and four attendants.

"One apiece to ride, and two apiece to carry everything. Not another mule to be had. Unpack the loads again and make them smaller!"

Fred came and sat with us that night before the charcoal brazier in his and Monty's room.

"They all talk of robbers on the road," he said. "Northward, through the Circassian Gates, or eastward it's all the same. There's a man in a room across the way who was stripped stark naked and beaten because they thought he might have money in his clothes. When he reached this place without a stitch on him he still had all his money in his clenched fists! Quite a sportsman — what? Imagine his juggling with it while they whipped him with knotted cords!"

"What have you heard about Kagig?"

"Nothing. But a lot about vukuart.* It's vague, but there's something in the air. You'll notice the Turkish muleteers are having nothing whatever to say to our Zeitoonli, although they've accepted the same service. Moslems are keeping to-gether, and Armenians are getting the silence cure. Armenians are even shy of speaking to one another. I've tried listening, and I've tried asking questions, although that was risky. I can't get a word of explanation. I've noticed, though, that the ugly mood is broadening. They've been polite to me, but I've heard the word shapkali applied more than once to you fellows. Means hatted man, you know. Not a serious insult, but implies contempt."

Nothing but comfort and respectability ever seemed able to make Fred gloomy. He discussed our present prospects with the air of an epicure ordering dinner. And Monty listened with his dark, delightful smile — the kindliest smile in all the world. I have seen unthoughtful men mistake it for a sign of weakness.

I have never known him to argue. Nor did he then, but

---

* Turkish word: happenings, a euphemism for massacre.

strode straight down into the khan yard, we sitting on the balcony to watch. He visited our string of mules first for an excuse, and invited a Kurdish chieftain (all Kurds are chieftains away from home) to inspect a swollen fetlock. With that subtle flattery he unlocked the man's reserve, passed on from chance remark to frank, good-humored questions, and within an hour had talked with twenty men. At last he called to one of the Zeitoonli to come and scrape the yard dung from his boots, climbed the stairs leisurely, and sat beside us.

"You're quite right, Fred," he said quietly.

Then there came suddenly from out the darkness a yell for help in English that brought three of us to our feet. Fred brushed his fierce mustaches upward with an air of satisfaction, and sat still.

"There's somebody down there quite wrong, and in line at last to find out why!" he said. "I've been waiting for this. Sit down."

We obeyed him, though the yells continued. There came blows suggestive of a woman on the housetops beating carpets.

"D'you recollect the man I mentioned at the consulate — the biped Peter Measel, missionary on his own account, who keeps a diary and libels ladies in it? Well, he's foul of a thalukdar* from Rajputana, and of a Prussian contractor, recruiting men for work on the Baghdad railway. I wasn't allowed to murder him. I see why now — finger of justice — I'd have been too quick. Sit down, you idiots! You've no idea what he wrote about Miss Vanderman. Let him scream, I like it!"

"Come along," said Monty. "If he were a bad-house keeper he has had enough!"

But Will had gone before us, headlong down the stairs with the speed off the mark that they taught him on the playing field at Bowdoin. When we caught up he was standing astride a prostrate being who sobbed like a cow with its throat cut, and a Rajput and a German, either of them six feet tall, were considering whether or not to resent the violence of his interference. The German was disposed to yield to numbers.

* Punjabi Word — landholder.

The Rajput not so.

"Why are you beating him?" asked Monty.

"Gott in Hinimel, who would not! He wrote of me in his diary — der Liminel! — that I shanghai laborers."

"Do you, or don't you?" asked Monty sweetly.

"Kreutz-blitzen! What is that to do with you — or with him? What right had he to write that people in France should pray for me in church?"

The Rajput all this while was standing simmering, as ready as a boar at bay to fight the lot of us, yet I thought with an air about him, too, of half-conscious surprise. Several times he took a half-pace forward to assert his right of chastisement, looked hard at Monty, and checked mid-stride.

"You've done enough," said Monty.

"Who are you that says so?" the German retorted.

"He — who — will — attend — to — it — that — you — do — no — more!" Monty's smooth voce had become without inflection.

"Bah! That is easy, isn't it? You are four to one!"

"Five to one!"

The Rajput's gruff throat thrilled with a new emotion. He sprang suddenly past me, and thrust himself between Monty and the German, who took advantage of the opportunity to walk away.

"Lord Montdidier, colonel sahib bahadur, burra salaam!"

He made no obeisance, but stood facing Monty eye to eye. The words, as be roiled them out, were like an order given to a thousand men. One almost heard the swish of sabers as the squadrons came to the general salute.

"I knew you, Rustum Khan, the minute I set eyes on you. Why were you beating this man?"

"Sahib bahadur, because he wrote in his book that people in France should pray for me in church, naming my honorable name, because, says he — but I will not repeat what he says. It is not seemly."

"How do you know what is in his diary?" Monty asked.

"That German read it out to me. We were sitting, he and I, discussing how the Turks intend to butcher the Armenians, as all the world knows is written. They say it shall happen soon. Said he to me — the German said to me — 'I know

another,' said he, 'who if I had my way should suffer first in
that event.' Saying which he showed the written book that he
had found, and read me parts of it. The German was for
denouncing the fellow as a friend of Armenians, but I was
for beating him at once, and I had my way."

"Where is the book?" demanded Monty.

"The German has it."

"The German has no right to it."

"I will bring it."

Rustum Khan strode off into the night, and Monty bent
over the sobbing form of the self-appointed missionary. We
were all alone in the midst of the courtyard, not even watched
from behind the wheels of arabas, for a fight or a thrashing
in the khans of Asia Minor is strictly the affair of him who
gets the worst of it.

"Will you burn that book of yours, Measel, if we protect
you from further assault?"

The man sobbed that he would do anything, but Monty
held him to the point, and at last procured a specific affirm-
ative. Then Rustum Khan came back with the offending
tome. It was bulky enough to contain an account of the sins
of Asia Minor.

Fred and I picked the poor fellow up and led him to where
the cooking places stood in one long row. Will carried the
book, and Rustum Khan stole wood from other folks' piles,
and fanned a fire. We watched the unhappy Peter Measel put
the book on the flames with his own hands.

"You're old enough to have known better than keep such
a diary!" said Monty, stirring the charred pages.

"I am at any rate a martyr!" Measel answered.

The man could walk by that time — he was presumably
abstemious and recovered from shock quickly. Monty sent
me to see him to his room, which turned out to be next the
German's, and until Will came over from our quarters with
first-aid stuff from our chest I spent the minutes telling the
German what should happen to him in case he should so far
forget discretion as to resume the offensive. He said nothing
in reply, but sat in his doorway looking up at me with an
expression intended to make me feel nervous of reprisals
without committing him to deeds.

Later, when we had done our best for "the martyred biped Measel," as Fred described him, Will and I found Rustum Khan with Fred and Monty seated around the charcoal brazier in Monty's room, deep in the valley of reminiscences. Our entry rather broke the spell, but Rustum Khan was not to be denied.

"You used to tell in those days, Colonel sahib bahadur," he said, addressing Monty with that full-measured compliment that the chivalrous, old East still cherishes, "of a castle of your ancestors in these parts. Do you remember, when I showed you the ruins of my family place in Rajputana, how you stood beside me on the heights, sahib, and vowed some day to hunt for that Crusaders' nest, as you called it?"

"That is the immediate purpose of this trip of ours," said Monty.

"Ah!" said the Rajput, and was silent for about a minute. Fred Oakes began to hum through his nose. He has a ridiculous belief that doing that throws keen inquirers off a scent.

"Colonel sahib, since I was a little butcha not as high as your knee I have spoken English and sat at the feet of British officers. Little enough I know, but by the beard of God's prophet I know this: when a British colonel sahib speaks of 'immediate purposes,' there are hidden purposes of greater importance!"

"That well may be," said Monty gravely. "I remember you always were a student of significant details, Rustum Khan."

"There was a time when I was in your honor's confidence."

Monty smiled.

"That was years ago. What are you doing here, Rustum Khan?"

"A fair enough question! I hang my head. As you know, sahib, I am a rangar. My people were all Sikhs for several generations back. We converts to Islam are usually more thoroughgoing than born Moslems are. I started to make the pilgrimage to Mecca, riding overland alone by way of Persia. As I came, missing few opportunities to talk with men, who should have been the lights of my religion, I have felt enthusiasm waning. These weeks past I have contemplated return without visiting Mecca at all. I have wandered to and fro, hoping for the fervor back again, yet finding none. And now, sahib, I find you — I, Rustum Khan, at a loose end for lack of inspiration. I have prayed. Colonel sahib bahadur, I believe thou art the gift of God!'"

Monty sought our eyes in turn in the lantern-lit darkness. We made no sign. None of us but he knew the Rajput, so it was plainly his affair.

"Suit yourself," said Will, and the rest of us nodded.

"We are traveling into the interior," said Monty, "in the rather doubtful hope that our absence from a coast city may in some way help Armenians, Rustum Khan."

The Rajput jumped to his feet that instant, and came to the salute.

"I might have known as much. Colonel Lord Montdidier sahib, I offer fealty! My blood be thine to spill in thy cause! Thy life on my head — thine honor on my life — thy way my way, and God be my witness!"

"Don't be rash, Rustum Khan. Our likeliest fate is to be taken prisoner by men of your religion, who will call you a renegade if you defend Armenians. And what are Armenians to you?"

"Ah, sahib! You drive a sharp spur into an open sore! I have seen too much of ill-faith — cruelty — robbery — torture — rapine — butchery, all in the name of God! It is this last threat to the Armenians that is the final straw! I took the pilgrimage in search of grace. The nearer I came to the place they tell me is on earth the home of grace, the more unfaith I see! Three nights ago in another place I was led aside and offered the third of the wealth of a fat Armenian if I would lend my sword to slit helpless throats — in the name of God, the compassionate, be merciful! My temper was about spoilt forever when that young idiot over the way described me in his book as — never mind how he described me — he paid the price! Sahib bahadur, I take my stand with the defenseless, where I know thou and thy friends will surely be! I am thy man!"

"It is not included in our plans to fight," said Monty.

"Sahib, there is always work for real soldiers!"

"What do you fellows say? Shall we let him come with us?"

"I travel at my own charges, sahib. I am well mounted and well armed."

"Sure, let him come with us!" said Will. "I like the man."

"He has my leave to come along to England afterward," said Fred, "if he'll guarantee to address me as the 'gift of God' in public!"

I left them talking and returned to see whether the "martyred biped Measel" needed further help. He was asleep, and as I listened to his breathing I heard voices in the next room. The German was talking in English, that being often the only tongue that ten men have in common. Through the partly opened door I could see that his room was crammed with men.

"They are spies, every one of them!" I heard him say. "The man I thrashed is of their party. You yourselves saw how they came to his rescue, and seduced the Indian by means of threats. This is the way of the English. ('Curse them!' said a voice.) They write notes in a book, and when that offense is detected they burn the book in a corner, as ye saw them do. I saw the book before they burned it. I thrashed the spy who wrote in the book because he had written in it reports on what it is proposed to do to infidels at the time ye know about. I tell you those men are all spies — one is as bad as the other. They work on behalf of Armenians, to bring about interference from abroad."

That he had already produced an atmosphere of danger to us I had immediate proof, for as I crossed the yard again I dodged behind an araba in the nick of time to avoid a blow aimed at me with a sword by a man I could not see.

"All your charming is undone!" I told Fred, bursting in on our party by the charcoal brazier. Almost breathless I reeled off what I had overheard. "They'll be here to murder us by dawn!" I said.

"Will they?" said Monty.

We were up and away two hours before dawn, to the huge delight of our Turkish muleteers, who consider a dawn start late, yet not too early for the servants of the khan, who knew enough European manners to stand about the gate and beg for tips. Nor were we quite too early for the enemy, who came out into the open and pelted us with clods of dung, the German encouraging from the roof. Fred caught him unaware full in the face with a well-aimed piece of offal. Then the khan keeper slammed the gate behind us and we rode into the unknown.

Chapter Four

"We are the robbers, effendi!"

THE ROAD

There is a mystery concerning roads
And he who loves the Road shall never tire.
For him the brooks have voices and the breeze
Brings news of far-off leafiness and leas
And vales all blossomy. The clinging mire
Shall never weary such an one, nor yet their loads
O'ercome the beasts that serve him. Rock and rill
Shall make the pleasant league go by as hours
With secret tales they tell; the loosened stone,
Sweet turf upturned, the bees' full-purposed drone,
The hum of happy insects among flowers,
And God's blue sky to crown each hill!
Dawn with her jewel-throated birds
To him shall be a new page in the Book
That never had beginning nor shall end,
And each increasing hour delights shall lend —
New notes in every sound — in every nook
New sights — new thoughts too wide for words,
Too deep for pen, too high for human song,
That only in the quietness of winding ways
From tumult and all bitterness apart
Can find communication with the heart —
Thoughts that make joyous moments of the days,
And no road heavy, and no journey long!

*T*he snow threatened in the mountains had not material-
ized, and the weather had changed to pure perfection. About
an hour after we started the khan emptied itself behind us in

a long string, jingling and clanging with horse and camel bells. But they turned northward to pass through the famed Circassian Gates, whereas we followed the plain that paralleled the mountain range — our mules' feet hidden by eight inches of primordial ooze.

"Wish it were only worse!" said Monty. "Snow or rain might postpone massacre. Delay might mean cancellation."

But there was no prospect whatever of rain. The Asia Minor spring, perfumed and amazing sweet, breathed all about us, spattered with little diamond-bursts of tune as the larks skyrocketed to let the wide world know how glad they were. Whatever dark fate might be brooding over a nation, it was humanly impossible for us to feel low-spirited.

Our Zeitoonli Armenians trudged through the mud behind us at a splendid pace — mountain-men with faces toward their hills. The Turks — owners of the animals another man had hired to us — rode perched on top of the loads in stoic silence, changing from mule to mule as the hours passed and watching very carefully that no mule should be overtaxed or chilled. In fact, the first attempt they made to enter into conversation with us was when we dallied to admire a view of Taurus Mountain, and one of them closed up to tell us the mules were catching cold in the wind. (If they had been our animals it might have been another story.)

Their contempt for the Zeitoonli was perfectly illustrated by the difference in situation. They rode; the Armenians walked. Yet the Armenians were less afraid; and when we crossed a swollen ford where a mule caught his forefoot between rocks and was drowning, it was Armenians, not Turks, who plunged into the icy water and worked him free without straining as much as a tendon.

The Turks were obsessed by perpetual fear of robbers. That, and no other motive, made them tolerate the hectoring of Rustum Khan, who had constituted himself officer of transport, and brought up the rear on his superb bay mare. As he had promised us he would, he rode well armed, and the sight of his pistol holsters, the rifle protruding stock-first from a leather case, and his long Rajput saber probably accomplished more than merely keeping Turks in countenance; it prevented them from scattering and bolting home.

His own baggage was packed on two mules in charge of an Armenian boy, who was more afraid of our Turks than they of robbers. Yet, when we demanded of our muleteers what sort of men, and of what nation the dreaded highwaymen might be they pointed at Rustum Khan's lean servant. At the khan the night before one of them had pointed out to Monty two Circassians and a Kurd as reputed to have a monopoly of robbery on all those roads.

Nevertheless, they made the new accusation without blinking.

"All robbers are Armenians — all Armenians are robbers!" they assured us gravely.

When we halted for a meal they refused to eat with our Zeitoonli, although they graciously permitted them to gather all the firewood, and accepted pieces of their pasderma (sun-dried meat) as if that were their due. As soon as they had eaten, and before we had finished, Ibrahim, their grizzled senior, came to us with a new demand. On its face it was not outrageous, because we were doing our own cooking, as any man does who has ever peeped into a Turkish servant's behind-the-scene arrangements.

"Send those Armenians away!" he urged. "We Turks are worth twice their number!"

"By the beard of God's prophet!" thundered Rustum Khan, "who gave camp-followers the right to impose advice?"

"They are in league with highwaymen to lead you into a trap!" Ibrahim answered.

Rustum Khan rattled the saber that lay on the rock beside him.

"I am hunting for fear," he said. "All my life I have hunted for fear and never found it!"

"Pekki!" said Ibrahim dryly. The word means "very well." The tone implied that when the emergency should come we should do well not to depend on him, for he had warned us.

We were marching about parallel with the course the completed Baghdad railway was to take, and there were frequent parties of surveyors and engineers in sight. Once we came near enough to talk with the German in charge of a party, encamped very sumptuously near his work. He had a numerous armed guard of Turks.

"A precaution against robbers?" Monty asked, and I did not hear what the German answered.

Rustum Khan laughed and drew me aside.

"Every German in these parts has a guard to protect him from his own men, sahib! For a while on my journey westward I had charge of a camp of recruited laborers. Therefore I know."

The German was immensely anxious to know all about us and our intentions. He told us his name was Hans von Quedlinburg, plainly expecting us to be impressed.

"I can direct you to good quarters, where you can rest comfortably at every stage, if you will tell me your direction," he said.

But we did not tell him. Later, while we ate a meal, he came and questioned our Turks very closely; but since they were in ignorance they did not tell him either.

"Why do you travel with Armenian servants?" he asked us finally before we moved away.

"We like 'em," said Monty.

"They'll only get you in trouble. We've dismissed all Armenian laborers from the railway works. Not trustworthy, you know. Our agents are out recruiting Moslems."

"What's the matter with Armenians?"

"Oh, don't you know?"

"I'm asking."

The German shrugged his shoulders.

"I'll tell you one thing. This will illustrate. I had an Armenian clerk. He worked all day in my tent. A week ago I found him reading among my private papers. That proves you can't trust an Armenian."

"Ample evidence!" said Monty without a smile, but Fred laughed as we rode away, and the German stared after us with a new set of emotions pictured on his heavy face.

Late in the afternoon we passed through a village in which about two hundred Armenian men and women were holding a gathering in a church large enough to hold three times the number. One of them saw us coming, and they all trooped out to meet us, imagining we were officials of some kind.

"Effendi," said their pastor with a trembling hand on Monty's saddle, "the Turks in this village have been washing their white garments!"

We had heard in Tarsus what that ceremony meant.

"It means, effendi, they believe their purpose holy! What shall we do — what shall we do?"

"Why not go into Tarsus and claim protection at the British consulate?" suggested Fred.

"But our friends of Tarsus warn us the worst fury of all will be in the cities!"

"Take to the hills, then!" Monty advised him.

"But how can we, sir? How can we? We have homes — property — children! We are watched. The first attempt by a number of us to escape to the hills would bring destruction down on all!"

"Then escape to the hills by twos and threes. You ask my advice — I give it."

It looked like very good advice. The slopes of the foothills seemed covered by a carpet of myrtle scrub, in which whole armies could have lain in ambush. And above that the cliffs of the Kara Dagh rose rocky and wild, suggesting small comfort but sure hiding places.

"You'll never make me believe you Armenians haven't hidden supplies," said Monty. "Take to the hills until the fury is over!"

But the old man shook his head, and his people seemed at one with him. These were not like our Zeitoonli, but wore the settled gloom of resignation that is poor half-brother to Moslem fanaticism, caught by subjection and infection from the bullying Turk. There was nothing we could do at that late hour to overcome the inertia produced by centuries, and we rode on, ourselves infected to the verge of misery. Only our Zeitoonli, striding along like men on holiday, retained their good spirits, and they tried to keep up ours by singing their extraordinary songs.

During the day we heard of the chicken, as Will called her, somewhere on ahead, and we spent that night at a kahveh, which is a place with all a khan's inconveniences, but no dignity whatever. There they knew nothing of her at all. The guests, and there were thirty besides ourselves, lay all around the big room on wooden platforms, and talked of nothing but robbers along the road in both directions. Every man in the place questioned each of us individually to find out why we had not been looted on our way of all we owned, and each man ended in a state of hostile incredulity because we vowed we had met no robbers at all. They shrugged their shoulders when we asked for news of Miss Gloria Vanderman.

There was no fear of Ibrahim and his friends decamping in the night, for the Zeitoonli kept too careful watch, waiting on them almost as thoughtfully as they fetched and carried for us, but never forgetting to qualify the service with a smile or a word to the Turks to imply that it was done out of pity for brutish helplessness.

These Zeitoonli of ours were more obviously every hour men of a different disposition to the meek Armenians of the places where the Turkish heel had pressed. But for our armed presence and the respect accorded to the Anglo-Saxon they would have had the whole mixed company down on them a dozen times that night.

"I'm wondering whether the Armenians within reach of the Turks are not going to suffer for the sins of mountaineers!" said Fred, as we warmed ourselves at the great open fire at one end of the room.

"Rot!" Will retorted. "Sooner or later men begin to dare assert their love of freedom, and you can't blame 'em if they show it foolishly. Some folk throw tea into harbors — some stick a king's head on a pole — some take it out for the present in fresh-kid stuff. These Zeitoonli are men of spirit, or I'll eat my hat!"

But if we ourselves had not been men of spirit, obviously capable of strenuous self-defense, our Zeitoonli would have found themselves in an awkward fix that night.

We supped off yogurt — the Turkish concoction of milk — cow's, goat's, mare's, ewe's or buffalo's (and the buffalo's is best) — that is about the only food of the country on which the Anglo-Saxon thrives. Whatever else is fit to eat the Turks themselves ruin by their way of cooking it. And we left before dawn in the teeth of the owner of the kahveh's warning.

"Dangerous robbers all along the road!" he advised, shaking his head until the fez grew insecure, while Fred counted out the coins to pay our bill. "Armenians are without compunction — bad folk! Aye, you have weapons, but so have they, and they have the advantage of surprise! May Allah the compassionate be witness, I have warned you!"

"There will be more than warnings to be witnessed!," growled Rustum Khan as he rode away. "Those others, who sharpened weapons all night long, and spoke of robbers, have been waiting three days at that kahveh till the murdering begins!"

That morning, on Rustum Khan's advice, we made our Turkish muleteers ride in front of us. The Zeitoon men marched next, swinging along with the hillman stride that eats up distance as the ticked-off seconds eat the day. And we rode last, admiring the mountain range on our left, but watchful of other matters, and in position to cut off retreat.

"The last time a Turk ran away from me he took my Gladstone bag with him!" said Fred. "No, only Armenians are dishonest. It was obedience to his prophet, who bade him take advantage of the giaour — quite a different thing! Ibrahim's sitting on my kit, and I'm watching him. You fellows suit yourselves!"

We passed a number of men on foot that morning all coming our way, but no Armenians among them. However, we exchanged no wayside gossip, because our Zeitoonli in front availed themselves of privilege and shouted to every stranger to pass at a good distance.

That is a perfectly fair precaution in a land where every one goes armed, and any one may be a bandit. But it leads to aloofness. Passers-by made circuits of a half-mile to avoid us, and when we spurred our mules to get word with them they mistook that for proof of our profession and bolted. We chased three men for twenty minutes for the fun of it, only desisting when one of them took cover behind a bush and fired a pistol at us with his eyes shut.

"Think of the lies he'll tell in the kahveh tonight about beating off a dozen robbers single-handed!" Will laughed.

"Let's chase the next batch, too, and give the kahveh gang an ear-full!"

"I rather think not," said Monty. "They'll say we're Armenian criminals. Let's not be the spark."

He was right, so we behaved ourselves, and within an hour we had trouble enough of another sort. We began to meet dogs as big as Newfoundlands, that attacked our unmounted Zeitoonli, refusing to be driven off with sticks and stones, and only retreating a little way when we rode down on them.

"Shoot the brutes!" Will suggested cheerfully, and I made ready to act on it.

"For the lord's sake, don't!" warned Monty, riding at a huge black mongrel that was tearing strips from the smock of one of our men. The owner of the dog, seeing its victim was Armenian, rather encouraged it than otherwise, leaning on a long pole and grinning in an unfenced field near by.

"The consul warned me they think more of a dog's life hereabouts than a man's. In half an hour there'd be a mob on our trail. Take the Zeitoonli up behind us."

Rustum Khan was bitter about what he called our squeamishness. But we each took up a man on his horse's rump, and the dogs decided the fun was no longer worth the effort, especially as we had riding whips. But skirmishing with the dogs and picking up the Armenians took time, so that our muleteers were all alone half a mile ahead of us, and had disappeared where the road dipped between two hillocks, when they met with the scare they looked for.

They came thundering back up the road, flogging and flopping on top of the loads like the wooden monkeys-on-a-stick the fakers used to sell for a penny on the curb in Fleet Street, glancing behind them at every second bound like men who had seen a thousand ghosts.

We brought them to a halt by force, but take them on the whole, now that they were in contact with us, they did not look so much frightened as convinced. They had made up their minds that it was not written that they should go any farther, and that was all about it.

"Ermenie!" said Ibrahim. And when we laughed at that he stroked his beard and vowed there were hundreds of Armenians ambushed by the roadside half a mile ahead. The others corrected him, declaring the enemy were thousands strong.

Finally Monty rode forward with me to investigate. We passed between the hillocks, and descended for another hundred yards along a gradually sloping track, when our mules became aware of company. We could see nobody, but their long ears twitched, and they began to make preparations preliminary to braying recognition of their kin.

Suddenly Monty detected movement among the myrtle bushes about fifty yards from the road, and my mule confirmed his judgment by braying like Satan at a sideshow. The noise was answered instantly by a chorus of neighs and brays from an unseen menagerie, whereat the owners of the animals disclosed themselves — six men, all smiling, and unarmed as far as we could tell — the very same six gypsies who had pitched their tent in the midst of the khan yard at Tarsus.

Then in a clearing at a little distance we saw women taking down a long low black tent, and between us and them a considerable herd of horses, mostly without halters but headed into a bunch by gypsy children. Somebody on a gray stallion came loping down toward us, leaping low bushes, riding erect with pluperfect hands and seat.

"I've seen that stallion before!" said I.

"And the girl on his back is looking for somebody who owns her heart!" smiled Monty. "Hullo! Are you the lucky man?'"

She reined the stallion in, and took a good, long look at us, shading her eyes with her hand but showing dazzling white teeth between coral lips. Suddenly the smile departed, and a look of sullen disappointment settled on her face, as she wheeled the stallion with a swing of her lithe body from the hips, and loped away. Never, apparently, did two men make less impression on a maiden's heart. The six gypsies stood staring at us foolishly, until one of them at last held his hand up palm outward. We accepted that as a peace signal.

"Are you waiting here for us?" Monty asked in English, and the oldest of the six — a swarthy little man with rather bowlegs — thought he had been asked his name.

"Gregor Jhaere," be answered.

For some vague reason Monty tried him next in Arabic and then in Hindustani, but without result. At last he tried halting Turkish, and the gypsy replied at once in German. As Monty used to get two-pence or three-pence a day extra when he was in the British army, for knowing something of that tongue, we stood at once on common ground.

"Kagig told us to wait here and bring you to him," said Gregor Jhaere.

"Where is Kagig?" Monty asked, and the man smiled blankly — much more effectively than if he had shrugged his shoulders.

"We obey Kagig at times," he said, as if that admission settled the matter. Then there was interruption. Rustum Khan came spurring down the road with his pistol holsters unbuttoned and his saber clattering like a sutler's pots and pans, to see whether we needed help. He had no sooner reined in beside us than I caught sight of Will, drawn between curiosity and fear lest the muleteers might bolt, standing in his stirrups to peer at us from the top of the track between the hillocks. Somebody else caught sight of him too.

There came a shrill about from over where the women were packing up, and everybody turned to look, Gregor Jhaere included. As hard as the gray stallion could take her in a bee line toward Will the daughter of the dawn with flashing teeth and blazing eyes was riding ventre a terre.

"Maga!" Gregor shouted at her, and then some unintelligible gibberish. But she took no more notice of him than if he had been a crow on a branch. In a minute she was beside Will, talking to him, and from over the top of the rise we could hear Fred shouting sarcastic remonstrance.

"She is bad!" Gregor announced in English. It seemed to be all the English he knew.

"Are you her father?" Monty asked, and Gregor answered in very slipshod German:

"She is the daughter of the devil. She shall be soundly thrashed! The chalana!* And he a Gorgio!"**

Suddenly Fred began to shout for help then, and we rode back, the gypsies following and Rustum Khan remaining on guard between them and their camp with his upbrushed black beard bristling defiance of Asia Minor. Our Turkish muleteers had decided to make a final bolt for it, and were using their whips on the Zeitoonli, who clung gamely to the reins. As soon as we got near enough to lend a hand the Turks resigned themselves with a kind of opportune fatalism. The Zeitoonli promptly turned the tables on them by laying hold

---

* Chalana — She jockey (a compliment).
**Gorgio — Gentile (an insult).

of a leg of each and tipping them off into the mud. Ibrahim showed his teeth, and reached for a hidden weapon as he lay, but seemed to think better of it. It looked very much as if those four Zeitoonli knew in advance exactly what the interruption in our journey meant.

Will was out of the running entirely, or else the rest of us were, depending on which way one regarded it. He had eyes for nobody and nothing but the girl, nor she for any one but him, and nobody could rightfully blame either of them. Yankee though he is, Will sat his mule in the western cowboy style, and he was wearing a cowboy hat that set his youth off to perfection. She looked fit to flirt with the lord of the underworld, answering his questions in a way that would have made any fellow eager to ask more. Strangely enough, Gregor Jhaere, presumably father of the girl appeared to have lost his anger at her doings and turned his back.

Fred, smiling mischief, started toward them to horn in, as Will would have described it, but at that moment about a dozen of the gypsy women came padding uproad, fostered watchfully by Rustum Khan, who seemed convinced that murder was intended somehow, somewhere. They brought along horses with them — very good horses — and Fred prefers a horse trade to triangular flirtation on any day of any week.

The gypsies promptly fell to and off-saddled our loads under Gregor Jhaere's eye, transferring them to the meaner-looking among the beasts the women had brought, taking great care to drop nothing in the mud. And at a word from Gregor two of the oldest hags came to lift us from our saddles one by one, and hold us suspended in mid-air while the saddles were transferred to better mounts. But there is an indignity in being held out of the mud by women that goes fiercely against the white man's grain, and I kicked until they set me back in the saddle.

Monty solved the problem by riding to higher, clean ground near the roadside, where we could stand on firm grass.

Seeing us dismounted, the gypsies underwent a subtle mental change peculiar to all barbarous people. To the gypsy and the Cossack, and all people mainly dependent on the horse, to be mounted is to signify participation in affairs. To be dismounted means to stand aside and "let George do it."

Gregor Jhaere became a different man. He grew noisy and in response to his yelped commands they swooped in unprovoked attack on our unhappy muleteers. Before we could interfere they had thrown each Turk face downward, our Zeitoonli helping, and were searching them with swift intruding fingers for knives, pistols, money.

The Turk leaves his money behind when starting on a journey at some other man's expense; but they did draw forth a most astonishing assortment of weapons. They were experts in disarmament. Maga Jhaere lost interest in Will for a moment, and pricked her stallion to a place where she could judge the assortment better. Without any hesitation she ordered one of the old women to pass up to her a mother-o'-pearl ornamented Smith & Wesson, which she promptly hid in her bosom. Judging by the sounds he made, that pistol was the apple of Ibrahim's old eye, but he had seen the last of it. When we interfered, and he could get to her stirrup to demand it back, Maga spat in his face; which was all about it, except that Monty made generous allowance for the thing when paying the reckoning presently. As our servants, those Turks were, of course, entitled to our protection, and besides that weapon we had to pay for five knives that were gone beyond hope of recovery.

Monty paid our Turks off (for it was evident that even had they been willing they would not have been allowed to proceed with us another mile). Then, as Ibrahim mounted and marshaled his party in front of him, he forgot manners as well as the liberal payment.

"Mashallah!" (God be praised!) he shouted, with the slobber of excitement on his lips and beard. "Now I go to make Armenians pay for this! Let the shapkali,* too, avoid me! Ya Ali, ya Mahoma, Alahu!" (Oh, Ali, oh, Mahomet, God is God!)

"Let's hope they haven't a spark of honesty!" said Monty cryptically, watching them canter away.

"Why on earth — ?"

"Let's hope they ride back to the consul and swear they haven't received one piaster of their pay. That would let him

---

* Shapkali — hatted man-foreigner.

know we're clear away!"

"Optimist!" jeered Will. "That consul's a Britisher. He'd take their lie literally, and deduce we're no good!"

For the moment the girl on the gray stallion had ridden away from Will and was giving regal orders to the mob of women and shrill children, who obeyed her as if well used to it. Gregor Jhaere and his men stood staring at us, Gregor shaking his head as if our letting the Turks go free had been a bad stroke of policy.

"Aren't you afraid to travel with all that mob of women and cattle?" asked Monty. "We've heard of robbers on the road."

"We are the robbers, effendi!" said Gregor with an air of modesty. The others smirked, but he seemed disinclined to overinsist on the gulf between us.

"Hear him!" growled Rustum Khan. "A thief, who boasts of thieving in the presence of sahibs! So is corruption, stinking in the sun!"

He added something in another language that the gypsies understood, for Gregor started as if stung and swore at him, and Maga Jhaere left her womenfolk to ride alongside and glare into his eyes. They were enemies, those two, from that hour forward. He, once Hindu, now Moslem, had no admiration whatever to begin with for unveiled women. And, since the gypsy claims to come from India and may therefore be justly judged by Indian standards, and has no caste, but is beneath the very lees of caste, he loathed all gypsies with the prejudice peculiar to men who have deserted caste in theory and in self-protection claim themselves above it. It was a case of height despising deep in either instance, she as sure of her superiority as he of his.

There might have been immediate trouble if Monty had not taken his new, restless, fresh horse by the mane and swung into the saddle.

"Forward, Rustum Khan!" be ordered. "Ride ahead and let those keen eyes of yours keep us out of traps!"

The Rajput obeyed, but as he passed Will he checked his mare a moment, and waiting until Will's blue eyes met his he raised a warning finger.

"Kubadar, sahib!"

Then he rode on, like a man who has done his duty.

"What the devil does he mean?" demanded Will.

"Kubadar means, 'Take care'!" said Monty. "Come on, what are we waiting for?"

That was the beginning, too, of Will's feud with the Rajput, neither so remorseless nor so sudden as the woman's, because he had a different code to guide him and also had to convince himself that a quarrel with a man of color was compatible with Yankee dignity. We could have wished them all three either friends, or else a thousand miles apart two hundred times before the journey ended.

As we rode forward with even our Zeitoonli mounted now on strong mules, Maga Jhaere sat her stallion beside Will with an air of owning him. She was likely a safer friend than enemy, and we did nothing to interfere. Monty pressed forward. Fred and I fell to the rear.

"Haide!"* shouted Gregor Jhaere, and all the motley swarm of women and children caught themselves mounts — some already loaded with the gypsy baggage, some with saddles, some without, some with grass halters for bridles. In another minute Fred and I were riding surrounded by a smelly swarm of them, he with big fingers already on the keys of his beloved concertina, but I less enamored than he of the company.

Women and children, loaded, loose and led horses were all mixed together in unsortable confusion, the two oldest hags in the world trusting themselves on sorry, lame nags between Fred and me as if proximity to us would solve the very riddle of the gypsy race. And last of all came a pack of great scrawny dogs that bayed behind us hungrily, following for an hour until hope of plunder vanished.

"That little she-devil who has taken a fancy to Will," said Fred with a grin, "is capable of more atrocities than all the Turks between here and Stamboul! She looks to me like Santanita, Cleopatra, Salome, Caesar's wife, and all the Borgia ladies rolled in one. There's something added, though, that they lacked."

"Youth," said I. "Beauty. Athletic grace. Sinuous charm."

"No, probably they all had all those."

---

* Haide! — Turkish, "Come on!"

"Then horsemanship."

"Perhaps. Didn't Cleopatra ride?"

"Then what?" said I, puzzled.

"Indiscretion!" he answered, jerking loose the catch of his infernal instrument.

"Don't be afraid, old ladies," he said, glancing at the harridans between us. "I'm only going to sing!"

He makes up nearly all of his songs, and some of them, although irreverent, are not without peculiar merit; but that was one of his worst ones.

The preachers prate of fallen man
And choirs repeat the chant,
While unco' guid with unction urge
Repression of the joys that surge,
And jail for those who can't.
The poor deluded duds forget
That something drew the sting
When Adam tiptoed to his fall,
And made it hardly hurt at all.
Of Mother Eve I sing!

CHORUS

Oh, Mother Eve, dear Mother Eve,
The generations come and go,
But daughter Eve's as live as you
Were back in Eden years ago!

Oh, hell's not hell with Eve to tell
Again the ancient tale,
But Eden's grassy ways and bowers
Deprived of Eve to ease the hours
Would very soon grow stale!
Red cherry lips that leap to laugh,
And chic and flick and flair
Can make black white for any one —
The task of Sisyphus good fun!
So what should Adam care!

CHORUS

Oh, daughter Eve, dear daughter Eve,
The tribulations go and come,
But no adventure's ever tame
With you to make surprises hum!

Chapter Five

"Effendi, that is the heart of Armenia burning."

THE PATTERAN

(I)

Aye-yee — I see — a cloud afloat in air af amethyst
I know its racing shadow falls on banks of gold
Where rain-rejoicing gravel warms the feeding roots
And smells more wonderful than wine.
I know the shoots of myrtle and of asphodel now stir the mould
Where wee cool noses sniff the early mist.
Aye-yee — the sparkle of the little springs I see
That tinkle as they hunt the thirsty rill.
I know the cobwebs glitter with the jeweled dew.
I see a fleck of brown — it was a skylark flew
To scatter bursting music, and the world is still
To listen. Ah, my heart is bursting too — Aye-yee!

Chorus:

(It begins with a swinging crash, and fades away.)
Aye-yee, aye-yah — the kites see far
(But also to the foxes views unfold) —
No hour alike, no places twice the same,
Nor any track to show where morning came,
Nor any footprint in the moistened mould
To tell who covered up the morning star.
    Aye-yee — aye-yah!

(2)

Aye-yee — I see — new rushes crowding upwards in the mere
Where, gold and white, the wild duck preens himself

Safe hidden till the sun-drawn, lingering mists melt.
I know the secret den where bruin dwelt.
I see him now sun-basking on a shelf
Of windy rock. He looks down on the deer,
Who flit like flowing light from rock to tree
And stand with ears alert before they drink.
I know a pool of purple rimmed with white
Where wild-fowl, warming for the morning flight,
Wait clustering and crying on the brink.
And I know hillsides where the partridge breeds. Aye-yee!

Chorus:

Aye-yee, aye-yah — the kites see far
(But also to the owls the visions change) —
No dawn is like the next, and nothing sings
Of sameness — very hours have wings
And leave no word of whose hand touched the range
Of Kara Dagh with opal and with cinnabar.
   Aye-yee, aye-yah!

(3)

Aye-yee — I see — new distances beyond a blue horizon flung.
I laugh, because the people under roofs believe
That last year's ways are this!
No roads are old! New grass has grown!
All pools and rivers hold New water!
And the feathered singers weave
New nests, forgetting where the old ones hung!
Aye-yah — the muddy highway sticks and clings,
But I see in the open pastures new
Unknown to busne* in the houses pent!
I hear the new, warm raindrops drumming on the tent,
I feel already on my feet delicious dew,
I see the trail outflung! And oh, my heart has wings!

Chorus:

Aye-yee, aye-yah — the kites see far
(But also on the road the visions pass) —
The universe reflected in a wayside pool,
A tinkling symphony where seeping waters drool,
The dance, more gay than laughter, of the windswept grass —
Oh, onward! On to where the visions are!
   Aye-yee — aye-yah!

---

* Busne — Gypsy word — Gentile, or non-gypsy.

*R*ussia, Rumania, Bulgaria, Bohemia, Persia, Armenia were all one hunting ground to the troupe we rode with. Even the children seemed to have a smattering of most of the tongues men speak in those intriguing lands. Will and the girl beside him conversed in German, but the old hag nearest me would not confess acquaintance with any language I knew. Again and again I tried her, but she always shook her head.

Fred, with his ready gift of tongues, attempted conversation with ten or a dozen of them, but whichever language he used in turn appeared to be the only one which that particular individual did not know. All he got in reply was grins, and awkward silence, and shrugs of the shoulders in Gregor's direction, implying that the head of the firm did the talking with strangers. But Gregor rode alone with Monty, out of earshot.

Maga (for so they all called her) flirted with Will outrageously, if that is flirting that proclaims conquest from the start, and sets flashing white teeth in defiance of all intruders. Even the little children had hidden weapons, but Maga was better armed than any one, and she thrust the new mother-o-pearl-plated acquisition in the face of one of the men who dared drive his horse between hers and Will's. That not serving more than to amuse him, she slapped him three times back-handed across the face, and thrusting the pistol back into her bosom, drew a knife. He seemed in no doubt of her willingness to use the steel, and backed his horse away, followed by language from her like forked lightning that disturbed him more than the threatening weapon. Gypsies are great believers in the efficiency of a curse.

Nothing could be further from the mark than to say that Will tried to take advantage of Maga's youth and savagery. Fred and I had shared a dozen lively adventures with him without more than beginning yet to plumb the depths of his respect for Woman. Only an American in all the world knows how to meet Young Woman eye to eye with totally unpatronizing frankness, and he was without guile in the matter. But not so she. We did not know whether or not she was Gregor Jhaere's daughter; whether or not she was truly the gypsy that she hardly seemed. But she was certainly daughter of the Near

East that does not understand a state of peace between the sexes. There was nothing lawful in her attitude, nor as much as the suspicion that Will might be merely chivalrous.

"America's due for sex-enlightenment!" said I.

"Warn him if you like," Fred laughed, "and then steer clear! Our America is proud besides imprudent!"

Fred off-shouldered all responsibility and forestalled anxiety on any one's account by playing tunes, stampeding the whole cavalcade more than once because the horses were unused to his clanging concertina, but producing such high spirits that it became a joke to have to dismount in the mud and replace the load on some mule who had expressed enjoyment of the tune by rolling in slime, or by trying to kick clouds out of the sky.

And strangely enough he brought about the very last thing he intended with his music — stopped the flirtation's immediate progress. Maga seemed to take to Fred's unchastened harmony with all the wildness that possessed her. Some chord he struck, or likelier, some abandoned succession of them touched off her magazine of poetry. And so she sang.

The only infinitely gorgeous songs I ever listened to were Maga's. Almighty God, who made them, only really knows what country the gypsies originally came from, but there is not a land that has not felt their feet, nor a sorrow they have not witnessed. Away back in the womb of time there was planted in them a rare gift of seeing what the rest of us can only sometimes hear, and of hearing what only very few from the world that lives in houses can do more than vaguely feel when at the peak of high emotion. The gypsies do not understand what they see, and hear, and feel; but they are aware of infinities too intimate for ordinary speech. And it was given to Maga to sing of all that, with a voice tuned like a waterfall's for open sky, and trees, and distances — not very loud, but far-carrying, and flattened in quarter-tones where it touched the infinite.

Fred very soon ceased from braying with his bellowed instrument. Her songs were too wild for accompaniment — interminable stanzas of unequal length, with a refrain at the end of each that rose through a thousand emotions to a crash of ecstasy, and then died away to dreaminess, coming to an end on an unfinished rising scale.

All the gypsies and our Zeitoonli and Rustum Khan's lean servant joined in the refrains, so that we trotted along under the snow-tipped fangs of the Kara Dagh oblivious of the passage of time, but very keenly conscious of touch with a realm of life whose existence hitherto we had only vaguely guessed at.

The animals refused to weary while that singing testified of tireless harmonies, as fresh yet as on the day when the worlds were born. We rattled forward, on and upward, as if the panorama were unrolling and we were the static point, getting out of nobody's way for the best reason in the world — that everybody hid at first sight or sound of us, except when we passed near villages, and then the great fierce-fanged curs chased and bayed behind us in short-winded fury.

"The dogs bark," quoted Fred serenely, "but the caravan moves on!"

An hour before dark we swung round a long irregular spur of the hills that made a wide bend in the road, and halted at a lonely kahveh — a windswept ruin of a place, the wall of whose upper story was patched with ancient sacking, but whose owner came out and smiled so warmly on us that we overlooked the inhospitable frown of his unplastered walls, hoping that his smile and the profundity of his salaams might prove prophetic of comfort and cleanliness within. Vain hope!

Maga left Will's side then, for there was iron-embedded custom to be observed about this matter of entering a road-house. In that land superstition governs just as fiercely as the rest those who make mock of the rule-of-rod religions, and there is no man or woman free to behave as be or she sees fit. Every one drew aside from Monty, and he strode in alone through the split-and-mended door, we following next, and the gypsies with their animals clattered noisily behind us. The women entered last, behind the last loaded mule, and Maga the very last of all, because she was the most beautiful, and beauty might bring in the devil with it only that the devil is too proud to dawdle behind the old hags and the horses.

We found ourselves in an oblong room, with stalls and a sort of pound for animals at one end and an enormous raised

stone fireplace at the other. Wooden platforms for the use of
guests faced each other down the two long sides, and the only
promise of better than usual comfort lay in the piles of
firewood waiting for whoever felt rich and generous enough
to foot the bill for a quantity.

But an agreeable surprise made us feel at home before ever
the fire leaped up to warm the creases out of saddle-weary
limbs. We had given up thinking of Kagig, not that we
despaired of him, but the gypsies, and especially Maga, had
replaced his romantic interest for the moment with their own.
Now all the man's own exciting claim on the imagination
returned in full flood, as he arose leisurely from a pile of skins
and blankets near the hearth to greet Monty, and shouted
with the manner of a chieftain for fuel to be piled on instantly
— "For a great man comes!" he announced to the rafters. And
the kahveh servants, seven sons of the owner of the place,
were swift and abject in the matter of obeisance. They were
Turks. All Turks are demonstrative in adoration of whoever
is reputed great. Monty ignored them, and Kagig came down
the length of the room to offer him a hand on terms of blunt
equality.

"Lord Montdidier," he said, mispronouncing the word
astonishingly, "this is the furthest limit of my kingdom yet.
Kindly be welcome!"

"Your kingdom?" said Monty, shaking hands, but not quite
accepting the position of blood-equal. He was bigger and
better looking than Kagig, and there was no mistaking which
was the abler man, even at that first comparison, with Kagig
intentionally making the most of a dramatic situation.

Kagig laughed, not the least nervously.

"Mirza," he said in Persian, "duzd ne giriftah padshah ast!"
(Prince, the uncaught thief is king.)

He was wearing a kalpak — the headgear of the Cossack,
which would make a high priest look outlawed, and a shaggy
goatskin coat that had seen more than one campaign. Un-
mistakably the garment had been slit by bullets, and repaired
by fingers more enthusiastic than adept. There was a pride of
poverty about him that did not gibe well with his boast of
being a robber.

"That's the first gink we've met in this land who didn't

claim to be something better than he looked!" Will whispered.

"Hopeless, I suppose!" Fred answered. "Never mind. I like the man."

It was evident that Monty liked him, too, for all his schooled reserve. Kagig ordered one of the owner's sons to sweep a place near the fire, and there he superintended the spreading of Monty's blankets, close enough to his own assorted heap for conversation without mutual offense. Will cleaned for himself a section of the opposite end of the platform, and Fred and I spread our blankets next to his. That left Rustum Khan in a quandary. He stood irresolute for a minute, eying first the gypsies, who had stalled most of their animals and were beginning to occupy the platform on the other side; then considering the wide gap between me and Monty. The dark-skinned man of breeding is far more bitterly conscious of the color line than any white knows how to be.

We watched, disinclined to do the choosing for him, racial instinct uppermost. Rustum Khan strolled back to where his mare was being cleaned by the lean Armenian servant, gave the boy a few curt orders, and there among the shadows made his mind up. He returned and stood before Monty, Kagig eying him with something less than amiability. He pointed toward the ample room remaining between Monty and me.

"Will the sahib permit? My izzat (honor) is in question."

"Izzat be damned!" Monty answered.

Rustum Khan colored darkly.

"I shared a tent with you once on campaign, sahib, in the days before — the good days before — those old days when —"

"When you and I served one Raj, eh? I remember," Monty answered. "I remember it was your tent, Rustum Khan. Unless memory plays tricks with me, the Orakzai Pathans had burned mine, and I had my choice between sharing yours or sleeping in the rain."

"Truly, huzoor."

"I don't recollect that I mouthed very much about honor on that occasion. If anybody's honor was in question then, I fancy it was yours. I might have inconvenienced myself, and dishonored you, I suppose, by sleeping in the wet. You can dishonor the lot of us now, if you care to, by — oh, tommyrot! Tell your man to put your blankets in the only empty place, and behave like a man of sense!"

"But, huzoor —"

Monty dismissed the subject with a motion of his hand, and turned to talk with Kagig, who shouted for yogurt to be brought at once; and that set the sons of the owner of the place to hurrying in great style. The owner himself was a true Turk. He had subsided into a state of kaif already over on the far side of the fire, daydreaming about only Allah knew what rhapsodies. But the Turks intermarry with the subject races much more thoroughly than they do anything else, and his sons did not resemble him. They were active young men, rather noisy in their robust desire to be of use.

The gypsies, with Gregor Jhaere nearest to the owner of the kahveh and the fireplace, occupied the whole long platform on the other side, each with his women around him — except that I noticed that Maga avoided all the men, and made herself a blanket nest in deep shadow almost within reach of a mule's heels at the far end. I believed at the moment that she chose that position so as to be near to Will, but changed my mind later. Several times Gregor shouted for her, and she made no answer.

The place had no other occupants. Either we were the only travelers on that road that night or, as seemed more likely, Kagig had exercised authority and purged the kahveh of other guests. Certainly our coming had been expected, for there was very good yogurt in ample quantity, and other food besides — meat, bread, cheese, vegetables.

When we had all eaten, and lay back against the stone wall looking at the fire, with great fanged shadows dancing up and down that made the scene one of almost perfect savagery, Gregor called again for Maga. Again she did not answer him. So he rose from his place and reached for a rawhide whip.

"I said she shall be thrashed!" he snarled in Turkish, and he made the whip crack three times like sudden pistol-shots. Will did not catch the words, and might not have understood them in any case, but Rustum Khan, beside me, both heard and understood.

"Atcha!" he grunted. "Now we shall see a kind of happenings. That girl is not a true gypsy, or else my eyes lie to me. They stole her, or adopted her. She lacks their instincts. The gitanas, as they call their girls, are expected to have aversion to white men. They are allowed to lure a white man to his ruin, but not to make hot love to him. She has offended against the gypsy law. The ataman* must punish. Watch the women. They take it all as a matter of course."

"Maga!" thundered Gregor Jhaere, cracking the great whip again. I thought that Kagig looked a trifle restless, but nobody else went so far as to exhibit interest, except that the old Turk by the fire emerged far enough out of kaif to open one eye, like a sly cat's.

The ataman shouted again, and this time Maga mocked him. So he strode down the room in a rage to enforce his authority, and dragged her out of the shadow by an arm, sending her whirling to the center of the floor. She did not lose her feet, but spun and came to a stand, and waited, proud as Satanita while he drew the whip slowly back with studied cruelty. The old Turk opened both eyes.

Nothing is more certain than that none of us would have permitted the girl to be thrashed. I doubt if even Rustum Khan, no admirer of gypsies or unveiled women, would have tolerated one blow. But Will was nearest, and he is most amazing quick when his nervous New England temper is aroused. He had the whip out of Gregor's hand, and stood on guard between him and the girl before one of us had time to move. The old Turk closed his eyes again, and sighed resignedly.

"Our preux chevalier — preux but damned imprudent!" murmured Fred. "Let's hope there's a gypsy here with guts enough to fight for title to the girl. It looks to me as if Will has claimed her by patteran** law. The only man with right to say whether or not a woman shall be thrashed is her owner. Once that right is established —"

"Touch her and I'll break your neck!" warned Will, without undue emotion, but truthfully beyond a shadow of a doubt.

The gypsy stood still, simmering, and taking the measure of the capable American muscles interposed between him and his legal prey. Every gypsy eye in the room was on him, and

---

* Ataman, gypsy headman.
**Patteran, a gypsy word: trail.

it was perfectly obvious that whatever the eventual solution of the impasse, the one thing he could not do was retreat. We were fewer in number, but much better armed than the gypsy party, so that it was unlikely they would rally to their man's aid. Kagig was an unknown quantity, but except that his black eyes glittered rather more brightly than usual he made no sign; and we kept quiet because we did not want to start a free-for-all fight. Will was quite able to take care of any single opponent, and would have resented aid.

Suddenly, however, Gregor Jhaere reached inside his shirt. Maga screamed. Rustum Khan beside me swore a rumbling Rajput oath, and we all four leapt to our feet. Maga drew no weapon, although she certainly had both dagger and pistol handy. Instead, she glanced toward Kagig, who, strangely enough, was lolling on his blankets as if nothing in the world could interest him less. The glance took as swift effect as an electric spark that fires a mine. He stiffened instantly.

"Yok!" he shouted, and at once there ceased to be even a symptom of impending trouble. Yok means merely no in Turkish, but it conveyed enough to Gregor to send him back to his place between his women and the Turk unashamedly obedient, leaving Maga standing beside Will. Maga did not glance again at Kagig, for I watched intently. There was simply no understanding the relationship, although Fred affected his usual all-comprehensive wisdom.

"Another claimant to the title!" he said. "A fight between Will and Kagig for that woman ought to be amusing, if only Will weren't a friend of mine. Watch America challenge him!"

But Will did nothing of the kind. He smiled at Maga, offered her a cigarette, which she refused, and returned to his place beyond Fred, leaving her standing there, as lovely in the glowing firelight as the spirit of bygone romance. At that Kagig shouted suddenly for fuel, and three of the Turk's seven hoydens ran to heap it on.

Instantly the leaping flames transformed the great, uncomfortable, draughty barn into a hall of gorgeous color and shadows without limit. There was no other illumination, except for the glow here and there of pipes and cigarettes, or matches flaring for a moment. Barring the tobacco, we lay like a baron's men-at-arms in Europe of the Middle Ages, with a captive woman to make sport with in the midst, only rather too self-reliant for the picture.

Feeling himself warm, and rested, and full enough of food, Fred flung a cigarette away and reached for his inseparable concertina. And with his eyes on the great smoked beams that now glowed gold and crimson in the firelight, he grew inspired and made his nearest to sweet music. It was perfectly in place — simple as the savagery that framed us — Fred's way of saying grace for shelter, and adventure, and a meal. He passed from Annie Laurie to Suwannee River, and all but made Will cry.

During two-three-four tunes Maga stood motionless in the midst of us, hands on her hips, with the fire-light playing on her face, until at last Fred changed the nature of the music and seemed to be trying to recall fragments of the song she had sung that afternoon. Presently he came close to achievement, playing a few bars over and over, and leading on from those into improvisation near enough to the real thing to be quite recognizable.

Music is the sure key to the gypsy heart, and Fred unlocked it. The men and women, and the little sleepy children on the long wooden platform opposite began to sway and swing in rhythm. Fred divined what was coming, and played louder, wilder, lawlessly. And Maga did an astonishing thing. She sat down on the floor and pulled her shoes and stockings off, as unselfconsciously as if she were alone.

Then Fred began the tune again from the beginning, and he had it at his finger-ends by then. He made the rafters ring. And without a word Maga kicked the shoes and stockings into a corner, flung her outer, woolen upper-garment after them, and began to dance.

There is a time when any of us does his best. Money — marriage — praise — applause (which is totally another thing than praise, and more like whisky in its workings) — ambition — prayer — there is a key to the heart of each of us that can unlock the flood tides of emotion and carry us nolens volens to the peaks of possibility. Either Will, or else Fred's music, or the setting, or all three unlocked her gifts that night. She danced like a moth in a flame — a wandering woman in the fire unquenchable that burns convention out of gypsy hearts, and makes the patteran — the trail — the only way worth while.

Opposite, the gypsies sprawled in silence on their platform, breathing a little deeper when deepest approval stirred them, a little more quickly when her Muse took hold of Maga and thrilled her to expression of the thoughts unknown to people of the dinning walls and streets.

We four leaned back against our wall in a sort of silent revelry, Fred alone moving, making his beloved instrument charm wisely, calling to her just enough to keep a link, as it were, through which her imagery might appeal to ours. Some sort of mental bridge between her tameless paganism and our twentieth-century twilight there had to be, or we never could have sensed her meaning. The concertina's wailings, mid-way between her intelligence and ours, served well enough.

My own chief feeling was of exultation, crowing over the hooded city-folk, who think that drama and the tricks of colored light and shade have led them to a glimpse of the hem of the garment of Unrest — a cheap mean feeling, of which I was afterward ashamed.

Maga was not crowing over anybody. Neither did she only dance of things her senses knew. The history of a people seized her for a reed, and wrote itself in figures past imagining between the crimson firelight; and the shadows of the cattle stalls.

Her dance that night could never have been done with leather between bare foot and earth. It told of measureless winds and waters — of the distances, the stars, the day, the night-rain sweeping down — dew dropping gently — the hundred kinds of birds-the thousand animals and creeping things — and of man, who is lord of all of them, and woman, who is lord of man — man setting naked foot on naked earth and glorying with the thrill of life, new, good, and wonderful.

One of the Turk's seven sons produced a saz toward the end — a little Turkish drum, and accompanied with swift, staccato stabs of sound that spurred her like the goads of overtaking time toward the peak of full expression — faster and faster — wilder and wilder — freer and freer of all limits, until suddenly she left the thing unfinished, and the drum-taps died away alone.

That was art — plain art. No human woman could have

finished it. It was innate abhorrence of the anticlimax that
sent her, having looked into the eyes of the unattainable, to
lie sobbing for short breath in her corner in the dark, leaving
us to imagine the ending if we could.

And instead of anticlimax second climax came. Almost
before the echoes of the drum-taps died among the dancing
shadows overhead a voice cried from the roof in Armenian,
and Kagig rose to his feet.

"Let us climb to the roof and see, effendim," he said,
pulling on his tattered goatskin coat.

"See what, Ermenie?" demanded Rustum Khan. The Rajput's eyes were still ablaze with pagan flame, from watching
Maga.

"To see whether thou hast manhood behind that swagger!"
answered Kagig, and led the way. No man ever yet explained
the racial aversions.

"Kopek! — dog, thou!" growled the Rajput, but Kagig took
no notice and led on, followed by Monty and the rest of us.
Maga and the gypsies came last, swarming behind us up the
ladder through a hole among the beams, and clambering on
to the roof over boxes piled in the draughty attic. Up under
the stars a man was standing with an arm stretched out toward
Tarsus.

"Look!" he said simply.

To the westward was a crimson glow that mushroomed
angrily against the sky, throbbing and swelling with hot life
like the vomit of a crater. We watched in silence for three
minutes, until one of the gypsy women began to moan.

"What do you suppose it is?" I asked then.

"I know what it is," said Kagig simply.

"Tell then."

"'Effendi, that is the heart of Armenia burning. Those are
the homes of my nation — of my kin!"

"And good God, where d'you suppose Miss Vanderman
is?" Fred exclaimed.

Will was standing beside Maga, looking into her eyes as if
he hoped to read in them the riddle of Armenia.

Chapter Six

"Passing the buck to Allah!"

LAUS LACHRIMABILIS

So now the awaited ripe reward —
Your cactus crown! Since I have urged
"Get ready for the untoward"
Ye bid me reap the wrath I dirged;
And I must show the darkened way,
Who beckoned vainly in the light!
I'll lead. But salt of Dead Sea spray
Were sweeter on my lips tonight!

Oh, days of aching sinews, when I trod the choking dust
With feet afire that could not tire, atremble with the trust
More mighty in my inner man than fear of men without,
The word I heard on Kara Dagh and did not dare to doubt —
Timely warning, clear to me as starlight after rain
When, sleepless on eternal hills, I saw the purpose plain
And left, swift-foot at dawn, obedient, to break
The news ye said was no avail — advice ye would not take!

Oh, — nights of tireless talking by the hearth of hidden fires —
On roofs, behind the trade-bales — among oxen in the byres —
Out in rain between the godowns, where the splashing puddles warn
Of tiptoeing informers; when I faced the freezing dawn
With set price on my head, but still the set resolve untamed,
Not melted by the mockery, by no suspicion shamed,
To hide by day in holes, abiding dark and wind and rain
That loosed me straining to the task ye ridiculed again!

Oh, weeks of empty waiting, while the enemy designed
In detail how to loot the stuff ye would not leave behind!
Worse weeks of empty agony when, helpless and alone,

I watched in hiding for the crops from that seed I had sown;

For dust-clouds that should prove at last Armenia awake —
A nation up and coming! I had labored for your sake,
I had hungered, I had suffered. Ye had well rewarded then
If ye had come, and hanged me just to prove that ye were men!

But all the pride was promises, the criticism jeers;
Ye had no heart for sacrifice, and I no time for tears.
I offered — nay, I gave! I squandered body and breath and soul,
I bared the need, I showed the way, I preached a goodly goal,
I urged you choose a leader, since your faith in me was dim,
I swore to serve the chief ye chose, and teach my lore to him,
So he should reap where I had sown. And yet ye bade me wait —
And waited till, awake at last, ye bid me lead too late!

And so, in place of ripe reward,
Your cactus crown! And I, who urged
"Get ready for the untoward"
Must drink the dregs of wrath I dirged!
Ye bid me set time's finger back!
And stage anew the opened fight!
I'll lead. But slime of Dead Sea wrack
Were sweeter on my lips this night!

*T*he first thought that occurred to each of us four was that
Kagig had probably lied, or that he had merely voiced his
private opinion, based on expectation. The glare in the distance seemed too big and solid to be caused by burning
houses, even supposing a whole village were in flames. Yet
there was not any other explanation we could offer. A distant
cloud of black smoke with bulging red under-belly rolled
away through the darkness like a tremendous mountain
range.

We stood in silence trying to judge how far away the thing
might be, Kagig standing alone with his foot on the parapet,
his goatskin coat hanging like a hussar's dolman, and Monty
pacing up and down along the roof behind us all. The gypsies
seemed able to converse by nods and nudges, with now and
then one word whispered. After a little while Maga whispered
in Will's ear, and he went below with her. All the gypsies
promptly followed. Otherwise in the darkness we might not

have noticed where Will went.

"That proves she is no gypsy!" vowed Rustum Khan, standing between Fred and me. "They, would have trusted one of their own kind."

"They call her Maga Jhaere," said I. "The ataman's name is Jhaere. Don't you suppose he's her father?"

"If he were her father he would have no fear," the Rajput answered. "All gypsies are alike. Their women will dance the nautch, and promise unchastity as if that were a little matter. But when it comes to performance of promises the gitana* is true to the Rom.** It is because she is no gypsy that they follow her now to watch. And it is because men say that Americans are Mormons and polygamous, and very swift in the use of revolvers, that all follow instead of one or two!"

"Go down then, and make sure they don't murder him!" commanded Monty, and Rustum Khan turned to obey with rather ill grace. He contrived to convey by his manner that he would do anything for Monty, even to the extent of saving the life of a man he disliked. At the moment when he turned there came the sound of a troop of horses galloping toward us.

"I will first see who comes," he said.

"The blood of Yerkes sahib on your head, Rustum Khan!" Monty answered. At that he went below.

But neither were we destined to remain up there very long. We heard colossal thumping in the kahveh beneath us and presently the Rajput's head reappeared through the opening in the roof.

"The fools are barricading the door," he shouted. "They make sure that an enemy outside could burn us inside without hindrance!"

At that Kagig came along the roof to our corner and looked into Monty's eyes. Fred and I stood between the two of them and the parapet, because for the first few seconds we were not sure the Armenian did not mean murder. His eyes glittered, and his teeth gleamed. It was not possible to guess whether or not the hand under his goatskin coat clutched a weapon.

---

* Gitana, gypsy young woman.

**Rom — Gypsy husband, or family man.

"It is now that you Eenglis sportmen shall endure a test!" he remarked.

Exactly as in the Yeni Khan in Tarsus when we first met him there was a moment now of intense repulsion, entirely unaccountable, succeeded instantly by a wave of sympathy. I laughed aloud, remembering how strange dogs meeting in the street to smell each other are swept by unexplainable antipathies and equally swift comradeship. He thought I laughed at him.

"Neye geldin?" he growled in Turkish. "Wherefore didst thou come? To cackle like a barren hen that sees another laying? Nichevo," he added, turning his back on me. And that was insolence in Russian, meaning that nobody and nothing could possibly be of less importance. He seemed to keep a separate language for each set of thoughts. "Let us go below. Let us stop these fools from making too much trouble," he added in English. "One man ought to stay on the roof. One ought to be sufficient."

Since he had said I did not matter, I remained, and it was therefore I who shouted down a challenge presently in round English at a party who clattered to the door on blown horses, and thundered on it as if they had been shatirs* hurrying to herald the arrival of the sultan himself. There was nothing furtive about their address to the decrepit door, nor anything meek. Accordingly I couched the challenge in terms of un-mistakable affront, repeating it at intervals until the leader of the new arrivals chose to identify himself.

"I am Hans von Quedlinburg!" he shouted. But I did not remember the name.

"Only a thief would come riding in such a hurry through the night!" said I. "Who is with you?"

Another voice shouted very fast and furiously in Turkish, but I could not make head or tail of the words. Then the German resumed the song and dance.

"Are you the party who talked with me at my construction camp?"

"We talk most of the time. We eat food. We whistle. We drink. We laugh!" said I.

---

* Shatir, the man who runs before a personage's horse.

"Because I think you are the people I am seeking. These are Turkish officials with me. I have authority to modify their orders, only let me in!"

"How many of you?" I asked. I was leaning over at risk of my life, for any fool could have seen my head to shoot at it against the luminous dark sky; but I could not see to count them.

"Never mind how many! Let us in! I am Hans von Quedlinburg. My name is sufficient."

So I lied, emphatically and in thoughtful detail.

"You are covered," I said, "by five rifles from this roof. If you don't believe it, try something. You'd better wait there while I wake my chief."

"Only be quick!" said the German, and I saw him light a cigarette, whether to convince me he felt confident or because he did feel so I could not say. I went below, and found Monty and Kagig standing together close to the outer door. They had not heard the whole of the conversation because of the noise the owner's sons had made removing, at their orders, the obstructions they had piled against the door in their first panic. Every one else had returned to the sleeping platforms, except the Turkish owner, who looked awake at last, and was hovering here and there in ecstasies of nervousness.

I repeated what the German had said, rather expecting that Kagig at any rate would counsel defiance. It was he, however, who beckoned the Turk and bade him open the door.

"But, effendi —"

"Chabuk! Quickly, I said!"

"Che arz kunam?" the Turk answered meekly, meaning "What petition shall I make?" the inference being that all was in the hands of Allah.

"Of ten men nine are women!" sneered Kagig irritably, and led the way to our place beside the fire. The Turk fumbled interminably with the door fastenings, and we were comfortably settled in our places before the new arrivals rode in, bringing a blast of cold air with them that set the smoke billowing about the room and made every man draw up his blankets.

"Shut that door behind them!" thundered Kagig. "If they come too slowly, shut the laggards out!"

"Who is this who is arrogant?" the German demanded in English.

He was a fine-looking man, dressed in civilian clothes cut as nearly to the military pattern as the tailor could contrive without transgressing law, but with a too small fez perched on his capable-looking head in the manner of the Prussian who would like to make the Turks believe he loves them. Rustum Khan cursed with keen attention to detail at sight of him. The man who had entered with him became busy in the shadows trying to find room to stall their horses, but Von Quedlinburg gave his reins to an attendant, and stood alone, akimbo, with the firelight displaying him in half relief.

"I am a man who knows, among other things, the name of him who bribed the kaimakam.* on Chakallu," Kagig answered slowly, also in English.

The German laughed.

"Then you know without further argument that I am not to be denied!" he answered. "What I say tonight the government officials will confirm tomorrow! Are you Kagig, whom they call the Eye of Zeitoon?"

"I am no jackal," said Kagig dryly, punning on the name Chakallu, which means "place of jackals."

The German coughed, set one foot forward, and folded both arms on his breast. He looked capable and bold in that attitude, and knew it. I knew at last who he was, and wondered why I had not recognized him sooner — the contractor who had questioned us near the railway encampment along the way, and had offered us directions; but his manner was as different now from then as a bully's in and out of school. Then he had sought to placate, and had almost cringed to Monty. Everything about him now proclaimed the ungloved upper hand.

His party, finding no room to stall their horses, had begun to turn ours loose, and there was uproar along the gypsy side of the room — no action yet, but a threatening snarl that promised plenty of it. Will was half on his feet to interfere, but Monty signed to him to keep cool; and it was Monty's aggravatingly well-modulated voice that laid the law down.

---

* Kaimakam, headman (Turkish).

"Will you be good enough," be asked blandly, "to call off your men from meddling with our mounts?" He could not be properly said to drawl, because there was a positive subacid crispness in his voice that not even a Prussian or a Turk on a dark night could have overlooked.

The German laughed again.

"Perhaps you did not hear my name," he said. "I am Hans von Quedlinburg. As overcontractor on the Baghdad railway I have the privilege of prior accommodation at all roadhouses in this province — for myself and my attendants. And in addition there are with me certain Turkish officers, whose rights I dare say you will not dispute."

Monty did not laugh, although Fred was chuckling in confident enjoyment of the situation.

"You need a lesson in manners," said Monty.

"What do you mean?" demanded Hans von Quedlinburg.

Monty rose to his feet without a single unnecessary motion.

"I mean that unless you call off your men — at once this minute from interfering with our animals I shall give you the lesson you need."

The German saluted in mock respect. Then he patted his breast pocket so as to show the outline of a large repeating pistol. Monty took two steps forward. The German drew the pistol with an oath. Will Yerkes, beyond Fred and slightly behind the German, coughed meaningly. The German turned his head, to find that he was covered by a pistol as large as his own.

"Oh, very well," he said, "what is the use of making a scene?" He thrust his pistol back under cover and shouted an order in Turkish. Monty returned to his place and sat down. The newcomers at the rear of the room tied their horses together by the bridles, and Hans von Quedlinburg resumed his well-fed smile.

"Let it be clearly understood," he said, "that you have interfered with official privilege."

"As long as you do your best in the way of manners you may go on with your errand," said Monty.

Suddenly Fred laughed aloud.

"The martyred biped!" he yelped.

He was right. Peter Measel, missionary on his own account, and sometime keeper of most libelous accounts, stepped out from the shadows and essayed to warm himself, walking past the German with a sort of mincing gait not calculated to assert his manliness. Hans von Quedlinburg stretched out a strong arm and hurled him back again into the darkness at the rear.

"Tchuk-tchuk! Zuruck!" he muttered.

It clearly disconcerted him to have his inferiors in rank assert themselves. That accounted, no doubt, for the meek self-effacement of the Turks who had come with him. Peter Measel did not appear to mind being rebuked. He crossed to the other side of the room, and proceeded to look the gypsies over with the air of a learned ethnologist.

"You speak of my errand," said Hans von Quedlinburg, "as if you imagine I come seeking favors. I am here incidentally to rescue you and your party from the clutches of an outlaw. The Turkish officials who are with me have authority to arrest everybody in this place, yourselves included. Fortunately I am able to modify that. Kagig — that rascal beside you — is a well-known agitator. He is a criminal. His arrest and trial have been ordered on the charge, among other things, of stirring up discontent among the Armenian laborers on the railway work. These gypsies are all his agents. They are all under arrest. You yourselves will be escorted to safety at the coast."

"Why should we need an escort to safety?" Monty demanded.

"Were you on the roof?" the German answered. "And is it possible you did not see the conflagration? An Armenian insurrection has been nipped in the bud. Several villages are burning. The other inhabitants are very much incensed, and all foreigners are in danger — yourselves especially, since you have seen fit to travel in company with such a person as Kagig."

"What has Peter Measel got to do with it?" demanded Fred. "Has he been writing down all our sins in a new book?"

"He will identify you. He will also identify Kagig's agents. He brings a personal charge against a man named Rustum Khan, who must return to Tarsus to answer it. The charge is robbery with violence."

Rustum Khan snorted.

"The violence was only too gentle, and too soon ended. As for robbery, if I have robbed him of a little self-conceit, I will answer to God for that when my hour shall come! How is it your affair to drag that whimpering fool through Asia at your tail — you a German and he English?"

The German had a hot answer ready for that, but the Turks had discovered Maga Jhaere in hiding in the shadows between two old women. She screamed as they tried to drag her forth, and the scream brought us all to our feet. But this time it was Kagig who was swiftest, and we got our first proof of the man's enormous strength. Fred, Will and I charged together round behind the newcomers' horses, in order to make sure of cutting off retreat as well as rescuing Maga. Monty leveled a pistol at the German's head. But Kagig did not waste a fraction of a second on side issues of any sort. He flew at the German's throat like a wolf at a bullock. The German fired at him, missed, and before he could fire again he was caught in a grip he could not break, and fighting for breath, balance and something more.

One of the gypsies, who had not seen the need of hurrying to Maga's aid, now proved the soundness of his judgment by divining Kagig's purpose and tossing several new faggots on the already prodigious fire.

"Good!" barked Kagig, bending the struggling German this and that way as it pleased him.

Seeing our man with the upper hand, Monty and Rustum Khan now hurried into the melee, where two Turkish officers and eight zaptieh were fighting to keep Maga from four gypsies and us three. Nobody had seen fit to shoot, but there was a glimmering of cold steel among the shadows like lightning before a thunderstorm. Monty used his fists. Rustum Khan used the flat of a Rajput saber. Maga, leaving most of her clothing in the Turk's hands, struggled free and in another second the Turks were on the defensive. Rustum Khan knocked the revolver out of an officer's hand, and the rest of them were struggling to use their rifles, when the German shrieked. All fights are full of pauses, when either side could snatch sudden victory if alert enough. We stopped, and turned to look, as if our own lives were not in danger.

Kagig had the German off his feet, face toward the flames, kicking and screaming like a madman. He whirled him twice — shouted a sort of war cry — hove him high with every sinew in his tough frame cracking — and hurled him head-foremost into the fire.

The Turks took the cue to haul off and stand staring at us. We all withdrew to easier pistol range, for contrary to general belief, close quarters almost never help straight aim, especially when in a hurry. There is a shooting as well as a camera focus, and each man has his own.

Pretty badly burnt about the face and fingers, Hans von Quedlinburg crawled backward out of the fire, smelling like the devil, of singed wool. Kagig closed on him, and hurled him back again. This time the German plunged through the fire, and out beyond it to a space between the flames and the back wall, where it must have been hot enough to make the fat run. He stood with a forearm covering his face, while Kagig thundered at him voluminous abuse in Turkish. I wondered, first, why the German did not shoot, and then why his loaded pistol did not blow up in the heat, until I saw that in further proof of strength Kagig had looted his pistol and was standing with one foot on it.

Finally, when the beautiful smooth cloth of which his coat was made bad taken on a stinking overlay of crackled black, the German chose to obey Kagig and came leaping back through the fire, and lay groaning on the floor, where the kahveh's owner's seven sons poured water on him by Kagig's order. His burns were evidently painful, but not nearly so serious as I expected. I got out the first-aid stuff from our medicine bag, and Will, who was our self-constituted doctor on the strength of having once attended an autopsy, disguised as a reporter, in the morgue at the back of Bellevue Hospital in New York City, beckoned a gypsy woman, and proceeded to instruct her what to do.

However, Hans von Quedlinburg was no nervous weakling. He snatched the pot of grease from the woman's hands, daubed gobs of the stuff liberally on his face and hands, and sat up — resembling an unknown kind of angry animal with his eyebrows and mustache burned off except for a stray,

outstanding whisker here and there. In a voice like a bull's at
the smell of blood he reversed what he had shouted through
the flames, and commanded his Turks to arrest the lot of us.

Kagig laughed at that, and spoke to him in English, I
suppose in order that we, too, might understand.

"Those Turks are my prisoners!" he said. "And so are you!"

It was true about the Turks. They had not given up their
weapons yet, but the gypsies were between them and the door,
and even the gypsy women were armed to the teeth and
willing to do battle. I caught sight of Maga's mother-o'-pearl
plated revolver, and the Turkish officer at whom she had it
leveled did not look inclined to dispute the upper hand.

"You Germans are all alike," sneered Kagig. "A dog could
read your reasoning. You thought these foreigners would turn
against me. It never entered your thick skull that they might
rather defy you than see me made prisoner. Fool! Did men
name me Eye of Zeitoon for nothing? Have I watched for
nothing! Did I know the very wording of the letters in your
private box for nothing? Are you the only spy in Asia? Am I
Kagig, and do I not know who advised dismissing all Armenians from the railway work? Am I Kagig, and do I not know
why? Kopek! (Dog!) You would beggar my people, in order
to curry favor with the Turk. You seek to take me because I
know your ways! Two months ago you knew to within a day
or two when these new massacres would begin. One month,
three weeks, and four days ago you ordered men to dig my
grave, and swore to bury me alive in it! What shall hinder me
from burning you alive this minute?"

There were five good hindrances, for I think that Rustum
Khan would have objected to that cruelty, even had he been
alone. Kagig caught Monty's eye and laughed.

"Korkakma!" he jeered. "Do not be afraid!" Then be
glanced swiftly at the Turks, and at Peter Measel, who was
staring all-eyes at Maga on the far side of the room.

"Order your pigs of zaptieh to throw their arms down!"

Instead, the German shouted to them to fire volleys at us.
He was not without a certain stormy courage, whatever
Kagig's knowledge of his treachery.

But the Turks did not fire, and it was perfectly plain that
we four were the reason of it. They had been promised an

easy prey — captured women — loot — and the remunerative task of escorting us to safety. Doubtless Von Quedlinburg had promised them our consul would be lavish with rewards on our account. Therefore there was added reason why they should not fire on Englishmen and an American. We had not made a move since the first scuffle when we rescued Maga, but the Turkish lieutenant had taken our measure. Perhaps he had whispered to his men. Perhaps they reached their own conclusions. The effect was the same in either case.

"Order them to throw their weapons down!" commanded Kagig, kicking the German in the ribs. And his coat had been so scorched in the fierce heat that the whole of one side of it broke off, like a cinder slab.

This time Hans von Quedlinburg obeyed. For one thing the pain of his burns was beginning to tell on him, but he could see, too, that he had lost prestige with his party.

"Throw down your weapons!" he ordered savagely.

But he had lost more prestige than he knew, or else he had less in the beginning than he counted on. The Turkish lieutenant — a man of about forty with the evidence of all the sensual appetites very plainly marked on his face — laughed and brought his men to attention. Then he made a kind of half-military motion with his hand toward each of us in turn, ignoring Kagig but intending to convey that we at any rate need not feel anxious.

It was Maga Jhaere who solved the riddle of that impasse. She was hardly in condition to appear before a crowd of men, for the Turks had torn off most of her clothes, and she had not troubled to find others. She was unashamed, and as beautiful and angry as a panther. With panther suddenness she snatched the lieutenant's sword and pistol.

It suited neither his national pride nor religious prejudices to be disarmed by a gypsy woman; but the Turk is an amazing fatalist, and unexpectedness is his peculiar quality.

"Che arz kunam?" he muttered — the perennial comment of the Turk who has failed, that always made Kagig bare his teeth in a spasm of contempt. "Passing the buck to Allah," as Will construed it.

But disarming the mere conscript soldiers was not quite so simple, although Maga managed it. They had less regard for their own skins than handicapped their officer, and yet more than his contempt for the female of any human breed.

They refused point-blank to throw their rifles down, bringing a laugh and a shout of encouragement from the German. But she screwed the muzzle of her pistol into the lieutenant's ear, and bade him enforce her orders, the gypsy women applauding with a chorus of "Ohs" and "Ahs." The lieutenant succumbed to force majeure, and his men, who were inclined to die rather than take orders from a woman, obeyed him readily enough. They laid their rifles down carefully, without a suggestion of resentment.

"So. The women of Zeitoon are good!" said Kagig with a curt nod of approval, and Maga tossed him a smile fit for the instigation of another siege of Troy.

The gypsy women picked the rifles up, and Maga went to hunt through the mule-packs for clothing. Then Kagig turned on us, motioning with his toe toward Hans von Quedlinburg, who continued to treat himself extravagantly from our jar of ointment.

"You do not know yet the depths of this man's infamy!" he said. "The world professes to loathe Turks who rob, sell and murder women and children. What of a German — a foreigner in Turkey, who instigates the murder — and the robbery — and the burning — and the butchery — for his own ends, or for his bloody country's ends? This man is an instigator!"

"You lie!" snarled Von Quedlinburg. "You dog of an Armenian, you lie!" Kagig ignored him.

"This is the German sportman who tried once to go to Zeitoon to shoot bears, as he said. But I knew he was a spy. I am not the Eye of Zeitoon merely because that title rolls nicely on the tongue. He has — perhaps he has it in his pocket now — a concession from the politicians in Stamboul, granting him the right to exploit Zeitoon — a place he has never seen! He has encouraged this present butchery in order that Turkish soldiers may have excuse to penetrate to Zeitoon that he covets. He wants you Eenglis sportmen out of the way. You were to be sent safely back to Tarsus, lest you should be witnesses of what must happen. Perhaps you do not believe all this?'"

He stooped down and searched the German's coat pockets with impatient fingers that tugged and jerked, tossing out handkerchief and wallet, cigars, matches that by a miracle had not caught in the heat, and considerable money to the floor. He took no notice of the money, but one of the old gypsy women crept out and annexed it, and Kagig made no comment.

"He has not his concession with him. I can prove nothing tonight. I said you shall stand a test. You must choose. This German and those Turks are my prisoners. You have nothing to do with it. You may go back to Tarsus if you wish, and tell the Turks that Kagig defies them! You shall have an escort as far as the nearest garrison. You shall have fifty men to take you back by dawn tomorrow."

At that Rustum Khan turned several shades darker and glared truculently.

"Who art thou, Armenian, to frame a test for thy betters?" he demanded, throwing a very military chest. And Will promptly bridled at the Rajput's attitude.

"You've no call to make yourself out any better than he is!" he interrupted. And at that Maga Jhaere threw a kiss from across the room, but one could not tell whether her own dislike of Rustum Khan, or her approval of Will's support of Kagig was the motive.

Fred began humming in the ridiculous way he has when be thinks that an air of unconcern may ease a situation, and of course Rustum Khan mistook the nasal noises for intentional insult. He turned on the unsuspecting Fred like a tiger. Monty's quick wit and level voice alone saved open rupture.

"What I imagine Rustum Khan means is this, Kagig: My friends and I have engaged you as guide for a hunting trip. We propose to hold you strictly to the contract."

Kagig looked keenly at each of us and nodded.

"In my day I have seen the hunters hunted!" he said darkly.

"In my day I have seen an upstart punished!" growled the Rajput, and sat down, back to the wall.

"Castles, and bears!" smiled Monty.

Kagig grinned.

"What if I propose a different quarry?"

"Propose and see!" Monty was on the alert, and therefore

to all outward appearance in a sort of well-fed, catlike, dally-
ing mood.

"This dog," said Kagig, and he kicked the German's ribs
again, "has said nothing of any other person he must rescue.
Bear me witness."

We murmured admission of the truth of that.

"Yet I am the Eye of Zeitoon, and I know. His purpose was
to leave his prisoners here and hurry on to overtake a lady —
a certain Miss Vanderman, who he thinks is on her way to
the mission at Marash. He desired the credit for her rescue
in order better to blind the world to his misdeeds! Nevertheless, now that she can be no more use to him, observe his
chivalry! He does not even mention her!"

The German shrugged his shoulders, implying that to
argue with such a savage was waste of breath.

"What do you know of Miss Vanderman's where-abouts?"
demanded Will, and Maga Jhaere, at the sound of another
woman's name, sat bolt upright between two other women
whose bright eyes peeped out from under blankets.

"I had word of her an hour before you came, effendi,"
Kagig answered. "She and her party took fright this afternoon, and have taken to the hills. They are farther ahead than
this pig dreamed" — once more he kicked Von Quedlinburg
— "more than a day's march ahead from here."

"Then we'll hunt for her first," said Monty, and the rest
of us nodded assent.

Kagig grinned.

"You shall find her. You shall see a castle. In the castle where
you find her you shall choose again! It is agreed, effendi!"

Then he ordered his prisoners made fast, and the gypsies
and our Zeitoonli servants attended to it, he himself, however, binding the German's hands and feet. Will went and put
bandages on the man's burns, I standing by, to help. But we
got no thanks.

"Ihr seit verruckt!" he sneered. "You take the side of bandits. Passt mal auf — there will be punishment!"

The Zeitoonli were going to tie Peter Measel, but he set up
such a howl that Kagig at last took notice of him and ordered
him flung, unbound, into the great wooden bin in which the
horse-feed was kept for sale to wayfarers. There he lay, and

slept and snored for the rest of that session, with his mouth close to a mouse-hole.

Then Kagig ordered our Zeitoonli to the roof on guard, and bade us sleep with a patriarchal air of authority.

"There is no knowing when I shall decide to march," be explained.

Given enough fatigue, and warmth, and quietness, a man will sleep under almost any set of circumstances. The great fire blazed, and flickered, and finally died down to a bed of crimson. The prisoners were most likely all awake, for their bonds were tight, but only Kagig remained seated in the midst of his mess of blankets by the hearth; and I think he slept in that position, and that I was the last to doze off. But none of us slept very long.

There came a shout from the roof again, and once again a thundering on the door. The move — unanimous — that the gypsies' right hands made to clutch their weapons resembled the jump from surprise into stillness when the jungle is caught unawares. A second later when somebody tossed dry fagots on the fire the blaze betrayed no other expression on their faces than the stock-in-trade stolidity. Even the women looked as if thundering on a kahveh door at night was nothing to be noticed. Kagig did not move, but I could see that he was breathing faster than the normal, and he, too, clutched a weapon. Von Quedlinburg began shouting for help alternately in Turkish and in German, and the owner of the place produced a gun — a long, bright, steel-barreled affair of the vintage of the Comitajes and the First Greek War. He and his sons ran to the door to barricade it.

"Yavash!" ordered Kagig. The word means slowly, as applied to all the human processes. In that instance it meant "Go slow with your noise!" and mine host so understood it.

But the thundering on the great door never ceased, and the kahveh was too full of the noise of that for us to hear what the Zeitoonli called down from the roof. Kagig arose and stood in the middle of the room with the firelight behind him. He listened for two minutes, standing stock-still, a thin smile flickering across his lean face, and the sharp satyrlike tops of his ears seeming to prick outward in the act of intelligence.

"Open and let them in!" he commanded at last.

"I will not!" roared the owner of the place. "I shall be tortured, and all my house!"

"Open, I said!"

"But they will make us prisoner!"

Kagig made a sign with his right hand. Gregor Jhaere rose and whispered. One by one the remaining gypsies followed him into the shadows, and there came a noise of scuffling, and of oaths and blows. As Gregor Jhaere had mentioned earlier, they did obey Kagig now and then. The Turks came back looking crestfallen, and the fastenings creaked. Then the door burst open with a blast of icy air, and there poured in nineteen armed men who blinked at the firelight helplessly.

"Kagig — where is Kagig?"

"You cursed fools, where should I be!"

"Kagig? Is it truly you?" Their eyes were still blinded by the blaze.

"Shut that door again, and bolt it! Aye — Kagig, Kagig, is it you!"

"It is Kagig! Behold him! Look!"

They clustered close to see, smelling infernally of sweaty garments and of the mud from unholy lurking places.

"Kagig it is! And has all happened as I, Kagig, warned you it would happen?"

"Aye. All. More. Worse!"

"Had you acted beforehand in the manner I advised?"

"No, Kagig. We put it off. We talked, and disagreed. And then it was too late to agree. They were cutting throats while we still argued. When we ran into the street to take the offensive they were already shooting from the roofs!"

"Hah!"

That bitter dry expletive, coughed out between set teeth, could not be named a laugh.

"Kagig, listen!"

"Aye! Now it is 'Kagig, listen!' But a little while ago it was I who was saying 'Listen!' I walked myself lame, and talked myself hoarse. Who listened to me? Why should I listen to you?"

"But, Kagig, my wife is gone!"

"Hah!"

"My daughter, Kagig!"

"Hah!'

A third man thrust himself forward and thumped the butt of a long rifle on the floor.

"They took my wife and two daughters before my very eyes, Kagig! It is no time for talking now — you have talked already too much, Kagi, — now prove yourself a man of deeds! With these eyes I saw them dragged by the hair down street! Oh, would God that I had put my eyes out first, then had I never seen it! Kagig —"

"Aye — Kagig!"

"You shall not sneer at me! I shot one Turk, and ten more pounced on them. They screamed to me. They called to me to rescue. What could I do? I shot, and I shot until the rifle barrel burned my fingers. Then those cursed Turks set the house on fire behind me, and my companions dragged me away to come and find others to unite with us and make a stand! We found no others! Kagig — I tell you — those bloody Turks are auctioning our wives and daughters in the village church! It is time to act!"

"Hah! Who was it urged you in season and out of season — day and night — month in, month out — to come to Zeitoon and help me fortify the place? Who urged you to send your women there long ago?"

"But Kagig, you do not appreciate. To you it is nothing not to have women near you. We have mothers, sisters, wives —"

"Nothing to me, is it? These eyes have seen my mother, ravished by a Kurd in a Turkish uniform!"

"Well, that only proves you are one with us after all! That only proves —"

"One with you! Why did you not act, then, when I risked life and limb a thousand times to urge you?"

"We could not, Kagig. That would have precipitated —"

He interrupted the man with an oath like the aggregate of bitterness.

"Precipitated? Did waiting for the massacre like chickens waiting for the ax delay the massacres a day? But now it is 'Come and lead us, Kagig!' How many of you are there left to lead?"

"Who knows? We are nineteen —"

"Hah! And I am to run with nineteen men to the rape of Tarsus and Adana?"

"Our people will rally to you, Kagig!"

"They shall."

"Come, then!"

"They shall rally at Zeitoon!"

"Oh, Kagig — how shall they reich Zeitoon? The cursed Turks have ordered out the soldiers and are sending regiments —"

"I warned they would!"

"The cavalry are hunting down fugitives along the roads!"

"As I foretold a hundred times!"

"They were sent to protect Armenians —"

"That is always the excuse!"

"And they kill — kill — kill! A dozen of them hunted me for two miles, until I hid in a watercourse! Look at us! Look at our clothes! We are wet to the skin — tired — starving! Kagig, be a man!"

He went back to his mess of blankets and sat down on it, too bitter at heart for words. They reproached him in chorus, coming nearer to the fire to let the fierce heat draw the stink out of their clothes.

"Aye, Kagig, you must not forget your race. You must not forget the past, Kagig. Once Armenia was great, remember that! You must not only talk to us, you must act at last! We summon you to be our leader, Kagig, son of Kagig of Zeitoon!"

He stared back at them with burning eyes — raised both bands to beat his temples — and then suddenly turned the palms of his hands toward the roof in a gesture of utter misery.

"Oh, my people!"

That glimpse he betrayed of his agony was but a moment long. The fingers closed suddenly, and the palms that had risen in helplessness descended to his knees clenched fists, heavy with the weight of purpose.

"What have you done with the ammunition?" he demanded.

"We had it in the manure under John Zimisces' cattle."

"I know that. Where is it now?"

"The Turks discovered it at dawn today. Some one had told. They burned Zimisces and his wife and sons alive in the straw!"

"You fools! They knew where the stuff was a week ago! A month ago I warned you to send it to Zeitoon, but somebody told you I was treacherous, and you fools listened! How much ammunition have you left now?"

"Just what we have with us. I have a dozen rounds."

"I ten."

"I nine."

"I thirty-three."

Each man had a handful, or two handfuls at the most. Kagig observed their contributions to the common fund with scorn too deep for expression. It was as if the very springs of speech were frozen.

"We summon you to lead us, Kagig!"

Words came to him again.

"You summon me to lead? I will! From now I lead! By the God who gave my fathers bread among the mountains, I will, moreover, be obeyed! Either my word is law —"

"Kagig, it is law!"

"Or back you shall go to where the Turks are wearing white, and the gutters bubble red, and the beams are black against the sky! You shall obey me in future on the instant that I speak, or run back to the Turks for mercy from my hand! I have listened to enough talk!"

"Spoken like a man!" said Monty, and stood up.

We all stood up; even Rustum Khan, who did not pretend to like him, saluted the old warrior who could announce his purpose so magnificently. Maga Jhaere stood up, and sought Will's eyes from across the room. Fred, almost too sleepy to know what he was doing (for the tail end of the fever is a yearning for early bed) undid the catch of his beloved instrument, and made the rafters ring. In a minute we four were singing "For he's a jolly good fellow," and Kagig stood up, looking like Robinson Crusoe in his goatskins, to acknowledge the compliment.

The noise awoke Peter Measel, and when we had finished making fools of ourselves I walked over to discover what he was saying. He was praying aloud — nasally — through the mouse-hole — for us, not himself. I looked at my watch. It was two hours past midnight.

"You fellows," I said, "it's Sunday. The martyred biped has just waked up and remembered it. He is praying that we may be forgiven for polluting the Sabbath stillness with immoral tunes!"

My words had a strange effect. Monty, and Fred, and Will laughed. Rustum Khan laughed savagely. But all the Armenians, including Kagig, knelt promptly on the floor and prayed, the gypsies looking on in mild amusement tempered by discretion. And out of the mouse-hole in the horse-feed bin came Peter Measel's sonorous, overriding periods:

"And, O Lord, let them not be smitten by Thine anger. Let them not be cut down in Thy wrath! Let them not be cast into hell! Give them another chance, O Lord! Let the Ten Commandments be written on their hearts in letters of fire, but let not their souls be damned forever more! If they did not know it was the Sabbath Day, O Lord, forgive them! Amen!"

It was a most amazing night.

Chapter Seven

"We hold you to your word!"

LIBERA NOS, DOMINE!

A priest, a statesman, and a soldier stood
Hand in each other's hand, by ruin faced,RConsulting to find succor if they could,
Till soon the lesser ones themselves abased,
Their sword and parchment on an altar laid
In deep humility the while the priest he prayed.

He prayed first for his church, that it might be
Upholden and acknowledged and revered,
And in its opal twilight men might see
Salvation if in truth enough they feared,
And if enough acknowledgment they gave
To ritual, and rosary, and creed that save.

Then prayed he for the state, that it should wean
Well-tutored counselors to do their part
Full profit and prosperity to glean
With dignity, although with contrite heart
And wisdom that Tradition wisdom ranks,
That church and state might stand and men give thanks.

Last prayed he for the soldier — longest, too,
That all the honor and the aims of war
Subserving him might carry wrath and rue
Unto repentance, and in trembling awe
The enemy at length should fault confess
And yield, to crave a peace of righteousness.

Behind them stood a patriot unbowed,
Not arrogant in gilt or goodly cloth,

Nor mincing meek, and yet not poorly proud;
With eyes afire that glittered not with wrath;
Aware of evil hours, and undismayed
Because he loved too well. He also prayed.

"Oh, Thou, who gavest, may I also give,
Withholding not — accepting no reward;
For I die gladly if the least ones live.
Twice righteous and two-edged be the sword,
'Neath freedom's banner drawn to prove Thy word
And smite me if I'm false!" His prayer was heard.

*T*he remainder of that night was nightmare pure and simple — mules and horses squealing in instinctive fear of action they felt impending — gypsies and Armenians dragging packs out on the floor, to repack everything a dozen times for some utterly godless reason — Rustum Khan seizing each fugitive Armenian in turn to question him, alternating fierce threats with persuasion — Kagig striding up and down with hands behind him and his scraggly black beard pressed down on his chest — and the great fire blazing with reports like cannon shots as one of the Turk's sons piled on fuel and the resinous wet wood caught.

The Turk and his other six sons ran away and hid themselves as a precaution against our taking vengeance on them. With situations reversed a Turk would have taken unbelievable toll in blood and agony from any Armenian he could find, and they reasoned we were probably no better than themselves. The marvel was that they left one son to wait on us, and take the money for room and horse-feed.

"Remember!" warned Monty, as we four sidled close together with our backs against the wall. "Until we're in actual personal danger this trouble is the affair of Kagig and his men!"

"I get you. If we horn in before we have to we'll do more harm than good. Give the Turks an excuse to call us outlaws and shoot instead of rescue us. Sure. But what about Miss Vanderman?" said Will.

"I foresee she's doomed!" Fred stared straight in front of him. "It looks as if we'll lose our little Willy too! One woman at a time, especially when the lady totes a mother-o'-pearl revolver and about a dozen knives! If you come out of this alive, Bill, you'll be wiser!"

"Fond of bull, aren't you! You'd jest on an ant-heap."

"There's nothing to discuss," said I. "If there's a lady in danger somewhere ahead, we all know what we're going to do about it."

Monty nodded.

"If we can find her and get word to the consul, that 'ud be one more lever for him to pull on."

"D'you suppose they'd dare molest an Englishwoman?" I asked, with the sudden gooseflesh rising all over me.

"She's American," said Will between purposely set lips. But I did not see that that qualified the unpleasantness by much.

One of the Armenians, whom Rustum Khan had finished questioning, went and stood in Kagig's way, intercepting his everlasting sentry-go.

"What is it, Eflaton?"

"My wife, Kagig!"

"Ah! I remember your wife. She fed me often."

"You must come with me and find her, Kagig — my wife and two daughters, who fed you often!"

"The daughters were pretty," said Kagig. "So was the wife. A young woman yet. A brave, good woman. Always she agreed with me, I remember. Often I heard her urge you men to follow me to Zeitoon and help to fortify the place!"

"Will you leave a good woman in the hands of Turks, Kagig? Come — come to the rescue!"

"It is too bad," said Kagig simply. "Such women suffer more terribly than the hags who merely die by the sword. Ten times by the count — during ten succeeding massacres I have seen the Turks sell Armenian wives and daughters at auction. I am sorry, Eflaton."

"My God!" groaned Will. "How long are we four loafers going to sit here and leave a white woman in danger on the road ahead?" He got up and began folding his blankets.

The Armenian whom Kagig had called Eflaton threw himself to the floor and shrieked in agony of misery. Rustum Khan stepped over him and came and stood in front of Monty.

"These men are fools," he said. "They know exactly what the Turks will do. They have all seen massacres before. Yet not one of them was ready when the hour set for this one came. They say — and they say the truth, that the Turks will murder all Europeans they catch outside the mission stations, lest there be true witnesses afterward whom the world will believe."

"But a woman — scarcely a white woman?" This from Will, with the tips of his ears red and the rest of his face a deathly white.

"Depending on the woman," answered Rustum Khan. "Old — unpleasing —" He made an upward gesture with his thumb, and a noise between his teeth suggestive of a severed windpipe. "If she were good-looking — I have heard say they pay high prices in the interior, say at Kaisarieh or Mosul. Once in a harem, who would ever know? The road ahead is worse than dangerous. Whoever wishes to save his life would do best to turn back now and try to ride through to Tarsus."

"Try it, then, if you're afraid!" sneered Will, and for a moment I thought the Rajput would draw steel.

"I know what this lord sahib and I will do," he said, darkening three or four shades under his black beard. "It was for men bewitched by gypsy-women that I feared!"

Will was standing. Nothing but Monty's voice prevented blows. He rapped out a string of sudden rhetoric in the Rajput's own guttural tongue, and Rustum Khan drew back four paces.

"Send him back, Colonel sahib!" he urged. "Send that one back! He and Umm Kulsum will be the death of us!"

Fred went off into a peal of laughter that did nothing to calm the Rajput's ruffled temper.

"Who was Umm Kulsum?" I asked him, divining the cause.

"The most immoral hag in Asian legend! The aggregated essence of all female evil personified in one procuress!"

"Say, I'll have to teach that gink —"

Monty got up and stood between them, but it was a new alarm that prevented blows. A fist-blow in the Rajput's face would have meant a blood feud that nothing less than a man's life could settle, and Monty looked worried. There came a new thundering on the door that brought everybody to his feet as if murder were the least of the charges against us. Only Kagig appeared at ease and unconcerned.

"Open to them!" he shouted, and resumed his pacing to and fro.

Our Armenian servants ran to the door, and in a minute returned to say that fifty mounted men from Zeitoon were drawn up outside. Kagig gave a curt laugh and strode across to us.

"I said you Eenglis sportmen should see good sport."

Monty nodded, with a hand held out behind him to warn us to keep still.

"I said you shall shoot many pigs!"

"Lead on, then."

"Turks are pigs!"

Monty did not answer. To have disagreed would have been like flapping a red cloth at a tiger. Yet to have agreed with him at once might have made him jump to false conclusions. The consul's last words to us had been insistent on the unwisdom of posing as anything but hunters, legitimately entitled to protection from the Turkish government.

"I would like you gentlemen for allies!"

"You are our servant at present."

"Would you think of holding me to that?" demanded Kagig with a gesture of extreme irritation. It is only the West that can joke at itself in the face of crisis.

"If not to that," said Monty blandly, "then what agreements do you keep?"

Kagig saw the point. He drew a deep impatient breath and drove it out again hissing through his teeth. Then he took grim hold of himself.

"Effendi," he said, addressing himself to Monty, but including all of us with eyes that seemed to search our hearts, "you are a lord, a friend of the King of Eengland. If I were less than a man of my word I could make you prisoner and oblige your friend the King of Eengland to squeeze these cursed Turks!"

Rustum Khan heard what he said, and made noise enough drawing his saber to be heard outside the kahveh, but Kagig did not turn his head. Three gypsies attended to Rustum Khan, slipping between him and their master, and our four

Zeitoonli servants cautiously approached the Rajput from behind.

"Peace!" ordered Monty. "Continue, Kagig."

Kagig held both hands toward Monty, palms upward, as if he were offering the keys of Hell and Heaven.

"You are sportmen, all of you. Shall I keep my word to you? Or shall I serve my nation in its agony?"

Monty glanced swiftly at us, but we made no sign. Will actually looked away. It was a rule we four had to leave the playing of a hand to whichever member of the partnership was first engaged; and we never regretted it, although it often called for faith in one another to the thirty-third degree. The next hand might fall to any other of us, but for the present it was Monty's play.

"We hold you to your word!" said Monty.

Kagig gasped. "But my people!"

"Keep your word to them too! Surely you haven't promised them to make us prisoner?"

"But if I am your servant — if I must obey you for two piasters a day, how shall I serve my nation?"

"Wait and see!" suggested Monty blandly.

Kagig bowed stiffly, from the neck.

"It would surprise you, effendi," he said grimly, "to know how many long years I have waited, in order that I may see what other men will do!"

Monty never answered that remark. There came a yell of "Fire!" and in less than ten seconds flames began to burst through the door that shut off the Turks' private quarters, and to lick and roar among the roof beams. The animals at the other end of the room went crazy, and there was instant panic, the Armenians outside trying to get in to help, and fighting with the men and animals and women and children who choked the way. Then the hay in the upper story caught alight, and the heat below became intolerable. Monty saw and instantly pounced on an ax and two crowbars in the corner.

"Through the wall!" he ordered.

Fred, Will and I did that work, he and Kagig looking on. It was much easier than at first seemed likely. Most of the stones were stuck with mud, not plaster, and when the first three or four were out the rest came easily. In almost no time we had a great gap ready, and the extra draft we made increased the holocaust, but seemed to lift the heat higher. Then some of the Zeitoonli saw the gap, and began to hurry blindfolded horses through it and in a very little while the place seemed empty. I saw the Turkish owner and several of his sons looking on in fatalistic calm at about the outside edge of the ring of light, and it occurred to me to ask a question.

"Hasn't that Turk a harem?" I asked.

In another second we four were hurrying around the building, and Will and I burst in the door at the rear with our crowbars. Monty and Fred rushed past us, and before I could get the smoke out of my eyes and throat they were hurrying out again with two old women in their arms — the women screaming, and they laughing and coughing so that they could hardly run. Then Will made my blood run cold with a new alarm.

"The biped!" he shouted. "The Measel in the corn-bin!"

They dropped the old ladies, and all four of us raced back to our hole in the wall — plunged into the hell-hot building, pulled the lid off the corn-bin (it was fastened like an ancient Egyptian coffin-lid with several stout Wooden pegs), dragged Measel out, and frog-marched him, kicking and yelling, to the open, where Fred collapsed.

"Measel," said Will, stooping to feel Fred's heart, "if you're the cause of my friend Oakes' death, Lord pity you!"

Fred sat up, not that he wished to save the "biped" any anguish, but the wise man vomits comfortably when he can, the necessity being bad enough without additional torment.

"See!" said a voice out of darkness. "He empties himself! That is well. It is only the end of the fever. Now he will be a man again. But the sahibs should have left that writer of characters in the corn-bin, where he could have shared the fate of his master without troubling us again!"

Rustum Khan strode into the light, with half his fierce beard burned away from having been the last to leave by the front entrance, and a decided limp from having been kicked by a frantic mule.

"What have you done with the German?" demanded Monty.

"I, sahib? Nothing. In truth nothing. It was the seven sons of the Turk — abetted I should say by gypsies. It was the German who set the place alight. The girl, Maga Jhaere they call her, saw him do it. She watched like a cat, the fool, hoping to amuse herself, while he burned off his ropes with a brand that fell his way out of the fire. When another brand jumped half across the room he set the place alight with it, tossing it over the party wall. He was an able rascal, sahib."

"Was?" demanded Monty.

"Aye, sahib, was! In another second he released the Turkish lieutenant and shouted in his ear to escape and say that Armenians burned this kahveh! Gregor Jhaere slew the Turk, however. And Maga followed the German into the open, where she denounced him to some of the Zeitoonli who recently arrived. They took him and threw him back into the fire — where he remained. I begin to like these Zeitoonli. I even like the gypsies more than formerly. They are men of some discernment, and of action!"

"Man of blood!" growled Monty. "What of the Turkish owner and his seven sons?"

"They shall burn, too, if the sahib say so!"

"If they burn, so shall you! Where is Kagig?"

"Seeing that the sahibs' horses are packed and saddled. I came to find the sahibs. According to Kagig it is time to go, before Turks come to take vengeance for a burned roadhouse. They will surely say Armenians burned it, whether or not there is a German to support their accusation!"

Then we heard Kagig's high-pitched "Haide — chabuk!" and picked up Peter Measel, and ran around the building to where the horses were already saddled, and squealing in fear of the flames. We left the Turk, and his wives and seven sons, to tell what tale they pleased.

Chapter Eight

"I go with that man!"

LO HERE! LO THERE!
Ye shall not judge men by the drinks they take,
Nor by unthinking oath, nor what they wear,
For look! the mitered liars protest make
And drinking know they lie, and knowing swear.
No oath is round without the rounded fruit,
Nor pompous promise hides the ultimate.
In scarlet as in overalls and tailored suit
Tomorrows truemen and the traitors wait
Untold by trick of blazonry or voice.
But harvest ripens and there come the reaping days
When each shall choose one path to bide the choice,
And ye shall know men when they face dividing ways.

*T*o those who have never ridden knee to knee with outlaws full pelt into unknown darkness, with a burning house behind, and a whole horizon lit with the rolling glow of murdered villages, let it be written that the sensation of so doing is creepy, most amazing wild, and not without unrighteous pleasure.

There was a fierce joy that burned without consuming, and a consciousness of having crossed a Rubicon. Points of view are left behind in a moment, although the proof may not be apparent for days or weeks, and I reckon our mental change from being merely hunters of an ancient castle and big game-tourists-trippers, from that hour. As we galloped behind

Kagig the mesmerism of respect for custom blew away in the wind. We became at heart outlaws as we rode — and one of us a privy councilor of England!

The women, Maga included, were on in front. The night around and behind us was full of the thunder of fleeing cattle, for the Zeitoonli had looted the owner of the kahveh's cows and oxen along with their own beasts and were driving them helter-skelter. The crackling flames behind us were a beacon, whistling white in the early wind, that we did well to hurry from.

It was Monty who called Kagig's attention to the idiocy of tiring out the cattle before dawn, and then Kagig rode like an arrow until he could make the gypsies hear him. One long keening shout that penetrated through the drum of hoofs brought them to a walk, but they kept Maga in front with them, screened from our view until morning by a close line of mounted women and a group of men. The Turkish prisoners were all behind among the fifty Armenians from Zeitoon, looking very comfortless trussed up on the mounts that nobody else had coveted, with hands made fast behind their backs.

A little before dawn, when the saw-tooth tips of the mountain range on our left were first touched with opal and gold, we turned off the araba track along which we had so far come and entered a ravine leading toward Marash. Fred was asleep on horseback, supported between Will and me and snoring like a throttled dog. The smoke of the gutted kahveh had dwindled to a wisp in the distance behind us, and there was no sight or sound of pursuit.

No wheeled vehicle that ever man made could have passed up this new track. It was difficult for ridden horses, and our loaded beasts had to be given time. We seemed to be entering by a fissure into the womb of the savage hills that tossed themselves in ever-increasing grandeur up toward the mist-draped heights of Kara Dagh. Oftener than not our track was obviously watercourse, although now and then we breasted higher levels from which we could see, through gaps between hill and forest, backward along the way we had come. There was smoke from the direction of Adana that smudged a whole skyline, and between that and the sea about a dozen sooty columns mushroomed against the clouds.

There was not a mile of the way we came that did not hold a hundred hiding places fit for ambuscade, but our party was too numerous and well-armed to need worry on that account. Monty and Kagig drew ahead, quite a little way behind the gypsies still, but far in front of us, who had to keep Fred upright on his horse.

"My particular need is breakfast," said I.

"And Will's is the woman!" said Fred, admitting himself awake at last. Will had been straining in the stirrups on the top of every rise his horse negotiated ever since the sun rose. It certainly was a mystery why Maga should have been spirited away, after the freedom permitted her the day before.

"Rustum Khan has probably made off with her, or cut her head off!" remarked Fred by way of offering comfort, yawning with the conscious luxury of having slept. "I don't see Rustum Khan. Let's hope it's true! That 'ud give the American lady a better chance for her life in case we should overtake her!"

Will and Fred have always chosen the most awkward places and the least excuse for horseplay, and the sleep seemed to have expelled the last of the fever from Fred's bones, so that he felt like a schoolboy on holiday. Will grabbed him around the neck and they wrestled, to their horses' infinite disgust, panting and straining mightily in the effort to unseat each other. It was natural that Will should have the best of it, he being about fifteen years younger as well as unweakened by malaria. The men of Zeitoon behind us checked to watch Fred rolled out of his saddle, and roared with the delight of fighting men the wide world over to see the older campaigner suddenly recover his balance and turn the tables on the younger by a trick.

And at that very second, as Will landed feet first on the gravel panting for breath, Maga Jhaere arrived full gallop from the rear, managing her ugly gray stallion with consummate ease. Her black hair streamed out in the wind, and what with the dew on it and the slanting sun-rays she seemed to be wearing all the gorgeous jewels out of Ali Baba's cave. She was the loveliest thing to look at — unaffected, unexpected, and as untamed as the dawn, with parted lips as red as the branch of budding leaves with which she beat her horse.

But the smile turned to a frown of sudden passion as she saw Will land on the ground and Fred get ready for reprisals. She screamed defiance — burst through the ranks of the nearest Zeitoonli — set her stallion straight at us — burst between Fred and me — beat Fred savagely across the face with her sap-softened branch — and wheeled on her beast's haunches to make much of Will. He laughed at her, and tried to take the whip away. Seeing he was neither hurt nor indignant, she laughed at Fred, spat at him, and whipped her stallion forward in pursuit of Kagig, breaking between him and Monty to pour news in his ear.

"A curse on Rustum Khan!" laughed Fred, spitting out red buds. "He didn't do his duty!"

He had hardly said that when the Rajput came spurring and thundering along from the rear. He seemed in no hurry to follow farther, but drew rein between us and saluted with the semi-military gesture with which he favored all who, unlike Monty, had not been Colonels of Indian regiments.

"I tracked Umm Kulsum through the dark!" he announced, rubbing the burned nodules out of his singed beard and then patting his mare's neck. "I saw her ride away alone an hour before you reached that fork in the road and turned up this watercourse. 'By the teeth of God,' said I, 'when a good-looking woman leaves a party of men to canter alone in the dark, there is treason!' and I followed."

I offered the Rajput my cigarette case, and to my surprise he accepted one, although not without visible compunction. As a Mohammedan by creed he was in theory without caste and not to be defiled by European touch, but the practices of most folk fall behind their professions. A hundred yards ahead of us Maga was talking and gesticulating furiously, evidently railing at Kagig's wooden-headedness or unbelief. Monty sat listening, saying nothing.

"What did you see, Rustum Khan?" asked Fred.

"At first very little. My eyes are good, but that gypsy-woman's are better, and I was kept busy following her; for I could not keep close, or she might have heard. The noise of her own clumsy stallion prevented her from hearing the lighter footfalls of my mare, and by that I made sure she was not expecting to meet an enemy. 'She rides to betray us to her friends!' said I, and I kept yet farther behind her, on the alert against ambush."

"Well?"

"She rode until dawn, I following. Then, when the light was scarcely born as yet, she suddenly drew rein at an open place where the track she had been following emerged out of dense bushes, and dismounted. From behind the bushes I watched, and presently I, too, dismounted to hold my mare's nostrils and prevent her from whinnying. That woman, Maga Jhaere, knelt, and pawed about the ground like a dog that hunts a buried bone!"

In front of us Maga was still arguing. Suddenly Kagig turned on her and asked her three swift questions, bitten off like the snap of a closing snuffbox lid. Whether she answered or not I could not see, but Monty was smiling.

"I suspect she was making signals!" growled Rustum Khan. "To whom — about what I do not know. After a little while she mounted and rode on, choosing unerringly a new track through the bushes. I went to where she had been, and examined the ground where she had made her signals. As I say, my eyes are good, but hers are better. I could see nothing but the hoof-marks of her clumsy gray brute of a stallion, and in one place the depressions on soft earth where she had knelt to paw the ground!"

Monty was beginning to talk now. I could see him smiling at Kagig over Maga's head, and the girl was growing angry. Rustum Khan was watching them as closely as we were, pausing between sentences.

"It may be she buried something there, but if so I did not find it. I could not stay long, for when she rode away she went like wind, and I needed to follow at top speed or else be lost. So I let my mare feel the spurs a time or two, and so it happened that I gained on the woman; and I suppose she heard me. Whether or no, she waited in ambush, and sprang out at me as I passed so suddenly that I know not what god of fools and drunkards preserved her from being cut down! Not many have ridden out at me from ambush and lived to tell of it! But I saw who she was in time, and sheathed my steel again, and cursed her for the gypsy that she half is. The other half is spawn of Eblis!"

A hundred yards ahead of us Kagig had reached a decision, but it seemed to be not too late yet in Maga's judgment to try to convert him. She was speaking vehemently, passionately, throwing down her reins to expostulate with both hands.

"Kagig isn't the man you'd think a young woman would choose to be familiar with," Fred said quietly to me, and I wondered what he was driving at. He is always observant behind that superficial air of mockery he chooses to assume, but what he had noticed to set him thinking I could not guess.

Rustum Khan threw away the cigarette I had given him, and went on with his tale.

"That woman has no virtue."

"How do you know?" demanded Will.

"She laughed when I cursed her! Then she asked me what I had seen."

"What did you say?"

"To test her I said I had seen her lover, and would know him again by his smell in the dark!"

"What did she say to that?'

"She laughed again. I tell you the woman has no shame! Then she said if I would tell that tale to Kagig as soon as I see him she would reward me with leave to live for one whole week and an extra hour in which to pray to the devil — meaning, I suppose, that she intends to kill me otherwise. Then she wheeled her stallion — the brute was trying to tear out the muscles of my thigh all that time — and rode away — and I followed — and here I am!"

"How much truth is there in your assertion that you saw her lover?" Will demanded.

"None. I but said it to test her."

"Why in thunder should she want it believed?"

"God knows, who made gypsies!"

At that moment the advance-guard rode into an open meadow, crossed by a shallow, singing stream at which Kagig ordered a halt to water horses. So we closed up with him, and he repeated to us what he had evidently said before to Monty.

"Maga says — I let her go scouting — she says she met a

man who told her that Miss Gloria Vanderman and a party of seven were attacked on the road, but escaped, and now have doubled on their tracks so that they are far on their return to Tarsus."

Rustum Khan met Monty's eyes, and his lips moved silently.

"What do you know, sirdar?" Monty asked him.

"The woman lies!"

Maga was glaring at Rustum Khan as a leopardess eyes an enemy. As he spoke she made a significant gesture with a finger across her throat, which the Rajput, if he saw, ignored.

"To what extent?" demanded Kagig calmly.

"Wholly! I followed her. She met no man, although she pawed the ground at a place where eight ridden horses had crossed soft ground a day ago."

Kagig nodded, recognizing truth — a rather rare gift.

If the Rajput's guess was wrong and Maga did know shame, at any rate she did not choose that moment to betray it.

"Oh, very well!" she sneered. "There were eight horses. They were galloping. The track was nine hours old."

Kagig nodded without any symptom of annoyance or reproach.

"There is an ancient castle in the hills up yonder," he said, "in which there may be many Armenians hiding."

He took it for granted we would go and find out, and Maga recognized the drift.

"Very well," she said. "Let that one go, and that one," pointing at Fred and me.

"You'll appreciate, of course," said Monty, "that it's out of the question for us to go forward until we know where that lady is."

Kagig bowed gravely.

"I am needed at Zeitoon," he answered.

Then Maga broke in shrilly, pointing at Will:

"Take that one for hostage!" she advised. "Bring him along to Zeitoon. Then the rest will follow!"

Kagig looked gravely at her.

"I shall take this one," he answered, laying a respectful hand on Monty's sleeve. "Effendi, you are an Eenglis lord. Be your life and comfort on my head, but I need a hostage for my

nation's sake. You others — I admit the urgency — shall hunt
the missionary lady. If I have this one" — again he touched
Monty — "I know well you will come seeking him! You,
effendi, you understand my — necessity?"

Monty nodded, smiling gravely. There was a fire at the back
of Monty's eyes and something in his bearing I had never
seen before.

"Then I go with my colonel sahib!" announced Rustum
Khan. "That gypsy woman will kill him otherwise!"

"Better help hunt for the lady, Rustum Khan."

"Nay, colonel sahib bahadur — thy blood on my head! I
go with thee — into hell and out beyond if need be!"

"You fellows agreeable?" asked Monty. "There is no disput-
ing Kagig's decision. We're at his mercy."

"We've got to find Miss Vanderman!" said Will.

"You are not at my mercy, effendi," grumbled Kagig. The
man was obviously distressed. "You are rather at my discretion. I am responsible. For my nation's sake and for my honor
I dare not lose you. Who has not seen how a cow will follow
the calf in a wagon? So in your case, if I hold the one — the
chief one — the noble one — the lord — the cousin of the
Eenglis king" (Monty's rank was mounting like mercury in
a tube as Kagig warmed to the argument) — "you others will
certainly hunt him up-hill and down-dale. Thus will my
honor and my country's cause both profit!"

Monty smiled benignantly.

"It's all one, Kagig. Why labor the point? I'm going with
you. Rustum Khan prefers to come with me." Kagig looked
askance at Rustum Khan, but made no comment. "One
hostage is enough for your purpose. Let me talk with my
friends a minute."

Kagig nodded, and we four drew aside.

"Now," demanded Fred, who knew the signs, "what special
quixotry do you mean springing?"

"Shut up, Fred. There's no need for you fellows to follow
Kagig another yard. He'll be quite satisfied if he has me in
keeping. That will serve all practical purposes. What you three
must do is find Miss Vanderman if you can, and take her
back to Tarsus. There you can help the consul bring pressure
to bear on the authorities."

"Rot!" retorted Fred. "Didums, you're drunk. Where did you get the drink?"

Monty smiled, for he held a card that could out-trump our best one, and he knew it. In fact he led it straight away.

"D'you mean to say you'd consider it decent to find that young woman in the mountains and drag her to Zeitoon at Kagig's tail, when Tarsus is not more than three days' ride away at most? You know the Turks wouldn't dare touch you on the road to the coast."

"For that matter," said Fred, "the Turks 'ud hardly dare touch Miss Vanderman herself."

"Then leave her in the hills!" grinned Monty. "Kagig tells me that the Kurds are riding down in hundreds from Kaisarich way. He says they'll arrive too late to loot the cities, but they're experts at hunting along the mountain range. Why not leave the lady to the tender ministrations of the Kurds!"

"One 'ud think you and Kagig knew of buried treasure! Or has he promised to make you Duke of Zeitoon?" asked Will. "Tisn't right, Monty. You've no call to force our band in this way."

"Name a better way," said Monty.

None of us could. The proposal was perfectly logical.

Three of us, even supposing Kagig should care to lend us some of his Zeitoonli horsemen, would be all too few for the rescue work. Certainly we could not leave a lady unprotected in these hills, with the threat of plundering Kurds overhanging. If we found her we could hardly carry her off up-country if there were any safer course.

"Time — time is swift!" said Kagig, pulling out a watch like a big brass turnip and shaking it, presumably to encourage the mechanism.

"The fact is," said Monty, drawing us farther aside, for Rustum Khan was growing restive and inquisitive, "I've not much faith in Kagig's prospects at Zeitoon. He has talked to me all along the road, and I don't believe he bases much reliance on his men. He counts more on holding me as hostage and so obliging the Turkish government to call off its murderers. If you men can rescue that lady in the hills and return to Tarsus you can serve Kagig best and give me my best chance too. Hurry back and help the consul raise Cain!"

That closed the arguments, because Maga Jhaere slipped past Kagig and approached us with the obvious intention of listening. She had discovered a knowledge of English scarcely perfect but astonishingly comprehensive, which she had chosen to keep to herself when we first met — a regular gypsy trick. Fred threw down the gauntlet to her, uncovering depths of distrust that we others had never suspected under his air of being amused.

"Now, miss!" he said, striding up to her. "Let us understand each other! This is my friend." He pointed to Monty. "If harm comes to him that you could have prevented, you shall pay!"

Maga tossed back her loose coils of hair and laughed.

"Never fear, sahib!" Rustum Khan called out. "If ought should happen to my Colonel sahib that Umm Kulsum shall be first to die. The women shall tell of her death for a generation, to frighten naughty children!"

"You hear that?" demanded Fred.

Maga laughed again, and swore in some outlandish tongue.

"I hear! And you hear this, you old —" She called Fred by a name that would make the butchers wince in the abattoirs at Liverpool. "If anything happens to that man, —" she pointed to Will, and her eyes blazed with lawless pleasure in his evident discomfort "— I myself — me — this woman — I alone will keel — keel — keel — torture first and afterwards keel your friend 'at you call Monty! I am Maga! You have heard me say what I will do! As for that Rustum Khan — you shall never see him no more ever!"

Kagig pulled out the enormous watch again. He seemed oblivious of Maga's threats — not even aware that she had spoken, although she was hissing through impudent dazzling teeth within three yards of him.

"The time," he said, "has fleed — has fled — has flown. Now we must go, effendi!"

"I go with that man!" announced Maga, pointing at Will, but obviously well aware that nothing of the kind would be permitted.

"Maga, come!" said Kagig, and got on his horse. "You gentlemen may take with you each one Zeitoonli servant. No, no more. No, the ammunition in your pockets must suffice.

Yes, I know the remainder is yours; come then to Zeitoon and get it! Haide — Haide! Mount! Ride! Haide, Zeitoonli! To Zeitoon! Chabuk!"

Chapter Nine

"And you left your friend to help me?"

WITH NEW TONGUES

Oh, bard of Avon, thou whose measured muse
Most sweetly sings Elizabethan views
To shame ungentle smiths of journalese
With thy sublimest verse, what words are these
That shine amid the lines like jewels set
But ere thine hour no bard had chosen yet?
Didst thou in masterly disdain of too much law
Not only limn the truths no others saw
But also, lord not slave of written word,
Lend ear to what no other poet heard
And, liberal minded on the Mermaid bench
With bow for blade and chaff for serving wench
Await from overseas slang-slinging Jack
Who brought the new vocabulary back?

So we three stood still in a row disconsolate, with three ragged men of Zeitoon holding our horses and theirs, and watched Monty ride away in the midst of Kagig's motley command, he not turning to wave back to us because he did not like the parting any better than we did, although he had pretended to be all in favor of it.

Kagig had left us one mule for our luggage, and the beast was unlikely to be overburdened, for at the last minute he had turned surly, and as he sat like a general of division to watch his patch-and-string command go by he showed how Eye of Zeitoon only failed him for a title in giving his other eye — the one he kept on us — too little credit. It was a good-looking crowd of irregulars that he reviewed, and every bearded, goatskin clad veteran in it had a word to say to him, and he an answer — sometimes a sermon by way of answer. But he saw every item that we removed from the common packs, and sternly reproved us when we tried to exceed what he considered reasonable. At that he based our probable requirements on what would have been surfeit of encumbrance for himself.

"Empty your pockets, effendim!" he ordered at last. "Six cartridges each for rifle, and six each for pistol must be all. Your cartridges I know they are. But my people are in extremity!"

When he rode away at last, sitting his horse in the fashion of a Don Cossack and shepherding Maga in front of him because she kept checking her gray stallion for another look at Will, he left us no alternative than to take to the mountains swiftly unless we cared to starve. We watched Monty's back disappear over a rise, with Rustum Khan close behind, and then Fred signed to one of the three Zeitoonli to lead on.

All three of the men Kagig had left with us were surly, mainly, no doubt, because they disliked separation from their friends. But there was fear, too, expressed in their manner of riding close together, and in the fidgety way in which they watched the smoke of burning Armenian villages that smudged the sky to our left.

"If they try to bolt after Kagig and leave us in the lurch I'm going to waste exactly one cartridge as a warning," Fred announced. "After that — !"

"Probably Kagig 'ud skin them if they turned up without us," remarked Will.

There was something in that theory, for we learned later what Kagig's ferocity could be when driven hard enough. But from first to last those men of Zeitoon never showed a symptom of treachery, although their resentment at having to turn their backs toward home appeared to deepen hourly.

With strange unreason they made no haste, whereas we were in a frenzy of impatience; and when Fred sought to improve their temper by singing the songs that had hitherto acted like charms on Kagig's whole command, they turned in their saddles and cursed him for calling attention to us.

"Inch goozek?" demanded one of them (What would you like?), and with a gesture that made the blood run cold he suggested the choice between hanging and disembowelment.

Will solved the speed problem by striving to push past them along the narrow track; and they were so determined to keep in front of us that within half an hour from the start our horses were sweating freely. Then we began to climb, dismounting presently to lead our horses, and all notions of speed went the way of other vanity.

Several times looking back toward our right hand we caught sight of Kagig's string threading its way over a rise, or passing like a line of ants under the brow of a gravel bank. But they were too far away to discern which of the moving specks might be Monty, although Kagig was now and then unmistakable, his air of authority growing on him and distinguishing him as long as he kept in sight.

We saw nothing of the footprints in soft earth that Maga had read so offhandedly. In fact we took another way, less cluttered up with roots and bushes, that led not straight, but persistently toward an up-towering crag like an eyetooth. Below it was thick forest, shaped like a shovel beard, and the crag stuck above the beard like an old man's last tooth.

But mountains have a discouraging way of folding and refolding so that the airline from point to point bears no relation to the length of the trail. The last kites were drooping lazily toward their perches for the night when we drew near the edge of the forest at last, and were suddenly brought to a halt by a challenge from overhead. We could see nobody. Only a hoarse voice warned us that it was death to advance another yard, and our tired animals needed no persuasion to stand still.

There, under a protruding lock as it were of the beard, we waited in shadow while an invisible somebody, whose rifle scraped rather noisily against a branch, eyed every inch of us at his leisure.

"Who are you?" he demanded at last in Armenian, and one of our three men enlightened him in long-drawn detail.

The explanation did not satisfy. We were told to remain exactly where we were until somebody else was fetched. After twenty minutes, when it was already pitch-dark, we heard the breaking of twigs, and low voices as three or four men descended together among the trees. Then we were examined again from close quarters in the dark, and there are few less agreeable sensations. The gooseflesh rises and the clammy cold sweat takes all the comfort out of waning courage.

But somebody among the shadowy tree-trunks at last seemed to think he recognized familiar attitudes, and asked again who we might be. And, weary of explanations that only achieved delay our man lumped us all in one invoice and snarled irritably:

"These are Americans!"

The famous "Open sesame" that unlocked Ali Baba's cave never worked swifter then. Reckless of possible traps no less than five men flung themselves out of Cimmerian gloom and seized us in welcoming arms. I was lifted from the saddle by a man six inches shorter than myself, whose arms could have crushed me like an insect.

"We might have known Americans would bring us help!" he panted in my ear. His breath came short not from effort, but excitement.

Fred was in like predicament. I could just see his shadow struggling in the embrace of an enthusiastic host, and some-where out of sight Will was answering in nasal indubitable Yankee the questions of three other men.

"This way! Come this way! Bring the horses, oh, Zeitoonli! Americans! Americans! God heard us — there have come Americans!"

Threading this and that way among tree-trunks that to our unaccustomed eyes were simply slightly denser blots on black-ness, Will managed to get between Fred and me.

"We're all of us Yankees this trip!" he whispered, and I knew he was grinning, enjoying it hugely. So often he had been taken for an Englishman because of partnership with us that he had almost ceased to mind; but he spared himself none of the amusement to be drawn out of the new turn of affairs, nor us any of the chaff that we had never spared him.

"Take my advice," he said, "and try to act you're Yanks for all you've got. If you can make blind men believe it, you may get out of this with whole skins!"

I expected the retort discourteous to that from Fred, who was between Will and me, shepherded like us by hard-breathing, unseen men. But he was much too subtly skilful in piercing the chain mail of Will's humor — even in that hour.

"Sure!" he answered. "I guess any gosh-durned rube in these parts 'll know without being told what neck o' the woods I hail from. Schenectady's my middle name! I'm —"

"Oh, my God!" groaned Will. "We don't talk that way in the States. The missionaries —"

"I'm the guy who put the 'oh!' in Ohio!" continued Fred. "I'm running mate to Colonel Cody, and I've ridden herd on half the cows in Hocuspocus County, Wis.! I can sing The Star-Spangled Banner with my head under water, and eat a chain of frankforts two links a minute! I'm the riproaring original two-gun man from Tabascoville, and any gink who doubts it has no time to say his prayers!"

There were paragraphs more of it, delivered at uneven intervals between deep gasps for breath as we made unsteady progress up-hill among roots and rocks left purposely for the confusion of an enemy. At first it filled Will with despair that set me laughing at him. Then Will threw seriousness to the winds and laughed too, so that the spell of impending evil, caused as much as anything by forced separation from Monty, was broken.

But it did better than put us in rising spirits. It convinced the Armenians! That foolish jargon, picked up from comic papers and the penny dreadfuls, convince more firmly than any written proof the products of the mission schools, whose one ambition was to be American themselves, and whose one pathetic peak of humor was the occasional glimpse of United States slang dropped for their edification by missionary teachers!

"By jimminy!" remarked an Armenian near me.

"Gosh-all-hemlocks!" said another.

Thenceforward nothing undermined their faith in us. Plenty of amused repudiation was very soon forthcoming from another source, but it passed over their heads. Fred and I, because we used fool expressions without relation to the context or proportion, were established as the genuine article; Will, perhaps a rather doubtful quantity with his conservative grammar and quiet speech, was accepted for our sakes. They took an arm on either side of us to help us up the hill, and in proof of heart-to-heart esteem shouted "Oopsidaisy!" when we stumbled in the pitchy dark. When we were brought to a stand at last by a snarled challenge and the click of rifles overhead, they answered with the chorus of Ta-ra-ra-boom-de-ay, a classic that ought to have died an unnatural death almost a quarter of a century before.

Suddenly we smelt Standard oil, and a man emerged through a gap in ancient masonry less than six feet away carrying a battered, cheap "hurricane" lantern whose cracked glass had been reinforced with patches of brown paper. He was armed to the teeth — literally. He had a long knife in his mouth, a pistol in his left hand, and a rifle slung behind him, but after one long look at us, holding the lantern to each face in turn, he suddenly discarded all appearances of ferocity.

"You know about pistols?" he demanded of me in English, because I was nearest, and thrust his Mauser repeater under my nose. "Why won't this one work? I have tried it every way."

"Lordy!" remarked Will.

"Lead on in!" I suggested. Then, remembering my new part, "It'll have to be some defect if one of us can't fix it!"

The gap-guard purred approval and swung his lantern by way of invitation to follow him as he turned on a naked heel and led the way. We entered one at a time through a hole in the wall of what looked like the dungeon of an ancient castle, and followed him presently up the narrow stone steps leading to a trapdoor in the floor above. The trapdoor was made of odds and ends of planking held in place by weights. When he knocked on it with the muzzle of his rifle we could hear men lifting things before they could open it.

When a gap appeared overhead at last there was no blaze of light to make us blink, but a row of heads at each edge of the hole with nothing but another lantern somewhere in the gloom behind them. One by one we went up and they made way for us, closing in each time to scan the next-comer's face; and when we were all up they laid the planks again, and piled heavy stones in place. Then an old man lighted another lantern, using no match, although there was a box of them beside him on the floor, but transferring flame patiently with a blade of dry grass. Somebody else lit a torch of resinous wood that gave a good blaze but smoked abominably.

"What has become of our horses?" demanded Fred, looking swiftly about him.

We were in a great, dim stone-walled room whose roof showed a corner of star-lit sky in one place. There were twenty men surrounding us, but no woman. Two trade-blankets sewn together with string hanging over an opening in the wall at the far end of the room suggested, nevertheless, that the other sex might be within ear-shot.

"The horses?" Fred demanded again, a bit peremptorily.

One of the men who had met us smirked and made apologetic motions with his hands.

"They will be attended to, effendi —"

"I know it! I guarantee it! By the ace of brute force, if a horse is missing —! Arabaiji!"

One of our three Zeitoonli stepped forward.

"Take the other two men, Arabaiji, and go down to the horses. Groom them. Feed them. If any one prevents you, return and tell me." Then he turned to our hosts. "Some natives of Somaliland once ate my horse for supper, but I learned that lesson. So did they! I trust I needn't be severe with you!"

There was no furniture in the room, except a mat at one corner. They were standing all about us, and perfectly able to murder us if so disposed, but none made any effort to restrain our Zeitoonli.

"Now we're three to their twenty!" I whispered, and Will nodded. But Fred carried matters with a high hand.

"Send a man down with them to show them where the horses are, please!"

There seemed to be nobody in command, but evidently one man was least of all, for they all began at once to order him below, and he went, grumbling.

"You see, effendi, we have no meat at all," said the man who had spoken first.

"But you don't look hungry," asserted Fred.

They were a ragged crowd, unshaven and not too clean, with the usual air of men whose only clothes are on their

backs and have been there for a week past. All sorts of clothes
they wore — odds and ends for the most part, probably
snatched and pulled on in the first moment of a night alarm.

"Not yet, effendi. But we have no meat, and soon we shall
have eaten all the grain."

"Well," said Fred, "if you need horse-meat, gosh durn you,
take it from the Turks!"

"Gosh durn you!" grinned three or four men, nudging one
another.

They were lost between a furtive habit born of hiding for
dear life, a desire to be extremely friendly, and a new suspicion
of Fred's high hand. Fred's next words added disconcertment.

"Where is Miss Vanderman?" he demanded, suddenly.

Before any one had time to answer Will made a swift move
to the wall, and took his stand where nobody could get behind
him. He did not produce his pistol, but there was that in his
eye that suggested it. I followed suit, so that in the event of
trouble we stood a fair chance of protecting Fred.

"What do you mean?" asked three Armenians together.

"Did you never see men try to cover a secret before?" Will
whispered.

"Or give it away?" I added. Six of the men placed themselves between Fred and the opening where the blankets hung,
ostentatiously not looking at the blankets.

"Have you an American lady with you?" Fred asked, and
as he spoke he reached a hand behind him. But it was not
his pistol that he drew. He carries his concertina slung to him
by a strap with the care that some men lavish on a camera.
He took it in both hands, and loosed the catch.

"Have you an American lady named Miss Vanderman with
you?" he repeated.

"Effendi, we do not understand."

He repeated in Armenian, and then in Turkish, but they
shook their heads.

"Very well," he said, "I'll soon find out. A mission-school
pupil might sing My Country, 'Tis of Thee or Suwannee River
or Poor Blind Joe. You know Poor Blind Joe, eh? Sung it in
school? I thought so. I'll bet you don't know this one."

He filled his impudent instrument with wind and forth-
with the belly of that ancient castle rang to the strains of a

tune no missionaries sing, although no doubt the missionary ladies are familiar with it yet from where the Arctic night shuts down on Bering Sea to the Solomon Islands and beyond — a song that achieved popularity by lacking national significance, and won a war by imparting recklessness to typhus camps. I was certain then, and still dare bet today that those ruined castle walls re-echoed for the first time that evening to the clamor of — a hot time in the old town tonight!

Seeing the point in a flash, we three roared the song together, and then again, and then once more for interest, the Armenians eying us spellbound, at a loss to explain the madness. Then there began to be unexplained movements behind the blanket hanging; and a minute later a woman broke through — an unmistakable Armenian, still good-looking but a little past the prime of life, and very obviously mentally distressed. She scarcely took notice of us, but poured forth a long flow of rhetoric interspersed with sobs for breath. I could see Fred chuckling as he listened. All the facial warnings that a dozen men could make at the woman from behind Fred's back could not check her from telling all she knew.

Nor were Will and I, who knew no Armenian, kept in doubt very long as to the nature of her trouble. We heard another woman's voice, behind two or three sets of curtains by the sound of it, that came rapidly nearer; and there were sounds of scuffling. Then we heard words.

"Please play that tune again, whoever you are! Do you hear me? Do you understand?"

"Boston!" announced Will, diagnosing accents.

"You bet your life I understand!" Fred shouted, and clanged through half a dozen bars again.

That seemed satisfactory to the owner of the voice. The scuffling was renewed, and in a moment she had burst through the crude curtains with two women clinging to her, and stood there with her brown hair falling on her shoulders and her dress all disarrayed but looking simply serene in contrast to the women who tried to restrain her. They tried once or twice to thrust her back through the curtain, although clearly determined to do her no injury; but she held her ground easily. At a rough guess it was tennis and boating that had done more for her muscles than ever strenuous house-work did for the Armenians.

"Who are you?" she asked, and Will laughed with delight.

"I reckon you'll be Miss Vanderman?' suggested Fred in outrageous Yankee accent. She stared hard at him.

"I am Miss Vanderman. Who are you, please.

I sat down on the great stone they had rolled over the trap, for even in that flickering, smoky light I could see that this young woman was incarnate loveliness as well as health and strength. Will was our only ladies' man (for Fred is no more than random troubadour, decamping before any love-affair gets serious). The thought conjured visions of Maga, and what she might do. For about ten seconds my head swam, and I could hardly keep my feet.

Will left the opening bars of the overture to Fred, with rather the air of a man who lets a trout have line. And Fred blundered in contentedly.

"I'll allow my name is Oakes — Fred Oakes," he said.

"Please explain!" She looked from one to the other of us.

"We three are American towerists, going the grand trip." (Remember, a score of Armenians were listening. Fred's intention was at least as much to continue their contentment as to extract humor from the situation.) "You being reported missing we allowed to pick you up and run you in to Tarsus. Air you agreeable?"

The women were still clinging to her as if their whole future depended on keeping her prisoner, yet without hurt. She looked down at them pathetically, and then at the men, who were showing no disposition to order her release.

"I don't understand in the least yet. I find you bewildering. Can you contrive to let us talk for a few minutes alone?"

"You bet your young life I can!"

Fred stepped to the wall beside us, but we none of us drew pistol yet. We had no right to presume we were not among friends.

"Thirty minutes interlude!" he announced. "The man who stands in this room one minute from now, or who comes back to the room without my leave, is not my friend, and shall learn what that means!"

He repeated the soft insinuation in Armenian, and then

in Turkish because he knows that language best. There is not an Armenian who has not been compelled to learn Turkish for all official purposes, and unconsciously they gave obedience to the hated conquerors' tongue, repressing the desire to argue that wells perennially in Armenian breasts. They had not been long enough enjoying stolen liberty to overcome yet the full effects of Turkish rule.

"And oblige me by leaving that lady alone with us!" Fred continued. "Let those dames fall away!"

Somebody said something to the women. Another Armenian remarked more or less casually that we should be unable to escape from the room in any case. The others rolled the great stone from the trap and shoved the smaller stones aside, and then they all filed down the stone stairs, leaving us alone — although by the trembling blankets it was easy to tell that the women had not gone far. The last man who went below handed the spluttering torch to Miss Vanderman, as if she might need it to defend herself, and she stood there shaking it to try and make it smoke less until the planks were back in place. She was totally unconscious of it, but with the torchlight gleaming on her hair and reflected in her blue eyes she looked like the spirit of old romance come forth to start a holy war.

"Now please explain!" she begged, when I had pushed the last stone in place. "First, what kind of Americans can you possibly be? Do you all use such extraordinary accents, and such expressions?"

"Don't I talk American to beat the band?" objected Fred. "Sit down on this rock a while, and I'll convince you."

She sat on the rock, and we gathered round her. She was not more than twenty-two or three, but as perfectly assured and fearless as only a well-bred woman can be in the presence of unshaven men she does not know. Fred would have continued the tomfoolery, but Will oared in.

"I'm Will Yerkes, Miss Vanderman."

"Oh!"

"I know Nurse Vanderman at the mission."

"Yes, she spoke of you."

"Fred Oakes here is —"

"Is English as they make them, yes, I know! Why the

amazing efforts to —"

"I stand abashed, like the leopard with the spots unchange-able!" said Fred, and grinned most unashamedly.

"They're both English."

"Yes, I see, but why —"

"It's only as good Americans that we three could hope to enter here alive. They're death on all other sorts of non-Ar-menians now they've taken to the woods. We supposed you were here, and of course we had to come and get you."

She nodded. "Of course. But how did you know?"

"That's a long story. Tell us first why you're here, and why you're a prisoner."

"I was going to the mission at Marash — to stay a year there and help, before returning to the States. They warned me in Tarsus that the trip might be dangerous, but I know how short-handed they are at Marash, and I wouldn't listen. Be-sides, they picked the best men they could find to bring me on the way, and I started. I had a Turkish permit to travel — a teskere they call it — see, I have it here. It was perfectly ridiculous to think of my not going."

"Perfectly!" Fred agreed. "Any young woman in your place would have come away!"

She laughed, and colored a trifle. "Women and men are equals in the States, Mr. Oakes."

"And the Turk ought to know that! I get you, Miss Van-derman! I see the point exactly!"

"At any rate, I started. And we slept at night in the houses of Armenians whom my guides knew, so that the journey wasn't bad at all. Everything was going splendidly until we reached a sort of crossroads — if you can call those goat-tracks roads without stretching truth too far — and there three men came galloping toward us on blown horses from the direction of Marash. We could hardly get them to stop and tell us what the trouble was, they were in such a hurry, but I set my horse across the path and we held them up."

"As any young lady would have done!" Fred murmured.

"Never mind. I did it! They told us, when they could get their breath and quit looking behind them like men afraid of ghosts, that the Turks in Marash — which by all accounts is a very fanatical place — had started to murder Armenians.

They yelled at me to turn and run.

" 'Run where?' I asked them. 'The Turks won't murder me!'

"That seemed to make them think, and they and my six men all talked together in Armenian much too fast for me to understand a word of it. Then they pointed to some smoke on the sky-line that they said was from burning Armenian homes in Marash.

" 'Why didn't you take refuge in the mission?' I asked them. And they answered that it was because the mission grounds were already full of refugees.

"Well, if that were true — and mind you, I didn't believe it — it was a good reason why I should hurry there and help. If the mission staff was overworked before that they would be simply overwhelmed now. So I told them to turn round and come to Marash with me and my six men."

"And what did they say?" we demanded together.

"They laughed. They said nothing at all to me. Perhaps they thought I was mad. They talked together for five minutes, and then without consulting me they seized my bridle and galloped up a goat-path that led after a most interminable ride to this place."

"Where they hold you to ransom?"

"Not at all. They've been very kind to me. I think that at the bottom of their thoughts there may be some idea of exchanging me for some of their own women whom the Turks have made away with. But a stronger motive than that is the determination to keep me safe and be able to produce me afterward in proof of their bona fides. They've got me here as witness, for another thing. And then, I've started a sort of hospital in this old keep. There are literally hundreds of men and women hiding in these hills, and the women are beginning to come to me for advice, and to talk with me. I'm pretty nearly as useful here as I would be at Marash."

"And you're — let's see — nineteen-twenty — one — two — not more than twenty-two," suggested Fred.

"Is intelligence governed by age and sex in England." she retorted, and Fred smiled in confession of a hit.

"Go on," said Will. "Tell us."

"There's nothing more to tell. When I started to run toward the — ah — music, the women tried to prevent me. They knew

Americans had come, and they feared you might take me away."

"They were guessing good!" grinned Will.

She shook her head, and the loosened coils of hair fell lower. One could hardly have blamed a man who had desired her in that lawless land and sought to carry her off. The Armenian men must have been temptation proof, or else there had been safety in numbers.

"I shall stay here. How could I leave them? The women need me. There are babies — daily — almost hourly — here in these lean hills, and no organized help of any kind until I came."

"How long have you been here?" I asked.

"Nearly two days. Wait till I've been here a week and you'll see."

"We can't wait to see!" Will answered. "We've a friend of our own in a tight place. The best we can do is to rescue you —"

"I don't need to be rescued!"

"— to rescue you — take you back to Tarsus, where you'll be safe until the trouble's over — and then hurry to the help of our own man."

"Who is your own man? Tell me about him."

"He's a prince."

"Really?"

"No, really an earl — Earl of Montdidier. White. White all through to the wish-bone. Whitest man I ever camped with. He's the goods."

"If you'd said less I'd have skinned you for an ingrate!" Fred announced.

"Monty is a man men love."

Miss Vanderman nodded. "Where is he?"

"On the way to a place called Zeitoon," answered Will.

"He's a hostage, held by Armenians in the hope of putting pressure on the Turks. Kagig — the Armenians, that's to say — let us go to rescue you, knowing that he was sufficiently important for their purpose."

"And you left your friend to help me?"

"Of course. What do you suppose?"

"And if I were to go with you to Tarsus, what then?"

"He says we're to ride herd on the consulate and argue."

"Will you?"

"Sure we'll argue. We'll raise particular young hell. Then back we go to Zeitoon to join him!"

"Would you have gone to Tarsus except on my account?"

Will hesitated.

"No. I see. Of course you wouldn't. Well. What do you take me for? You did not know me then. You do now. Do you think I'd consent to your leaving your fine friend in pawn while you dance attendance on me? Thank you kindly for your offer, but go back to him! If you don't I'll never speak to one of you again!"

Chapter Ten

"When I fire this Pistol —"

THESE LITTLE ONES

If Life were what the liars say
And failure called the tune
Mayhap the road to ruin then
Were cluttered deep wi' broken men;
We'd all be seekers blindly led
To weave wi' worms among the dead,
If Life were what the liars say
And failure called the tune.

But Life is Father of us all
(Dear Father, if we knew!)
And underneath eternal arms
Uphold. We'll mock the false alarms,
And trample on the neck of pain,
And laugh the dead alive again,
For Life is Father to us all,
And thanks are overdue!

If Truth were what the learned say
And envy called the tune
Mayhap 'twere trite what treason saith
That man is dust and ends in death;
We'd slay with proof of printed law
Whatever was new that seers saw,
If Truth were what the learned say
And envy called the tune.

But Truth is Brother of us all
(Oh, Brother, if we knew!)
Unspattered by the muddied lies

That pass for wisdom of the wise —
Compassionate, alert, unbought,
Of purity and presence wrought, —
Big Brother that includes us all
Nor knows the name of Few!

If Love were what the harlots say
And hunger called the tune
Mayhap we'd need conserve the joys
Weighed grudgingly to girls and boys,
And eat the angels trapped and sold
By shriven priests for stolen gold,
If Love were what the harlots say
And hunger called the tune.

But Love is Mother of us all
(Dear Mother, if we knew!) —
So wise that not a sparrow falls,
Nor friendless in the prison calls
Uncomforted or uncaressed.
There's magic milk at Mercy's breast,
And little ones shall lead us all
When Trite Love calls the tune!

*N*aturally, being what we were, with our friend Monty held
in durance by a chief of outlaws, we were perfectly ready to
kidnap Miss Vanderman and ride off with her in case she
should be inclined to delay proceedings. It was also natural
that we had not spoken of that contingency, nor even considered it.

"We never dreamed of your refusing to come with us," said
Will.

"We still don't dream of it!" Fred asserted, and she turned
her head very swiftly to look at him with level brows. Next
she met my eyes. If there was in her consciousness the slightest
trace of doubt, or fear, or admission that her sex might be
less responsible than ours, she did not show it. Rather in the
blue eyes and the athletic poise of chin, and neck, and
shoulders there was a dignity beyond ours.

Will laughed.

"Don't let's be ridiculous," she said. "I shall do as I see fit."

Fred's neat beard has a trick of losing something of its trim when he proposes to assert himself, and I recognized the symptoms. But at the moment of that impasse the Armenians below us had decided that self-assertion was their cue, and there came great noises as they thundered with a short pole on the trap and made the stones jump that held it down.

At that signal several women emerged from behind the hanging blankets — young and old women in various states of disarray — and stood in attitudes suggestive of aggression. One did not get the idea that Armenians, men or women, were sheeplike pacifists. They watched Miss Vanderman with the evident purpose of attacking us the moment she appealed to them.

"If you don't roll the stones away I think there'll be trouble," she said, and came and stood between Will and me. Fred got behind me, and began to whisper. I heard something or other about the trap, and supposed he was asking me to open it, although I failed to see why the request should be kept secret; but the women forestalled me, and in a moment they had the stones shoved aside and the men were emerging one by one through the opening.

Then at last I got Fred's meaning. There was a second of indecision during which the Armenians consulted their womenfolk, in two minds between snatching Miss Vanderman out of our reach or discovering first what our purpose might be. I took advantage of it to slip down the stone stairs behind them.

The opening in the castle wall was easy to find, for the star-lit sky looked luminous through the hole. Once outside, however, the gloom of ancient trees and the castle's shadow seemed blacker than the dungeon had been. I groped about, and stumbled over loose stones fallen from the castle wall, until at last one of our own Zeitoonli discovered me and, thinking I might be a trouble-maker, tripped me up. Cursing fervently from underneath his iron-hard carcass I made him recognize me at last. Then he offered me tobacco, unquestionably stolen from our pack, and sat down beside me on a rock while I recovered breath.

It took longer to do that than he expected, for he had enjoyed the advantage of surprise while hampered by no compunctions on the ground of moderation. When the ag-

ony of windlessness was gone and I could question him he
assured me that the horses were well enough, but that he and
his two companions were hungry. Furthermore, he added, the
animals were very closely watched — so much so that the other
two, Sombat and Noorian, were standing guard to watch the
watchers.

"But I am sure they are fools," he added.

This man Arabaiji had been an excellent servant, but decidedly supercilious toward the others from the time when
he first came to us in the khan at Tarsus. Regarding himself
as intelligent, which he was, he usually refused to concede
that quality, or anything resembling it, to his companions.

"That is why I was looking for you when you hit me in the
dark with that club of a fist of yours," I answered. "I wanted
to speak with you alone because I know you are not a fool."

He felt so flattered that he promptly let his pipe go out.

"While Sombat and Noorian are keeping an eye on the
horses, I want you to watch for trouble up above here," I said.
"In case the people of this place should seek to make us
prisoner, then I want you to gallop, if you can get your horse,
and run otherwise, to the nearest —"

He checked me with a gesture and one word.

"Kagig!"

"What about him?" I demanded.

"If I were to bring Turks here, Kagig would never rest until
my fingers were pulled off one by one!"

"If you were to bring Turks here, or appeal to Turks," said
I, "Kagig would never get you."

"How not?"

"Unless he should find your dead carcass after my friends
and I had finished with it!"

"What then?"

He lighted his pipe again by way of reestablishing himself
in his own esteem, and it glowed and crackled wetly in the
dark beside me in response to the workings of his intelligence.

"In case of trouble up here, and our being held prisoner,
go and find other Armenians, and order them in Kagig's
name to come and rescue us."

"Those who obey Kagig are with Kagig," he answered.

"Surely not all?"

"All that Kagig could gather to him after eleven years!"

"In that case go to Kagig, and tell him."

"Kagig would not come. He holds Zeitoon."

"Are you a fool?"

"Not I! The other two are fools."

"Then do you understand that in case these people should make us prisoner —"

He nodded. "They might. They might propose to sell you to the Turks, perhaps against their own stolen womenfolk."

"Then don't you see that if you were gone, and I told them you had gone to bring Kagig, they would let us go rather than face Kagig's wrath?"

"But Kagig would not come."

"I know that. But how should they know it?"

I knew that be nodded again by the motion of the glowing tobacco in his pipe. It glowed suddenly bright, as a new idea dawned on him. He was an honest fellow, and did not conceal the thought.

"Kagig would not send me back to you," he said. "He is short of men at Zeitoon."

"Never mind," said I. "In case of trouble up above here, but not otherwise, will you do that?"

"Gladly. But give it me in writing, lest Kagig have me beaten for running from you without leave."

That was my turn to jump at a proposal. I tore a sheet from my memorandum book, and scribbled in the dark, knowing be could not read what I had written.

"This writing says that you did not run away until you had made quite sure we were in difficulties. So, if you should run too soon, and we should not be in difficulties after all, Kagig would learn that sooner or later. What would Kagig do in that case?"

"He would throw me over the bridge at Zeitoon — if he could catch me! Nay! I play no tricks."

"Good. Then go and hide. Hide within call. Within an hour, or at most two hours we shall know how the land lies. If all should be well I will change that writing for another one, and send you to Kagig in any case. No more words now — go and hide!"

He put his pipe out with his thumb, and took two strides

into a shadow, and was gone. Then I went back through the
gap in the dungeon wall, and stumbled to the stairs. Apparently not missing me yet, they had covered up the trap, and
I had to hammer on it for admission. They were not pleased
when my head appeared through the hole, and they realized
that I had probably held communication with our men. I
suppose Fred saw by my face that I had accomplished what
I went for, because he let out a laugh like a fox's bark that
did nothing toward lessening the tension.

On the other hand it was quite clear that during my
absence Miss Vanderman had not been idle. Excepting the
two men who had admitted me, every one was seated — she
on the floor among the women, with her back to the wall,
and the rest in a semicircle facing them. Two of the women
had their arms about her, affectionately, but not without a
hint of who controlled the situation.

"What have you been doing?" Fred demanded, and be
laughed at Gloria Vanderman with an air of triumph.

"Making preparations," I said, "to take Miss Vanderman
to Tarsus."

I wish I could set down here a chart of the mixed emotions
then expressed on that young lady's face. She did not look at
Will, knowing perhaps that she already had him captive of
her bow and spear. Neither did Will look at us, but sat tracing
figures with a forefinger in the dust between his knees, wondering perhaps how to excuse or explain, and getting no
comfort.

If my guess was correct, Gloria Vanderman was about
equally distracted between the alternative ignominy of sub-
mitting her free will to Armenians or else to us. Compassion
for the women in their predicament weighed one way —
knowledge that our friend Monty was in durance vile contingent on her actions pulled heavily another Fred was frankly
enjoying himself, which influenced her strongly toward the
Armenian side, she being young and, doubtless the idol of a
hundred heart-sick Americans, contemptuous of forty-year-
old bachelors.

"Of course we shall not let you go!" one of the Armenians
assured her in quite good English, and I began fumbling at
the pistol in my inner pocket, for if Arabaiji was to run to

Zeitoon, then the sooner the better. But it needed only that imputation of helplessness to tip the beam of Miss Gloria's judgment.

"You can attend to the sick ones. You can play music for us all. Doubtless these other two have qualifications."

I was too busy admiring Gloria to know what effect that announcement had on Fred and Will. She shook herself free from the women, and stood up, splendid in the flickering yellow light. There was a sort of swift move by every one to be ready against contingencies, and I judged it the right moment to spring my own surprise.

"When I fire this pistol," I said, producing it, "a man will start at once for Zeitoon to warn Kagig. He has a note in his pocket written to Kagig. Judge for yourselves how long it will take Kagig and his men to reach this place!"

The nearest man made a very well-judged spring at me and pinned my elbows from behind. Another man knocked the pistol from my hand. The women seized Gloria again. But Fred was too quick — drew his own pistol, and fired at the roof.

"Twice, Fred!" I shouted, and he fired again.

"There!" said I. "Do what you like. The messenger has gone!"

And then Gloria shook herself free a last time, and took command.

"Is that true?" she demanded.

I nodded. "The best of our three men was to start on his way the minute he heard the second shot."

Then I was sure she was Boadicea reincarnate, whether the old-time British queen did or did not have blue eyes and brown hair.

"I will not have brave men brought back here on my account! Kagig must be a patriot! He needs all his men! I don't blame him for making a hostage of Lord Montdidier! I would do the same myself!"

Will had evidently given her a pretty complete synopsis of our adventure while I was outside talking with Arabaiji. It is always a mystery to the British that Americans should hold themselves a race apart and rally to each other as if the rest of the Anglo-Saxon race were foreigners, but those two had

obeyed the racial rule. They understood each other — swiftly
— a bar and a half ahead of the tune.

"This old castle is no good!" she went on, not raising her
voice very high, but making it ring with the wholesomeness
of youth, and youth's intolerance of limits. "The Turks could
come to this place and burn it within a day if they chose!"

"The Turks won't trouble. They'll send their friends the
Kurds instead," Fred assured her.

"Ah-h-h-gh !" growled the Armenians, but she waved them
back to silence.

"How much food have you? Almost none! How much
ammunition?"

"Ah-h-h-h!" they chorused in a very different tone of voice.

"D'you mean you've got cartridges here?" Fred demanded.

"Fifty cases of cartridges for government Mauser rifles!"
bragged the man who was nearest to Will.

"Gee! Kagig 'ud give his eyes for them!" (Will devoted his
eyes to the more poetic purpose of exchanging flashed encouragement with Gloria.)

"Men, women and children — how many of you are there?"

"Who knows? Who has counted? They keep coming."

"No, they don't. You've set a guard to keep any more away
for fear the food won't last — I know you have! Well — what
does it matter how many you are? I say let us all go to Zeitoon
and help Kagig!"

"Oh, bravo!" shouted Fred, but it was Will's praise that
proved acceptable and made her smile.

"Second the motion!"

I added a word or two by way of make-weight, that did
more as a matter of fact than her young ardor to convince
those very skeptical men and women. No doubt she broke
up their determination to sit still, but it was my words that
set them on a course.

"Kagig will be angry when he comes. He's a ruthless man,"
said I, and the Armenians, men as well as women, sought one
another's eyes and nodded.

"Kagig must be more of a ruthless bird than we guessed!"
Will whispered.

Counting women, there was less than a score of refugees
in the room, and if we had only had them to convince, our

work was pretty nearly done. There was the guard among the trees down-hill that we knew about still to be converted, or perhaps coerced. But just at the moment when we felt we held the winning hand, there came a ladder thrust down through the hole in the corner of the roof, and a man whom they all greeted as Ephraim began to climb down backward. He was so loaded with every imaginable kind of weapon that he made more noise than a tinker's cart.

Nor was Ephraim the only new arrival. Man after man came down backward after him, each man cursed richly for treading on his predecessor's fingers — a seeming endless chain of men that did not cease when the room was already uncomfortably overcrowded. Some of these men wore clothes that suggested Russia, but the majority were in rags. The ladder swayed and creaked under them, and finally, at a word from Ephraim, the last-comers sat on the upper rungs, bending the frail thing with their weight into a complaining loop.

Several of the newcomers had torches, and their acrid smoke turned the twice-breathed air of the place into evil-tasting fog.

Three men put their faces close to Ephraim's and proceeded to enlighten him as to what had passed. He seemed to be recognized as some sort of chieftain, and carried himself with a commanding air, but so many men talked at once, and all in Armenian, that we could not pick out more than a word or two here and there. Even Fred, with his gift of tongues, could hardly make head or tail of it.

We three pressed through the swarm and took our stand beside Gloria, not hesitating to thrust the other women aside. They dragged at their menfolk to call attention to us, but the argument was too hot to be missed, and the women clawed and screamed in vain.

"I believe we could get out!" I shouted in Will's ear. But he shook his head. At least six men were standing on the trap, and we could not have driven them off it because there was no other space on the floor that they could occupy. So I turned to Fred.

"Couldn't we shake those ruffians off the ladder, and climb up it and escape?" I shouted. But Fred shook his head, and went on listening, trying to follow the course of the dispute.

At last somebody with louder lungs than any other man made Ephraim understand that it was I who sent the messenger to Zeitoon. Instantly that solved the problem to his mind. I should be hanged, and that would be all about it. He gesticulated. The men swarmed down off the ladder to the already overcrowded floor, and mistaking Will for me several men started to thrust him forward. A face appeared through the hole in the roof and its owner was sent running for a rope. I had not recovered my pistol, and my rifle was slung at my back where I could not possibly get at it for the crowd. But Fred had a Colt repeater handy in his hip-pocket and he promptly screwed the muzzle of it into Ephraim's ear. What he said to him I don't know, but Ephraim's convictions underwent a change of base and he began to yell for silence. The men who had seized Will let go of him just as the rope with a disgusting noose in the end was lowered through the roof. And then Ossa was imposed on Pelion.

A new face appeared at the hole. Not that we could see the face. We could only see the form of a man who shook the bloody stump of a forearm at us, and shrieked unintelligible things. After thirty seconds even the men in the far corner were aware of him, and then there was stony silence while he had his say. He repeated his message a dozen times, as if he had it by heart exactly, spitting foam out of his mouth and never ceasing to shake the butchered stump of an arm. At about the dozenth time he fainted and fell headlong down the ladder bringing up on the shoulders of the men below.

"What does he say?" I bellowed in Fred's car. But Fred was forcing his way closer to Gloria, to tell her.

"He says the Kurds are coming! He says two regiments of Kurdish cavalry have been turned loose by the Turks with orders to 'rescue' Armenians. They are on their way, riding by night for a wonder. They cut both his hands off, but he got away by shamming dead. He says they are cutting off the feet of people and bidding them walk to Tarsus. They are taking the women and girls for sale. Old women and very little children they are making what they call sport with. Have you heard of Kurds? Their ideas of sport are worse than the Red-man's ever were."

Every tongue in the room broke loose. In another second

every man was still. They looked toward Ephraim. He who could order a hanging so glibly should shoulder the new responsibility.

But Ephraim was not ready with a plan, and could not speak English. Wild-eyed, he seized the lapel of my coat in trembling fingers, and with a throat grown suddenly parched, crackled a question at me in Armenian. I could have understood Volopuk easier.

"What does he say, Fred?"

"He wants to know how soon Kagig can be here."

"Kagig!" Ephraim echoed, clutching at my collar. "Yes, yes, yes! Kagig! Come — how soon?"

"We shall be all right," said another man in English over on the far side of the room. His hoarse voice sounded like a bellow in the silence. "Kagig will come presently. Kagig will butcher the Kurds. Kagig will certainly save us."

"Kagig!" Ephraim insisted. "Come — how soon?"

But I knew Kagig would not come, that night or at any time, and Ephraim shook me in frenzied impatience for an answer.

Chapter Eleven

"That man's dose is death, and he dies unshriven!"

"MALE AND FEMALE CREATED HE THEM"

The ancient orders pass. The fetters fall.
All-potent inspiration stirs dead peoples to new birth.
And over bloodied fields a new, clear call
Rings kindlier on deadened ears of earth.
Man — male — usurping — unwise overlord,
Indoctrinated, flattered, by himself betrayed
And all-betraying since with idiot word
He bade his woman bear and be afraid,
Awakes to see delusion of the past
Unmourned along with all injustice die,
Himself by woman wisdom blessed at last
And her unchallenged right the reason why.

*N*ow for a moment I became the unwilling vortex of that mob of anxious men and women — I who by, my own confession knew Kagig, I who had sent Kagig a message, I who five minutes ago was on the verge of being hanged in the greasy noose that still swung above the ladder through the hole in the roof — I who therefore ought to be thoroughly plastic-minded and obedient to demands.

The place had become as evil smelling as the Black Hole of Calcutta. Everybody was sweating, and they shoved and milled murderously in the effort to get near me and learn, each with his own ears from my lips, just when Kagig might be expected. Ephraim, their presumptive leader, got shuffled to the outside of the pack — the only silent man between the four walls, watchful for new opportunity.

With my clothing nearly torn off and cars in agony from bellowed questions, the only remedy I could think of was to yell to Fred to start up a tune on his concertina; I had seen him change a crowd's temper many a time in just that way. But even supposing my advice had been good, he could not get his arms free, and it was Gloria Vanderman who saved that day.

Whoever has tried to write down the quality that makes the college girl, United States or English, what she is has failed, just as whoever has tried to muzzle or discredit her has failed. She is something new that has happened to the world, not because of men and women and the priests and pundits, but in spite of them. Part of the reason can be given by him who knows history enough, and commands almost unlimited leisure and page; but that would only be the uninteresting part that we could easily dispense with. The college girl has happened to the world, as light did in Genesis 1:3.

Gloria Vanderman, with her back against the wall, struggled and contrived to get her foot on Will's bent knee. Another struggle sent her breast-high above the sea of sweating faces. There was fitful light enough to see her by, because the man who held a pine torch was privileged. If there had not been hot sparks scattering from the thing doubtless they would have closed in on him and crushed it down, and out, but he had elbow-room, and accordingly Gloria's face glowed golden in its frame of disordered chestnut hair. One heard her voice because it was clear, and sweet with reasonableness, so that it vibrated in an unobstructed orbit.

"Surely you are not cowards?" she began, and they grew silent, because that idea called for consideration.

"Kagig is a patriot. Kagig is fighting for all Armenia. Surely you are not the men to let brave Kagig be tempted away from his post of danger at Zeitoon? If I know you men and women you will hasten to meet Kagig, taking your food, and weapons, and children with you. You will hurry — hurry — hurry to meet him — to meet him as near Zeitoon as possible, so as to turn him back to his post of duty!"

Then Ephraim saw his chance. Some whisperer translated to him and he owned a voice that was worth gold for political purposes.

He took up the tale in Armenian, working himself up into a splendid fervor, and so amplifying the argument that he could almost fairly claim it as his own before he was half-done. She had introduced the light, but he exploited it, and he knew his nation — knew the tricks of speech most likely to spur them into action.

Within five minutes they were shoving the stones off the trap at imminent risk of anybody's legs, and the ladder bent groaning under the weight of twice as many as it ought to bear, as half of them essayed the short cut over the roof. A blast of sweet air through the opened trap ejected most of the smoky ten-times-breathed stuff out with the climbers; and as the room emptied and we wiped the grimy sweat from our faces I heard Will talking to Gloria Vanderman in a new tongue — new, that is to say, to the old world.

"Good goods! Stampeded 'em! They'll vote for you for any office — your pick! If that guy Ephraim plans buttering the slide we'll set him on it — watch!"

"You bet," she answered sentimentally. "I wasn't cheer leader for nothing. Besides, I delivered the valedictory — say, what are we waiting here for?"

"Come on, then!" I urged her. "We'll leave our mule-load behind in case they've eaten your horse. Come with us to the stables and —"

But she interrupted me.

"You men go down and get the horses. Do what you can with the crowd. I'll get the women into something like order if that's possible, and we'll all meet wherever there's open ground and moonlight at the foot of the hill."

"I'll come with you," Will proposed. "You'll need —"

"No you won't! The women are easy. They've been taught to obey orders! It'll take all the wit you three men own between you to get the men in line! Let's get busy!"

The men had treated the hanging blankets with the respect the ancient Jews accorded to the veil of the Holy of Holies. (We learned afterward that there was an Armenian man of the party who had followed a circus one summer all across the

States, and had brought that sensible precaution home with him as rule number one for successful management of mixed assemblies.) Gloria Vanderman made a run for the curtain and dived behind it. We heard the women welcome her.

"Let's go!" said Will.

Will had ever been our ladies' man in all our wanderings, because women could never resist his unaffected comradeship. Even among Americans he was rare in his gift of according to women equality not only of liberty, but of understanding and good sense, and it went like wine to the heads of some we had met, so that Will was seldom without a sex-problem on his hands and ours. But Will was too good a comrade to be surrendered to any woman lightly.

"Damn that chicken!" murmured Fred by way of praying fervently, pausing in the breach in the wall to rub his shin. "Feel that bruise, will you! No young woman ever brought me luck yet!"

"What are you waiting for?" complained a voice from outer darkness. "Come on, you rummies!"

Fred sat down on the protruding stone that had injured his shin, and detained me with his arm across the opening.

"Mark my words! In order that that young woman may be educated to consider Will Yerkes a paragon of unimaginable virtues, we — you and I — are going to have to do what he calls 'hustle.' We're going to see speed, and we're going to sweat, trying to catch up. There isn't a scatterbrained adventure conceivable that we're not going to be forced into, nor an imaginable peril that we're not going to have to pull him out of. We're going to be cursed for our trouble, and ridiculed to make amusement for her majesty. And at the end of it all we're going to be patronized for a couple of ignorant damned fools who don't know better than be bachelors. What's worse, we're going to submit tamely. What is infinitely worse, we're going to like it! There are times when I doubt the sanity of my whole sex!"

"Have you guys taken root?" demanded the familiar voice and we heard Will's returning footsteps.

"No, America. But I have to sit down when my shin hurts and I'm seized with the gift of prophecy."

"Huh! We'll find Miss Vanderman tired of waiting for us

with the women. Since when has a crack on the shin made a baby of you? You used to be tough enough!"

"D'you get the idea?" chuckled Fred. "We're coming, Will, we're coming."

Perfectly unconsciously Will took the lead, and most outrageously he drove us. Not that his driving was not shrewd, for his usually practical and quick mind seemed to take on added brilliancy. And since we first joined partnership — he and Monty and Fred and I — we had always been contented to follow the lead of whichever held it at the moment. But there was new efficiency, and impatience of a brand-new kind that would not rest until every man and animal had been rummaged in darkness out of that old ruin, and men, horses, cows, goats, bags of grain, and fifty cases of cartridges were driven down through the forest like water forced through a sieve, and were gathered in the only open space discoverable.

There we cooled our heels, fearful and full of vague imaginings until Miss Vanderman should bring the women, not at all encouraged by shouts in the distance that well might be the exulting of plundering Kurds, nor by occasional rifle-shots that sounded continually nearer, nor by the angry crimson glow of burning roofs that lighted half the horizon.

We waited an hour, Will objecting whenever either of us proposed to return and speed Miss Vanderman.

"Aw, what's the use? D'you suppose she doesn't know we're waiting?"

At last Fred proposed that Will himself go and investigate. He went through the form of demurring, but yielded gracefully.

"The spirit," Fred chuckled, "is weak, and the flesh is willing!"

Will handed his mule's reins to an Armenian and started alone up-hill through the pitch-dark forest; and because the world is mixed of unexpectedness and grim jest in fairly equal proportions, five minutes after he left us Gloria Vanderman came leading the women by another path.

To avoid confusion with our part, and for sake of silence, she had led them a circuit, and except for the occasional wail of a child and a little low talking that blended like the hum of insects with the night, they made very little noise. The rear was brought up by the strongest women carrying the sick and wounded on litters that had been improvised in a hurry, and like most things of the sort were much too heavy.

"Your mule is ready," said I. But she shook her head.

"You gentlemen must give your mules up to the sick and wounded. We well ones can walk."

I did not know how to answer her, although I knew she was wrong. The way to organize a marching column is not to level down to the ability of the weakest, although the pace of the weakest may have to be the measure of speed. We, who had to protect the column and shepherd it, would need our mounts; without them we should all be at the mercy of any enemy, with no corresponding gain to any one except the litter-bearers. All the same, I did not care to take issue with that capable young woman then and there. She would have put me in the wrong and left me speechless and indignant, after the fashion that is older than poor Shylock's tale.

But Fred is made of sterner stuff than I, and was never above amusing himself at the expense of anybody's dignity.

"Will is the youngest," he answered. "Besides, he's keeping us all waiting with his love-affairs! He ought to be made to walk!"

"His love-affairs?"

"He went into the woods to see a woman," Fred answered imperturbably. "Let him forfeit his mule. Here he comes. Did you find her, America?"

Will emerged out of gloom with a grin on his face.

"Just my luck!" he said simply. "What are we waiting for? I can hear the Kurds. Let's start."

At that Gloria got excited.

"D'you mean you're willing to leave a woman behind alone in that forest?" she demanded, and Will's jaw dropped.

Fred nudged my ribs.

"Come on! We've given 'em a ground for their first quarrel. They'll never thank us if we wait a week. Mount! Walk — ride!"

We sent our two Zeitoonli in advance to show the way. True to his word, Arabaiji had left us, mule and all, and we missed him as we strove to get the unwieldy column marshaled and moving in line. We did not see Will and Gloria again that night, except when they passed between us, walking, arguing — Will explaining — we sitting on our mules on either side of the track until the last of the swarm tailed by. Then we brought up the rear together, to drive the stragglers and look out for pursuit.

"Not that I know what the devil we'll do if the Kurds get after us!" said Fred.

"Let's hope they make for the castle tonight, and waste time plundering that."

"Piffle!" he answered.

"Why?"

"Because, you ass, if they get to the place and find if empty they'll deduce, being less than idiots, that we're not far off and that we're at their mercy in the open! Let's hope to God they funk attacking in the dark, and wait out of range of the walls until daylight. In that case we've a chance. Otherwise — I've still got six rifle cartridges, and four for my pistol. How many have you?"

"Six of each."

"Then you owe me one for my pistol."

I passed it to him.

"So. Now we're good for exactly twenty-two Kurds between us. If we're pursued I propose to give those two young lovers a chance by making every cartridge count from behind cover."

"They'd hear the shooting and —"

"Not if we drop far enough behind."

"They'd hear shooting and Will, at any rate, would ride back."

"He couldn't! He'd have to look after the girl and the column."

"All the same — Will's —"

"I know he is. Very well. I'll arrange it another way. You wait behind here."

So I rode along slowly, and he spurred his horse to a trot. But he did not hold the trot long. I could hear him objurgating, coaxing, encouraging, explaining, and the shrill voices of women answering, as he tried at one and the same time to pass the unfortunates in the dark and to make them see the grim necessity for speed. Soon I grew as busy as he, bullying litter-bearers and mothers burdened with crying babies. In times of massacre and war, survivors are not necessarily those who enjoyed the best of it. Nearly-drowned men brought to life again would forego the process if the choice were theirs, and there were nearly twenty women who would have preferred death to that night's march. But I did not dare load my horse with babies, since it would likely be needed before dawn for sterner work.

It was more than an hour before Fred loomed in sight again, standing beside his horse in wait for me. He, too, had resisted the temptation to relieve mothers of their living loads (not that they ever expected it).

"How did you manage?" I asked, for I could tell by his air that the errand had been successful.

"I lied to him."

"Of course. What did you say?"

"Said if the straggling got bad you and I might fall a long way behind and fire our pistols, so as to give the impression Kurds are in pursuit. That would tickle up the rear-end to a run!"

"And he believed that?" Will knew as well as I Fred's not exactly subtle way of maneuvering to get the post of greatest danger for himself.

"He'd have believed anything! He's head-, heart-, and heels-over-end in love with the girl, and she's as bad as he is. They're talking political economy and international jurisprudence. When I reached 'em they'd just arrived at the conclusion that the United States can save the world, maybe — maybe not, but nothing else can. I was decidedly de trop. They're pretty to watch. No, he hasn't kissed her yet — you could tell that even in the dark. It's my belief he won't for a long time; America's way with women is beyond belief. They're telling each other all they know, and like, and dislike, and believe, and hope. It 'ud take a bullet to divide their destinies. I delivered my message, and they were so devilish polite you'd think I was the parson come to marry 'em. They'd forgotten my very existence. When it dawned on 'em who I was they were so keen to be rid of me they'd have agreed to anything at all. So it was easy."

"Good."

"No, it's bad. Will's a friend of mine. I hate to see him squandered on a woman. However, I did better than that."

"How so?"

As I spoke there loomed out of the darkness just ahead of us eight men surrounding something on the track, their rifles sticking up above their shoulders.

"I've found eight men with rifles all alike that fit the ammunition in the boxes. It's stolen Turkish government ammunition, by the way. The rifles come from the same source. The point is that a man caught with a stolen government rifle and ammunition in his possession would be tortured. Incidentally the men seem game. Therefore, if we have to fight a rear-guard action we can reasonably count on them. Haide!" he called to the eight men, and they picked up the case of cartridges, and resumed the march just ahead of us.

Fred lit his pipe contentedly, as he always is contented when he can make satisfactory arrangements to sacrifice himself unselfishly and pretend to himself he is a cynic. Whether because the armed guard of their own people put new courage in them, or because rifles at their rear made them more afraid, the stragglers gave less trouble for the next few hours. Perhaps they were growing more used to the march, and some of them were numb with anxiety, while not so weary yet that feet would not carry them forward.

Somewhere in advance a man with a high tenor voice began to sing a wild folk-song, of the sort that is common to all countries whose heritage is hope unstrangled. He and others like him with love and music in their brave hearts sang the tortured column through its night of agony, keeping alive faint hope that hell must have an end. Dawn broke sweet and calm. For it makes no matter if a nation writhes in agony, or man wreaks hate on man, the wind and the sky still whisper and smile; and the scent of wild flowers is not canceled by the stench of tired humanity.

Fred knocked his pipe out and rode to the top of shoulder of rock beside the track, beckoning to me to follow. We could see our column, astonishingly long drawn, winding like a line of ants in and out and over, following the leaders in a dream because there seemed nothing else to do or dream about. Once I thought I caught sight of Will on his horse, passing between trees, but I was not sure. Fred turned his horse about and looked in the direction we had come from. Presently, be nudged me.

"That smoke might be the castle we were in last night. See — it's red underneath. What'll you bet me Kurds don't show up in pursuit before the day's an hour old?"

That was nothing to bet about, and that kind of dawn is not the hour for roseate optimism.

"If they come," said I, "I hope I don't live to see what they'll do to the women."

Fred met my eyes and laughed.

"That's all right," he said. "You ride on. This rock commands the track. I'll follow later when pursuit's called off."

"Ride on yourself!" I answered, and he chuckled as he lighted his pipe again.

One of the men had a kerosene can filled with odds and ends of personal belongings. I turned them out in a hollow of the rock, and sent him to fill the can with drinking water at a spring. Then Fred and I chose stations, and Fred went to vast pains lecturing every one of us on how to keep cover. We had nothing to eat, and therefore no notion of putting up anything but a short fight. Our best point was the surprise that unexpected, organized resistance would be likely to produce on plundering Kurds.

It was pleasant enough where we lay, and reminded both of us of far less strenuous days. The little animals that are always curious to the point of their undoing came out and investigated our tracks as soon as the noise of the stragglers had ceased. The Armenians took no notice of the wild life; persecuted people seldom do, having their own hard case too much in mind; but Fred knew the name of nearly every bird and animal that showed itself, and even ceased smoking as his interest increased.

"Ever go fishing as a boy?" he asked.

"Didn't I!"

"Get up before daylight and escape from the house by the back way —"

"Stealing bread and cheese from the pantry on the way out —"

"And stopping where the grass was long near the watering place to dig worms —"

"And unchain the dog with frantic efforts to keep him

from barking —"

"Yes, but the rascal always would do it — bark and wake everybody! Lucky if nobody saw you as you slipped through the gate into the fields!"

"Ah! But then what a time the dog had — it was almost as good fun as the fishing to watch him scamper. And how hungry he got — and he ate more than his share of the bread and cheese, so that you'd have had to go home early because of the aching void if it hadn't been for the cottage where they gave a fellow milk out of a brown dish."

"Yumm! Didn't that country milk taste good! Snff — snff — they were mornings just like this at home when I went fishing. Cool and sweet and full of scent. Snff — snff!"

We sat still behind the ledge and let the air and scenery revive kind memories. The only noise was what our horses made cropping the grass in a hollow behind us, for the Armenians were well content to ruminate. Most likely they would have fallen asleep if we had not been there to keep an eye on them, for prolonged subjection to too much fear is soporific, so that tortured poor wretches sleep on the tightened rack.

I was very nearly asleep myself, having had practically none of it for two nights in succession, and had taken to watching the horses to keep my mind busy, when the movement of my horse's ears struck me as peculiar. Presently he ceased grazing and raised his head. I thought he was going to whinny, and turned to see Fred squinting down his rifle at something that was not in the range of my vision.

"Here they come!" he whispered.

As he spoke a Kurd stepped out from between the trees, and we could see that he had tied his horse to a branch in the gloom behind him. He had the long sleeves reaching nearly to the ground peculiar to his race, and the unmistakable sheeny nose and cruel lips. From the rifle that he carried cavalierly over his shoulder hung a woman's undergarment, with a dark stain on it that looked suspiciously like blood. My horse whinnied then, and his beast answered. At that he brought his rifle to the "ready" and nearly jumped out of his skin.

"I'm judge, jury, witness, prosecutor and executioner!" Fred whispered. "That man's dose is death, and he dies unshriven!"

Then he fired, and Fred could not miss at that range if he tried. The Kurd clapped a hand to his throat and fell backward, and one of our Armenians ran before we could stop him to seize the tied horse, and any other plunder. One of the things he brought back with him, besides the horse and rifle and ammunition belt, was a woman's finger with the ring not yet removed. He said he found it in the cartridge pouch.

In proof that organized defense was the last thing they reckoned on, nine more Kurds came galloping down the track pell-mell toward the place where they had heard the solitary rifle-shot, doubtless supposing their own man had come upon the quarry. We fired too fast, for the Armenians were not drilled men, but we dropped two horses and five Kurds, and the remaining four fled, with the riderless animals stampeding in their wake.

"What next?" said I, as Fred wiped out his rifle-barrel.

"They'll return in greater force. We'd better change ground. D'you notice how this rock is covered by that other one a quarter of a mile to the right? Higher ground, too, and the last place they'll look — come on!"

The man with the water-can spilled it all, for the sake of his medley of possessions, and I had to send him all the way back for more. But we took up our new stand at last with the horses well hidden and enough to drink to last the day out, and then had to wait half an hour before any Kurds came back to the attack.

They came on the second time with infinite precaution, lurking among the trees on the outskirts of the clearing and firing several random shots at our old position in the hope of drawing our fire. Finally, they emerged from the forest thirty strong and rushed our supposed hiding place at full gallop.

They were not even out of pistol range. Fred used the Mauser rifle taken from the dead Kurd, and then we both emptied our pistols at the fools, the Armenians meanwhile keeping up a savage independent fire so ragged and rapid that it might have been the battle of Waterloo.

The Kurds never knew whether or not we were another

party or the first one. They never discovered whether our former post was deserted or not. We never knew how many of them we hit, for after about a dozen had tumbled out of the saddle the remainder galloped for their lives. For minutes afterward we heard them crashing and pounding away in the distance to find their friends.

Our loot consisted of two wounded prisoners and four good horses, in addition to rifles and cartridges. We let the dead lie where they were for a warning to other scoundrels, and we looked on while our Armenians searched the bodies for anything likely to be of slightest use. They found almost nothing originally Kurdish, but more Armenian trinkets than would have stocked a traveling merchant's show-case, including necklaces and earrings.

Fred took the two prisoners aside and in Persian, which every Kurd can understand and speak after a fashion, offered them their choice between telling the whole truth or being handed over to Armenians. And as there isn't a bloody rascal in the world but suspects his intended victims of worse hankerings than his own, they loosed their tongues and told more than the truth, adding whatever they thought likely to please Fred.

"They say there were only about fifty of them in this raiding party to begin with, and several came to trouble before they met us. Seems there are Armenians hidden here and there who are able to give an account of themselves. Ten or twelve elected to stay near the castle we were in last night. They've burned it, but they have some captured women and propose to enjoy themselves. Shall we ride back and break in on the party?"

He meant what he said, but it was out of the question. "The party we've just trounced will give the alarm," I objected. "We'd only ride into a trap. Besides, you've no proof these prisoners are not lying to you."

"They say their raiding party is the only one within thirty miles. They rode ahead of the regiments to get first picking."

"We're none of us fit for anything but food and sleep," said I, and Fred had to concede the point.

Fortunately the food problem was solved for the moment by the Kurds, who had a sort of cheese with them whose awful taste deprived one of further appetite. We ate, and tied our two wounded prisoners on one horse; and as we had nothing to treat their wounds with except water they finished their trip in exquisite discomfort. Surprise that we should attend to their wounds at all, added to their despondency after they had time to consider what it meant. There was only one burden to their lamentation:

"What are you going to do with us? We will tell what we know! We will name names! We are your slaves! We kiss feet! Ask, and we will answer!"

They thought they were being kept alive for torture, and we let them keep on thinking it. Fred tied their horse to his own saddle and towed them along, singing at the top of his lungs to keep the rest of us awake; and for all his noise I fell asleep until he reached for his concertina and, the humor of the situation dawning on him, commenced a classic of his own composition, causing the morning to re-echo with irreverence, and making all of us except the prisoners aware of the fact that life is not to be taken seriously, even in Armenia. The prisoners intuitively guessed that the song had reference to ways and means they would rather have forgotten.

"Ow! My name it is 'orrible 'Enery 'Emms,
And I 'ails from a 'ell of a 'ole!
The things I 'ave thought an' the deeds I 'ave did
Are remarkable lawless an' better kep' hid,
So if Morgan you think of, an' Sharkey an' Kidd,
Forget 'em! To name such beginners as them's
An insult, so shivver my soul! Yow!
In every port o' the whole seven seas
I 'ave two or three wives on the rates,
For I'm free wi' my fancy an' fly wi' my picks,
And I've promised 'em plenty, an' given 'em nix,
But have left ev'ry one in a 'ell of a fix!
'Ooever said Bluebeard was brother to me's
Either jealous or misunderstates!

"Wow! For awful atrocity, murder an' theft,
For battery, arson and hate,
From breakin' the Sabbath to coveting cows,
An' false affidavits an' perjurin' vows,
I'm adept at whatever the law disallows,
And the gallowsmen gape at the noose that I left,
For I flit while the bally fools wait!"

Fred kept us awake all right. Like most of his original songs, that one had sixty or seventy verses.

Chapter Twelve

"America's way with a woman is beyond belief!"

CUI BONO?

Did caution keep the gates of Greece,
Ye saints of "safety first!"
Twixt Thessaly and Locris when
Leonidas' thousand men
Died scornful of the proffered peace
Of Xerxes the accurst?
Watch ye have kept, ward ye have kept,
But watch and ward were vain
If love and gratitude have slept
While ye stood guard for gain.

Or ye, who count the niggard cost
In time and coin and gear
Of succoring the under-dog,
How often have ye seen a hog,
Establishing his glutton boast,
Survive a famine year?
Fast ye have kept, feast ye have made;
Vain were the deeds and doles
If it was fear that ye obeyed
To save your coward souls.

Ye banish beauty to the stews
For lack of eyes that see,
And stifle joy with deadly rote
As empty as the texts ye quote,
The while forgiveness ye refuse
Lest wrath dishonored be.
Gray are your days, drab are your ways,

Strong are your fashioned bars,
But, ye who ask if service pays —
Who polishes the stars?

Spring in Armenia is almost as much like heaven as heaven itself could be, if it were not for the unspeakable Turk, but his blight rests on everything. I could have kept awake that morning without Fred's irreverent music, simply for sake of the scenery, if its freshness had been untainted. But there hung a sickly, faint pall of smoke that robbed the green landscape of all liveliness. One breathed weariness instead of wine.

We could not possibly have lost the way, because our crawling column had left a swath behind it of trampled grass and trodden crossing-places where the track wound and re-wound in a game of hide-and-seek with tinkling streams. But we began to wonder, nevertheless, why we caught up with nobody.

It was drawing on to ten in the morning, and I had dozed off for about the dozenth time, with my horse in pretty much the same condition, when I heard Will's voice at last, and looked up. He was standing alone on a ledge overlooking the track, but I could see the ends of rifles sticking up close by. If we had been an enemy, we should have stood small chance against him.

"Where are the rest of you?" I asked, and he laughed!

"Women, kids and wounded all swore a pitched battle was raging behind them. Most of them wanted to turn back and lend a hand. I thought you guys mighty cruel to put all that scare into a crowd in their condition — but I see —"

"Guests, America! My country's at peace with Turkey! Where shall we stow our guests?"

"There's a village below here."

He jerked a thumb over his shoulder. But behind him was the apex of a spur thrust out in midcurve of the mountain-side, and one could not see around that. We had emerged out of the straggling outposts of the forest high above the plain, and to our right the whole panorama lay snoozing in haze. The path by which we had turned our backs on Monty and

Kagig went winding away and away below, here and there an
infinitesimal thin line of slightly lighter color, but more often
suggested by the contour of the hills. Our Zeitoonli in their
zeal to return to their leader had been evidently cutting
corners. If the smudge of smoke to the right front overhung
Marash, then we were probably already nearer Zeitoon than
when we and Kagig parted company.

"Come up and see for yourselves," said Will.

Fred passed the line that held his prisoners in tow to an
Armenian, and we climbed up together on foot. Around the
corner of the spur, within fifty feet of where Will stood, was
an almost sheer escarpment, and at the foot of that, a thousand feet below us, with ramparts of living rock on all four
sides, crouched a little village fondled in the bosom of the
mountains.

"They've piled down there and made 'emselves at home.
The place was deserted, prob'ly because it 'ud be too easy to
roll rocks down into it. But I can't make 'em listen. Ours is
a pretty chesty lot, with guts, and our taking part with 'em
has stiffened their courage. They claim they're goin' to hold
this rats' nest against all the Turks and Kurds in Asia Minor!"

"That's where the rest of us are," said Will

"Where's Miss Vanderman?"

"Asleep — down in the village. The're all asleep. You guys
go down there and sleep, too. I'll follow, soon as I've posted
these men on watch. That small square hut next the big one
in the middle is ours. She's in the big one with a crowd of
women. Now don't make a fool row and wake her! Tie your
horses in the shade where you see the others standing in line;
there's a little corn for them, and a lot of hay that the owners
left behind."

So we undertook not to wake the lady, and left Will there
carefully choosing places, in which the men fell fast asleep
almost the minute his back was turned. Sleep was in the air
that morning — not mere weariness of mind and limb that a
man could overcome, but inexplicable coma. Whole armies
are affected that way on occasion. There was a man once
named Sennacherib.

"Sleepy hollow!" said Fred, and as he spoke his horse
pitched forward, almost spilling him; the rope that held the

prisoners in tow was all that saved the lot of them from rolling down-hill. Fred dismounted, and drove the horse in front of him with a slap on the rump, but the beast was almost too sleepy to make the effort to descend.

There was no taint of gas or poison fumes. The air tasted fresh except for the faint smoke, and the birds were all in full song. Yet we all had to dismount, and to let the prisoners walk, too, because the horses were too drowsy to be trusted. The path that zigzagged downward to the village was danger-ous enough without added risk, and the eight Armenian riflemen refused point-blank to lead the way unless they might drive the animals ahead of them.

Even so, neither we nor they were properly awake ,when we reached the village. We tied up the horses in a sort of dream — fed them from instinct and habit — and made our way to the hut Will had pointed out like men who walked in sleep.

Nobody was keeping watch. Nobody noticed our arrival. Men and women were sleeping in the streets and under the eaves of the little houses. Nothing seemed awake but the stray dogs nosing at men's feet and hunting hopelessly among the bundles.

The little house Will had reserved for our use contained a stool and a string-cot. On the stool was food — cheese and very dry bread; and because even in that waking dream we were conscious of hunger, we ate a little of it. Then we lay down on the floor and fell asleep — we, and the prisoners, and the eight Armenian riflemen. Within a quarter of an hour Will followed us into the house, but we knew nothing about that. Then he, too, fell asleep, and until two or three hours after dark we were a village of the dead.

To this day there is no explaining it. Certainly no human watch or ward saved us from destruction at the hands of roving enemies. I was awakened at last by a brilliant light, and the effort made by our two prisoners, still tied together, to crawl across my body. I threw them off me, and sat up, rubbing my eyes and wondering where I was.

In the door stood Kagig, with a lantern in his right hand thrust forward into the room. His eyes were ablaze with excitement, and between black beard and mustache his teeth showed in a grin mixed of scorn and amusement.

Next I beard Will's voice: "Jimminy!" and Will sat up. Then Fred gave tongue:

"That you, Kagig? Where's Monty? Where's Lord Montdidier?"

Kagig strode into the room, set the lantern on the floor, struck the remnants of the food from off the little stool, and sat down. I could see now that he was deathly tired.

"He is in Zeitoon," he answered.

Noises from outside began then to assert themselves in demonstration that the village was awake at last — also that the population had swollen while we slept. I could hear the restless movement of more than twice the number of horses we had had with us.

Kagig began to laugh — a sort of dry cackle that included wonder as well as rebuke. He threw both hands outward, palms upward, in a gesture that complemented the motion of shoulders shrugged up to his ears.

"All around — high hills! From every side from fifty places rocks could have been rolled upon you! So — and so you sleep!"

"I set guards!" Will exploded.

"Eleven guards I found — all together in one place — fast asleep!"

He showed his splendid teeth and the palms of his hands again in actual enjoyment of the situation. For the first time then I saw there was wet blood on his goatskin coat.

"Kagig — you're wounded!"

He made a gesture of impatience.

"It is nothing — nothing. My servant has attended to it."

So Kagig had a servant. I felt glad of that. It meant a rise from vagabondage to position among his people.

Of all earthly attainments, the first and most desirable and last to let go of is an honest servant — unless it be a friend. (But the difference is not so distinct as it sounds.)

A huge fear suddenly seized Fred Oakes.

"You said Monty is in Zeitoon — alive or dead? Quick, man! Answer!"

"Should I leave Zeitoon," Kagig answered slowly, unless I left a better man in charge behind me? He is alive in Zeitoon — alive — alive! He is my brother! He and I love one purpose

with a strong love that shall conquer! You speak to me of
Lord what-is-it? Hah! To me forever he is Monty, my brother
— my — "

"Where's Miss Vanderman?" I interrupted.

"Here!" she said quietly, and I turned my head to discover
her sitting beside Will in the shadow cast by Kagig's lantern.
She must have entered ahead of Kagig or close behind him,
unseen because of his bulk and the tricky light that he swung
in his right hand.

Kagig went on as if he had not heard me.

"There is a castle — I think I told you? — perched on a crag
in the forest beside Zeitoon. My men have cut a passage to
it through the trees, for it had stood forgotten for God knows
how long. Later you shall understand. There came Arabaiji,
riding a mule to death, saying you and this lady are in danger
of life at the hands of my nation. I did not believe that, but
Monty — he believed it."

"And I'll wager you found him a hot handful!" laughed
Fred. "Not so hot. Not so hot. But very determined. Later
you shall understand. He and I drove a bargain."

"Dammit!" Fred rose to his feet. "D'you mean you used
our predicament as a club to drive him with?"

Kagig laughed dryly.

"Do you know your friend so little, and think so ill of me?
He named terms, and I agreed to them. I took a hundred
mounted men to find you and bring you to Zeitoon, spreading them out like a fan, to scour the country. Some fell in
with a thing the Turks call a hamidieh regiment; that is a
rabble of Kurds under the command of Tenekelis."

"What are they?"

"Tenekelis? The word means 'tin-plate men.' We call them
that because of the tin badges given them to wear in their
headdress. In no other way do they resemble officers. They
are brigands favored by official recognition, that is all. Their
purpose is to pillage Armenians. While you slept in this
village, and your watchmen slept up above there, that whole
rabble of bandits with their tin-plate officers passed within
half a mile, following along the track by which you came! If
you had been awake — and cooking — or singing — or making
any sort of noise they must have heard you! Instead, they

turned down toward the plain a little short distance too soon
— and my men met them — and there was a skirmish — and
I rallied my other men, and attacked them suddenly. We
accounted for two of the tin-plate men, and so many of the
thing they call a regiment that the others took to flight.
Jannam! (My soul!) But you are paragons of sleepers!"

"Do you never sleep?" I asked him.

"Shall a man keep watch over a nation, and sleep?" he
answered. "Aye — here a little, there a little, I snatch sleep
when I can. My heart burns in me. I shall sleep on my horse
on the way back to Zeitoon, but the burning within will
waken me by fits and starts."

He got up and stood very politely in front of Gloria
Vanderman, removing his Cossack kalpak for the first time
and holding it with a peculiar suggestion of humility.

"You shall be put to no indignity at the hands of my
people," he said. "They are not bad people, but they have
suffered, and some have been made afraid. They would have
kept you safe. But now you shall have twenty men if you wish,
and they shall deliver you safely into Tarsus. If you wish it, I
will send one of these gentlemen with you to keep you in
countenance before my men; they are foreigners to you, and
no one could blame you for fearing them. The gentleman
would not wish to go, but I would send him!"

She shook her head, pretty merrily for a girl in her predicament.

"I was curious to meet you, Mr. Kagig, but that's nothing
to the attraction that draws me now. I must meet the other
man — is it Monty you all call him — or never know a
moment's peace!"

"You mean you will not go to Tarsus?"

"Of course I won't!"

"Of course!" laughed Fred. "Any young woman —"

"Of course?" Kagig repeated the extravagant gesture of
shrugged shoulders and up-turned palms. "Ah, well. You are
American. I will not argue. What would be the use?"

He turned his back on us and strode out with that air that
not even the great stage-actors can ever acquire, of becoming
suddenly and utterly oblivious of present company in the
consciousness of deeds that need attention. Generals of com-

mand, great captains of industry, and a few rare statesmen have it; but the statesmen are most rare, because they are trained to pretend, and therefore unconvincing. The generals and captains are detested for it by all who have never humbled themselves to the point where they can think, and be unselfishly absorbed. Kagig stepped out of one zone of thought into the next, and shut the door behind him.

A minute later we heard his voice uplifted in command, and the business of shepherding those women and children was taken out of our hands by a man who understood the business. The intoxicating sounds that armed men make as they evolve formation out of chaos in the darkness came in through open door and windows, and in another moment Kagig was back again with a hand on each door-post.

"You have brought all those cartridges!"

He thrust out both hands in front of him, and made the knuckles of every finger crack like castanets. In another second he was gone again. But we knew we were now forgiven all our sins of omission.

Somewhere about midnight, with a nearly full moon rising in a golden dream above the rim of the ravine, we started. And no wheeled vehicle could have followed by the track we took. It was no mean task for men on foot, and our burdened animals had to be given time. Whether or not Kagig slept, as he had said he would, on horse-back, he kept himself and our prisoners out of sight somewhere in the van; and this time the rear was brought up by a squadron of ragged irregular horse that would have made any old campaigner choke with joy to look at them.

Drill those men knew very little of — only sufficient to make it possible to lead them. No two men were dressed alike, and some were not even armed alike, although stolen Turkish government rifles far predominated. But they wore unanimously that dare-devil air, not swaggering because there is no need, that has been the key to most of the sublime surprises of all war. The commander, whose men sit that way in the saddle and toss those jokes shoulder over shoulder down the line, dare tackle forlorn hopes that would seem sheer leap-year lunacy to the martinet with twenty times their number.

"Who'd have thought it?" said Fred. "We've all heard the

Turk was a first-class fighting man, but I'd rather command fifty of these, than any five hundred Turks I ever saw.

There was no gainsaying that. Whoever had seen armies with an understanding eye must have agreed.

"Turks don't hate Armenians for their faults," I answered. "From what I know of the Turk he likes sin, and prefers it cardinal. If Armenians were mere degenerates, or murdering ruffians like the Kurds, the Turk would like them."

Fred laughed.

"Then if a Turk liked me, you'd doubt my social fitness?"

"Sure I would, if he liked you well enough to attract attention. The fact that the Turk hates Armenians is the best advertisement Armenians have got."

We were entering the heart of savage hills that tossed themselves in ever increasing grandeur up toward the mist-draped crags of Kara Dagh, following a trail that was mostly watercourse. The simple savagery of the mountains laid naked to view in the liquid golden light stirred the Armenians behind us to the depths of thought; and theirs is a conscious-ness of warring history; of dominion long since taken from them, and debauched like pearls by swine; of hope, eternally upwelling, born of love of their trampled fatherland. They began to sing, and the weft and woof of their songs were grief for all those things and a cherished, secret promise that a limit had been set to their nation's agony.

In his own way, with his chosen, unchaste instrument Fred is a musician of parts. He can pick out the spirit of old songs, even when, as then, he hears them for the first time, and make his concertina interpret them to wood and wind and sky. Indoors he is a mere accompanist, and in polite society his muse is dumb. But in the open, given fair excuse and the opportunity, he can make such music as compels men's ears and binds their hearts with his in common understanding.

Because of Fred's concertina, quite without knowing it, those Armenians opened their hearts to us that night, so that when a day of testing came they regarded us unconsciously as friends. Taught by the atrocity of cruel centuries to mistrust even one another, they would surely have doubted us other-wise, when crisis came. Nobody knows better than the Turk how to corrupt morality and friendship, and Armenia is honeycombed with the rust of mutual suspicion. But real music is magic stuff. No Turk knows any magic.

At dawn, twisting and zigzagging in among the ribs of rock-bound hills, we sighted the summit of Beirut Dagh all wreathed in jeweled mist. Then the only life in sight except ourselves was eagles, nervously obsessed with goings-on on the horizon. I counted as many as a dozen at one time, wheeling swiftly, and circling higher for a wider view, but not one swooped to strike.

Once, as we turned into a track that they told us led to El Oghlu, we saw on a hill to our left a small square building, gutted by fire. Twenty yards away from it, on top of the same round hill, strange fruit was hanging from a larger oak than any we had seen thereabouts — fruit that swung unseemly in the tainted wind.

"Turks!" announced one of Kagig's men, riding up to brag to us. "That square building is the guard-house for the zaptieh, put there by the government to keep check on robbers. They are the worst robbers!"

The man spoke English with the usual mission-school air suggestive of underdone pie. As a rule they go to school at such great sacrifice, and then so limited for funds, that they have to get by heart three times the amount an ordinary, undriven youth can learn in the allotted time. But by heart they have it. And like the pie they call to mind, only the surface of their talk is pale. Because their heart is in the thing, they under-stand.

"By hanging Turkish police," said Fred, "you only give the Turks a good excuse for murdering your friends."

"Come!" said the man of Zeitoon. "See."

He led the way down a path between young trees to a clearing where a swift stream gamboled in the sun. Down at the end of it, where the grass sloped gently upward toward the flanks of a great rock was a little row of graves with a cross made of sticks at the head of each — clearly not Turkish graves.

"Three men — eleven women," our guide said simply.

"You mean that the Turkish police —"

"There were fifteen on their way to Zeitoon. One survived, and reached Zeitoon, and told. Then he died, and we rode down to avenge them all. The Turks took the three men and beat them on the feet with sticks until the soles of their feet swelled up and burst. Then they made them walk on their tortured feet. Then they beat them to death. Shall I say what they did to the women?"

"What did you do to the Turks?" said I.

"Hanged them. We are not animals — we simply, hanged them."

Somewhere about noon we rode down a gorge into the village of El Oghlu. It was a miserable place, with a miserable, tiny kahveh in the midst of it, and Kagig set that alight before our end of the column came within a quarter of a mile of it. We burned the rest of the village, for he sent back Ephraim to order no shelter left for the regiments that would surely come and hunt us down. But the business took time, and we were farther than ever behind Kagig when the last wooden roof began to cockle and crack in the heat.

Will and Gloria were somewhere on in front, and Fred and I began to put on speed to try to overtake them. But from the time of leaving the burned village of El Oghlu there began to be a new impediment.

"We are not taking the shortest way," said Ephraim. "The shortest way is too narrow — good for one or two men in a hurry, but not for all of us."

We were gaining no speed by taking the easier road. There began to be vultures in evidence, mostly half-gorged, flopping about from one orgy to the next. And out from among the rocks and bushes there came fugitive Armenians — famished and wounded men and women, clinging to our stirrups and begging for a lift on the way to Zeitoon. Zeitoon was their one hope. They were all headed that way.

Fred detached a dozen mounted men to linger behind on guard against pursuit, and the rest of us overloaded our horses with women and children, giving up all hope of overtaking Gloria and Will, forgetting that they had come first on the scene. In my mind I imagined them riding side by side, Will with his easy cowboy seat, and Gloria looking like a boy except for the chestnut hair. But that imagination went the way of other vanities.

There was neither pleasure nor advantage in striding slowly beside my laboring horse, nor any hope of mounting him again myself. So I walked ahead and, being now horseless, ceased to be mobbed by fugitives. At the end of an hour I overtook two horses loaded with little children; but there was no sign of Gloria and Will, and losing zest for the pursuit as the sun grew stronger I sat down by the ways-side on a fallen tree.

It was then that I heard voices that I recognized. The first was a woman's.

"I'm simply crazy to know him."

A man's, that I could not mistake even amid the roar of a city, answered her.

"You've a treat in store. Monty is my idea of a regular he-man."

"Is he good-looking?"

"Yes. Stands and looks like a soldier. I've seen a plainsman in Wyoming who'd have matched him to a T all except the parted hair and the mustache."

"I like a mustache on a tall man."

"It suits Monty. The first idea you get of him is strength — strength and gentleness; and it grows on you as you know him better. It's not just muscles, nor yet will-power, but strength that makes your heart flutter, and you know for a moment how a woman must feel when a fellow asks her to be his wife. That's Monty."

I got up and retraced a quarter of a mile, to wait for Fred where I could not accuse myself of "listening in."

"Fred," I said, when he overtook me at last and we strode along side by side, "you were right. America's way with a woman is beyond belief!"

I told him what I had heard, and he thought a while.

"How about Maga Jhaere's way, when she and Will and the Vanderman meet?" he said at last, smiling grimly.

Chapter Thirteen

"'Take your squadron and go find him, Rustum Khan!' And I, sahib, obeyed my lord bahadur's orders."

"TOMORROW WE DIE"

All that is cynical; all that refuses
Trust in an altruist aim;
Every specious plea that excuses
Greed in necessity's name;
Studied indifference; scorn that amuses;
Cleverness, shifting the blame;
Selfishness, pitying trust it abuses —
Treason and these are the same.
Finally, when the last lees ye shall turn from
(E'en intellectuals flinch in the end!)
Ashes of loneliness then ye shall learn from —
All that's worth keeping's the faith of a friend.

*N*ever to be forgotten is that journey to Zeitoon. We threaded toward the heart of opal mountains along tracks that nothing on wheels — not even a wheel-barrow — could have followed. Perpetually on our right there kept appearing brilliant green patches of young rice, more full of livid light than flawless emeralds. And, as in all rice country, there were countless watercourses with frequently impracticable banks along which fugitives felt their way miserably, too fearful of pursuit to risk following the bridle track.

There is a delusion current that fugitives go fast. But it

stands to reason they do not; least of all, unarmed people
burdened with children and odds and ends of hastily
snatched household goods. We found them hiding everywhere to sleep and rest lacerated feet, and there was not a mile
of all that distance that did not add twenty or thirty stragglers
to our column, risen at sight of us out of their lurking places.
We scared at least as many more into deeper hiding, without
blame to them, for there was no reason why they should know
us at a distance from official murderers. Hamidieh regiments,
the militia of that land, wear uniforms of their own choosing,
which is mostly their ordinary clothes and weapons added.

With snow-crowned Beirut Dagh frowning down over us,
and the track growing every minute less convenient for horse
or man, word came from the rear that the hamidieh were truly
on our trail. Then we had our first real taste of what Armenians could do against drilled Turks, and even before Fred
and I could get in touch with Will and Gloria we realized
that whether or not we took part with them there was going
to be no stampede by the menfolk.

Nothing would persuade Gloria to go on to Zeitoon and
announce our coming. Kagig came galloping back and found
us four met together by a little horsetail waterfall. He ordered
her peremptorily to hurry and find Monty, but she simply
ignored him. In another moment he was too bent on shepherding the ammunition cases to give her a further thought.

Men began to gather around him, and he to issue orders.
They had either to kill him or obey. He struck at them with
a rawhide whip, and spurred his horse savagely at every little
clump of men disposed to air their own views.

"You see," he laughed, "unanimity is lacking!" Then his
manner changed back to irritation. "In the name of God,
effendim, what manner of sportmen are you? Will not each
of you take a dozen men and go and destroy those cursed
Turks?" (They call every man a Turk in that land who thinks
and acts like one, be he Turk, Arab, Kurd or Circassian.)

It was all opposed to the consul's plan, and lawless by any
reckoning. To attack the troops of a country with which our
own governments were not at war was to put our heads in a
noose in all likelihood. Perhaps if he had called us by any
other name than "sportmen" we might have seen it in that

light, and have told him to protect us according to contract.
But he used the right word and we jumped at the idea,
although Gloria, who had no notions about international
diplomacy, was easily first with her hat in the ring.

"I'll lead some men!" she shouted. "Who'll follow me?"
Her voice rang clear with the virtue won on college playing
fields.

"Nothing to it!" Will insisted promptly. "Here, you, Kagig
— I'll make a bargain with you!"

"Watch!" Fred whispered. "Will is now going to sell two
comrades in the market for his first love! D'you blame him?
But it won't work!"

"Send Miss Vanderman to Zeitoon with an escort and we
three —"

"What did I tell you?" Fred chuckled.

"— will fight for you all you like!"

But Gloria had a dozen men already swarming to her, with
never a symptom of shame to be captained by a woman; and
others were showing signs of inclination. She turned her back
on us, and I saw three men hustle a fourth, who had both
feet in bandages, until he gave her his rifle and bandolier. She
tossed him a laugh by way of compensation, and be seemed
content, although he had parted with more than the equiva-
lent of a fortune.

"That girl," said Kagig, from the vantage point of his great
horse, "is like the brave Zeitoonli wives! They fight! They can
lead in a pinch! They are as good as men — better than men,
for they think they know less!"

Fred swiftly gathered himself a company of his own, the
older men electing to follow his lead. Gloria had the cream
of the younger ones — men who in an earlier age would have
gone into battle wearing a woman's glove or handkerchief —
twenty or thirty youths blazing with the fire of youth. Will
went hot-foot after her with most of the English-speaking
contingent from the mission schools. Kagig had the faithful
few who had rallied to him from the first — the fighting men
of Zeitoon proper, including all the tough rear-guard who
had sent the warning and remained faithfully in touch with
the enemy until their chief should come.

That left for me the men who knew no English, and

Ephraim was enough of a politician to see the advantage to himself of deserting Fred's standard for mine; for Fred could talk Armenian, and give his own orders, but I needed an interpreter. I welcomed him at the first exchange of compliments, but met him eye to eye a second later and began to doubt.

"I'm going to hold these men in reserve," I told him, "until I know where they'll do most good. You know this country? Take high ground, then, where we can overlook what's going on and get into the fight to best advantage."

"But the others will get the credit," he began to object.

"I'll ask Kagig for another interpreter. Wait here."

At that he yielded the point and explained my orders to the men, who began to obey them willingly enough. But he went on talking to them rapidly as we diverged from the path the others had taken and ascended a trail that wild goats would have reveled in, along the right flank of where fighting was likely to take place. I did not doubt be was establishing notions of his own importance, and with some success.

Firing commenced away in front and below us within ten minutes of the start, but it was an hour before I could command the scene with field-glasses, and ten minutes after that before I could make out the positions of our people, although the enemy were soon evident — a long, irregular, ragged-looking line of cavalry thrusting lances into every hole that could possibly conceal an Armenian, and an almost equally irregular line of unmounted men in front of them, firing not very cautiously nor accurately from under random cover.

It became pretty evident, after studying the positions for about fifteen minutes and sweeping every contour of the ground through glasses, that the enemy had no chance whatever of breaking through unless they could outflank Kagig's line. I held such impregnable advantage of height and cover and clear view that the men I had with me were ample to prevent the turning of our right wing. Our left flank rested on the brawling Jihun River that wound in and out between the rice fields and the rocky foot-hills. There lay the weakness of our position, and more than once I caught sight of Kagig spurring his horse from cover to cover to place his men. Once

I thought I recognized Fred, too, over near the river-bank; but of Will or of Gloria I saw nothing.

It was obvious that if reserves were needed anywhere it would be over on that left flank by the fordable Jihun. Ephraim saw that, and proceeded to preach it like gospel to the men before consulting me. Then, arrogant in the consciousness of majority approval, he came and advised me.

"Those — ah — hamidieh not coming this — ah — way. We cross over to — ah — other side. Then Kagig is being pleased with us. I give orders — yes?"

He did not propose to wait for my consent, but I detained him with a hand on his shoulder. It would have taken us two hours to get into position by the river-bank.

"Find out how many of the men can ride," I ordered.

Taken by surprise he called out the inquiry without stopping to discover my purpose first. It transpired there were seventeen men who had been accustomed to horseback riding since their youth. That would leave nine men for another purpose. I separated sheep from goats, and made over the nine to Ephraim.

"You and these nine stay here," I ordered, "and hold this flank until Kagig makes a move." I did not doubt Kagig would fall back on Zeitoon as soon as he could do that with advantage. Neither did I doubt Ephraim's ability to spoil my whole plan if be should see fit. Yet I had to depend on his powers as interpreter.

There are two ways of relieving a weak wing, and the obvious one of reinforcing it is not of necessity the best. I could see through the glasses a bowl of hollow grazing ground in which the dismounted Kurds had left their horses; and I could count only five men guarding them. Most of the horses seemed to be tied head to head by the reins, but some were hobbled and grazing close together.

"Tell these seventeen men I have chosen that I propose to creep up to the enemy's horses and steal or else stampede them," I ordered.

Ephraim hesitated. Glittering eyes betrayed fear to be left out of an adventure, disgust to see his own advice ignored, and yet that he was alert to the advantage of being left with a lone command.

"But we should — ah — cross to the — ah — other side and — ah — help Kagig," he objected. Perhaps he hoped to build political influence on the basis of his own account to Kagig afterward of how be had argued for the saner course.

"Please explain what I have said — exactly!"

He continued to hesitate. I could see the Kurdish riflemen responding to orders from their rear and beginning to concentrate in the direction of our left wing. Our center, where Gloria and Will were probably concealed by rocks and foliage, poured a galling fire on them, and they had to reform, and detach a considerable company to deal with that; but two-thirds of their number surged toward our left, and if my plan was to succeed almost the chief element was time.

"But Kagig will —"

One of the men had a hide rope, very likely looted from the village we had burned. I took it from him and tied a running noose in the end. Then I made the other end fast to the roots of a tree that had been rain-washed until they projected naked over fifty feet of sheer rock.

"Now," I said, "explain what I said, or I'll hang you in sight of both sides!"

I wondered whether he would not turn the tables and hang me. I knew I would not have been willing to lessen Kagig's chances by shooting any of them if they had decided to take Ephraim's part. But the politician in the man was uppermost and he did not force the issue.

"All right, effendi — oh, all right!" he answered, trying to laugh the matter off.

"Explain to them, then!"

I made him do it half a dozen times, for once we were on our way along the precipitous sides of the hills the only control I should have would be force of example, aided to some extent by the sort of primitive signals that pass muster even in a kindergarten. If they should talk Turkish to me slowly I might understand a little here and there, but to speak it myself was quite another matter; and in common with most of their countrymen, though they understood Turkish perfectly and all that went with it, they would rather eat dirt than foul their months with the language of the hated conqueror.

But, once explained, the plan was as obvious as the risk

entailed, and they approved the one as swiftly as they despised the other. The Kurds below were not oblivious to the risk of reprisals from the hills, and we spent five minutes picking out the men posted to keep watch, making careful note of their positions. At the point where we decided to debouch on to the plain there were two sentries taking matters fairly easy, and I told off four men to go on ahead and attend to those as silently as might be.

Then we started — not close together, for the Kurds would certainly be looking out for an attack from the hills in force, and would not be expecting individuals — but one at a time, two Armenians leading, and the rest of them following me at intervals of more than fifty yards.

At the moment of starting I gave Ephraim another order, and within two hours owed my life and that of most of my men to his disobedience.

"You stay here with your handful, and don't budge except as Kagig moves his line! Few as you are, you can hold this flank safe if you stay firm."

He stayed firm until the last of my seventeen had disappeared around the corner of the cliff; and five minutes later I caught sight of him through the glasses, leading his following at top speed downward along a spur toward the plain. The Kurds on the lookout saw him too and, concentrating their attention on him, did not notice us when we dodged at long intervals in full sunlight across the face of a white rock.

There was little leading needed; rather, restraining, and no means of doing it. Instead of keeping the formation in which we started off, those in the rear began to overtake the men in front and, rather than disobey the order to keep wide intervals, to extend down the face of the hill, so that within fifteen minutes we were in wide-spaced skirmishing order. Then, instead of keeping along the hills, as I had intended, until we were well to the rear of the Kurdish firing-line, they turned half-left too soon, and headed in diagonal bee line toward the horses, those who had begun by leading being last now, and the last men first. Being shorter-winded than the rest of them and more tired to begin with, that arrangement soon left me a long way in the rear, dodging and crawling laboriously and stopping every now and then to watch the development of the battle. There was little to see but the flash of rifles; and they explained nothing more than that the Kurds were forcing their way very close to our center and left wing.

Not all the fighting had been done that day under organized leadership. I stumbled at one place and fell over the dead bodies of a Kurd and an Armenian, locked in a strangle-hold. That Kurd must have been bold enough to go pillaging miles in advance of his friends, for the two had been dead for hours. But the mutual hatred had not died off their faces, and they lay side by side clutching each other's throats as if passion had continued after death.

The sight of Ephraim and his party hurrying across their front toward Kagig's weak left wing had evidently convinced the Kurds that no more danger need be expected from their own left. There can have been no other possible reason why we were unobserved, for the recklessness of my contingent grew as they advanced closer to the horses, and from the rear I saw them brain one outpost with a rock and rush in and knife another with as little regard for concealment as if these two had been the only Kurds within eagle's view. Yet they were unseen by the enemy, and five minutes later we all gathered in the shelter of a semicircle of loose rocks, to regain wind for the final effort.

"Korkakma!" I panted, using about ten per cent. of my Turkish vocabulary, and they laughed so loud that I cursed them for a bunch of fools. But the man nearest me chose to illustrate his feeling for Turks further by taking the corner of his jacket between thumb and finger and going through the motions of squeezing off an insect — the last, most expressive gesture of contempt.

The horses were within three hundred yards of us. On rising ground between us and the Kurdish firing-line was a little group of Turkish officers, and to our right beyond the horses was miscellaneous baggage under the guard of Kurds, of whom more than half were wounded. I could see an obviously Greek doctor bandaging a man seated on an empty ammunition box.

But our chief danger was from the mounted scoundrels who were so busy murdering women and children and wounded men half a mile away to the rear. They had come along working the covert like hunters of vermin, driving lances into every possible lurking place and no doubt skewering their own wounded on occasion, for which Armenians would afterward be blamed. We could hear them chorusing with glee whenever a lance found a victim, or when a dozen of them gave chase to some panic-stricken woman in wild flight. Through the glasses I could see two Turkish officers with them, in addition to their own nondescript "tin-plate men"; and if officers or men should get sight of us it was easy to imagine what our fate would be.

That thought, and knowledge that Gloria Vanderman and Will and Fred were engaged in an almost equally desperate venture within a mile of me (evidenced by dozens of wild bullets screaming through the air) suggested the idea of taking a longer chance than any I had thought of yet. A moment's consideration brought conviction that the effort would be worth the risk. Yet I had no way of communicating with my men!

I pointed to the Turkish officers clustered together watching the effort of their firing-line. From where we lay to the horses would be three hundred yards; from the horses to those officers would be about two hundred and fifty yards farther at an angle of something like forty degrees. Counting their orderlies and hangers-on we outnumbered that party by two to one; and "the fish starts stinking from the head" as the proverb says. With the head gone, the whole Kurdish firing-line would begin to be useless.

I tried my stammering Turkish, but the men were in no mood to be patient with efforts in that loathly tongue. None of them knew a word in English. I tried French — Italian — smattering Arabic — but they only shook their heads, and began to think nervousness was driving me out of hand. One of them laid a soothing hand on my shoulder, and repeated what sounded like a prayer.

To lose the confidence of one's men under such circumstances at that stage of the game was too much. I grew really rattled, and at random, as a desperate man will I stammered off what I wanted to say in the foreign tongue that I knew best, regardless of the fact that Armenians are not black men, and that there is not even a trace of connection between their language and anything current in Africa. Zanzibar and Armenia are as far apart as Australia and Japan, with about as much culture in common.

To my amazement a man answered in fluent Kiswahili! He had traded for skins in some barbarous district near the shore of Victoria Nyanza, and knew half a dozen Bantu languages. In a minute after that we had the plan well understood and truly laid; and, what was better, they had ceased to believe me a victim of nerves — a fact that gave me back the nerve that had been perilously close to vanishing.

We paid no more attention to the firing-line, nor to the mounted Kurds who were drawing the coverts nearer and nearer to us. It was understood that we were to sacrifice ourselves for our friends, and do the utmost damage possible before being overwhelmed. We shook hands solemnly. Two or three men embraced each other. The five who by common consent were reckoned the best rifle shots lay down side by side with me among the rocks, and the remainder began crawling out one by one on their stomachs toward the horses, with instructions to take wide open order as quickly as possible, with the idea of making the Kurds believe our numbers were greater than they really were.

When I judged they were half-way toward the horses we six opened fire on the Turkish officers. And every single one of us missed! At the sound of our volley the devoted horse-thieves rose to their feet and rushed on the horse-guards, forgetting to fire on them from sheer excitement, and as a matter of fact one of them was shot dead by a horse-guard before the rest remembered they had deadly weapons of their own.

I remedied the first outrageous error to a slight extent by killing the Turkish colonel's orderly, missing the commander himself by almost a yard. My five men all missed with their second shots, and then it was too late to pull off the complete coup we had dared to hope for. The entire staff took cover, and started a veritable hail of fire with their repeating pistols, all aimed at us, and aimed as wildly as our own shots had been.

Meanwhile the mounted Kurds at the rear had heard the firing and were coming on full pelt, yelling like red Indians.

I could see, in the moment I snatched for a hurried glance in that direction, that the purpose of cutting loose and stampeding the horses was being accomplished; but even that comparatively simple task required time, and as the Kurds galloped nearer, the horses grew as nervous as the men who sought to loose them.

But conjecture and all caution were useless to us six bent on attacking the colonel and his staff. We crawled out of cover and advanced, stopping to fire one or two shots and then scrambling closer, giving away our own paucity of numbers, but increasing the chance of doing damage with each yard gained. And our recklessness had the additional advantage of making the staff reckless too. The colonel kept in close hiding, but the rest of them began dodging from place to place in an effort to outflank us from both sides, and I saw four of them bowled over within a minute. Then the remainder lay low again, and we resumed the offensive.

The next thing I remember was hearing a wild yell as our party seized a horse apiece and galloped off in front of the oncoming Kurds — straight toward Kagig's firing-line. That, and the yelling of the horsemen in pursuit drew the attention of the riflemen attacking Kagig to the fact that most of their horses were running loose and that there was imminent danger to their own rear. I only had time to get a glimpse of them breaking back, for the Turkish colonel got my range and sent a bullet ripping down the length of the back of my shooting jacket. That commenced a duel — he against me — each missing as disgracefully as if we were both beginners at the game of life or death, and I at any rate too absorbed to be aware of anything but my own plight and of oceans of unexplained noise to right and left. I knew there were galloping horses, and men yelling; but knowledge that the Turkish military rifle I was using must be wrongly sighted, and that my enemy had no such disadvantage, excluded every other thought.

I had used about half the cartridges in my bandolier when a Kurd's lance struck me a glancing blow on the back of the head. His horse collapsed on top of me, as some thundering warrior I did not see gave the stupendous finishing stroke to rider and beast at once.

There followed a period of semi-consciousness filled with enormous clamor, and upheavings, and what might have been earthquakes for lack of any other reasonable explanation, for I felt myself being dragged and shaken to and fro. Then, as the weight of the fallen horse was rolled aside there surged a tide of blissful relief that carried me over the border of oblivion.

When I recovered my senses I was astride of Rustum Khan's mare, with a leather thong around my shoulders and the Rajput's to keep me from falling. We were proceeding at an easy walk in front of a squadron of ragged-looking irregulars whom I did not recognize, toward the center of the position Kagig had held. Kagig's men were no longer in hiding, but standing about in groups; and presently I caught sight of Fred and Will and Kagig standing together, but not Gloria Vanderman. A cough immediately behind us made me turn my head. The Turkish colonel, who had fought the ridiculously futile duel with me, was coming along at the mare's tail with his hands tied behind him and a noose about his neck made fast to one of the saddle-rings.

"Much obliged, Rustum Khan!" I said by way of letting him know I was alive. "How did you get here?"

"Ha, sahib! Not going to die, then? That is good! I came because Colonel Lord Montdidier sahib sent me with a squadron of these mountain horsemen — fine horsemen they are — fit by the breath of Allah to draw steel at a Rajput's back!"

"He sent you to find me?"

"Ha, sahib. To rescue you alive if that were possible."

"How did he know where I was?"

"An Armenian by name of Ephraim came and said you had gone over to the Turks. Certain men he had with him corroborated, but three of his party kept silence. My lord sahib answered 'I have hunted, and camped, and fought beside that man — played and starved and feasted with him. No more than I myself would he go over to Turks. He must have seen an opportunity to make trouble behind the Turks' backs. Take your squadron and go find him, Rustum Khan!' And I, sahib, obeyed my lord bahadur's orders."

"Where is Lord Montdidier now?"

"Who knows, sahib. Wherever the greatest need at the

moment is."

"Tell me what has happened."

"You did well, sahib. The loosing of the horses and the shooting behind their backs put fear into the Kurds. They ceased pressing on our left wing. And I — watching from behind cover on the right wing — snatched that moment to outflank them, so that they ran pell-mell. Then I saw the mounted Kurds charging up from the rear, and guessed at once where you were, sahib. The Kurds were extended, and my men in close order, so I charged and had all the best of it, arriving by God's favor in the nick of time for you, sahib. Then I took this colonel prisoner. Only once in my life have I seen a greater pile than his of empty cartridge cases beside one man. That was the pile beside you, sahib! How many men did you kill, and he kill? And who buried them?"

"Where is Miss Vanderman?" I asked, turning the subject.

"God knows! What do I know of women? Only I know this: that there is a gypsy woman bred by Satan out of sin itself, who will make things hot for any second filly in this string! Woe and a woman are one!"

Not caring to listen to the Indian's opinions of the other sex any more than he would have welcomed mine about the ladies of his own land, I made out my injuries were worse than was the case, and groaned a little, and grew silent.

So we rode without further conversation up to where Fred and Will were standing with Kagig, and as I tumbled off into Fred's arms I was greeted with a chorus of welcome that included Gloria's voice.

"That's what I call using your bean!" she laughed, in the slangy way she had whenever Will had the chance to corrupt her Boston manners.

"It feels baked," I said. "I used it to stop a Kurd's lance with. Hullo! What's the matter with you?"

"I stopped a bullet with my forearm!"

She was sitting in a sort of improvised chair between two dwarfed tree-trunks, and if ever I saw a proud young woman that was she. She wore the bloody bandage like a prize diploma.

"And I've seen your friend Monty, and he's better than the accounts of him!"

I glanced at Will, alert for a sign of jealousy.

"Monty is the one best bet!" he said. And his eyes were generous and level, as a man's who tells the whole truth.

Chapter Fourteen

"Rajput, I shall hang you if you make more trouble!"

"LO, THIS IS THE MAN —"

(Psalm 52)

Choose, ye forefathers of tomorrow, choose!
These easy ways there be
Uncluttered by the wrongs each other bears,
And warmly we shall walk who can not see
How thin some other fellow's garment wears,
Nor need to notice whose.

Choose, ye stock-owners in tomorrow, choose!
The road these others tread
Is littered deep with jetsam and the bones
Of their dishonored dead.
What altruism for defeat atones?
Have ye not much to lose?

Choose, ye inheritors of ages, choose!
What owe ye to the past?
The burly men who Magna Charta wrung
From tyranny entrenched would stand aghast
To see the ripples from that stone they flung,
They, too, had selfish views.

Choose, ye investors in the future, choose!
Ye need pick cautious odds;
Tomorrow's fruit is seeded down today,
And unwise purpose like the unknown gods
Tempts on a wasteful way.
"Ware well what guide ye use!

*W*e went and bivouacked by the brawling Jihun under a roof of thatch, whose walls were represented by more or less upright wooden posts and debris; for Kagig would not permit anything to stand even for an hour that Turks could come and fortify. None of us believed that the repulse of that handful of Kurdish plunderers and the capture of a Turkish colonel would be the end of hostilities — rather the beginning.

Kagig, when Gloria asked him what he proposed to do with Rustum Khan's prisoner, smiled cynically and ordered him searched by two of the Zeitoonli standing guard. Rustum Khan was standing just out of low ear-shot absorbed in contemplation of the lie of the country. I noticed that Fred began to look nervous, but he did not say anything. Will was too busy fussing with Gloria's wound, making a new bandage for it and going through the quite unnecessary motions of keeping up her spirits, to observe any other phenomena. An Armenian woman named Anna, who had attached herself to Gloria because, she said, her husband and children had been killed and she might as well serve as weep, sat watching the two of them with quiet amusement.

The Turk offered no further objection than a shrug of his fatalist shoulders and a muttered remark about Ermenie and bandits. Even when the mountaineers laughed at the chink of stolen money in all his pockets he did not exhibit a trace of shame. They shook him, and pawed him, and poured out gold in little heaps on the ground (out of the magnanimity of his official heart he had doubtless left all silver coin for his hamidieh to pouch); but Kagig only had eyes for the papers they pulled out of his inner pocket and tossed away. He pounced on them.

"Hah!" he laughed. "There! Did I tell you? These are his orders — signed by a governor's secretary — countersigned by the governor himself — to 'set forth with his troops and rescue Armenians in the Zeitoon district.' Rescue them! Have you seen? Did you observe his noble rescue work? Here — see the orders for yourselves! Observe how the Stamboulis propose to prove their innocence after the event!"

Since they were written in Turkish they were of no conceivable use to any one but Fred and Rustum Khan. Fred glanced

over them, and shouted to Rustum Khan to come and look.
That was a mistake, for it called the Rajput's attention to what
had been happening to his prisoner. He came striding toward
us with his black beard bristling and eyes blazing with anger.

"Who searched him?" he demanded.

"He was searched by my order," Kagig answered in the calm
level voice that in a man of such spirit was prophetic of
explosion.

"Who gave thee leave to order him searched, Armenian?"

"I left you his money," Kagig answered with biting scorn,
pointing to the little heaps of gold coin on the ground.

I had no means of knowing what peaks of friction had
already been attained between the two, and it was not likely
that I should instantly choose sides against the man who
within the hour had saved my life at peril of his own. But
Will saw matters in another light, and Fred began humming
through his nose. Will left Gloria and walked straight up to
Rustum Khan. He had managed to shave himself with cold
Jihun water and some laundry soap, and his clean jaw suggested standards set up and sworn to since ever they gave the
name of Yankee to men possessed by certain high ideals.

"Kagig needs no leave from any one to order prisoners
searched!" he said, shaping each word distinctly.

Rustum Khan spluttered, and kicked at a heap of coin.

"Perhaps you have bargained for your share of all loot? I
have heard that in America men —"

"Rajput!" said Kagig, looking down on him from slightly
higher ground, "I will hang you if you make more trouble!"

At that I interfered. I was not the only one in Rustum
Khan's debt; it was likely his brilliant effort at the critical
moment had saved our whole fighting line. Besides, I saw the
Turk grinning to himself with satisfaction at the rift in our
good will.

"Suppose we refer this dispute to Monty," I proposed,
reasoning that if it should ever get as far as Monty, tempers
would have died away meanwhile. Not that Monty could not
have handled the problem, tempers and all.

"I refer no points of honor," growled the Rajput. "I have
been insulted."

"Rot!" exclaimed Fred, getting to his feet. When his usually neat beard has not been trimmed for a day or two he looks more truculent than he really is. "I've been listening. The insolence was on the other side."

"Do you deny Kagig's right to question prisoners?" I asked, thinking I saw a way out of the mess.

"Can I not question him?" Rustum Khan turned on me with a gesture that made it clear he held me to no friendship on account of service rendered.

He strode toward his prisoner, with heaven knows what notion in his head, but Fred interposed himself. The likeliest thing at that moment was a blow by one or the other that would have banished any chance of a returning reign of reason. Rustum Khan turned his back to the Turk and thrust out his chest toward Fred as if daring him to strike. Even the kites seemed to expect bloodshed and circled nearer.

It was Gloria who cut the Gordian knot. It was her un-wounded hand, not Fred's, that touched the Rangar's breast.

"Rustum Khan," she said, "I think better of you than to believe you would take advantage of our ignorance. You're a soldier. We are only civilians trying to help a tortured nation. We know nothing of Rajput customs. Won't you go to Lord Montdidier and tell him about it, and ask him to decide? We'll all obey Monty, you know."

Rustum Khan looked down at her bandaged wrist, and then into violet eyes that were not in the least degree afraid of him but only looking diligently for the honor he so boasted.

"Who can refuse a beautiful young woman?" he said, beginning to melt. But he refused to meet her eyes again, or even to acknowledge our existence.

"I give you the prisoner!" He made her a motion of arrogant extravagance with his right hand as if performing the act of transfer. Then he turned on his heel with a little simultaneous mock salute, and striding to his bay mare, mounted and rode away.

Kagig took over the prisoner at once without comment and began to question him under a tree twenty yards away, paying no attention to the riflemen who matched one an-other, laughing, for the plundered money. We four went back to the shelter of the thatch roof, for the plan was to remain behind with the company of Zeitoonli whom Kagig had placed carefully at vantage points, and give stragglers a chance to save themselves before we resumed the journey to Zeitoon.

Naturally enough, Rustum Khan and his fiery unreason was the subject we discussed, and Fred laid law down as to how he should be dealt with whenever the chance should come to bring him to book. But Rustum Khan was a bagatelle compared to what was coming, if we had only known it. While we talked I saw Gregor Jhaere, the ataman of gypsies, ride down the track on a brown mule and dismount within ten yards of Kagig. He hobbled his mule, and went and sat close by Kagig and the Turk, engaging in a three-cornered talk with them. Kagig seemed to have expected him, for there was no sign of greeting or surprise.

There was nothing disturbing about Gregor's arrival on the scene; he was evidently helping Kagig to cross-examine the Turk and check up facts. Within their limits gypsies are about the best spies obtainable because of their ability to take advantage of credulity and their own immeasurable unbelief in protest or appearances. It was the individual who followed Gregor at a distance, and dismounted from a gray stallion quite a long way off in order not to draw attention to herself, who made my blood turn cold. I caught sight of Maga Jhaere first because the others had their backs toward her. Then the expression of my face brought Fred to his feet. By that time Magi had vanished out of view unaware that any one had seen her, creeping like a pantheress from rock to rock.

"What's the matter?" Fred demanded, sitting down again, ill-tempered with himself for being startled.

"Maga Jhaere!"

"How exciting!" said Gloria. "I'm crazy to meet her."

But Will looked less excited and more anxious than I had ever seen him, and we all three laughed.

"All right!" he said. "I tell you it's no joke. That woman believes she's got her hooks in."

We tried to go on talking naturally, but lapsed into uncomfortable silence as the minutes dragged by and no Maga put in her appearance. Fred began humming through his nose again in that ridiculous way that he thinks seems unconcerned, but that makes his best friends yearn to smite him hip and thigh.

"I guess you were mistaken," Will said at last, spreading out his shoulders with relief at the mere suggestion. But I was facing the direction of Zeitoon, as he was not, and again the expression of my face betrayed the facts.

There were two large stones leaning together, with a small triangular gap between them, less than thirty feet from where we sat. In that gap I could see a pair of eyes, and nothing else. They had almost exactly the expression of a panther's that is stalking, not its quarry, but its mortal foe. In spite of having seen Maga approaching, I would have believed them an animal's eyes, only that from experience I knew an animal's eyes betray fear and anger without reason, whereas these blazed with the desperate reasoning that holds fear in contempt. Panthers can hate, be afraid, sweep fear aside with anger, and plan painstakingly for murderous attack; but it is only behind human eyes that one may recognize the murder — purpose based on argument.

"I see her," I said. "I suspect she's got a pistol, and —"

I had not known until that moment that the short hair was standing up the back of my head, but I felt it go down with a creepy cold chill as I spoke. Then once more it rose. Knowing she was seen and recognized, Maga got to her feet and stood on the larger of the two stones, looking down on us. Her hands were on her hips, and I could see no weapon, but her lips moved in voiceless imprecation.

"Are you Maga Jhaere?" asked Gloria, first of us all to recover some measure of self-command.

Maga nodded. She was barefooted, clothed only in bodice and leather jacket and a rather short ochre-colored skirt that blew in the gaining wind and showed the outline of her lithe young figure. Her long black hair billowed and galloped in the wind behind her.

"I am Maga Jhaere," she said slowly, addressing Gloria. "Who are you?"

"My name is Gloria Vanderman."

"And that man beside you — who is he?"

Gloria did not answer. Will looked more embarrassed than the devil caught in daylight, and Fred recovered his mental equilibrium sufficiently to chuckle.

"Is he your husband?"

"No."

"Then what you want with 'im?"

No one said a word. Only, Fred made a movement with his hand behind him that Maga noticed and spurned with a toss of her chin.

"You coming to Zeitoon?"

Gloria nodded. Glancing over toward Kagig I saw that he was aware of Maga and was watching her out of the corner of his eye while he talked with Gregor and the Turk. They were both getting angry with the Turk and using gestures suggestive of impending agony by way of emphasis. The Turk was growing fidgety.

Maga spread her arms out as if she were embracing all the universe and called it hers.

"Then — if you ar-re coming to Zeitoon — you choose first a 'usband. There are — many 'usbands. Some 'ave lost a wife — some 'ave sick wife — some not yet never 'ad no wife. Plenty Armenians — also two other men there — but you let that one — Will — alone! Choose a 'usband — marry, 'im — then you come to Zeitoon! If you come without a 'usband — I will keel you — do you understand?"

"Now then, America!" grinned Fred in a stage aside that Maga could hear as clearly as if it had been intended for her. "Let's see the eagle scream for liberty!"

"Eagle scream?" said Maga, almost screaming herself. "What you know about eagles? You ol' fool! That man Will is thinking you ar-re 'is frien'. You ar-re not 'is frien'! Let 'im come with me, an' I will show 'im what ar-re eagles — what is freedom — what is knowledge — what is life! I know. You ol' fool, you not know! You ol' fool, you marry that woman — then you can bring 'er to Zeitoon an' she is safe! Otherwise —"

She reached in the bosom of her blouse and drew out, not the mother-o'-pearl-plated pistol that I feared, but a knife with an eighteen-inch blade of glittering steel. Instantly Fred covered her with his own repeater, but she laughed in his face.

"You ol' fool, you ar-re afraid to shoot me!"

If she meant that Fred would feel squeamish about shooting before she hurled the knife, then she was certainly right. But she knew better than to make one preliminary motion.

And Kagig knew better than to permit further pleasantries. I saw him whisper to Gregor, and the gypsy ataman started on hands and knees to creep round behind her. But Maga's eyes were practiced like those of all other wild creatures in detecting movement behind her as well as in front. She spat, and gave vent to a final ultimatum.

"You 'ave 'eard. I said — you let that man Will Yerr-kees alone! An' don't you dare come to Zeitoon without a 'usband!"

Then she turned and dodged Gregor, and ran for her gray stallion — mounted the savage brute with a leap from six feet away, and rode like the wind toward the gut of the pass that shut off Zeitoon from our view. A minute later a shell from a small-bore cannon screamed overhead, and burst a hundred yards beyond us on a sheet of rock.

"Not bad for a ranging shot!" said Fred, suddenly as self-possessed as if the world never held such a thing as an untamed woman.

"Observe, you sportsmen all!" Kagig exclaimed, getting to his feet. "The Turkish nobility are proceeding to rescue poor Armenians. Behold, their charity comes even from the cannon's mouth! It is time to go now, lest it overtake us! No cannon can come in sight of Zeitoon. Follow me."

With his usual sudden oblivion of everything but the main objective Kagig mounted and rode away, followed by Gregor in charge of the prisoner, and by a squadron or so of mounted Zeitoonli who attempted no formation but came cantering as each detachment realized that their leader was on the move. We found ourselves last, without an armed man between us and the enemy, although without a doubt there were still dozens of fugitive poor wretches who had not had the courage or perhaps the strength to overtake us yet.

Kagig had had the forethought to leave comparatively fresh mules for us to ride, and there was not any particular reason for hurry. Will went ahead, with Gloria and Anna beside him on one mule — Gloria laughing him out of countenance because of his nervousness on her account, but he insistent on the danger in case of repeated gun-fire. Fred rode slowly beside me in the rear, for we still hoped to encourage a few stray fugitives to come out of their hiding holes and follow us to safety.

A second cannon shot, not nearly so well aimed as the first had been, went screaming over toward our left and landed without bursting among low bushes. A third and a fourth followed it, and the last one did explode. That was plainly too much for some one who had dodged into hiding when the second shot fell; we saw him come rushing out from cover like a lunatic, unconscious of direction and only intent on shielding the top of his head with his hands.

"Is the poor devil hurt?" I said, wondering. But Fred broke into a roar of laughter; and he is not a heartless man — merely gifted more than usual with the hunter's eye that recognizes sex and species of birds and animals at long range. I can see farther than Fred can, but at recognizing details swiftly I am a blind bat compared to him.

"The martyred biped!" he laughed. "Peter Measel by the God of happenings!"

We rode over toward him, and Peter it was, running with his eyes shut. He screamed when we stopped him, and sobbed instead of talking when we pulled him in between our mules and offered him two stirrup leathers to hold. He seemed to think that standing between the mules would protect him from the artillery fire, and as we were not in any hurry we took advantage of that delusion to let him recover a modicum of nerve.

And the moment that began to happen he was the same sweet Peter Measel with the same assurance of every other body's wickedness and his own divinity, only with something new in his young life to add poignancy.

"What were you doing there?" demanded Fred, as we got him to towing along between us at last.

"I was looking for her."

"For whom?"

"For Maga Jhaere."

Fred allowed his ribs to shake in silent laughter that annoyed the mule, and we had to catch Measel all over again because the beast's crude objections filled the martyred biped full of the desire to run.

"Somebody must save that girl!" he panted. "And who else can do it? Who else is there?"

"There's only you!" Fred agreed, choking down his mirth.

"I'm glad you agree with me. At least you have that much blessedness, Mr. Fred. D'you know that girl was willing to be a murderess? Yes! She tried to murder Rustum Khan. Rustum Khan ought to be hanged, for he is a villain — a black villain! But she must not have blood on her hands — no, no!"

"Why didn't she murder him?" demanded Fred. "Qualms at the last moment?"

"No. I'm sorry to say no. She has no Godlikeness yet. But that will come. She will repent. I shall see to that. It was I who prevented her, and she all but murdered me! She would have murdered me, but Kagig held her wrist; and to punish her he gave an order that I should preach to her morning, afternoon, and evening — three times a day. So I had my opportunity. There was a guard of gypsy women set to see that she obeyed."

"Continue," said Fred. "What happened?"

"She broke away, and came down to see the fighting."

"Why did you follow her? Weren't you afraid?"

"Oh, Mr. Fred, if you only knew! Yet I felt impelled to find her. I could not trust her out of sight."

"Why not? She seems fairly well able to look after herself."

"Oh, I can not allow wickedness. I must make it to cease! It entered my head that she intended to find Kagig!"

"Well? Why not?"

"Oh, Mr. Fred — tell me! You may know — you perhaps as well as any one, for you are such an ungodly man! What are her relations with Kagig? Does he — is he — is there wickedness between them?"

"Dashed if I know. She's a gypsy. He's a fine half-savage. Why should it concern you?"

"Oh, I could not endure it! It would break my heart to believe it!"

"Then why think about it?"

"How can I help it? I love her! Oh, I love her, Mr. Fred! I never loved a woman in all my life before. It would break my heart if she were to be betrayed into open sin by Kagig! Oh, what shall I do? What shall I do? I love her! What shall I do?"

"Do?" said Fred, looking forward in imagination to new worlds of humor, "why — make love, if you love her! Make hot love and strong!"

"Will you help me, Mr. Fred?" the biped stammered. "You see, she's rather wild — a little unconventional — and I've never made love even to a sempstress. Will you help me?"

"Certainly!" Fred chuckled. "Certainly. I'll guarantee to marry her to you if you'll dig up the courage. Have you a ring?"

Peter Measel produced a near-gold ring with a smirk almost of recklessness, a plain gold ring whose worn appearance called to mind the finger taken from a dead Kurd's cartridge pouch. It may be that Measel bought it, but neither Fred nor I spoke to him again, for half an hour.

Chapter Fifteen
"Scenery to burst the heart!"

THE REBEL'S HYMN
The seeds that swell within enwrapping mould,
Gray buds that color faintly in the northing sun,
Deep roots that lengthen after winter's rest,
The flutter of year's youth in April's breast
As young leaves in the warming hour unfold —
These and my heart are one!

Go dam the river-course with carted earth;
Or bind with iron bands that riven stone
That century on century has slept
Until into its heart a tendril crept,
And in the quiet majesty of birth
New nature broke into her own!
Or bid the sun stand still! Or fashion wings
To herd the heaven's stars and make them be
Subservient to will and rule and whim!
Or rein the winds, and still the ocean's hymn!
More surely ye shall manage all these things
Than chain the Life in me!

Great mountains shedding the reluctant snow,
Vision of the finish of the thing begun,
Spirit of the beauty of the torrent's song,
Unconquerable peal of carillon,
And secrets that in conquest overflow —
These and my heart are one!

*Y*et another night we were destined to spend on the Zeitoon road, for we had not the heart to leave behind us the stragglers who balked fainting in the gut of the pass. Some were long past the stage where anything less than threats could make impression on them, and only able to go forward in a dull dream at the best. But there were numbers of both men and women unexpectedly capable of extremes of heroism, who took the burden of misery upon themselves and exhibited high spirits based on no evident excuse. Nothing could overwhelm those, nothing discourage them.

"To Zeitoon!" somebody shouted, as if that were the very war-cry of the saints of God. Then in a splendid bass voice he began to sing a hymn, and some women joined him. So Fred Oakes fell to his old accustomed task, and played them marching accompaniments on his concertina until his fingers ached and even he, the enthusiast, loathed the thing's bray. In one way and another a little of the pall of misery was lifted.

Kagig sent us down bread and yogurt at nightfall, so that those who had lived thus far did not die of hunger. Women brought the food on their heads in earthen crocks — splendid, good-looking women with fearless eyes, who bore the heavy loads as easily as their mountain menfolk carried rifles. They did not stay to gossip, for we had no news but the stale old story of murder and plunder; and their news was short and to the point.

"Come along to Zeitoon!" was the burden of it, carried with a singsong laugh. "Zeitoon is ready for anything!"

Before we had finished eating, each two of them gathered up a poor wretch from our helpless crowd and strode away into the mountains with a heavier load than that they brought.

"Come along to Zeitoon!" they called back to us. But even Fred's concertina, and the hymns of the handful who were not yet utterly spent, failed to get them moving before dawn.

We did not spend the night unguarded, although no armed men lay between us and the enemy. We could hear the Kurds shouting now and then, and once, when I climbed a high rock, I caught sight of the glow of their bivouac fires. Imagination conjured up the shrieks of tortured victims, for we had all seen enough of late to know what would happen to any luckless straggler they might have caught and brought to make sport by the fires. But there was no imagination about the calls of Kagig's men, posted above us on invisible dark crags and ledges to guard against surprise. We slept in comfortable consciousness that a sleepless watch was being kept — until fleas came out of the ground by battalions, divisions and army corps, making rest impossible.

But even the flea season was a matter of indifference to the hapless folk who lay around us, and although we fussed and railed we could not persuade them to go forward before dawn broke. Then, though, they struggled to their feet and started without argument. But an hour after the start we reached the secret of the safety of Zeitoon, without which not even the valor of its defenders could have withstood the overwhelming numbers of the Turks for all those scores of years; and there was new delay.

The gut of the pass rose toward Zeitoon at a sharp incline — a ramp of slippery wet clay, half a mile long, reaching across from buttress to buttress of the impregnable hills. It was more than a ridden mule could do to keep its feet on the slope, and we had to dismount. It was almost as much as we ourselves could do to make progress with the aid of sticks, and we knew at last what Kagig had meant by his boast that nothing on wheels could approach his mountain home. The poor wretches who had struggled so far with us simply gave up hope and sat down, proposing to die there. The martyred biped copied them, except that they were dry-eyed and he shed tears. "To think that I should come to this — that I should come to this!" he sobbed. Yet the fool must have come down by that route, and have gone up that way once.

We should have been in a quandary but for the sound of axes ringing in the mountain forest on our left — a dense dark growth of pine and other evergreens commencing about a hundred feet above the naked rock that formed the northerly side of the gorge. Where there were axes at work there was in all likelihood a road that men could march along, and our refugees sat down to let us do the prospecting.

"It would puzzle Napoleon to bring cannon over this approach, and the Turks don't breed Napoleons nowadays!" Fred shouted cheerily. "Give me a hundred good men and I'll hold this pass forever! Wait here while I scout for a way round."

He tried first along the lower edge of the line of timber, encouraged by ringing axes, falling trees, and men shouting in the distance.

"It looks as if there once had been a road here," he shouted down to us, "but nothing less than fire would clear it now, and everything is sopping wet. I never saw such a tangle of roots and rocks. A dog couldn't get thought!"

Will volunteered to cross to the right-hand side and hunt over there for a practicable path. Gloria stayed beside me, and I had my first opportunity to talk with her alone. She was very pale from the effects of the wound in her wrist, which was painful enough to draw her young face and make her eyes burn feverishly. Even so, one realized that as an old woman she would still be beautiful.

I watched the eagles for a minute or two, wondering what to say to her, and she did not seem to object to silence, so that I forced an opening at last as clumsily as Peter Measel might have done it.

"What is it about Will that makes all women love him?" I asked her.

"Oh, do they all love him?"

"Looks like it!" said I.

She still wore the bandolier they had stripped from the man with the bandaged feet, although Will had relieved her of the rifle's weight. To the bottom of the bandolier she had tied the little bag of odds and ends without which few western women will venture a mile from home. Opening that she produced a small round mirror about twice the size of a dollar piece, and offered it to me with a smile that disarmed the rebuke.

"Perhaps it's his looks," she suggested.

I took the mirror and studied what I saw in it. In spite of a cracking headache due to that and the gaining sun (for I had lost my hat when the Kurd rode me down with his lance) the episode of Rustum Khan carrying me back out of death's door on his bay mare had not lingered in memory. There had been too much else to think about. Now for the first time I realized how near that lance-point must have come to finishing the chapter for me. I had washed in the Jihun when we bivouacked, but had not shaved; later on, my scalp had bled anew, so that in addition to unruly hair tousled and matted with dry blood I had a week-old beard to help make me look like a graveyard ghoul.

"I beg pardon!" I said simply, handing her the mirror back.

At that she was seized with regret for the unkindness, and utterly forgot that I had blundered like a bullock into the sacred sanctuary of her newborn relationship to Will.

"Oh, I don't know which of you is best!" she said, taking my hand with her unbandaged one. "You are great unselfish splendid men. Will has told me all about you! The way you have always stuck to your friend Monty through thick and thin — and the way you are following him now to help these tortured people — oh, I know what you are — Will has told me, and I'm proud —"

The embarrassment of being told that sort of thing by a young and very lovely woman, when newly conscious of dirt and blood and half-inch-long red whiskers, was apparently not sufficient for the mirth of the exacting gods of those romantic hills. There came interruption in the form of a too-familiar voice.

"Oh, that's all right, you two! Make the most of it! Spoon all you want to! My girl's in the clutches of an outlaw! Kiss her if you want to — I won't mind!"

I dropped her hand as if it were hot lead. As a matter of fact I had hardly been conscious of holding it.

"Oh, no, don't mind me!" continued the "martyred biped" in a tone combining sarcasm, envy and impudence.

"Shall I kill him?" I asked.

"No! no!" she said. "Don't be violent — don't —"

Peter Measel, whom we had inevitably utterly forgotten, was sitting up with his back propped against a stone and his legs stretched straight in front of him, enjoying the situation with all the curiosity of his unchastened mind. I hove a lump of clay at him, but missed, and the effort made my headache worse.

"If you think you can frighten me into silence you're mistaken!" he sneered, getting up and crawling behind the rock to protect himself. But it needed more than a rock to hide him from the fury that took hold of me and sent me in pursuit in spite of Gloria's remonstrance.

Viewed as revenge my accomplishment was pitiful, for I had to chase the poor specimen for several minutes, my headache growing worse at every stride, and he yelling for mercy like a cur-dog shown the whip, while the Armenians — women and little children as well as men — looked on with mild astonishment and Gloria objected volubly. He took to the clay slope at last in hope that his light weight would give him the advantage; and there at last I caught him, and clapped a big gob of clay in his mouth to stop his yelling.

Even viewed as punishment the achievement did not amount to much. I kicked him down the clay slope, and he was still blubbering and picking dirt out of his teeth when Will shouted that he had found a foot-track.

"Do you understand why you've been kicked?" I demanded.

"Yes. You're afraid I'll tell Mr. Yerkes!"

"Oh, leave him!" said Gloria. "I'm sorry you touched him. Let's go!"

"It was as much your fault as his, young woman!" snarled the biped, getting crabwise out of my reach. "You'll all be sorry for this before I'm through with you!"

I was sorry already, for I had had experience enough of the world to know that decency and manners are not taught to that sort of specimen in any other way than by letting him go the length of his disgraceful course. Carking self-contempt must be trusted to do the business for him in the end. Gloria was right in the first instance. I should have let him alone.

However, it was not possible to take his threat seriously, and more than any man I ever met he seemed to possess the knack of falling out of mind. One could forget him more swiftly than the birds forget a false alarm. I don't believe any of us thought of him again until that night in Zeitoon.

The path Will had discovered was hardly a foot wide in places, and mules could only work their way along by rubbing hair off their flanks against the rock wall that rose nearly sheer on the right hand. From the point of view of an invading army it was no approach at all, for one man with a rifle posted on any of the overhanging crags could have held it against a thousand until relieved. It was a mystery why Kagig, or some one else, had not left a man at the foot of the clay slope to tell us about this narrow causeway; but doubtless Kagig had plenty to think about.

He and most of his men had gone struggling up the clay slope, as we could tell by the state of the going. But they were old hands at it and knew the trick of the stuff. We had all our work cut out to shepherd our poor stragglers along the track Will found, and even the view of Zeitoon when we turned round the last bend and saw the place jeweled in the morning mist did not do much to increase the speed.

As Kagig had once promised us, it was "scenery to burst the heart!" Not even the Himalayas have anything more ruggedly beautiful to show, glistening in mauve and gold and opal, and enormous to the eye because the summits all look down from over blowing cloud-banks.

There were moss-grown lower slopes, and waterfalls plunging down wet ledges from the loins of rain-swept majesty; pine trees looming blue through a soft gray fog, and winds whispering to them, weeping to them, moving the mist back and forth again; shadows of clouds and eagles lower yet, moving silently on sunny slopes. And up above it all was snow-dazzling, pure white, shading off into the cold blue of infinity.

Men clad in goatskin coats peered down at us from time to time from crags that looked inaccessible, shouting now and then curt recognition before leaning again on a modern rifle to resume the ancient vigil of the mountaineer, which is beyond the understanding of the plains-man because it includes attention to all the falling water voices, and the whispering of heights and deeps.

We came on Zeitoon suddenly, rising out of a gorge that was filled with ice, or else a raging torrent, for six months of the year. Over against the place was a mountainside so exactly suggesting painted scenery that the senses refused to believe it real, until the roar and thunder of the Jihun tumbling among crags dinned into the ears that it was merely wonderful, and not untrue.

The one approach from the southward — that gorge up which we trudged — was overlooked all along its length by a hundred inaccessible fastnesses from which it seemed a hand-

ful of riflemen could have disputed that right of way forever.
The only other line of access that we could see was by a
wooden bridge flung from crag to crag three hundred feet
high across the Jihun; and the bridge was overlooked by
buildings and rocks from which a hail of lead could have
been made to sweep it at short range.

Zeitoon itself is a mountain, next neighbor to the Beirut
Dagh, not as high, nor as inaccessible; but high enough, and
inaccessible enough to give further pause to its would-be
conquerors. Not in anything resembling even rows, but in
lawless disorder from the base to the shoulder of the mountain, the stone and wooden houses go piling skyward, overlooking one another's roofs, and each with an unobstructed
view of endless distances. The picture was made infinitely
lovely by wisps of blown mist, like hair-lines penciled in the
violet air.

Distances were all foreshortened in that atmosphere, and
it was mid-afternoon before we came to a halt at last face to
face with blank wall. The track seemed to have been blocked
by half the mountain sitting down across it. We sat down to
rest in the shadow of the shoulder of an overhanging rock,
and after half an hour some one looked down on us, and
whistled shrilly. Kagig with a rifle across his knees looked
down from a height of a hundred and fifty feet, and laughed
like a man who sees the bitter humor of the end of shams.

"Welcome!" he shouted between his hands. And his voice
came echoing down at us from wall to wall of the gorge. Five
minutes later he sent a man to lead us around by a hidden
track that led upward, sometimes through other houses, and
very often over roofs, across ridiculously tiny yards, and in
between walls so closely set together that a mule could only
squeeze through by main force.

We stabled the mules in a shed the man showed us, and
after that Kagig received us four, and Anna, Gloria's self-constituted maid, in his own house. It was bare of nearly everything but sheer necessities, and he made no apology, for he
had good taste, and perfect manners if you allowed for the
grim necessity of being curt and the strain of long responsibility.

A small bench took the place of a table in the main large

room. There was a fireplace with a wide stone chimney at one end, and some stools, and also folded skins intended to be sat on, and shiny places on the wall where men in goatskin coats had leaned their backs.

Two or three of the gypsy women were hanging about outside, and one of the gypsies who had been with him in the room in the khan at Tarsus appeared to be filling the position of servitor. He brought us yogurt in earthenware bowls — extremely cool and good it was; and after we had done I saw him carry down a huge mess more of it to the house below us, where many of the stragglers we had brought along were quartered by Kagig's order.

"Where's Monty?" Fred demanded as soon as we entered the room.

"Presently!" Kagig answered — rather irritably I thought. He seemed to have adopted Monty as his own blood brother, and to resent all other claims on him.

The afternoon was short, for the shadow of the surrounding mountains shut us in. Somebody lighted a fire in the great open chimney-place, and as we sat around that to revel in the warmth that rests tired limbs better than sleep itself, Kagig strode out to attend to a million things — as the expression of his face testified.

Then in came Maga, through a window, with self-betrayal in manner and look of having been watching us ever since we entered. She went up to Will, who was squatted on folded skins by the chimney corner, and stood beside him, claiming him without a word. Her black hair hung down to her waist, and her bare feet, not cut or bruised like most of those that walk the hills unshod, shone golden in the firelight. I looked about for Peter Measel, expecting a scene, but he had taken himself off, perhaps in search of her.

She had eyes for nobody but Gloria, and no smile for any one. Gloria stared back at her, fascinated.

"You married?" she asked; and Gloria shook her head. "You 'eard me, what I said back below there!"

Gloria nodded.

"You sing?"

"Sometimes."

"You dance?"

"Oh, yes. I love it."

"Ah! You shall sing — you shall dance — against me! First you sing — then I sing. Then you dance — then I dance — tonight — you understan'? If I sing better as you sing — an' if I dance better as you dance — then I throw you over Zeitoon bridge, an' no one interfere! But if you sing better as I sing — an' if you dance better as I dance — then you shall make a servant of me; for I know you will be too big fool an' too chicken 'earted to keel me, as I would keel you! You understan'?"

It rather looked as if an issue would have to be forced there and then, but at that minute Gregor entered, and drove her out with an oath and terrific gesture, she not seeming particularly afraid of him, but willing to wait for the better chance she foresaw was coming. Gregor made no explanation or apology, but fastened down the leather window-curtain after her and threw more wood on the fire.

Then back came Kagig.

"Where the devil's Monty?" Fred demanded.

"Come!" was the only answer. And we all got up and followed him out into the chill night air, and down over three roofs to a long shed in which lights were burning. All the houses — on every side of us were ahum with life, and small wonder, for Zeitoon was harboring the refugees from all the district between there and Tarsus, to say nothing of fighting men who came in from the hills behind to lend a hand. But we were bent on seeing Monty at last, and had no patience for other matters.

However, it was only the prisoners he had led us out to see, and nothing more.

"Look, see!" he said, opening the heavy wooden door of the shed as an armed sentry made way for him. (Those armed men of Zeitoon did not salute one another, but preserved a stoic attitude that included recognition of the other fellow's right to independence, too.) "Look in there, and see, and tell me — do the Turks treat Armenian prisoners that way?"

We entered, and walked down the length of the dim interior, passing between dozens of prisoners lying comfortably enough on skins and blankets. As far as one could judge, they had been fed well, and they did not wear the look of neglect or ill-treatment. At the end, in a little pen all by himself, was the colonel whom Rustum Khan had made a present of to Gloria.

"What's the straw for?" Fred demanded.

"Ask him!" said Kagig. "He understands! If there should be treachery the straw will be set alight, and he shall know how pigs feel when they are roasted alive! Never fear — there will be no treachery!"

We followed him back to his own house, he urging us to make good note of the prisoners' condition, and to bear witness before the world to it afterward.

"The world does not know the difference between Armenians and Turks!" he complained again and again.

Once again we arranged ourselves about his open chimney-place, this time with Kagig on a foot-stool in the midst of us. Heat, weariness, and process of digestion were combining to make us drowsily comfortable, and I, for one, would have fallen asleep where I sat. But at last the long-awaited happened, and in came Monty striding like a Norman, dripping with dew, and clean from washing in the icy water of some mountain torrent.

"Oh, hello, Didums!" Fred remarked, as if they had parted about an hour ago. "You long-legged rascal, you look as if you'd been having the time of your life!"

"I have!" said Monty. And after a short swift stare at him Fred looked glum. Those two men understood each other as the clapper understands the bell.

Chapter Sixteen

"What care I for my belly, sahib, if you break my heart?"

"IT WAS VERY GOOD"

(Genesis 1:31)

I saw these shambles in my youth, and said
There is no God! No Pitiful presides
Over such obsequies as these. The end
Alike is darkness whether foe or friend,
Beast, man or flower the event abides.
There is no heaven for the hopeful dead —
No better haven than forgetful sod
That smothers limbs and mouth and ears and eyes,
And with those, love and permanence and strife
And vanity and laughter that they thought was life,
Making mere compost of the one who dies.
To whose advantage? Nay, there is no God!
But He, whose other name is Pitiful, was pleased
By melting gentleness whose measures broke
The ramps of ignorance and keeps of lust,
Tumbling alike folly and the fool to dust,
To teach me womanhood until there spoke
Still voices inspiration had released,
And I heard truly. All the voices said:
Out of departed yesterday is grown today;
Out of today tomorrow surely breaks;
Out of corruption the inspired awakes;
Out of existence earth-clouds roll away
And leave all living, for there are no dead!

*A*fter we had made room for Monty before the fire and some one had hung his wet jacket up to dry, we volleyed questions at him faster than he could answer. He sat still and let us finish, with fingers locked together over his crossed knee and, underneath the inevitable good humor, a rather puzzled air of wishing above all things to understand our point of view. Over and over again I have noticed that trait, although he always tried to cover it under an air of polite indifference and easy tolerance that was as opaque to a careful observer as Fred's attempts at cynicism.

In the end he answered the last question first.

"My agreement with Kagig?"

"Yes, tell them!" put in Kagig. "If I should, they would say I lied!"

"It's nothing to speak of," said Monty offhandedly. "It dawned on our friend here that I have had experience in some of the arts of war. I proposed to him that if he would take a force and go to find you, I would help him to the limit without further condition. That's all."

"All, you ass? Didums, I warned you at the time when you let them make you privy councilor that you couldn't ever feel free again to kick over traces! Dammit, man, you can be impeached by parliament!"

"Quite so, Fred. I propose that parliament shall have to do something at last about this state of affairs."

"You'll end up in an English jail, and God help you! — social position gone — milked of your last pound to foot the lawyers' bills — otherwise they'll hang you!"

"Let 'em hang me after I'm caught! I've promised. Remember what Byron did for Greece? I don't suppose his actual fighting amounted to very much, but he brought the case of Greece to the attention of the public. Public opinion did the rest, badly, I admit, but better badly and late than never. I'm in this scrimmage, Fred, until the last bell rings and they hoist my number."

"Fine!" exclaimed Gloria, jumping to her feet. "So am I in it to a finish!"

Monty smiled at her with understanding and approval.

"Almost my first duty, Miss Vanderman," he said kindly,

"will be to arrange that you can not possibly come to harm or be prejudiced by any course the rest of us may decide on."

"Quite so!" Will agreed with a grin, and Fred began chuckling like a schoolboy at a show.

"Nonsense!" she answered hotly. "I've come to harm already — see, I'm wounded — I've been fighting — I'm already prejudiced as you call it! If you're an outlaw, so am I!"

She flourished her bandaged wrist and looked like Joan of Arc about to summon men to sacrifice. But the argument ready on her lips was checked suddenly. The night was without wind, yet the outer door burst open exactly as if a sudden hurricane had struck it, and Maga entered with a lantern in her hand. She tried to kick the door shut again, but it closed on Peter Measel who had followed breathlessly, and she turned and banged his head with the bottom of the lantern until the glass shattered to pieces.

"That fool!" she shouted. "Oh, that fool!" Then she let him come in and close the door, giving him the broken lantern to hold, which he did very meekly, rubbing the crown of his head with the other hand; and she stood facing the lot of us with hands on her hips and a fine air of despising every one of us. But I noticed that she kept a cautious eye on Kagig, who in return paid very little attention to her.

"Fight?" she exclaimed, pointing at Gloria. "What does she know about fighting? If she can fight, — let her fight me! I stand ready — I wait for 'er! Give 'er a knife, an' I will fight 'er with my bare 'ands!"

Gloria turned pale and Will laid a hand on her shoulder, whispering something that brought the color back again.

"Maga!"

Kagig said that one word in a level voice, but the effect was greater than if he had pointed a pistol. The fire died from her eyes and she nodded at him simply. Then her eyes blazed again, although she looked away from Gloria toward a window. The leather blind was tied down at the corners by strips of twisted hide.

She began to jabber in the gypsy tongue — then changed her mind and spat it out in English for our joint benefit.

"All right. She is nothing to do with me, that woman, and she shall come to a rotten end, I know, an' that is enough.

But there is some one listening! Not a woman — not with spunk enough to be a woman! That dirty horse-pond drinking unshaven black bastard Rustum Khan is outside listening! You think 'e is busy at the fortifying? Then I tell you, No, 'e is not! 'E is outside listening!"

The surprising answer to that assertion was a heavy saber thrust between the window-frame and blind and descending on the thong. Next followed Rustum Khan's long boot. Then came the man himself with dew all over his upbrushed beard, returning the saber to its scabbard with an accompanying apologetic motion of the head.

"Aye, I was listening!" He spoke as one unashamed. "Umm Kulsum" (that was his fancy name for Maga) "spoke truth for once! I came from the fortifying, where all is finished that can be done tonight. I have been the rounds. I have inspected everything. I report all well. On my way hither I saw Umm Kulsum, with that jackal trotting at her heel —" he made a scornful gesture in the direction of Peter Measel, who winced perceptibly, at which Fred Oakes chuckled and nudged me "— and I followed Umm Kulsum, to observe what harm she might intend."

"Black pig!" remarked Maga, but Rustum Khan merely turned his splendid back a trifle more toward her. His color, allowing for the black beard, was hardly darker than hers.

"Why should I not listen, since my heart is in the matter? Lord sahib — Colonel sahib bahadur! — take back those words before it is too late! Undo the promise made to this Armenian! What is he to thee? Set me instead of thee, sahib! What am I? I have no wives, no lands any longer since the money-lenders closed their clutches on my eldest son, no hope, nor any fellowship with kings to lose! But I can fight, as thou knowest! Give me, sahib, to redeem thy promise, and go thou home to England!"

"Sit down, Rustum Khan!"

"But, sahib —"

"Sit down!" Monty repeated.

"I will not see thee sacrificed for this tribe of ragged people, Colonel sahib!"

Monty rose to his feet slowly. His face was an enigma. The Rajput stood at attention facing him and they met each other's eyes — East facing West — in such fashion that manhood seemed to fill the smoky room. Every one was silent. Even Maga held her breath. Monty strode toward Rustum Khan; the Rajput was the first to speak.

"Colonel sahib, I spoke wise words!"

It seemed to me that Monty looked very keenly at him before he answered.

"Have you had supper, Rustum Khan? You look to me feverish from overwork and lack of food."

"What care I for my belly, sahib, if you break my heart?" the Rajput answered. "Shall I live to see Turks fling thy carcass to the birds? I have offered my own body in place of thine. Am I without honor, that my offer is refused?"

Monty answered that in the Rajput tongue, and it sounded like the bass notes of an organ.

"Brother mine, it is not the custom of my race to send substitutes to keep such promises. That thou knowest, and none has reason to know better. If thy memories and honor urge thee to come the way I take, is there no room for two of us?"

"Aye, sahib!" said the Rajput huskily. "I said before, I am thy man. I come. I obey!"

"Obey, do you?" Monty laid both hands on the Rajput's shoulders, struck him knee against knee without warning and pressed him down into a squatting posture. "Then obey when I order you to sit!"

The Rajput laughed up at him as suddenly sweet-tempered as a child.

"None other could have done that and not fought me for it!" he said simply. "None other would have had the strength!" he added.

Monty ignored the pleasantry and turned to Maga, so surprising that young woman — that she gasped.

"Bring him food at once, please!"

"Me? I? I bring him food? I feed that black —"

"Yes!" snapped Kagig suddenly. "You, Maga!"

Maga's and Kagig's eyes met, and again he had his way with her instantly. Peter Measel, standing over by the door, looked wistful and sighed noisily.

"Why should you obey him?" he demanded, but Maga

ignored him as she passed out, and Fred nudged me again.

"A miracle!" he whispered. "Did you hear the martyred biped suggest rebellion to her? He'll be offering to fight Kagig next! Guess what is Kagig's hold over the girl — can you?"

But a much greater miracle followed. Rather than disobey Monty again; rather than seem to question his authority, or differ from his judgment in the least, Rustum Khan forbore presently from sending for his own stripling servant and actually accepted food from Maga's hands.

As a Mohammedan, he made in theory no caste distinctions. But as a Rajput be had fixed Hindu notions without knowing it, and almost his chief care was lest his food should be defiled by the touch of outcasts, of whom he reckoned gypsies lowest, vilest and least cleansable. Nevertheless he accepted curds that had been touched by gypsy fingers, and ate greedily, in confirmation of Monty's diagnosis; and after a few minutes he laid his head on a folded goatskin in the corner, and fell asleep.

Then Monty sent a servant to his own quarters for some prized possession that he mentioned in a whisper behind his hand. None of us suspected what it might be until the man returned presently with a quart bottle of Scotch whisky. Kagig himself got mugs down from a shelf three inches wide, and Monty poured libations. Kagig, standing with legs apart, drank his share of the strong stuff without waiting; and that brought out the chief surprise of the evening.

"Ah-h-h!" he exclaimed, using the back of his hand to wipe mobile lips. "Not since I drank in Tony's have I tasted that stuff! The taste makes me homesick for what never was my home, nor ever can be! Tony's — ah!"

"What Tony's?" demanded Will, emerging from whispered interludes with Gloria like a man coming out of a dream.

"Tony's down near the Battery."

"What — the Battery, New York — ?"

"Where else? Tony was a friend of mine. Tony lent me money when I landed in the States without a coin. It was right that I should take a last drink with Tony before I came away forever."

Fred reached into the corner for a lump of wood and set it down suggestively before the fire. Kagig accepted and sat down on it, stretching his legs out rather wearily.

"I noticed you've been remembering your English much better than at first," said Will. "Go on, man, tell us!"

Kagig cleared his throat and warmed himself while his eyes seemed to search the flames for stories from a half-forgotten past.

"Weren't the States good enough for you?" Will suggested, by way of starting him off.

"Good enough? Ah!" He made all eight fingers crack like castanets. "Much too good! How could I live there safe and comfortable — eggs and bacon — clean shirt — good shoes — an apartment with a bath in it — easy work — good pay — books to read — kindness — freedom — how could I accept all that, remembering my people in Armenia?"

He ran his fingers through his hair, and stared in the fire again — remembering America perhaps.

"There was a time when I forgot. All young men forget for a while if you feed them well enough. The sensation of having money in my pocket and the right to spend it made me drunk. I forgot Armenia. I took out what are called first papers. I was very prosperous — very grateful."

He lapsed into silence again, holding his head bowed between his hands.

"Why didn't you become a citizen?" asked Will.

"Ah! Many a time I thought of it. I am citizen of no land — of no land! I am outlaw here — outlaw in the States! I slew a Turk. They would electrocute me in New York — for slaying the man who — have you heard me tell what happened to my mother, before my very eyes? Well — that man came to America, and I slew him!"

"Why did you leave Armenia in the first place?" asked Gloria, for he seemed to need pricking along to prevent him from getting off the track into a maze of silent memory.

"Why not? I was lucky to get away! That cursed Abdul Hamid had been rebuked by the powers of Europe for butchering Bulgars, so he turned on us Armenians in order to prove to himself that he could do as he pleased in his own house. I tell you, murder and rape in those days were as common as flies at midsummer! I escaped, and worked my passage in the stoke-hole of a little merchant steamer — they were little ships in those days. And when I reached America without money or friends they let me land because I had been told by the other sailors to say I was fleeing from religious persecution. The very first day I found a friend in Tony. I cleaned his windows, and the bar, and the spittoons; and he lent me money to go where work would be plentiful. Those were the days when I forgot Armenia."

He began to forget our existence again, laying his face on his forearms and staring down at the floor between his feet.

"What brought it back to memory?" asked Gloria.

"The Turk brought it back — Fiamil — who bought my mother from four drunken soldiers, and ill-treated her before my eyes. He came to the Turkish consulate, not as consul but in some peculiar position; and by that time I was thriving as head-waiter and part-owner of a New York restaurant. Thither the fat beast came to eat daily. And so I met him, and recognized him. He did not know me.

"Remember, I was young, and prosperous for the first time in all my life. You must not judge me by too up-right stand-ards. At first I argued with myself to let him alone. He was nothing to me. I no longer believed in God. My mother was long dead, and Armenia no more my country. My money was accumulating in a savings bank. I was proud of it, and I remember I saw visions of great restaurants in every city of America, all owned by me! I did not like to take any step that should prevent that flow of money into the savings bank.

"But Fiamil inflamed my memory, and I saw him every day. And at last it dawned on me what his peculiar business in America must be. He was back at his old games, buying women. He was buying American young women to be shipped to Turkey, all under the seal of consular activity. One day, after he had had lunch and I had brought him cigarettes and coffee, he made a proposal. And although I did not care very deeply for the women of a free land who were willing to be sold into Turkish harems, nevertheless, as I said, he in-flamed my memory. A love of Armenia returned to me. I remembered my people, I remembered my mother's shame, and my own shame.

"After a little reflection I agreed with Fiamil, and met him that night in an upstairs room at a place he frequented for his purposes. I locked the door, and we had some talk in there, until in the end he remembered me and all the details of my mother's death. After that I killed him with a corkscrew and my ten fingers, there being no other weapon. And I threw his body out of the window into the gutter, as my mother's body had been thrown, myself escaping from the building by another way.

"Not knowing where to hide, I kept going — kept going; and after two days I fell among sportmen — cow-punchers they called themselves, who had come to New York with a circus, and the circus had gone broke. To them I told some of my story, and they befriended me, taking me West with them to cook their meals; and for a year I traveled in cow camps. In those days I remembered God as well as Armenia, and I used to pray by starlight.

"And Armenia kept calling — calling. Fiamil had wakened in me too many old memories. But there was the money in the savings bank that I did not dare to draw for fear the police might learn my address, yet I had not the heart to leave behind.

"So I took a sportman into my confidence, and told him about my money, and why I wanted it. He was not the foreman, but the man who took the place of foreman when the real foreman was too drunk — the hungriest man of all, and so oftenest near the cook-fire. When I had told him, he took me to a township where a lawyer was, and the lawyer drew up a document, which I signed.

"Then the sportman — his name was Larry Atkins, I remember — took that document and went to draw the money on my behalf. And that was the last I saw of him. Not that he was not sportman — all through. He told me in a letter afterward that the police arrested him, supposing him to be me, but that he easily proved he was not me, and so got away with the money. Enclosed in the package in which the letter came were his diamond ring and a watch and chain, and he also sent me an order to deliver to me his horse and saddle.

"He explained he had tried to double my money by gambling, but had lost. Therefore he now sent me all he had left, a fair exchange being no robbery. Oh, he was certainly sportman!

"So I sold his watch and chain and the horse — but the diamond ring I kept — behold it! — see, on Maga's hand! — it was a real diamond that a woman had given him; and with the proceeds I came back to Armenia. In Armenia I have ever since remained, with the exception of one or two little journeys in time of war, and one or two little temporary hidings, and a trip into Persia, and another into Russia to get ammunition.

"How have I lived? Mostly by robbery! I rob Turks and all friends of Turks, and such people as help make it possible for Turks as a nation to continue to exist! I — we — I and my men — we steal a cartridge sooner than a piaster — a rifle sooner than a thousand rubles! Outlaws must live, and weapons are the chief means! I am the brains and the Eye of Zeitoon, but I have never been chieftain, and am not now. Observe my house — is it not empty? I tell you, if it had not been for my new friend Monty there would have been six or seven rival chieftains in Zeitoon tonight! As it is, they sulk in their houses, the others, because Monty has rallied all the fighting men to me! Now that Monty has come I think there will be unity forever in Zeitoon!"

He turned toward Monty with a gesture of really magnificent approval. Caesar never declined a crown with greater dignity.

"You, my brother, have accomplished in a few days what I have failed to do in years! That is because you are sportman! Just as Larry Atkins was sportman! He sent me all he had, and could not do more. I understood him. Why did he do it? Simply sportman — that is all! Why do you do this? Why do you throw your life into the hot cauldron of Zeitoon? Because you are sportman! And my people see, and understand. They understand, as they have never understood me! I will tell you why they have never understood me. This is why:

"I have always kept a little in reserve. At one time money in a bank. At another time money buried. Sometimes a place to run and hide in. Now and then a plan for my own safety in case a defense should fail. Never have I given absolutely quite all, burning all my bridges. Had I been Larry Atkins I would not have gambled with the money of a man who

trusted me; but, having lost the money, I would not have sent
my diamond and the watch and chain! Neither, if the horse
and saddle bad been within my reach would I have sent an
order to deliver those! That is why Zeitoon has never altogether trusted me! Some, but never all, until tonight!

"My brother —"

He stood up, with the motions of a man who is stiff with
weariness.

"I salute you! You have taught me my needed lesson!"

"I wonder!" whispered Fred to me. "Remember Peter at the
fireside? Methinks friend Kagig doth too much protest! We'll
see. Nemesis comes swiftly as a rule."

I shoved Fred off his balance, rolled him over, and sat on
him, because cynicism and iconoclasm are twin deities I
neither worship nor respect. But at times Fred Oakes is gifted
with uncanny vision. While he struggled explosively to throw
me off, the door began resounding to steady thumps, and at
a sign from Kagig, Maga opened it.

There strode in nine Armenians, followed closely by one
of the gypsies of Gregor Jhaere's party, who whispered to
Maga through lips that hardly moved, and made signals to
Kagig with a secretive hand like a snake's head. I got off Fred's
stomach then, and when he had had his revenge by emptying
hot pipe ashes down my neck he sat close beside me and
translated what followed word for word. It was all in Armenian, spoken in deadly earnest by hairy men on edge with
anxiety and yet compelled to grudging patience by the presence of strangers and knowledge of the hour's necessity.

When the gypsy had finished making signals to Kagig be
sat down and seemed to take no further interest. But a little
later I caught sight of him by the dancing fire-light creeping
along the wall, and presently he lay down with his head very
close to Rustum Khan's. Nothing points more clearly to the
clarifying tension of that night than the fact that Rustum
Khan with his notions about gypsies could compel himself
to lie still with a gypsy's head within three inches of his own,
and sham sleep while the gypsy whispered to him. I was not
the only one who observed that marvel, although I did not
know that at the time.

The nine Armenians who had entered were evidently influential men. Elders was the word that occurred as best describing them. They were smelly with rain and smoke and the close-kept sweat beneath their leather coats — all of them bearded — nearly all big men — and they strode and stood with the air of being usually heard when they chose to voice opinion. Kagig stood up to meet them, with his back toward the fire — legs astraddle, and hands clasped behind him.

"Ephraim says," began the tallest of the nine, who had entered first and stood now nearest to Kagig and the firelight, "that you will yourself be king of Armenia!"

"Ephraim lies!" said Kagig grimly. "He always does lie. That man can not tell truth!"

Two of the others grunted, and nudged the first man, who made an exclamation of impatience and renewed the attack.

"But there is the Turk — the colonel whom your Indian friend took prisoner — he says —"

"Pah! What Turk tells the truth?"

"He says that the Indian — what is his name? Rustum Khan — was purposing to use him as prisoner-of-war, whereas in accordance with a private agreement made beforehand you were determined to make matters easy for him. He demands of us better treatment in fulfillment of promise. He says that the army is coming to take Zeitoon, and to make you governor in the Sultan's name. He offered us that argument thinking we are your dupes. He thought to —"

"Dupes?" snarled Kagig. "How long have ye dealt with Turks, and how long with me, that ye take a Turk's word against mine?"

"But the Turk thought we are your friends," put in a harsh-voiced man from the rear of the delegation. "Otherwise, how should he have told us such a thing?"

"If he had thought you were my friends," Kagig answered, "he would never have dared. If you had been my friends, you would have taken him and thrown him into Jihun River from the bridge!"

"Yet he has said this thing," said a man who had not spoken yet.

"And none has heard you deny it, Kagig!" added the man nearest the door.

"Then hear me now!" Kagig shouted, on tiptoe with anger.

Then he calmed himself and glanced about the room for a glimpse of eyes friendly to himself. "Hear me now. Those Turks — truly come to set a governor over Zeitoon. I forgot that the prisoner might understand English. I talked with this friend of mine —" he made a gesture toward Monty. "Perhaps that Turk overheard, he is cleverer than he looks. I had a plan, and I told it to my friend. The Turk was near, I remember, eating the half of my dinner I gave him."

"Have you then a plan you never told to us?" the first man asked suspiciously.

"One plan? A thousand! Am I wind that I should babble into heedless ears each thought that comes to me for testing? First it was my plan to arouse all Armenia, and to overthrow the Turk. Armenia failed me. Then it was my plan to arouse Zeitoon, and to make a stand here to such good purpose that all Armenia would rally to us. Bear me witness whether Zeitoon trusted me or not? How much backing have I had? Some, yes; but yours?

"So it was plain that if the Turks sent a great army, Zeitoon could only hold out for a little while, because unanimity is lacking. And my spies report to me that a greater army is on the way than ever yet came to the rape of Armenia. These handful of hamidieh that ye think are all there is to be faced are but the outflung skirmishers. It was plain to me that Zeitoon can not last. So I made a new plan, and kept it secret."

"Ah-h-h! So that was the way you took us into confidence? Always secrets behind secrets, Kagig! That is our complaint!"

"Listen, ye who would rather suspect than give credit!" He used one word in the Armenian. "It was my plan — my new plan, that seeing the Turks insist on giving us a governor, and are able to overwhelm us if we refuse, then I would be that governor!"

"Ah-h-h! What did we say! Unable to be king, you will be governor!"

"I talked that over with my new friend, and he did not agree with me, but I prevailed. Now hear my last word on this matter: I will not be governor of Zeitoon! I will lead against this army that is coming. If you men prevent me, or disobey me, or speak against me, I will hang you — every one! I will accept no reward, no office, no emolument, no title — nothing! Either I die here, fighting for Zeitoon, or I leave Zeitoon when the fighting is over, and leave it as I came to it — penniless! I give now all that I have to give. I burn my bridges! I take inviolable oath that I will not profit! And by the God who fed me in the wilderness, I name my price for that and take my payment in advance! I will be obeyed! Out with you! Get out of here before I slay you all! Go and tell Zeitoon who is master here until the fight is lost or won!"

He seized a great firebrand and charged at them, beating right and left, and they backed away in front of him, protesting from under forearms raised to protect their faces. He refused to hear a word from them, and drove, them back against the door.

Strange to say, it was Rustum Khan who gave up all further pretense at sleeping and ran round to fling the door open — Rustum Khan who took part with Kagig, and helped drive them out into the dark, and Rustum Khan who stood astraddle in the doorway, growling after them in Persian — the only language he knew thoroughly that they likely understood:

"Bismillah! Ye have heard a man talk! Now show yourselves men, and obey him, or by the beard of God's prophet there shall be war within Zeitoon fiercer than that without! Take counsel of your womenfolk! Ye —" (he used no drawing room word to intimate their sex) — "are too full of thoughts to think!"

Then he turned on Kagig, and held out a lean brown hand. Kagig clasped it, and they met each other's eyes a moment.

"Am I sportman?" Kagig asked ingenuously.

"Brother," said Rustum Khan, "next after my colonel sahib I accept thee as a man fit to fight beside!"

We were all standing. A free-for-all fight had seemed too likely, and we had not known whether there were others outside waiting to reinforce the delegation. Rustum Khan sought Monty's eyes.

"You have the news, sahib?"

Kagig laughed sharply, and dismissed the past hour from his mind with a short sweep of the hand.

"No. Tell me," said Monty.

"The gypsy brought it. A whole division of the Turkish regular army is on the march. Their rear-guard camps tonight a day's march this side of Tarsus. Dawn will find the main body within sight of us. Half a brigade has hurried forward to reinforce the men we have just beaten. Are there any orders?"

Fred's face fell, and my heart dropped into my boots. A division is a horde of men to stand against.

"No," said Monty. "No orders yet."

"Then I will sleep again," said Rustum Khan, and suited action to the word, laying his head on the same folded goatskin he had used before and breathing deeply within the minute.

Nobody spoke. Rustum Khan's first deep snore had not yet announced his comment on the situation, and we all stood waiting for Kagig to say something. But it was Peter Measel who spoke first.

"I will pray," he announced. "I saw that gypsy whispering to the Indian, and I know there is treachery intended! O Lord — O righteous Lord — forgive these people for their bloody and impudent plans! Forgive them for plotting to shed blood! Forgive them for arrogance, for ambition, for taking Thy name in vain, for drinking strong drink, for swearing, for vanity, and for all their other sins. Forgive above all the young woman of the party, who is not satisfied with a wound already but looks forward with unwomanly zest to further fighting! Forgive them for boasting and —"

"Throw that fool out!" barked Kagig suddenly.

"O Lord forgive —"

Fred was nearest the door, and opened it. Maga laughed aloud. I was nearest to Peter Measel, so it was I who took him by the neck and thrust him into outer darkness. Kagig kicked the door shut after him; but even so we heard him for several minutes grinding out condemnatory prayers.

"Now sleep, sportmen all!" said Kagig, blessing us with both hands. "Sleep against the sport tomorrow!"

Chapter Seventeen

"I knew what to expect of the women!"

"AND DELILAH SAID —"

Always at fault is the fellow betrayed
(Majorities murder to prove it!)
As Samson discovered, Delilah lies,
The stigma's stuck on by the cynical wise,
And nothing can ever remove it.
We'll cast out Delilah and spit on her dead,
(That revenge is remarkably human),
And pity the victim of underhand tricks
So be that it's moral (the sexes don't mix);
But, oh, think what the cynical wise would have said
If Judas were only a woman!

*W*e slept until Monty called us, two hours before dawn, although I was conscious most of the night of stealthy men and women who stepped over me to get at Kagig and whisper to him. His marvelous spy system was working full blast, and he seemed to run no risks by letting the spies report to any one but himself. Fred, who slept more lightly than I did, told me afterward that the women principally brought him particulars of the workings of local politics; the men detailed news of the oncoming concrete enemy.

There was breakfast served by Maga in the dark — hot milk, and a strange mess of eggs and meat. For some reason no one thought of relighting the fire, and although the ashes glowed we shivered until the food put warmth in us.

By the light of the smoky lamp I thought that Monty wore a strangely divided air, between gloom and exultation. Fred had been wide awake and talking with him since long before first cock-crow and was obviously out of sorts, shaking his head at intervals and unwilling more than to poke at his food with a fork. I crossed the room to sit beside them, and came in for the tail end of the conversation.

"I might have known it, Didums, when I let you go on alone. I'll never forgive myself. I had a premonition and disobeyed it. You pose as a cast-iron materialist with no more ambition than money enough to retrieve your damned estates, and all the while you're the most romantic ass who ever wore out saddle-leather! Found it, have you? Then God help us all! I know what's coming! You're about to 'vert back to Crusader days, and try to do damsilly deeds of chivalry without the war-horse or the suit of mail!"

"No need for you to join me, Fred. You take charge of the others and get them away to safety."

"Take charge of hornets! I'd leave you, of course, like a shot! But can you see Will Yerkes, for instance, riding off and leaving you to play Don Quixote? Damn you, Didums, can't you see — ?"

"Destiny, Fred. Manifest destiny."

"Can't you see crusading is dead as a dead horse?"

"So am I, old man. I'm no use but to do this very thing. I can serve these people. If I'm killed, there'll be a howl in the papers. If I'm taken, there'll be a row in parliament."

"You don't intend to be taken — I know you!"

"Honest, Fred, I —"

"Have I known you all these years to be fooled now? Smelling rats 'ud be subtle to it — I can feel the air bristling! You mean to raise the Montdidier banner and die under it, last of your race. But you're not last, you bally ass!"

"Last in the direct line, Fred."

"Yes, but there's that rotter Charles ready to inherit! If you're bent on suicide —"

"I'm not. You know I'm not."

"— you might have the decency to kill that miserable cousin first and bring the line to an end in common honor! He'll survive you, and as sure as I sit here and swear at you, he'll bring the Montdidier name into worse disgrace than Judas Iscariot's!"

"I've no intention of suicide, Fred. I assure you —"

But Fred waved the argument aside contemptuously, and stood up to gather our attention.

"Listen!" He thrust forward his Van Dyke beard that valiantly strove to hide a chin like a piece of flint. "Monty has found the robbers' nest that used to belong to his infernal ancestors. I charge any of you who count yourselves his friends to help me prevent him from behaving like an idiot!"

"That'll do, Fred!" said Monty, pressing him back against the wall. "The fact is," he twisted at his black mustache and eyed us each for a second in turn, looking as handsome as the devil, "that I have found what I originally set out to look for. It overlooks Zeitoon, hidden among trees. I propose to use it. As for quixotism — is there any one here not willing to fight in the last ditch to help Kagig and these Armenians?"

"I'm with you!" laughed Gloria, and she and Will had a scuffle over near the fireplace.

"I knew what to expect of the women," said Monty rather bitterly. "I'm speaking to Fred and the men!"

"Where's Peter Measel?" I asked. But the others did not see the connection.

"Come along," said Monty. "Seems to me we're wasting time," and he strode out through the window on to the roof of the house below — usually the shortest way from point to point in Zeitoon. Kagig followed him, and then Rustum Khan. The stars were no longer shining in the pale sky overhead, but it was dark where we were because of the mountains that shut out the dawn. Fred came last, grumbling and stumbling, too disturbed to look where he was going.

"Fancy me acting Cassandra at my time of life and none to believe me!" he muttered. Then, louder: "I warn you all! I know that fellow Monty. If he comes out of this alive it'll be because we haul him out by the hair! Won't you listen?"

Outside the window I remembered the field-glasses I had laid down in a corner, and returned to get them. In the room were Maga and the woman Anna, who had appointed herself Gloria Vanderman's maid; they were apparently about to sweep the floor and tidy the place, but as I crossed the room an older gypsy woman entered by the door, and she and Maga promptly drove Anna out through the window after my party. Then the old woman came close to me, her beady bright eyes fixed on mine, and went through the suggestive gypsy motions that invite the crossing of a palm with silver.

There seemed at first no excuse for listening to her. Every gypsy will beg, whether there is need or not, and knowledge of their habits did not make me less short-tempered; besides I had no silver within reach, nor time to waste.

"Not now!" I said, pushing her aside.

But Maga came to her rescue, and clutched my arm.

"See!" she said, and took a Maria Theresa dollar from some hiding place in her skirt. "I give silver for you. So." The old hag pouched the coin with exactly the same avidity with which she would have taken it from me. "Now she will make magic. Then I see. Then I tell you something. You listen!"

It began to dawn on me that I would better listen after all. Every human is superstitious, whether or not he admits if to himself; but the particular fraud of pretending to tell fortunes never did happen to find the joint in my own armor. It seemed likely these two women had some plan that included the preliminary deception of myself, and the sooner I knew something about it the better. So I sat down on Kagig's stool, to give them a better opinion of their advantage over me, there being nothing like making the enemy too confident. Then I held out the palm of my hand for inspection and tried to look like a man pretending he does not believe in magic. Whatever Maga thought, the old hag was delighted. She began to croak an incantation, shuffling first with one foot, then with the other, and finally with both together in a weird dance that almost shook her old frame apart. Then she went through a pantomime of finger-pointing, as if transferring from herself to Maga the gift of divining about me.

Presently, standing a little to one side of me, with eyes on the old hag's and my hand held between her two, Maga began chanting in English. The fact that her voice was musical and low where the bag's had been high-pitched and rasping heightened interest, if nothing else.

"You now four men," she began, with a little pause, and something like a swallow between each sentence. "You all love one another ver' much. You all like Kagig. Kagig is liking you. But Turks are coming presently, and they keel Kagig — keel heem, you understan'? That man Monty is also keel — keel dead. That man Fred — I not know — I not see. You I see — you I see two ways. First way, you marry that woman Gloria — you go away — all well — all good. Second way — you not marry her. Then you all die — dam' quick — Monty, Fred, Will, you, Gloria, everybody — an' Zeitoon is all burn' up by bloody Turks!"

She paused and looked at me sidewise under lowered eyelids. I stared straight in front of me, as if in the state of self-hypnotism that is the fortune-teller's happy hunting-ground.

"You understan'?"

"Yes," I said. "I think I see. But how shall I marry Miss Gloria? Suppose she does not want me?"

"You must! Never mind what she want! Listen! This is only way to save your frien's and Zeitoon! I am giving men — four — five — six men. They are seizing Gloria. You go with them. They take you safe away. Then Zeitoon is also safe, an' your frien's are also safe."

"Monty, too?" I asked.

"Yes, then he is also safe." But — I felt her hands tremble slightly as she said that.

"Do you mean I should leave him?" I asked.

"You must! You must!" She almost screamed at me, and shook my hand between her two palms as if by that means to drive the fact into my consciousness. The old hag had her eyes fixed on my right temple as if she would burn a hole there, and between them they were making a better than amateur effort to control me by suggestion. It seemed wise to help them deceive themselves. Maga let go my hand gently, and began passing her ten fingers very softly through my hair, and there are other men who will bear me witness that there exists sensation less appealing than when a pretty girt does that.

"You must!" she said again more quietly. "That is the only way to save Zeitoon. God is angry."

"What do you know about God?" I asked unguardedly, knowing well that whatever their open pretenses, gypsies despise all religion except diabolism. They study creeds for the sake of plunder, just as hunters study the habits of the wild.

"Maybe nothing — maybe much! Peter Measel, he say —"

She paused, as if in doubt whether she was using the right argument. And in that moment I recalled what Rustum Khan had once said about her being no true gypsy.

"Go on," I urged her. "Peter Measel is an expert. He's a high priest. He knows it all."

"Peter Measel is saying, God is ver' angry with Zeitoon and is sending to destroy such bloody people what plan fighting and rebellion."

"I'll think it over," I said, moving to get up. But independent thinking was the last thing that Maga intended to permit me.

"No, no! No, no, no! You must dee-cide now — at once! There is no time. Now — now I give you five — six mens — now they seize that woman Gloria — now you carry 'er away into the mountains — now you make 'er yours — your own, you understan', so as she is ashamed to deny it afterward — yes? — you see?"

"Where are the men?" I demanded.

"I fetch them quick!"

I could see the hilt of her knife, and the bulge of her repeating pistol, but I could also feel the weight of my own loaded Colt against my hip. I did not doubt I could escape before her men could arrive on the scene, but that would have been to leave some secret only part uncovered. There was obviously more behind this scheme than met the ear. It is my experience that if we throw fear to the winds, and are willing to wait in tight places for the necessary inspiration, then we get it.

"Very well," I said. "I agree. Bring your men."

"You wait. I get 'em."

I nodded, and she said something in the gypsy language to the old hag, who went out through the door in a hurry. Alone with Maga I felt less than half as safe as I had been. She proceeded to make use of every moment in the manner they say makes millionaires.

"Gloria, she is ver' nice girl!" She made a wonderful gesture of both hands that limned in empty air the curves of her detested rival. "You will love her. By-and-by she love you — also ver' much."

The thought flashed through my head again that I ought to escape whole while I had the chance; but the answer to that was the certainty that she would thence-forward be on guard against me without having given me any real information. I was perfectly convinced there was a deep plot underlying the foolishness she had proposed. The fact that she considered me so venial and so gullible was no proof that the hidden purpose was not dangerous. The mystery was how to seem to be fooled by her and yet get in touch with my friends. Then suddenly I recalled that she and the hag had been trying to use the gypsy's black art. Unless they can trick their victim into a mental condition in which innate superstition becomes uppermost, players of that dark game are helpless.

Yet gypsies are more superstitious than any one else. Hanging to her neck by a skein of plaited horse-hair was the polished shell of a minute turtle — smaller than a dollar piece.

"Give me that," I said, "for luck," and she jumped at the idea.

"Yes, yes — that is to bring you luck — ver' much luck!"

She snatched it off and hung it around my neck, pushing the turtle-shell down under my collar out of sight.

"That is love-token!" she whispered. "Now she love you immediate'! Now you 'ave ver' much luck!"

The last part of her prophecy was true. The luck seemed to change. That instant the key was given me to escape without making her my relentless enemy, a voice that I would know among a million began shouting for me petulantly from somewhere half a dozen roofs away.

"What in hell's keeping you, man? Here's Monty getting up a tourist party to his damned ancestral nest and you're delaying the whole shebang! Good lord alive! Have you fallen in love with a woman, or taken the belly-ache, or fallen down a well, or gone to sleep again, or all of them, or what?"

"Coming, Fred!" I shouted. "Coming!"

"You'd better!"

He began playing cat-calls on his concertina — imitation bugle-calls, and fragments of serenades. For a second Maga looked reckless — then suspicious — then, as it began to dawn on her from studying my face that I, too, was afraid of Fred, relieved.

"Does he know anything?" I asked her.

"He? That Fred? No! No, no, no! An' you no tell 'im. You 'ear me? You no tell 'im! You go now — go to 'im, or else 'e is get suspicious — understan'? My men — they go an' get that woman. When they finish getting that woman, then I send for you an' you come quick — understan'?"

I nodded.

"Listen! If you tell your frien's — if you tell that Frrred, or those others — then I not only keel you, but my men put out your eyes first an' then pull off your toes an' fingers — understan'?"

I shrugged my shoulders, suggesting an attempt to seem at ease.

"Besides — I warn you! You tell Kagig anything against me an' Kagig is at once your enemy!"

I nodded, and tried to look afraid. Perhaps the speculation that the last boast started in my mind helped give me a look that convinced her.

Fred began calling again.

"You go!" she ordered imperiously, with a last effort to impress me with her mental predominance. "Go quickly!"

I made motions of hand and face as nearly suggestive of underhanded cunning as I could compass, and climbed out through the window without further invitation. Seeing me emerge, Fred beckoned from fifty yards away and turned his back. Morning was just beginning to descend into the valley, suddenly bright from having finished all the dawn delays among the crags higher up; but there were deep shadows here and especially where one roof overhung another.

Jumping from roof to roof to follow Fred, I was suddenly brought up short by a figure in shadow that gesticulated wildly without speaking. It was below me, in a narrow, shallow runway between two houses, and I had been so impressed by my interview with Maga that assassination was the first thought ready to mind. I sprang aside and tried to check myself, missed footing, and fell into the very runway I had tried to avoid.

A friend unmistakable, Anna — Gloria's self-constituted maid — ran out of the darkest shadow and kept me from scrambling to my feet.

"Wait!" she whispered. "Don't be seen talking to me. Listen!"

My ankle pained considerably and I was out of breath. I was willing enough to lie there.

"Maga has made a plot to betray Zeitoon! She has been talking with that Turkish colonel who was captured. I don't know what the plot is, but I listened through a chink in the wall of the prison, and I heard him promise that she should have Will Yerkes!"

"What else did you hear?"

"Nothing else. There was wind whistling, and the straw made a noise."

At that moment Fred chose to turn his head to see whether I was following. Not seeing me, he came back over the roofs, shouting to know what had happened. I got to my feet but, although he hardly looks the part, he is as active as a boy, and he had scrambled to a higher roof that commanded a view of my runway before my twisted ankle would permit me to escape.

"So that's it, eh? A woman!"

"Keep an eye on Miss Gloria!" I whispered to Anna, and she ducked and ran.

If I had had presence of mind I would have accepted the insinuation, and turned the joke on Fred. Instead, I denied it hotly like a fool, and nothing could have fed the fires of his spirit of raillery more surely.

"I've unearthed a plot," I began, limping along beside him.

"No, sir! It was I who unearthed the two of you!"

"See here, Fred —"

"Look? I'd be ashamed! No, no — I wasn't looking!"

"Fred, I'm serious!"

"Entanglements with women are always serious!"

"I tell you, that girl Maga —"

"Two of 'em, eh? Worser and worser! You'll have Will jealous into the bargain!"

"Have it your own way, then!" I said, savage with pain (and the reasons he did not hesitate to assign to my strained ankle were simply scandalous). "I'll wait until I find a man with honest ears."

"Try Kagig!" he advised me dryly.

And Kagig I did try. We came on him at our end of the bridge that overhung the Jihun River. Our party were waiting on the far side, and Fred hurried over to join them. Kagig was listening to the reports of a dozen men, and while I waited to get his ear I could see Fred telling his great joke to the party. It was easy to see that Gloria Vanderman did not enjoy the joke; nor did I blame her. I did not blame her for sending word there and then to Anna that her services would not be required any more.

As soon as Kagig saw me he dismissed the other men in various directions and made to start across the bridge. I called to him to wait, and walked beside him.

"I've uncovered a plot, Kagig," I began. "Maga Jhaere has been talking with the Turkish prisoner."

"I know it. I sent her to talk with him!"

"She has bargained with him to betray Zeitoon!"

For answer to that Kagig turned his head and stared sharply at me — then went off into peals of diabolic laughter. He had not a word to offer. He simply utterly, absolutely, unqualifiedly disbelieved me — or else chose to have it appear so.

Chapter Eighteen

"Per terram et aquam."

AND HE WHO WOULD SAVE HIS LIFE
SHALL LOSE IT

The fed fools beat their brazen gong
For gods' ears dulled by blatant praise,
Awonder why the scented fumes
And surplices at evensong
Avail not as in other days.
Shrunken and mean the spirit fails
Like old snow falling from the crags
And priest and pedagog compete
With nostrums for the age that ails,
But learn not why the spirit lags.
Tuneless and dull the loose lyre thrums
Ill-plucked by fingers strange to skill
That change and change the fever'd chords,
But still no inspiration comes
Though priest and pundit labor still.
Lust-urged the clamoring clans denounce
Whate'er their sires agreed was good,
And swift on faith and fair return
With lies the feud-leaders pounce
Lest Truth deprive them of their food.
Dog eateth dog and none gives thanks;
All crave the fare, but grudge the price
Their nobler forbears proudly paid,
That now for moonstruck madness ranks —
The only true coin — Sacrifice!

*T*he man who is a hero to himself perhaps exists, but the
surface indications are no proof of it. I don't pretend to be

satisfied, and made no pretense at the time of being satisfied with my share in Maga's treachery. But I claim that it was more than human nature could have done, to endure the open disapproval of my friends, begun by Fred's half-earnest jest, and continued by my own indignation; and at the same time to induce them to take my warning seriously.

Will avoided me, and walked with Gloria, who made no particular secret of her disgust. Fred naturally enough kept the joke going, to save himself from being tripped in his own net. He had probably persuaded himself by that time that the accusation was true, and therefore equally probably regretted having made it; for he would have been the last man in the world to give tongue about an offense that he really believed a friend of his had committed.

Monty, who believed from force of habit every single word Fred said, walked beside me and was good enough to give me fatherly advice.

"Not the time, you know, to fool with women. I don't pretend, of course, to any right to judge your private conduct, but — you can be so awfully useful, you know, and all that kind of thing, when you're paying strict attention. Women distract a man."

All, things considered, I might have done worse than decide to say no more about the plot, but to keep my own eyes wide open. (I was particularly sore with Gloria, and derived much unwise consolation from considering stinging remarks I would make to her when the actual truth should out.)

Monty began making the best of my, in his eyes, damaged character by explaining the general dispositions he and Kagig had made for the defense of Zeitoon.

"According to my view of it," he said, "this bridge we've just crossed is the weakest point — or was. I think we can hold that clay ramp you came up yesterday against all comers. But there's a way round the back of this mountain that leads to the dismantled fort you see on this side of the river. That is the fort built by the Turkish soldiers whom Kagig told us the women of Zeitoon threw one by one over the bridge."

He stopped (we had climbed about two hundred feet of a fairly steep track leading up the flank of Beirut Dagh) and let the others gather around us.

"You see, if the enemy can once establish a footing on this hill, they'll then command the whole of Zeitoon opposite with rifle fire, even if they don't succeed in bringing artillery round the mountain."

Between us and Zeitoon there now lay a deep, sheer-sided gash, down at the bottom of which the Jihun brawled and boiled. I did not envy any army faced with the task of crossing it, even supposing the bridge should not be destroyed. But they would not need to cross in order to make the town untenable.

"The Zeitoonli are, you might say, superstitious about that bridge," Monty went on. "They refuse as much as to consider making arrangements to blow it up in case of need. Another remarkable thing is that the women claim the bridge defense as their privilege. That doesn't matter. They look like a crowd of last-ditch fighters, and we're awfully short of men. But we're almost equally short of ammunition; and if it ever gets to the point where we're driven in so that we have to hold that bridge, we shall be doling out cartridges one by one to the best shots! I have tried to persuade the women to leave the bridge until there's need of defending it, and to lend us a hand elsewhere meanwhile; but they've always held the bridge, and they propose to do the same again. Even Kagig can't shift them, although the women have been his chief supporters all along."

Fred interrupted, pointing toward a few acres of level land to our left, below Zeitoon village but still considerably above the river level.

"Is that Rustum Khan?"

"He it is," said Kagig. "A devil of a man — a wonder of a devil — no friend of mine, yet I shook hands with him and I salute him! A genius! A cavalryman born. Our people are not cavalrymen. No place for horses, this. Yet, as you have seen, there are some of us who can ride, and that Rustum Khan found many others — refugees from this and that place. See how he drills them yonder — see! It was the gift of God that so many horses fell into our hands. Some of the refugees brought horses along for food. Instead, Rustum Khan took men's corn away, to feed the hungry horses!"

"We could never have held the place without Rustum Khan," said Monty. "As it is we've a chance. The last thing the Turks will expect from us is mounted tactics. Allowing for plenty of spare horses, we shall have two full squadrons — one under Rustum Khan, and one I'll lead myself. From all accounts they're bringing an awful number of men against us, and we expect them to try to force the clay ramp. In that case — but come and see."

He led on up-hill, and after a few minutes the well-worn track disappeared, giving place to a newly cleared one. Trees had been cut down roughly, leaving stumps in such irregular profusion that, though horses could pass between them easily, no wheeled traffic could have gone that way. The undergrowth and the tree-trunks had been piled along either side, so that the new path was fenced in. It was steep and crooked, every section of it commanded by some other section higher up, with plenty of crags and boulders that afforded even better cover than the trees.

"Discovered this the first day I got here," said Monty. "Asked about bears, and a man offered to show me where a dozen of them lived. I was curious to see where a dozen bears could live in amity together — didn't believe a word of it. We set out that afternoon, and didn't reach the top until midnight. Worst climb I ever experienced. Lost ourselves a hundred times. Next day, however, Kagig agreed to let me have as many men as could be crowded together to work, and I took a hundred and twenty. Set them to cutting this trail and another one. They worked like beavers. But come along and look."

"How about the bears?" Fred demanded. "Did you get them?"

"Smelt 'em. Saw one — or saw his shadow, and heard him. Followed him up-hill by the smell, and so found the castle wall. Haven't seen a bear since."

"Hssh!" said Kagig, and sprang up-hill ahead of us to take the lead. "There are guards above there, and they are true Zeitoonli — they will shoot dam' quick!"

They did not shoot, because we all lay in the shadow of a great rock as soon as we could see a ragged stone wall uplifted against the purple sky, and Kagig whistled half a dozen times.

We plainly heard the snap of breech-blocks being tested.

"They are weary of talking fight!" Kagig whispered.

But the sixth or seventh whistle was answered by a shout, and we began to climb again. Close to the castle the tree-cutters had been able to follow the line of the original road fairly closely, and there were places underfoot that actually seemed to have been paved. Finally we reached a steep ramp of cemented stone blocks, not one of which was out of place, and went up that toward an arch — clear, unmistakable, round Roman that had once been closed by a portcullis and an oak gate. All of the woodwork had long ago disappeared, but there was little the matter with the masonry.

Under the echoing arch we strode into a shadowy courtyard where the sun had not penetrated long enough to warm the stones. In the midst of it a great stone keep stood as grim and almost as undecayed as when Crusaders last defended it. That castle had never been built by Crusaders; they had found it standing there, and had added to it, Norman on to Roman.

The courtyard was littered with weeds that Kagig's men had slashed down, and here and there a tree had found root room and forced its way up between the rough-hewn paving stones. Animals had laired in the place, and had left their smell there together with an air of wilderness. But now a new-old smell, and new-old sounds were awakening the past. There were horses again in the stables, whose roof formed the fighting-platform behind the rampart of the outer wall.

Monty led the way to the old arched entrance of the keep, and pointed upward to a spot above the arch where some one had been scraping and scrubbing away the stains of time. There, clean white now in the midst of rusty stonework, was a carved device — shield-shaped — two ships and two wheat-sheaves; and underneath on a scroll the motto in Latin — Per terram et aquam — By land and sea — in token that the old Montdidiers held themselves willing to do duty on either element. The same device and the same motto were on the gold signet ring on Monty's little finger.

"What's happening on top of the keep?" demanded Will.

Fred laughed aloud. We could not see up from inside, for at least one of the stone floors remained intact.

"Can't you guess?" demanded Fred. "Didn't I tell you the

man has 'verted to Crusader days?"

But Monty explained.

"There's an old stone socket up there that used to hold the flagpole. Two or three fellows have been kind enough to haul a tree up there, and they're trimming it to fit."

"If we were wise we'd hang you to it, Didums, and save you from a lousy Turkish jail!"

"Thank you, Fred," Monty answered. "There are capitulations still, I fancy. No Turk can legally try me, or imprison me a minute. I'm answerable to the British consul."

"They're fine, legal-minded sticklers for the rules, the Turks are!" Fred retorted.

"But we've a net laid for the Turks!" smiled Monty.

Fred shook his head. Monty led the way toward stone steps, whose treads bad been worn into smooth hollows centuries before by the feet of men in armor.

Up above on the outer rampart we could see Kagig's sentries outlined against the sky, protected against the chilly mountain air by goatskin outer garments and pointed goat-skin hats. We mounted the stone stair, holding to a baluster worn smooth by the rub of countless forgotten hands, as perfect yet as on the day when the masons pronounced it finished; and emerged on to a wide stone floor above the stables, guarded by a breast-high parapet pierced by slits for archers.

From below the breathing of the pines came up to us, peculiarly audible in spite of the Titan roar of Jihun River. Immediately below us was a ledge of forest-covered rock, and beyond that we could see sheer down the tree-draped flank of Beirut Dagh to the foaming water. We leaned our elbows on the parapet, and stared in silence all in a row, stared at in turn by the more than half-suspicious sentries.

"How does it feel, old man" asked Will at last, "standing on ramparts where your ancestors once ruled the roost?"

"Stranger than perhaps you think," Monty answered, not looking to right or left, or downward, but away out in front of him toward the sky-line on top of the opposite hills.

"I bet I know," said Will. "You hate to see the old order passing. You'd like the old times back."

"You're wrong for once, America!" Monty turned his back

on the parapet and the view, and with hands thrust deep
down in his pockets sought for words that could explain a
little of his inner man. Fred had perhaps seen that mood
before, but none of the rest of us. Usually he would talk of
anything except his feelings. He felt the difficulty now, and
checked.

"How so?" demanded Will.

"I've watched the old order passing. I'm part of it. I'm
passing, too."

Gloria watched him with melting eyes. Fred turned his back
and went through the fruitless rigmarole of trying to appear
indifferent, going to the usual length at last of humming
through his nose.

"That's what I said. You'd like these castle days back again."

"You're wrong, Will. I pray they never may come back. The
place is an anachronism. So am I! — useless for most modern
purposes. You'd have to tear castle or me so to pieces that
we'd be unrecognizable. The world is going forward, and I'm
glad of it. It shall have no hindrance at my hands."

"If men were all like you —" began Gloria, but he checked
her with a frown.

"You can call this castle a robbers' nest, if you like. It's easy
to call names. It stood for the best men knew in those days
— protection of the countryside, such law and order as men
understood, and the open road. It was built primarily to keep
the roads safe. There are lots of things in England and
America today, Will, that your descendants (being fools) will
sneer at, just as it's the fashion today to sneer at relics of the
past like this — and me!"

"Who's sneering? Not I! Not we!"

"This castle was built for the sake of the countryside. I've
a mind to see it end as it began — that's all."

"Aw — what's eating you, Monty?"

"Shut up croaking, you old raven!" grumbled Fred.

"Show us the view you promised. This isn't it, for there
isn't a Turk in sight."

Monty knew better than mistake Fred's surliness for anything but friendship in distress. Without another word he led
the way along the parapet toward a ragged tower at the
southern corner. It had been built by Normans, evidently

added to the earlier Roman wall.

"Now tell me if the old folk didn't know their business," said Monty. "Very careful, all! The steps inside are rough. The roof has fallen in, and the ragged upper edge that's left probably accounts for the castle remaining undetected from below all these years — looks like fangs of discolored rock."

We followed him through the doorless gap in the tower wall, and up broken stone stairs littered with fragments of the fallen roof, until we stood at last in a half-circle around the jagged rim, our feet wedged between rotten masonry, breasts against the saw-edge parapet, and heads on a level with the eagles. From that dizzy height we had a full view between the mountains, not only of the immediate environs of Zeitoon, but of most of the pass — up which we ourselves had come, and of some of the open land beyond it.

"D'you see Turks now?"

Monty pointed, but there was no need. Dense masses of men were bivouacked beyond the bottom of the wide clay ramp. Through the glasses I could see artillery and supply wagons. They were coming to make a thorough job of "rescuing" Zeitoon this time! After a while I was able to make out the dark irregular line of Kagig's men, and here and there the lighter color of freshly dug entrenchments. None of Zeitoon's defenders appeared to be thrown out beyond the clay ramp, but they evidently flanked it on the side of the pass that was farthest from us.

"Now look this way, and you'll understand."

Monty pointed to our right, and the significance of the voices we had heard so close to us when Fred was searching for a path around the clay on the morning of our arrival, was made plain instantly. Down from the ledge on which the castle stood to a point apparently within a few yards of the clay ramp there had been cut a winding swath through the forest, along which four horses abreast could be ridden, or as many men marched.

"How did you do all that in time?" demanded Will. "It looks like one of those contractor's jobs in the States — put through while you wait and to hell with everything!"

"It follows the old road," Monty answered. "There was too much cobble-paving for the trees to take hold, and most of

what they had to cut was small stuff. That accounts, too, for
the freedom from stumps. But, do you get the idea? The trees
between the end of the cutting and the clay ramp are cut
almost through — ready to fall, in fact. I'm afraid of a wind.
If it blows, our screen may fall too soon! But if the Turks try
to storm the ramp, we'll draw them on. Then, hey — presto!
Down go the remaining trees, and into the middle of 'em
rides our cavalry!"

"What's the use of cavalry four abreast?" demanded Fred,
in no mood to be satisfied with anything.

"Rustum Khan is concentrating all his energy on teaching
that one maneuver," Monty answered. "We come —"

"Thought it 'ud be 'we!' Your place is at the rear, giving
orders!"

"We come down the track at top speed, and the impetus
will carry us clear across the ramp. Some of the horses'll go
down, because the slope is slippery. But the remainder will
front form squadron, and charge down hill in line. Then
watch!"

"All right," Fred grumbled. "But how about you rear while
all that's going on? The Turk must have worked his way
around Beirut Dagh on former occasions — or how else could
he ever have built and held that dismantled fort? What's to
stop him from doing it again?"

"It's a fifteen-mile fight ahead of him," Monty answered,
"with riflemen posted at every vantage-point all the way —"

"Who is in charge of the riflemen?"

Kagig leaned back until he looked in danger of falling, and
tapped his breast significantly three times.

"I — I have picked the men who will command those
riflemen and women!"

"Well," Fred grumbled, "what are your plans for us?"

"For the last time, Fred, I want you, old man, to help me
to persuade these others to escape into the hills while there's
still a chance, and I want you to go with them."

"I also!" exclaimed Kagig. "I also desire that!"

"Now you've got that off your chest, Didums, suppose you
talk sense," suggested Fred. "What are your plans?"

Monty recognized the unalterable, and set his face.

"You first, Miss Vanderman. There's one way in which we

can always use a gentlewoman's services."

"Mayn't I fight?" she begged, and we all laughed.

"'Fraid not. No. The women have cleared out several houses for a hospital. Please go and superintend."

"Damn!" exclaimed Gloria, Boston fashion, not in the least under her breath.

"I am sending word," said Kagig, "that they shall obey you or learn from me!"

"The rest of us," Monty went on, "will know better what to do when we know what the Turk intends, but I expect to send all of you from time to time to wherever the fighting is thickest. Kagig, of course, will please himself, and my orders are subject to his approval."

"I'll go, then," said Gloria. "Good-bye!" And she kissed Will on the mouth in full view of all of us, he blushing furiously, and Kagig cracking all his finger-joints.

"Go with her, Will!" urged Monty, as she disappeared down the steps. "Go and save yourself. You're young. I've notions of my own that I've inherited, and the world calls me a back number. You go with Miss Vanderman!"

I seconded that motion.

"Go with her, Will! I've warned you she's unsafe alone! Go and protect her!"

Will grinned, wholly without malice.

"Thanks!" he said. "She's a back number, too. So'm I! If I left Monty in this pinch she'd never look at me, and I'd not ask her to! Inherited notions about merit and all that kind of thing, don't you know, by gosh! No, sir! She and I both sat into this game. She and I both stay! Wish Esau would open the ball, though. I'm tired of talking."

Chapter Nineteen

"Such drilling as they have had — such little drilling!"

ICH DIEN

Is honor out of fashion and the men she named
Fit only to be buried and defamed
Who dared hold service was true nobleness
And graced their service in a fitting dress?
Are manners out of date because the scullions scoff
At whosoever shuns the common trough
Liking dry bread better than the garbled stew
Nor praising greed because the style is new?
Let go the ancient orders if so be their ways
Are trespassing on decency these days.
So I go, rather than accept the trampled spoil
Or gamble for what great men earned by toil.
For rather than trade honor for a mob's foul praise
I'll keep full fealty to the ancient ways
And, hoisting my forebear's banner in the face of hell,
Will die beneath it, knowing I die well!

*F*ifteen minutes after Gloria Vanderman left us I saw a banner go jerkily mounting up the newly placed flagpole on the keep. A man blew a bugle hoarsely by way of a salute. I raised my hat. Monty raised his. In a moment we were all standing bare-headed, and the great square piece of cloth caught the wind that whistled between two crags of Beirut Dagh.

Fred, our arch-iconoclast, stood uncovered longest.

"Who the devil made it for you?" he inquired.

Stitched on the banner in colored cloth were the two wheat-sheaves and two ships of the Montdidiers, and a scroll stretched its length across the bottom, with the motto doubtless, although in the wind one could not read it.

"The women. Good of 'em, what? Miss Vanderman drew it on paper. They cut it out, and sat up last night sewing it."

"I suppose you know that's filibustering, to fly your private banner on foreign soil?"

"They may call it what they please," said Monty. "I can't well fly the flag of England, and Armenia has none yet. Let's go below, Fred, and see if there's any news."

"Yes, there is news," said Kagig, leading the way down. "I did not say it before the lady. It is not good news."

"That's the only kind that won't keep. Spit it out!" said Will.

Kagig faced us on the stable roof, and his finger-joints cracked again.

"It is the worst! They have sent Mahmoud Bey, against us. I would rather any six other Turks. Mahmoud Bey is not a fool. He is a young successful man, who looks to this campaign to bolster his ambition. He is a ruthless brute!"

"Which Turk isn't?" asked Will.

"This one is most ruthless. This Mahmoud is the one who in the massacres of five years ago caused Armenian prisoners to have horse-shoes nailed to their naked feet, in order, he said, that they might march without hurt. He will waste no time about preliminaries!"

Kagig was entirely right. Mahmoud Bey began the overture that very instant with artillery fire directed at the hidden defenses flanking the clay ramp. Next we caught the stuttering chorus of his machine guns, and the intermittent answer of Kagig's riflemen.

"Now, effendim, one of you down to the defenses, please! There is risk my men may use too many cartridges. Talk to them — restrain them. They might listen to me, but —" His long fingers suggested unhappy fragments of past history.

"You, Fred!" said Monty, and Fred hitched his concertina to a more comfortable angle.

Fred was the obvious choice. His gift of tongues would

enable him better than any of us to persuade, and if need were, compel. We had left our rifles leaning by the wall at the castle entrance, and in his cartridge bag was my oil-can and rag-bag. I asked him for them, and he threw them to me rather clumsily. Trying to catch them I twisted for the second time the ankle I had hurt that morning. Fred mounted and rode out through the echoing entrance without a backward glance, and I sat down and pulled my boot off, for the agony was almost unendurable.

"That settles your task for today," laughed Monty. "Help him back to the top of the tower, Will. Keep me informed of everything you see. Will — you go with Kagig after you've helped him up there."

"All right," said Will. "Where's Kagig bound for?"

"Round behind Beirut Dagh," Kagig announced grimly. "That's our danger-point. If the Turks force their way round the mountain —" He shrugged his expressive shoulders. Only he of all of us seemed to view the situation seriously. I think we others felt a thrill rather of sport than of danger.

I might have been inclined to resent the inactivity assigned to me, only that it gave me a better chance than I had hoped for of watching for signs of Maga Jhaere's promised treachery. Will helped me up and made the perch comfortable; then he and Kagig rode away together. Presently Monty, too, mounted a mule, and rode out under the arch, and fifteen minutes later fifty men marched in by twos, laughing and joking, and went to saddling the horses in the semicircular stable below me. After that all the world seemed to grow still for a while, except for the eagles, the distant rag-slitting rattle of rifle-fire, and the occasional bursting of a shell. Most of the shells were falling on the clay ramp, and seemed to be doing no harm whatever.

Away in the distance down the pass, out of range of the fire of our men, but also incapable of harm themselves until they should advance into the open jaws below the clay ramp, I could see the Turks massing in that sort of dense formation that the Germans teach. Even through the glasses it was not possible to guess their numbers, because the angle of vision was narrow and cut off their flanks to right and left; but I sent word down to Monty that a frontal attack in force seemed to be already beginning.

For an hour after that, while the artillery fire increased but our rifle-fire seemed to dwindle under Fred's persuasive tongue, I watched Monty mustering reinforcements in the gorge below the town. He overcame some of the women's prejudice, for it was a force made up of men and women that he presently led away. I was rather surprised to see Rustum Khan, after a talk with Monty, return to his squadron and remain inactive under cover of the hill; that fire-eater was the last man one would expect to remain willingly out of action. However, twenty minutes later, Rustum Khan appeared beside me, breathing rather hard. He begged the glasses of me, and spent five minutes studying the firing-line minutely before returning them.

"The lord sahib has more faith in these undrilled folk than I have!" he grumbled at last. "Observe: he goes with that bullet-food of men and women mixed, to hide them in reserve behind the narrow gut at the head of the ramp. The Turks are fools, as Kagig said, and their general is also a fool, in spite of Kagig. They propose to force that ramp. You see that by Frredd sahib's orders the firing on our side has grown greatly less. That is to draw the Turks on. See! It has drawn them! They are coming! The lord sahib will send for Frredd sahib to take command of that reserve, to man the top of the ramp in case the Turks succeed in climbing too far up it. Then he himself will gallop back to take charge of my squadron below there; and I take charge of his squadron up here. He and I are interchangeable, I having drilled all the men in any case — such drilling as they have had — such little, little drilling!"

The Turks began their advance into the jaws of that defile with a confidence that made my heart turn cold. What did they know? What were they depending on in addition to their weight of numbers? Mahmoud Bey had evidently hurried up almost his whole division, and was driving them forward into our trap as if he knew he could swallow trap and all. Not even foolish generals act that way. It needs a madman. Kagig had said nothing about Mahmoud being mad.

"Listen, Rustum Khan!" I said. "Go with a message to Lord Montdidier. Tell him the whole Turkish force is in motion and coming on as if their general knows something for certain that we don't know at all. Tell him that I suspect treachery at our rear, and have good reason for it!"

Rustum Khan eyed me for a minute as if he would read the very middle of my heart.

"Can you ride?" he asked.

"Of course," I answered. "It's only walking that I can't do."

"Then leave those glasses with me, and go yourself!"

"Why won't you go?" I asked.

"Because here are fifty men who would lack a leader in that case."

The answer was honest enough, yet I had my qualms about leaving the post Monty had assigned to me. The thought that finally decided me was that I would have opportunity to gallop past the hospital, two hundred yards over the bridge on the Zeitoon side, and make sure that Gloria was safe.

"Have you seen Maga Jhaere anywhere?" I asked.

"No," said the Rajput, swearing under his breath at the mere mention of her name.

"Then help me down from here. I'll go."

He muttered to himself, and I think he thought I was off to make love to the woman; but I was past caring about any one's opinion on that score. Five minutes later I was trotting a good horse slowly down the upper, steeper portion of the track toward Zeitoon, swearing to myself, and dreading the smoother going where I should feel compelled to gallop whether my ankle hurt or not. As a matter of fact I began to suspect a broken bone or ligament, for the agonizing pain increased and made me sit awkwardly on the horse, thus causing him to change his pace at odd intervals and give me more pain yet. However, gallop I had to, and I reached the bridge going at top speed, only to be forced to rein in, chattering with agony, by a man on foot who raced to reach the bridge ahead of me, and made unmistakable signals of having an important message to deliver.

He proved to be from Kagig, with orders to say that every man at his disposal was engaged by a very strong body of Turks who had spent the night creeping up close to their first objective, and had rushed it with the bayonet shortly after dawn.

"Order the women to stand ready by the bridge!" were the last words (the man had the whole by heart), and then there was a scribbled note from Will by way of make-weight.

"This end of the action looks pretty serious to me. We're badly outnumbered. The men are fighting gamely, but — tell Gloria for God's sake to look out after herself !"

I could hear no firing from that direction, for the great bulk of Beirut Dagh shut it off.

"How far away is the fighting?" I demanded.

"Oh, a long way yet."

I motioned to him to return to Kagig, and sent my horse across the bridge, catching sight of Gloria outside the hospital directly after I had crossed it. She waved her hand to me; so, seeing she was safe for the present, I let the message to her wait and started down the valley toward Monty as fast as the horse could go. I had my work cut out to drive him into the din of firing, for it was evidently his first experience of bursting shells, and even at half-a-mile distance he reared and plunged, driving me nearly crazy with pain. I found Monty shepherding the reserves he had brought down, watching through glasses from over the top of the spur that formed the left-hand wall of the gut of the pass.

"I left Rustum Khan in my place," I began, expecting to be damned at once for absenting without leave.

"Glad you came," he said, without turning his head.

I gave him my message, he listening while he watched the pass and the oncoming enemy.

"I tried to warn you of treachery this morning!" I said hotly. Pain and memory did nothing toward keeping down choler. "Where's Peter Measel? Seen him anywhere? Where's Maga Jhaere? Seen her, either? Those Turks are coming on into what they must know is a trap, with the confidence that proves their leaders have special information! Look at them! They can see this pass is lined, with our riflemen, yet on they come! They must suspect we've a surprise in store — yet look at them!"

They were coming on line after line, although Fred had turned the ammunition loose, and the rifle-fire of our well-hidden men was playing havoc. Monty seemed to me to look more puzzled than afraid. I went on telling him of the message Kagig had sent, and offered him Will's note, but he did not even look at it.

"Ah!" he said suddenly. "Now I understand! Yes, it's treachery. I beg your pardon for my thoughts this morning."

"Granted," said I, "but what next?"

"Look!" he said simply.

There were two sudden developments. What was left of the first advancing company of Turks halted below the ramp, and with sublime effrontery, born no doubt of knowledge that we had no artillery, proceeded to dig themselves a shallow trench. The Zeitoonli were making splendid shooting, but it was only a question of minutes until the shelter would be high enough for crouching men.

The second disturbing factor was that in a long line extending up the flank of the mountain, roughly parallel to the lower end of the track that Monty had caused to be cut from the castle, the trees were coming down as if struck by a cyclone! There must have been more than a regiment armed with axes, cutting a swath through the forest to take our secret road in flank!

That meant two things clearly. Some one had told Mahmoud of our plan to charge down from the height and surprise him, thus robbing us of all the benefit of unexpectedness; and, when the charge should take place, our men would have to ride down four abreast through ambush. And, if Mahmoud had merely intended placing a few men to trap our horsemen, he would never have troubled to cut down the forest. Plainly, he meant to destroy our mounted men at point-blank range, and then march a large force up the horse-track, so turning the tables on us. Considering the overwhelming numbers he had at his disposal, the game to me looked almost over.

Not so, however, to Monty. He glanced over his shoulder once at the men and women waiting for his orders, and I saw the women begin inspiriting their men. Then he turned on me.

"Now damn your ankle," he said. "Try to forget it! Climb up there and tell Fred to choose a hundred men and bring them down himself to oppose the enemy in front if he comes over the top of that ditch. Then you gallop back and get word to Rustum Khan to bring both squadrons down here. Tell him to stay by Fred and hold his horses until the last minute. Then you get all the women you can persuade to follow you, and man the castle walls! Hurry, now — that's all!"

There was a man holding my horse. I tied the horse securely to a tree instead, and told the man to help me climb, little suspecting what a Samson I had happened on. He laughed, seized me in his arms, and proceeded to carry me like a baby up the goat-track leading to the hidden rifle-pits and trenches. I persuaded him to let me get up on his shoulders, and in that way I had a view of most of what was happening.

Monty led his men and women at a run across the top of the ramp flanked by the full fire of the entrenched company below; and his action was so unexpected that the Turks fired like beginners. There were not many bodies lying quiet, nor writhing either when the last woman had disappeared among the trees on the far side. Those that did writhe were very swiftly caused to cease by volleys aimed at them in obedience to officers' orders. It began to look as if Gloria's hospital would not be overworked.

The tables were now turned on the Turks, except in regard to numbers. In the first place, as soon as Monty's command had penetrated downward through the trees parallel with the side of the ramp, he had the entrenched company in flank. It did not seem to me that he left more than ten or fifteen men to make that trench untenable, but the Turks were out of it within five minutes and in full retreat under a hot fire from Fred's men.

Then Monty pushed on to the far side of the castle road and held the remaining fringe of trees in such fashion that the Turks could not guess his exact whereabouts nor what number he had with him. Cutting down trees in a hurry is one thing, but cutting them down in face of hidden rifle-fire is most decidedly another, especially when the ax men have been promised there will be no reprisals.

The tree-felling suddenly ceased, and there began a close-quarters battle in the woods, in which numbers had less effect than knowledge of the ground and bravery. The Turk is a brave enough fighter, but not to be compared with moun-tain-Armenians fighting for their home, and it was easy to judge which held the upper hand.

I found Fred smoking his pipe and enjoying himself hugely, with half a dozen runners ready to carry word to whichever section of the defenses seemed to him to need counsel. He could see what Monty had done, and was in great spirits in consequence.

"I've bagged two Turk officers to my own gun," he announced. "Murder suits me to a T."

I gave him the message.

"Piffle!" he answered. "They can never take the ramp by frontal attack! The right thing to do is hold the flanks, and wither 'em as they cone!"

"Monty's orders!" I said, "and I've got to be going."

"Damn that fellow Didums!" he grumbled. "All right. But it's my belief he's turning a classy little engagement into a bloody brawl! Cut along! I'll pick my hundred and climb down there."

Cutting along was not so easy. My magnificent human mount was hit by a bullet — a stray one, probably, shot at a hazard at long range. He fell and threw me head-long; and the agony of that experience pretty nearly rendered me unconscious. However, he was not hit badly, and essayed to pick me up again. I refused that, but he held on to me and, both of us being hurt in the leg on the same side, we staggered together down the goat-track.

Down below we found the horse plunging in a frenzy of fear, and he nearly succeeded in breaking away from both of us, dragging us out into full view of the enemy, who volleyed us at long range. Fortunately they made rotten shooting, and one ill-directed hail of lead screamed on the far side, causing the horse to plunge toward me. The Armenian took me by the uninjured foot and flung me into the saddle, and I left up-pass with a parting volley scattering all around, and both hands locked into the horse's mane. He needed neither whip nor spur, but went for Zeitoon like the devil with his tail on fire.

I suppose one never grows really used to pain, but from use it becomes endurable. When Anna ran out to stop me by the great rock on which the lowest Zeitoon houses stand, and seized me by the foot, partly to show deference, partly in token that she was suppliant, and also partly because she was utterly distracted, I was able to rein the horse and listen to her without swearing.

"She is gone!" she shouted. "Gone, I tell you! Gloria is gone! Six men, they come and take her! She is resisting, oh, so hard — and they throw a sack over her — and she is gone, I tell you! She is gone!"

"Where is Maga?"

"Gone, too!"

"In which direction did they take Miss Gloria?"

"I do not know!"

I rode on. There were crowds of women near the bridge, all armed with rifles, and I hurried toward them.

But they refused to believe that any one in Zeitoon would do such a thing as kidnap Gloria, and while I waited for Anna to come and convince them a man forced himself toward me through the crowd. He was out of breath. One arm was in a bloody bandage, but in the other hand he held a stained and crumpled letter.

It proved to be from Will, addressed to all or any of us.

"Kagig is a wonder!" it ran, "He has put new life into these men and we've thrashed the Turk soundly. How's Gloria? Kagig says, 'Can you send us reinforcements?' If so we can follow up and do some real damage. Send 'em quick! Make Gloria keep cover!

WILL

Chapter Twenty

"So few against so many! I see death, and I am not sorry!"

THOU LAND OF THE GLAD HAND

Thou land of the Glad Hand, whose frequent boast
Is of the hordes to whom thou playest host!
Whose liberty is full! whose standard high
Has reached and taken stars from out the sky!
Whose fair-faced women tread the streets unveiled,
Unchallenged, unaffronted, unassailed!
Whose little ones in park and meadow laugh,
Nor know what cost that precious cup they quaff,
Nor pay in stripes and bruises and regret
Ten times each total of a parent's debt!
Thou nation born in freedom — land of kings
Whose laws protect the very feathered things,
Uplifting last and least to high estate
That none be overlooked — and none too great!
Is all thy freedom good for thee alone?
Is earth thy footstool? Are the clouds thy throne?
Shall other peoples reach thy hand to take
That gladdens only thee for thine own sake?

*T*o get word to Rustum Khan was simple enough, for he himself came riding down to get news. The minute he learned what Monty wanted of him he turned his horse back up-hill at a steady lope, and I began on the next item in the program.

Nor was that difficult. The reading aloud of Will's letter, translated to them by Anna, convinced the women that their beloved bridge was in no immediate danger, and no less than three hundred of them marched off to reinforce Kagig's men behind Beirut Dagh. I reckoned that by the time they reached the scene of action we would have a few more than three thousand men and women in the field under arms — against Mahmoud Bey's thirty thousand Turks!

There remained to scrape together as many as possible to man the castle walls; and what with wounded, and middle-aged women, and men whose weapons did not fit the plundered Turkish ammunition, I had more than a hundred volunteers in no time. The only disturbing feature about this new command of mine was that it contained more than a sprinkling of the type of malcontents who had bearded Kagig in his den the night before. Those looked like thoroughly excellent fighting men, if only they could have been persuaded to agree to trust a common leader.

Not one of them but knew a thousand times more of Zeitoon, and their people, and the various needs of defense than, for instance, I did. Yet they clustered about me for lack of confidence in one another, and shouted after the women who marched away advice to watch lest Kagig betray them all. Not for nothing had the unspeakable Turk inculcated theories of misrule all down the centuries!

I led them up to the castle, they carrying with them food enough for several days. We passed Rustum Khan coming down with the horsemen, and I fell behind to have word with him.

"Which of these men shall I pick to command the rest?" I asked him. "You've more experience of them."

"Any that you choose will be pounced on by the rest as wolves devour a sheep!" the Rajput answered.

"Should I have them vote on it?"

"They would elect you," he answered.

"I've got to be free to look for Miss Gloria. She's kidnapped — disappeared utterly!"

Rustum Khan swore under his breath, using a language that I knew no word of.

"A woman again, and more trouble!" he said at last grimly. "Let like cure like then! Choose a woman herdsman!" he grinned. "It may be she will surprise them into obedience!"

"I'll take your advice," said I, although I resented his insinuation that they were a herd — so swiftly does command make partisans.

"The last thing you may take from me, sahib!" he answered.

"How so?"

"So few against so many! I see death and I am not sorry. Only may I die leading those good mountain-men of mine!"

It was part and parcel of him to praise those he had drilled and scorn the others. I shook hands and said nothing. It did not seem my place to contradict him.

"Let us hope these people are the gainers by our finish!" he called over his shoulder, riding on after his command. "They are not at all bad people — only un-drilled, and a little too used to the ways of the Turk! Good-bye, sahib!"

Within the castle gate I found a woman, whom they all addressed as Marie, very busy sorting out the bundles they had thrown against the wall. She was putting all the food together into a common fund, and as I entered she shouted to her own nominees among the other women to get their cooking pots and begin business.

Still pondering Rustum Khan's advice, in the dark whether or not be meant it seriously, I chose Marie Chandrian to take command. She made no bones about it, but accepted with a great shrill laugh that the rest of them seemed to recognize — and to respect for old acquaintance' sake. She turned out to have her husband with her — an enormous, hairy man with a bull's voice who ought to have been in one or other of the firing-lines but had probably held back in obedience to his better half. She made him her orderly at once, and it was not long before every soul in the castle had his or her place to hold.

Then I mounted once more and rode at top speed down the new road that Monty was defending, taking another horse this time, not so good, but much less afraid of the din of battle.

I found Monty scarcely fifty paces from the track, on the outside edge of the fringe of trees that the Turks had been unable to cut down. There were numbers of wounded laid out on the track itself, with none to carry them away; and the Turks were keeping up a hot fire from behind the shelter of

the felled trees and standing stumps. The outside range was
two hundred yards, and there were several platoons of the
enemy who had crept up to within thirty or forty yards and
could not be dislodged.

I pulled Monty backward, for he could not hear me, and
he and I stood behind two trees while I told him what I had
done, shouting into his ear.

"I've got to go and find Gloria!" I said finally, and he
frowned, and nodded.

"Go first and take a look at the ramp through the trees.
Tell me what's happening."

So I limped down to the end of the track and made my
way cautiously through the lower fringe of trees that had been
cut three-parts through in readiness for felling in a hurry. Just
as I got there the Turks began a new massed advance up the
ramp, as if in direct proof of Monty's mental alertness.

The men posted on the opposite flank to where I was
opened a terrific fire that would have made poor Kagig bite
his lips in fear for the waning ammunition. Then Fred came
into action with his hundred, throwing them in line into the
open along the top, where they lay down to squander cartridges — squandering to some purpose, however, for the
Turkish lines checked and reeled.

But Mahmoud Bey had evidently given orders that this
advance should be pressed home, and the Turks came on,
company after company, in succeeding waves of men. There
were some in front with picks and shovels, making rough
steps in the slippery clay; and I groaned, hating to go and tell
Monty that it was only a matter of minutes before the frontal
attack must succeed and the pass be in enemy hands.

"Here goes Armenia's last chance!" I thought; and I waited
to see the beginning of the end before limping back to Monty.

And it was well I did wait. I had actually forgotten Rustum
Khan and his two squadrons. Nor would I ever have believed
without seeing it that one lone man could so inspirit and
control that number of aliens whom he had only as much as
drilled a time or two. It said as much for the Zeitoonli as for
Rustum Khan. Without the very ultimate of bravery, good
faith, and intelligence on their part he could never have come
near attempting what he did.

He brought his two squadrons in line together suddenly over the brow of the ramp, galloped them forward between Fred's extended riflemen, and charged down-hill, the horses checking as they felt the slippery clay under foot and then, unable to pull up, careering head-long, urged by their riders into madder and madder speed, with Rustum Khan on his beautiful bay mare several lengths in the lead.

Cavalry usually starts at a walk, then trots, and only gains its great momentum within a few yards of the enemy. This cavalry started at top speed, and never lost it until it buried itself into the advancing Turks as an avalanche bursts into a forest! No human enemy could ever have withstood that charge. Many of the horses fell in the first fifty yards, and none of these were able to regain their feet in time to be of use. Some of the riders were rolled on and killed. And some were slain by the half-dozen volleys the astonished Turks found time to greet them with. But more than two-thirds of Rustum Khan's men, armed with swords of every imaginable shape and weight, swept voiceless into an enemy that could not get out of their way; and regiments in the rear that never felt the shock turned and bolted from the wrath in front of them.

I climbed out to the edge of the trees, and yelled for Fred, waving both arms and my hat and a branch. He saw me at last, and brought his hundred men down the ramp at a run.

"Join Monty," I shouted, "and help him clear the woods."

He led his men into the trees like a pack of hounds in full cry, and I limped after them, arriving breathless in time to see the Turks in front of Monty in full retreat, fearful because the Rajput's cavalry had turned their flank. Then Monty and Fred got their men together and swung them down into the pass to cover Rustum Khan's retreat when the charge should have spent itself.

The Rajput had managed to demoralize the Turkish infantry, but Mahmoud's guns were in the rear, far out of reach. Bursting shells did more destruction as he shepherded the squadrons back again than bullet, bayonet and slippery clay combined to do in the actual charge itself. Monty gave orders to throw down the fringe of trees and let them through to the castle road, so saving them from the total annihilation in store if they had essayed to scramble up the slippery ramp. And then Fred's men joined Monty's contingent, helping them fortify the new line — deepening and reversing the trench the Turks had dug below the ramp, and continuing that line along through the remaining edge of trees that still stood between the enemy and the castle road.

But by cutting down the fringe at the end of the road to let Rustum Khan through we had forfeited the last degree of secrecy. If the Turks could come again and force the gut of the pass, nothing but the hardest imaginable fighting could prevent them from swinging round at that point and making use of our handiwork.

"That castle has become a weakness, not a strength, Colonel sahib!" said Rustum Khan, striding through the trees to where Monty and Fred and I were standing. "I have lost seven and thirty splendid men, and three and forty horses. One more such charge, and —"

"No, Rustum Khan. Not again," Monty answered.

"What else?" laughed the Rajput. "That castle divides our forces, making for weakness. If only —"

"We must turn it to advantage, then, Rustum Khan!"

"Ah, sahib! So speaks a soldier! How then?"

"Mahmoud knows by now that the trees are down," said I. "His watchers must have seen them fall. Some of the trees are lying outward toward the ramp."

"Exactly," said Monty. "His own inclination will lead him to use our new road, and we must see that he does exactly that. The guns are making the ramp too hot just now for amusement, but let some one — you, Fred — run a deep ditch across the top of the ramp; and if we can hold them until dark we'll have connected ditches dug at intervals all the way down."

Looking over the top of the trees I could just see the Montdidier standard bellying in the wind.

"I'll bet you Mahmoud can see that, too!" said I, drawing the others' attention to it.

"Let's hope so," Monty answered quietly. "Now, Rustum Khan, find one of those brave horsemen of yours who is willing to be captured by the enemy and give some false information. I want it well understood that our only fear is of a night attack!"

"You say, Colonel sahib, there will be no further use for cavalry?"

"Not for a charge down that ramp, at any rate!"

"Then send me! My word will carry conviction. I can say that as a Moslem I will fight no longer on the side of Christians. They will accept my information, and then hang me for having led a charge into their infantry. Send me, sahib!"

Monty shook his head. Rustum Khan seemed inclined to insist, but there came astonishing interruption. Kagig appeared, with arms akimbo, in our midst.

"Oh, sportmen all!" he laughed. "This day goes well!"

"Thank God you're here!" said Monty. "Now we can talk."

"That Will — what is his name? — Will Yerkees is a wonderful fighter!" said Kagig, snapping his fingers and making the joints crack.

"He accuses you of that complaint," said I.

"Me? No. I am only enthusiast. The road behind Beirut Dagh is rough and narrow. The Turks had hard work, and less reason for eagerness than we. So we overcame them. They have fallen back to where they were at dawn, and they are discouraged" — he made his finger-joints crack again — "discouraged! The women feel very confident. The men feet exactly as the women do! The Turks are preparing to bivouac where they lie. They will attack no more today — I know them!"

"Listen, Kagig!" Monty drew us all together with a gesture of both hands. "These Turks are too many for us, if we give them time. Our ammunition won't last, for one thing. We must induce Mahmoud to attack tonight — coax him up this castle road, and catch him in a trap. It can be done. It must be done!"

"I know the right man to send to the Turk to tell him things!" Kagig answered slowly with relish.

"That is my business!" growled Rustum Khan, but Kagig laughed at him.

"No Turk would believe a word you say — not one leetle word!" he said, snapping his fingers. "You are a good fighter. I saw your charge from the castle tower; it was very good. But

I will send an Armenian on this errand. Go on, Lord Monty;
I know the proper man."

"That's about the long and short of it," said Monty. "If we
can induce Mahmoud to attack tonight, we've a fair chance
of hitting him so hard that he'll withdraw and let us alone.
Otherwise —"

Kagig's finger-joints cracked harder than ever as his quick
mind reviewed the possibilities.

"Have you any idea what can have happened to Miss
Vanderman?" I asked him.

"Miss Vanderman? No? What? Tell me!"

He seemed astonished, and I told him slowly, lest he miss
one grain of the enormity of Maga's crime. But instead of
appearing distressed he shook his bands delightedly and
rattled off a very volley of cracking knuckles.

"That is the idea! We have Mahmoud caught! I know
Mahmoud! I know him! The man I shall choose shall tell
Mahmoud that Gloria Vanderman — the beautiful American
young lady, who is outlawed because of her fighting on behalf
of Armenians — who — who could not possibly be claimed
by the American consul, on account of being outlawed — is
in the castle tonight and can be taken if he only will act
quickly! Oh, how his eyes will glitter! That Mahmoud — he
buys women all the time! A young — beautiful — athletic
American girl — Mahmoud will sacrifice three thousand men
to capture her!"

Monty ground his teeth. Fred turned his back, and filled
his pipe. Rustum Khan brushed his black beard upward with
both hands.

"Suppose you go now and try to find Miss Vanderman,"
said Monty rather grimly to me. "If you find her, hide her
out of harm's way and communicate with Will!"

So Fred helped me on the horse and I rode back to the
castle, where I explained the details of the fighting below to
the defenders, and then rode on down to Zeitoon by the other
road. It was wearing along into the afternoon, and I had no
idea which way to take to look for Gloria; but I did have a
notion that Maga Jhaere might be looking out for me. There
was a chance that she might have been in earnest in persuad-
ing me to elope, and that if I rode alone she might show

herself — she or else Gloria's captors.

Failing signs of Maga Jhaere or her men, I proposed to ride behind Beirut Dagh in search of Will, and to get his quick Yankee wit employed on the situation.

So, instead of crossing the bridge into Zeitoon I guided my horse around the base of the mountain, riding slowly so as to ease the pain in my foot and to give plenty of opportunity to any one lying in wait to waylay me.

It happened I guessed rightly. The track swung sharp to the left after a while, and passed up-hill through a gorge between two cliffs into wilder country than any I had yet seen in Armenia. From the top of the cliff on the right-hand side a pebble was dropped and struck the horse — then another — then a third one. I thought it best to take no notice of that, although the horse made fuss enough.

The third pebble was followed by a shrill whistle, which I also decided to ignore, and continued to ride on toward where a clump of scrawny bushes marked the opening out of a narrow valley. I heard the bushes rustle as I drew near them, and was not surprised to see Maga emerge, looking hot, impatient and angry, although not less beautiful on that account.

"Fool!" she began on me. "Why you wait so long? Another half-hour and it is too late altogether! Come now! Leave the horse. Come quick!"

Wondering what important difference half an hour should make, it occurred to me that Will was probably impatient long ago at receiving no news of Gloria. If I judged Will rightly, he would be on his way to look for her.

"Come quick!" commanded Maga.

"I can't climb that cliff," said I. "I've hurt my foot."

"I help you. Come!"

She stepped up close beside me to help me down, but that instant it seemed to me that I heard more than one horse approaching.

"Quick!" she commanded, for she heard them, too, and held out her arms to help me. "Quick! I have two men to help you walk!"

I could have reached my pistol, but so could she have reached hers, and her hand and eye were quicker than forked lightning. Besides, to shoot her would have been of doubtful benefit until Gloria's whereabouts were first ascertained. She put an arm round me to pull me from the saddle, and that settled it. I fell on her with all my weight, throwing her backward into the bushes, and kicking the horse in the ribs with my uninjured foot. The horse took fright as I intended, and went galloping off in the direction of the approaching sounds.

I had not wrestled since I was a boy at school, and then never with such a spitting puzzle of live wires as Maga proved herself. I had the advantage of weight, but I had told her of my injured foot, and she worked like a she-devil to damage it further, fighting at the same time with left and right wrist alternately to reach pistol and knife.

I let go one wrist, snatched the pistol out of her bosom and threw it far away. But with the free and she reached her knife, and landed with it into my ribs. The pain of the stab sickened me; but the knowledge that she had landed fooled her into relaxing her hold in order to jump clear. So I got hold of both wrists again, and we rolled over and over among the bushes, she trying like an eel to wriggle away, and I doing my utmost to crush the strength out of her. We were interrupted by Will's voice, and by Will's strong arms dragging us apart.

"Catch her!" I panted. "Hold her! Don't let her go!"

"Never fear!" he laughed.

"Her men have kidnapped Gloria! Tie her hands!"

Will had two men with him, one of whom was leading my runaway horse. They gazed open-eyed while Will tied Maga's wrists behind her back.

"Kagig — what will he say?" one of them objected, but Will laughed.

"What you do with me?" demanded Maga.

"Take you to Kagig, of course. Where's Miss Vanderman?"

Then suddenly Maga's whole appearance changed. The defiance vanished, leaving her as if by magic supple again, subtle, suppliant, conjuring back to memory the nights when she had danced and sung. The fire departed from her eyes and they became wet jewels of humility with soft love lights glowing in their depths.

"You do not want that woman!" she said slowly, smiling at Will. "You give 'er to this fool!" She glanced at my bleeding ribs, as if the blood were evidence of folly. "You take me, Will Yerkees! Then I teach you all things — all about people — all about land, and love, and animals, and water, and the air — I teach you all!"

She paused a moment, watching his face, judging the effect of words. He stood waiting with a look of puzzled distress that betrayed regret for her tied wrists, but accepted the necessity. Perhaps she mistook the chivalrous distress for tenderness.

"I 'ave tried to make that man Kagig king! I 'ave tried, and tried! But 'e is no good! If 'e 'ad obeyed me, I would 'ave made 'im king of all Armenia! But 'e is as good as dead already, because Mahmoud the Turk is come to finish 'im — so!" She spat conclusively. "So now I make you king instead of 'im! You let that Gloria Vanderman go to this fool, an' I show you 'ow to make all Armenians follow you an' overthrow the Turks, an' conquer, an' you be king!"

Will laughed. "Better stick to Kagig! I'm going to take you to him!"

"You take me to 'im?"

She flashed again, swift as a snake to illustrate resentment. "Yes."

"Then I tell 'im things about you, an' 'e believe me!"

"Let's bargain," laughed Will. "Show me Miss Vanderman, alive and well, and —"

"Steady the Buffs!" I warned him. "Gloria's not far away. There were pebbles dropped on my horse. There may be a cave above this cliff — or something of the sort."

Will nodded. "— and I won't tell Kagig you made love to me!" he continued.

"Poof! Pah! Kagig, 'e know that long ago!"

Will turned to his two men and bade them tie the horses to a bush.

"How are the ribs?" he asked me.

"Nothing serious," said I.

"Do you think you can watch her if I tie her feet?"

"She's slippery and strong! Better tie her to a tree as well!"

So between them Will and the two men trussed her up like

a chicken ready for the market, making her bound ankles fast
to the roots of a bush. Then he led the two men up the
cliff-side, and Maga lay glaring at me as if she hoped hate
could set me on fire, while I made shift to stanch my wound.

But she changed her tactics almost before Will was out of
sight beyond a boulder, beginning to scream the same words
over and over in the gypsy tongue and struggling to free her
feet until I thought the thongs would either burst or strip the
flesh from her.

The screams were answered by a shout from up above. Then
I heard Will shout, and some one fired a pistol. There came
a clatter of loose stones, and I got to my feet to be ready for
action — not that my hurts would have let me accomplish
much.

A second later I saw three of Gregor Jhaere's gypsies scurrying along the cliff-side, turning at intervals to fire pistols
at some one in pursuit. So I joined in the fray with my Colt
repeater, and flattered myself I did not do so badly. The first
two shots produced no other effect than to bring the run-
aways to a halt. The next three shots brought all three men
tumbling head over heels down the cliff-side, rolling and
sliding and scattering the stones.

One fell near Maga's feet and lay there writhing. The other
two came to a standstill in a hideous heap beside me, and I
stooped to see if I could recognize them.

What happened after that was almost too quick for the
senses to take in. One of the gypsies came suddenly to life
and seized me by the neck. The other grasped my feet, and
as I fell I saw the third man slash loose Maga's thongs and
help her up.

My two assailants rolled me over on my back, and while
one held me the other aimed blows at my head with the butt
of his empty pistol. Once he hit me, and it felt like an
explosion. Twice by a miracle I dodged the blows, growing
weaker, though, and hopeless. He aimed a fourth blow, taking
his time about it and making sure of his aim, and I waited
in the nearest approach to fatalistic calm I ever experienced.

In a strange abstraction, in which every movement seemed
to be slowed down into unbelievable leisureliness, I saw the
butt of the pistol begin to approach my eye — near — nearer.

Then suddenly I heard a woman scream, and a shot ring out.

Instead of the pistol butt the gypsy's brains splashed on my face, and the man collapsed on top of me. Next I realized that Gloria Vanderman was wiping my face with a cloth of some kind, holding a hot pistol in her other hand, while Will was standing laughing over me, and Maga Jhaere with the other gypsy had disappeared altogether.

"Did you shoot Maga?" I mumbled.

"No," Will laughed. "I'd hate to shoot a woman who'd offered to make me king! She ought to be hung, though, for a horse-thief! She and that other gypsy got away with the mounts! Never mind — there are four of us to carry you, if Gloria lends a hand!"

But I have no notion how they carried me. All I remember is recovering consciousness that evening in the castle, to discover myself copiously bandaged, and painfully stiff, but not so much of an invalid after all.

Chapter Twenty-One

"Those who survive this night shall have brave memories!"

FRAGMENT

Oh, fear and hate shall have their spate
(For both of the twain are one)
And lust and greed devour the seed
That else had growth begun.
Fiercely the flow of death shall go
And short the good man's shrift!
All hell's awake full toll to take,
And passions hour is swift.

But there be cracks in evil's tracks
Where seed shall safe abide,
And living rocks shall breast the shocks
Of overflowing tide.
Castle and wall and keep shall fall,
Prophet and plan shall fail,
And they shall thank nor wit nor rank
Who in the end prevail.

*L*ooking back after this lapse of time there seems little difference between the disordered dreams of unconsciousness and the actual waking turmoil of that night. At first as I came slowly to my senses there seemed only a sea of voices all about me, and a constant thumping, as of falling weights.

There were great pine torches set in the rusty old rings on the wall, and by their fitful light I saw that I lay on a cot in

the castle keep. Monty, Fred, Will, Kagig and Rustum Khan
were conversing at a table. Gloria sat on an up-ended pine
log near me. A dozen Armenians, including the "elders" who
had disagreed with Kagig, stood arguing rather noisily near
the door.

"What is the thumping?" I asked, and Gloria hurried to
the cot-side. But I managed to sit up, and after she had given
me a drink I found that my foot was still the most injured
part of me. It was swollen unbelievably, whereas my bandaged
head felt little the worse for wear, and the knife-wound did
not hurt much.

"They're bringing in wood," she answered.

"Why all that quantity?"

The thumping was continuous, not unlike the noise good
stevedores make when loading against time.

"To burn the castle!"

At that moment Rustum Khan left the table, and seeing
me sitting up strode over.

"Good-bye, sahib!" he said, reaching out for my hand.

"The lord sahib has given me a post of honor and I go to
hold it. Those who survive this night shall have brave memories!"

I got to my feet to shake hands with him, and I think he
appreciated the courtesy, for his stern eyes softened for a
moment. He saluted Gloria rather perfunctorily as became
his attitude toward women, and strode away to a point
half-way between the door and Monty. There he turned,
facing the table.

"Lord sahib bahadur!" he said sonorously.

Monty got up and stood facing him.

"Salaam!"

"Salaam, Rustum Khan!" Monty answered, returning the
salute, and the others got to their feet in a hurry, and stood
at attention.

Then the Rajput faced about and went striding through
the doorless opening into the black night — the last I was
destined to see of him alive.

"May we all prove as faithful and brave as that man!" said
Monty, sitting down again, and Kagig cracked his knuckles.

Gloria and I went over and sat at the table, and seeing me

in a state to understand things Monty gave me a précis of the situation.

-"We're making a great beacon of this castle," he said. "Three hundred men and women are piling in the felled logs and trees and down-wood — everything that will burn. We shall need light on the scene. Rustum Khan has gone to hold the clay ramp and make sure the Turks turn up this castle road. Fred is to hold the corner; we've fortified the Zeitoon side of the road, and Fred and his men are to make sure the Turks don't spread out through the trees. Kagig, Will and I, with twenty-five very carefully picked men for each of us, wait for the Turks at the bottom of the road and put up a feint of resistance. Our business will be to make it look as little like a trap and as much like a desperate defense as possible. We hope to make it seem we're caught napping and fighting in the last ditch."

"Last ditch is true enough!" Fred commented cheerfully. Fred was obviously in his best humor, faced by a situation that needed no cynicism to discolor it — full of fight and perfectly contented.

"Practically all of the rest of the men and women who are not watching the enemy on the other side of Beirut Dagh," Monty went on, "are hidden, or will be hidden in the timber on either side of the road. We're hoping to God they'll have sense enough to keep silent until the beacon is lighted. You're to light the beacon, since you're recovering so finely — you and Miss Vanderman."

"Yes, but when?" said I.

"When the bugles blow. We've got six bugles —"

"Only two of them are cornets and one's a trombone," Fred put in.

"And when they all sound together, then set the castle alight and kill any one you see who isn't an Armenian!"

"Or us!" said Fred. "You're asked not to kill one of us!"

"As a matter of fact," said Monty, "I rather expect to be near you by that time, because we don't want to give the signal until as many Turks as possible are caught in the road like rats. At the signal we dose the road at both ends; Rustum Khan and Fred from the bottom end, and we at the top."

"Most of the murder," Fred explained cheerfully, "will be

done by the women hidden in the trees on either flank. As long as they don't shoot across the road and kill one another it'll be a picnic!"

"How do you know the Turks will walk into the trap?" I asked.

"Ten 'traitors,'" said Monty, "have let themselves get caught at intervals since noon. One of Kagig's spies has got across to us with news that Mahmoud means to finish the hash of Zeitoon tonight. His men have been promised all the loot and all the women."

"Except one!" Fred added with a glance at Gloria.

"Two! Except two!" remarked Kagig with a glance at the door. We looked, and held our breath.

Maga Jhaere stood there, with a hand on the masonry on each side!

"You fool, Kagig, what you fill this castle full of wood for?" she demanded.

Kagig beckoned to her.

"To burn little traitoresses!" he answered tenderly. "Come here!"

She walked over to him, and he put his arm around her waist, looking up from his seat into her face as if studying it almost for the first time. She began running her fingers through his hair.

"Is she not beautiful?" he asked us naively. Then, not waiting for an answer: "She is my wife, effendim. You would not have me be revengeful — not toward my wife, I think?"

"Your wife? Why didn't you tell us that before?"

Gloria seemed the most surprised, as well as the most amused, although we were all astonished.

"Not tell you before? Oh — do you remember Abraham — in the Bible — yes? She has been my best spy now and then. As Kagig's wife what good would she be? Yet, had I not married her, I should have lost the services of most of my best spies — Gregor Jhaere for one. He is not her father, no. They call her their queen. She is daughter of another gypsy and of an Armenian lady of very good family. She has always hoped to see me a monarch!"

He laughed, and cracked his finger-joints.

"To make of me a monarch, and to reign beside me!

Ha-ha-ha! I did those gypsies a favor by marrying her, for she was something of a problem to them, no gypsy being good enough in her eyes, and no busne (Gentile) caring for the honor until I saw and fell in love! Oh, yes, I fell in love! I, Kagig, the old adventurer, I fell in love!"

He drew her down and kissed her as tenderly as if she were a little child; then rose to his feet.

"You forgive her, effendim?" he asked. "You forgive her for my sake?"

None answered him. Perhaps he asked too much.

"Never mind me, then, effendim. Not for my sake, but for the good work she has so often done, and for the work she shall do — you forgive her?"

We all looked toward Gloria. It was her prerogative. Gloria took Maga's left hand in her right.

"I don't blame you," she said, "for coveting Will. I've coveted him myself! But you needn't have let your men handle me so roughly!"

"No?" said Maga blandly. "Then why did you 'urt two of them so badly that they run away? Did not you shoot that other one? So — I give 'im to you. I give you that Will Yerkees —"

"Thanks!" put in Will, but Maga ignored the interruption.

"— not because you are cleverer than me — or more beautiful. You are uglee! You can not dance, and as for fighting, I could keel you with one 'and! But because I like Kagig better after all!"

At that Kagig suddenly dismissed all such trivialities as treachery and matrimony from his mind with one of his Napoleonic gestures.

"It is time, effendim, to be moving!" He led the way out without another word, I limping along last and the Armenian "elders" following me.

It was pitchy dark in the castle courtyard, and without the light from numerous kerosene lanterns it would not have been possible to find the way between the heaped-up logs. There was only a crooked, very narrow passage left between the keep and the outer gate, and they had long ago left off using the gate for the lumber, but were hoisting it over the wall with ropes. One improvised derrick squealed in the darkness, and the logs came in by twos and tens and dozens. No sooner were we out of the keep than women came and tossed in logs through the door and windows, until presently that building, too, contained fuel enough to decompose the stone. And over the whole of it, here, there and everywhere, men were pouring cans and cans of kerosene, while other men were setting dry tinder in strategic places.

There was no moon that night. Or if there was a moon, then the dark clouds hid it. No doubt Mahmoud thought he had a night after his own heart for the purpose of overwhelming our little force; for how should he know that we were ready for the massed battalions forming to storm the gorge again. At a little after eight o'clock Mahmoud resumed the offensive with his artillery, and a messenger that Monty sent down to watch returned and reported the shells all bursting wild, with Rustum Khan's men taking careful cover in the ditches they had zigzagged down the whole face of the ramp.

An hour later the Turk's infantry was reported moving, and shortly before ten o'clock we heard the opening rattle of Rustum Khan's stinging defense. There was intended to be no deception about that part of our arrangements; nor was there. The oncoming enemy was met with a hail of destruction that checked and withered his ranks, and made the succeeding companies only too willing to turn at the castle road instead of struggling straight forward.

Nor was the turn accomplished without further loss; for our Zeitoonli, still entrenched on the flank of the pass, loosed a murderous storm of lead through the dark that swept every inch of the open castle road, and the turn became a shambles.

But Mahmoud had reckoned the cost and decided to pay it. Company after company poured up the gorge in the rear of the front ones, and turned with a roar up the road, butchered and bewildered, but ever adding to the total that gained shelter beyond the first turn in the road.

Those, however, had to deal at once with Monty, Will and Kagig, who opened on them guerrilla warfare from behind trees — never opposing them sufficiently to check them altogether, but leading them steadily forward into the two-mile trap. From where I stood on the top of the castle wall I could judge pretty accurately how the fight went; and I marveled at the skill of our men that they should retire up the road so slowly, and make such a perfect impression of desperate defense. Gloria refused from the first to remain inactive beside me, but went through the trees down the line of the road, crossing at intervals from side to side, urging and begging our ambushed people to be patient and reserve their fire until the chorus of bugles should blow.

About eleven o'clock a breathless messenger came to say that the Turks had renewed the attack on the other side of Beirut Dagh; but I did not even send him on to Kagig. If the attack was a feint, as was probable, intended to distract us from the main battle, then there were men enough there to deal with it. If, on the other hand, Mahmoud had divided forces and sent a formidable number around the mountain, then our only chance was nevertheless to concentrate on our great effort, and defeat the nearest first. There was not the slightest wisdom in sending down a message likely to distract Monty or Will or Kagig from their immediate task.

The women kept piling in the pine trees, until I thought the very weight of lumber might defeat our purpose by delaying the blaze too long. But Kagig had requisitioned every drop of kerosene in Zeitoon, and the stuff was splashed on with the recklessness that comes of throwing parsimony to the winds. Then I grew afraid lest they should fire the stuff too soon, or lest some stray spark from a man's pipe or an overturned lantern should do the work. Every imaginable fear presented itself, because, having no active part in the fighting, I had nothing to distract me from self-criticism. It became almost a foregone conclusion after a while that the night's work was destined to be spoiled entirely by some oversight or stupidity of mine.

The battle down in the valley dinned and screamed like the end of the world, although the Turks could not use their artillery for fear of slaughtering their own men. I could hear Fred hotly engaged, holding the corner of the turn where the Turks were seeking in vain to widen it. Probably the Turks supposed he was put there with a hundred men to defend the road, instead of to drive their thinned battalions up it.

In the end it was an accident that set the bugles blowing, and probably that accident saved our fortunes. Monty

shouted to a man to run and ask for news of the fighting
below. Mistaking the words in the din, the messenger ran to
the rock in the clearing on which the musicians waited, and
a minute later the first bars of the Marseillaise rang clearly
through the trees.

The almost instant answer was a volley from each side of
the road that sounded like the explosion of the whole world.
And the Turks hardly half into the trap yet! Monty and Will
and Kagig brought their men back up the road at the double,
as the only way to escape the fire of our ambushed friends. I
was two minutes fumbling with matches in the wind before
I could light the kindling set ready in the entrance arch; and
it was about three minutes more before the first long flame
shot skyward and the beacon we had set began to do its
appointed work.

Then, though, that castle proved to be a very Vesuvius, for
the draught poured in through the doorless arch and hurried
the hot flames skyward to be mushroomed roaring against
the belly of black clouds. None of us knew then where
Mahmoud was, nor that he had given the order that minute
to his trapped battalions to halt, face the trees on either side,
and advance in either direction in order to widen their front.

The firing of the castle, for some mad reason of the sort
that mothers every catastrophe, caused them to disobey that
order and, instead, to charge forward at the double. In a
moment the new fury (for it was not panic, nor yet exactly
the reverse) communicated itself all along the road, and the
regiments at the rear, in spite of the murderous fire from our
ambush, yelled and milled to drive the men in front more
swiftly.

Then Fred saw the castle flames, and led his men forward
to plug up the lower end of the road. Next Rustum Khan saw
it, and advanced three hundred down the ramp to hold the
ditch at the bottom and prevent reserves from coming to the
rescue.

It was then, so he told us afterward, that Fred realized who
was the person in authority who had sought to change the
line of battle at the critical moment. Mahmoud himself,
surrounded by his staff, had ridden forward to see what the
true nature of the difficulty might be, and had got caught in

the trap when Fred closed it and Rustum Khan cut off the flow of men!

Fred did his best by rapid fire to put an end to Mahmoud, staff and all. But the light from the castle did not reach down in among the trees, and when he told the nearest men who the target was that only made the shooting wilder. Nor was Mahmoud a man without decision. Realizing that he was trapped, at any rate from behind, he galloped forward with his staff, scattering bewildered men to right and left of him, to find out whether the trap could not be forced from the upper end, knowing that there were plenty of men on the road already to account for any possible total we could bring against them, if only they could be led forward and deployed.

So it came about that Mahmoud on a splendid war-horse, and five of his mounted staff, arrived at the head of the oncoming column; and Kagig saw them in a moment when the flare from the castle roared like a rocket hundreds of feet high and scattered all the shadows on that section of the road. Kagig passed the word along, but it was Monty who devised the instant plan, and one of Will's men who came running to find me.

So I forgot pain and disability in the excitement of having a part to play. Gloria had found her way back to the castle, and it was she who rallied all the men and women who had worked at piling fuel, and brought them to where I lay. Then I begged her to get back somewhere and hide, but she laughed at me.

Our business was to burry down the road and plug it against Mahmoud and his men, while Kagig got behind him by sheer hand-to-hand fighting, and Monty and Will approached him from the flanks. We had to be cautious about shooting, because of Kagig, for one thing, but for another, Will had sent the message, "Don't kill Mahmoud." And that, of course, was obvious. Mahmoud alive would be worth a thousand to us of any Mahmoud dead.

Gloria ran down the road beside me, and Will caught sight of her in the dancing light. I heard him shout something in United States English about women and hell-fire and burned fingers, but beyond that it was not polite, and was intended for me as much as for Gloria, I did not get the gist of it. Then the battle closed up around us, and we all fought hand to hand — women harder than the men — to close in on Mahmoud and drag him from his horse.

Three times in the fitful dark and even more deceptive dancing light we almost had him. But the first time he fought free, and his war-horse kicked a clear way for him for a few yards through the scrimmage. Then Kagig closed in on him from the rear. But three of the staff engaged Kagig alone, and twenty or thirty of Mahmoud's infantry drove Kagig's men back on the still advancing column. Kagig went down, fighting and shouting like a Berserker, and Monty let Mahmoud go to run to Kagig's rescue.

Monty did not go alone, for his men leapt after him like hounds. But he fought his way in the lead with a clubbed rifle, and stood over Kagig's body working the weapon like a flail. That was all I saw of that encounter, for Mahmoud decided to attempt escape by the upper way again, and it was I who captured him. I landed on him through the darkness with my clenched fist under the low hung angle of his jaw and, seizing his leg, threw him out of the saddle. There Gloria helped me sit on him; and the greater part of what we had to do was to keep the women from tearing him to pieces.

At last Gloria and I, with a dozen of them, took Mahmoud up-hill and made him sit down in full firelight with his back against a rock. He had nothing to say for himself, but stared at Gloria with eyes that explained the whole philosophy of all the Turks; and she, for sake of the decency that was her birthright, went and stood on the far side of the rock and kept the bulge of it between them.

Then I sent for Kagig, and Monty, and Will; And after they had seen to the barricading of the upper end of the road with fallen trees and a fairly wide ditch, Kagig and Will came, followed by half a dozen of the elders, who had been lending a stout hand during that part of the night's work. Kagig was out of breath, but apparently not hurt much.

They came so slowly that I wondered. Gloria, who could see much farther through the dark than I, gave a little scream and ran forward. I saw then by a sudden burst of flame from the castle that they were carrying something heavy, and I guessed what it was although my heart rebelled against belief;

but I did not dare leave Mahmoud, who seemed inclined to take advantage of the first stray opportunity. I stuck my pistol into his ear and dared him to move hand or foot.

Gloria came back in tears, and took Mahmoud's cape and my jacket, and spread them on the ground. On these they laid Monty very tenderly, Kagig looking on with cracking finger-joints that I could hear quite plainly in spite of the awful rage of battle that thundered and crashed and screamed among the woods. It was as one sometimes hears the ticking of a watch beneath the pillow in a nightmare.

Monty was alive, but in spite of what Gloria could do the dark blood was welling out from a sword gash on his right side, and we had not a surgeon within miles of us. From somewhere out of the darkness Maga appeared, bringing water, her face all black with the filth of fighting among trees, and her eyes on fire.

Monty seemed to be listening to the noise of battle — Kagig to think of nothing but his loss. He pointed at Mahmoud, who was eying Monty curiously.

"See the prisoner!" he said. "Ha! I would give a hundred of him a hundred times for Monty, my brother!"

Monty turned his head to see Mahmoud, and appeared partly satisfied.

"You hold the key," he said painfully. "Mahmoud will make terms. But it will take time to stop the fighting. You must send down reserves to Fred and Rustum Khan — that is where the strain is — you must see that surely — the enemy from below will be trying to come forward, and those in the trap to return. Fred and Rustum Khan are bearing all the brunt. Relieve them!"

It did not look good to me that Will should leave Gloria again; and Kagig must surely stay there to do the bargaining. So I took Monty's hand to bid him good-bye, and limped off through the dark to try to find men who would come with me to the shambles below. It wag Kagig and Will together who overtook me, picked me off my feet, and dragged me back, and Will went down alone, with a wave of the hand to Gloria, and a laugh that might have made the devil think he liked it.

Then began the conference, I holding a mere watching brief

with a pistol reasonably close to Mahmoud's ear. And for a
time, while Monty lived, the elders supported Kagig and
insisted on the full concession of his demands. But Monty,
with his head on Gloria's lap, died midway of the proceedings; and after that the elders' suspicion of Kagig reawoke, so
that Mahmoud took courage and grew more obstinate. Kagig
called them aside repeatedly to make them listen to his views.

"You fools!" he swore at them, cracking his knuckles and
twisting at his beard alternately. "Do you not realize that
Mahmoud is ambitious! Do you not understand that he must
yield all, if you insist! Otherwise we hang him here to a tree
in sight of the burning castle and his own men! No ambitious
rascal is ever willing to be hanged! Insist! Insist!"

"Ah, Kagig!" one of them answered. "Speak for yourself.
You would not like to be hanged perhaps! But we must
concede him something, or how shall he satisfy ambition?
He must be able to go back with something to his credit in
order to satisfy the politicians."

"Oh, my people! Oh, my people!" grumbled Kagig. "Can
you never see?"

But they went back to Mahmoud with a fresh proposal,
milder than the first; and eventually, after yielding point by
point, until Kagig begged them kindly to blow his brains out
and bury him with Monty, they reached a basis on which
Mahmoud was willing to capitulate — or to oblige them, as
he expressed it.

He won his main point: Zeitoon was to accept a Turkish
governor. They won theirs, that the governor was to bring no
troops with him, but to be contented with a body-guard of
Zeitoonli. For the rest: Mahmoud was to go free, taking his
wounded with him, but surrendering all the uninjured Turkish soldiers in the trap as hostages for the release of all
Armenian prisoners taken anywhere between Tarsus and Zeitoon. It was agreed there were to be no subsequent reprisals
by either side, and that hostages were not to be released until
after Mahmoud's army corps should have returned to whence
it came.

Kagig wrote the terms in Turkish by the light of the
holocaust in Monty's ancestral keep, and Mahmoud signed
the paper in the presence of ten witnesses. But whether he,

or his brother Turks, have kept, for instance, the last clause of the agreement, history can answer.

Chapter Twenty-Two

"God go with you to the States, effendim!"

ARMENIA

First of the Christian nations; the first of us all to feel
The fire of infidel hatred, the weight of the pagan heel;
Faithfullest down the ages tending the light that burned,
Tortured and trodden therefore, spat on and slain and spurned;
Branded for others' vices, robbed of your rightful fame,
Clinging to Truth in a truthless land in the name of the ancient Name;
Generous, courteous, gentle, patient under the yoke,
Decent (hemmed in a harem land ye were ever a one-wife folk);
Royal and brave and ancient — haply an hour has struck
When the new fad-fangled peoples shall weary of raking muck,
And turning from coward counsels and loathing the parish lies,
In shame and sackcloth offer up the only sacrifice.
Then thou who hast been neglected, who hast called o'er a world in vain
To the deaf deceitful traders' ears in tune to the voice of gain,
Thou Cinderella nation, starved that our appetites might live,
When we come with a hand outstretched at last — accept it, and forgive!

*T*he fighting lasted nearly until dawn, because of the difficulty of conveying Mahmoud's orders to the Turks, and Kagig's orders to our own tree-hidden firing-line. But a little before sunrise the last shot was fired, at about the time when most of the castle walls fell in and a huge shower of golden sparks shot upward to the paling sky. The cease fire left all Zeitoon's defenders with scarcely a thousand rounds of rifle ammunition between them; but Mahmoud did not know that.

An hour after dawn Fred joined us. He had the news of Monty's death already, and said nothing, but pointed to something that his own men bore along on a litter of branches. A minute or two later they laid Rustum Khan's corpse beside Monty's, and we threw one blanket over both of them.

I don't remember that Fred spoke one word. He and Monty had been closer friends than any brothers I ever knew. No doubt the awful strain of the fighting at the corner of the woods had left Fred numb to some extent; but he and Monty had never been demonstrative in their affection, and, as they had lived in almost silent understanding of each other, hidden very often for the benefit of strangers by keen mutual criticism, so they parted, Fred not caring to make public what he thought, or knew, or felt.

Kagig, not being in favor with the elders, vanished, Maga following with food for him in a leather bag, and we saw neither of them again until noon that day, by which time we ourselves had slept a little and eaten ravenously. Then he came to us where we still sat by the great rock with Mahmoud under guard (for nobody would trust him to fulfill his agreement until all his troops had retired from the district, leaving behind them such ammunition and supplies as they had carried to the gorge below the ramp).

We had laid both bodies under the one blanket in the shade, and Kagig pointed to them.

"I have found the place — the proper place, effendim!" he said simply. "Maga has made it fit."

Not knowing what he meant by that last remark, we invited some big Armenians to come with us to carry our honored dead, and followed Kagig one by one up a goat track (or a bear track, perhaps it was) that wound past the crumbled and blackened castle wall and followed the line of the mountain. Here and there we could see that Kagig had cleared it a little on his way back, and several times it was obvious that there had been a prepared, frequented track in ancient days.

"It took time to find," said Kagig, glancing back, "but I thought there must be such a place near such a castle."

Presently we emerged on a level ledge of rock, from a square hole in the midst of which a great slab had been levered away with the aid of a pole that lay beside it. All around the opening Maga had spread masses of wild flowers, and either she or Kagig had spread out on the rock the great banner with its ships and wheat-sheaves that the women had made by night in Monty's honor.

We could read the motto plainly now — Per terram et aquam — By land and sea; and Kagig pointed to some marks on the stone slab. Moss had grown in them and lichens, but he or else Maga had scraped them clean; and there on the stone lay the same legend graven bold and deep, as clear now as when the last crusader of the family was buried there, lord knew how many centuries before.

The tomb was an enormous place — part cave, and partly hewn — twenty feet by twenty by as many feet deep at the most conservative guess; and on four ledges, one on each side, not in their armor, but in the rags of their robes of honor, lay the bones of four earlier Montdidiers — all big men, broad-shouldered and long of shin and thigh.

We did not need to go down into the tomb and break the peace of centuries. Under the very center of the opening was a raised table of hewn rock, part of the cavern floor, about eight feet by eight that seemed to have been left there ready for the next man, or next two men when their time should come.

Down on to that we lowered Monty's body carefully with leather ropes, and then Rustum Khan's beside him, Rustum Khan receiving Christian burial, as neither he nor his proud ancestors would have preferred. But his line was as old as Monty's, and he died in the same cause and the selfsame battle, so we chose to do his body honor; and if the prayers that Fred remembered, and the other cheerfuller prayers that Gloria knew, were an offense to the Rajput's lingering ghost, we hoped he might forgive us because of friendship, and esteem, and the homage we did to his valor in burying his body there.

We covered Monty's body with the banner the women had made, and Rustum Khan's with flowers, for lack of a better shroud; then levered and shoved the great slab back until it rested snugly in the grooves the old masons had once cut so accurately as to preserve the bones beneath.

Then, when Gloria had said the last prayer:

"What next, Kagig?" Will demanded.

Kagig was going to answer, but thought better of it and strode away in the lead, we following. He did not stop until we reached the open and the smoking ruins of the castle walls. When he stopped:

"Has any one seen Peter Measel?" I asked.

"Forget him!" growled Will.

"Why?" demanded Maga. "Will you bury him in that same hole with them two?"

"Has any one seen him?" I asked again, uncertain why I asked, but curious and insistent.

"Sure!" said Maga. "Yes. Me I seen 'im. I keel 'im — so — with a knife — las' night! You not believe?"

Whether we believed or not, the news surprised us, and we waited in silence for an explanation.

"You not believe? Why not? That dog! 'E make of me a dam-fool! 'E tell me about God. 'E say God is angry with Zeitoon, an' Kagig is as good as a dead man, an' I shall take advantage. 'E 'ope 'e marry me. I 'ope if Kagig die I marry Will Yerkees, but I agree with Measel, making pretend, an' 'e run away to talk 'is fool secrets with the Turks. Then I make my own arrangements! But Mahmoud is not succeeding, and I like Kagig better after all. An' then last night in the darkness Peter Measel he is coming on a 'orse with Mahmoud because Mahmoud is not trusting him out of sight. An' I see him, an' 'e see me, an' 'e call me, an' I go to 'im through all the fighting, an' 'e get off the 'orse an' reach out 'is arms to me, an' I keel 'im with my knife — so! An' now you know all about it!"

"What next?" Will demanded dryly.

"Next?" said Kagig. "You effendim make your escape! The Turks will surely seek to be revenged on you. I will show you a way across the mountains into Persia."

"And you?" I asked.

"Into hiding!" he answered grimly. "Maga — little Maga, she shall come with me, and teach me more about the earth and sky and wind and water! Perhaps at last some day she shall make me — no, never a king, but a sportman."

"Come with us," said Will. "Come to the States."

"No, no, effendi. I know my people. They are good folk. They mistrust me now, and if I were to stay among them where they could see me and accuse me, and where the Turks could make a peg of me on which to hang mistrust, I should be a source of weakness to them. Nevertheless, I am ever the Eye of Zeitoon! I shall go into hiding, and watch! There will come an hour again — infallibly — when the Turks will seek to blot out the last vestige of Armenia. If I hide faithfully, and watch well, by that time I shall be a legend among my people, and when I appear again in their desperation they will trust me."

Will met Gloria's eyes in silence for a moment.

"I've a mind to stay with you, Kagig, and lend a hand," he said at last.

"Nay, nay, effendi!"

"We can attach ourselves to some mission station, and be lots of use," Gloria agreed.

"Use?" said Kagig, cracking his fingers. "The missions have done good work, but you can be of much more use — you two. You have each other. Go back to the blessed land you come from, and be happy together. But pay the price of happiness! You have seen. Go back and tell!"

"Tell about Armenian atrocities?" said Will. "Why, man alive, the papers are full of them at regular intervals!"

Kagig made a gesture of impatience.

"Aye! All about what the Turks have done to us, and how much about us ourselves? America believes that when a Turk merely frowns the Armenian lies down and holds his belly ready for the knife! Who would care to help such miserable-minded men and women? But you have seen otherwise. You know the truth. You have seen that Armenia is undermined by mutual suspicion cunningly implanted by the Turk. You have also seen how we rally around one man or a handful whom we know we dare trust!"

"True enough!" said Will. "I've wondered at it."

"Then go and tell America," Kagig almost snarled with blazing eyes, "to come and help us! To give us a handful of armed men to rally round! Tell them we are men and women, not calves for the shambles! Tell them to reach us out but one finger of one hand for half a dozen years, and watch us grow into a nation! Preach it from the house-tops! Teach it! Tell it to the sportmen of America that all we need is a handful to rally round, and we will all be sportmen too! Go and tell them — tell them!"

"You bet we will!" said Gloria.

"Then go!" said Kagig. "Go by way of Persia, lest the Turks find ways of stopping up your mouths. Monty has died to help us. I live that I may help. You go and tell the sportmen all. Tell them we show good sport in Zeitoon — in Armenia! God go with you all, effendim!"

Printed in the United States
27457LVS00001B/88